GENTLEMEN PREFER VILLAINS

C. ROCHELLE

CONTENTS

Typos & Languages	vii
Warning, Content & Triggers	ix
A Note on Superhero & Villain Identities	xiii
Stalk C. Rochelle	xv
1. Simon	1
2. Wolfgang	9
3. Simon	17
4. Wolfgang	25
5. Simon	35
6. Wolfgang	43
7. Wolfgang	51
8. Simon	61
9. Simon	67
10. Wolfgang	75
11. Simon	83
12. Wolfgang	91
13. Simon	99
14. Wolfgang	107
15. Simon	117
16. Simon	127
17. Wolfgang	135
18. Wolfgang	143
19. Simon	153
20. Simon	163
21. Simon	167
22. Wolfgang	177
23. Wolfgang	187
24. Simon	197
25. Simon	205
26. Wolfgang	215
27. Wolfgang	225
28. Simon	235
29. Simon	243
30. Wolfgang	251
31. Wolfgang	261

32. Wolfgang	267
33. Simon	275
34. Simon	285
35. Wolfgang	295
36. Simon	305
37. Wolfgang	313
38. Simon	321
39. Wolfgang	329
40. Wolfgang	337
41. Simon	345
42. Simon	353
43. Wolfgang	361
44. Simon	363
45. Simon	371
46. Wolfgang	379
47. Wolfgang	389
Epilogue	399
Reviews	409
Villainous Things Playlist	411
Wolfy & Simon Prints Available	413
Books by C. Rochelle	415
About the Author	417
Author's Note & Acknowledgments	419
Glossary	421

Copyright © 2023 C. Rochelle

First Printing: 2023

All rights reserved. No part of this publication may be reproduced, distributed, or transmitted in any form or by any means without the prior written permission of the author, except in the case of brief quotations embodied in critical reviews and certain other noncommercial uses permitted by copyright law.

Author's Note: The characters and events portrayed in this book are fictitious. Any similarity to real persons, living or dead, is coincidental and not intended by the author. All characters in this story are 18 years of age and older, and all sexual acts are consensual.

If you've read this, the leather gloves stay on.

ISBN: 9798387797804

Cover design by divineconception

TYPOS & LANGUAGES

While many people have gone over this book to find typos and other mistakes, we are only human. **If you spot an error, please do NOT report it to Amazon.**

I *want* to hear from you if there's an issue, so I can fix it. Send me an email at **crochelle.author@gmail.com** or **use the form** found pinned in my FB group or in my link in bio on TT & IG.

Glossary Note: Gentlemen Prefer Villains is an international romp, featuring locations and characters where English is not the first language. Non-English words are written phonetically and italicized. Please use your Kindle translate feature or reference the handy glossary in the back of this book for definitions.

A Note on Simon-Speak: Simon was born in France - to a Parisian mother who marries well and often - and has lived and traveled throughout Europe. While he's fluent in French (several languages, actually), he chooses to only access it when he's cursing on the streets or getting freaky in the sheets. Otherwise, he's speaking English, with a decidedly British flavor to it.

As the author, I did my best to have my characters sound authentic - and brought in British, French, and German authors/readers to check my work - but if something's way off, please contact me directly. Please also keep in mind that this is a work of fiction, people speak uniquely in the real world, and our tiny tyrant especially does whatever the fuck he wants.

SLANG NOTE: There is always a bit of slang peppered into my writing. When in doubt, use Google, or contact me using the methods above if you truly believe it's a typo.

WARNING, CONTENT & TRIGGERS

Gentlemen Prefer Villains is an MM romance between a villain and a "normie." Our men find other men in tight supersuits incredibly attractive. **This is not your kid's superhero book.** This is *Sin City* and *The Boys* having a love child with extra spicy Spideypool and is **meant for 18+ adults** who can handle such things.

The **Villainous Things** series contains standalone books (each with HEAs) that feature interconnected characters and an overarching plot. You should read them in order (starting with **Not All Himbos Wear Capes**).

Please do not hesitate to email the author directly with any questions or suggestions for adding to the TWs.

NOW THE GOOD STUFF

Content, Tropes & Kinks:

- Superheroes/villains (and the "normies" who love them)
- MM romance (love is love)

- Dual POV
- A James Bond meets Catch Me If You Can international romp
- A Venus flytrap that's treated better than most humans
- Fated mates + hurt/comfort
- Casual and not-so-casual psychopaths experiencing possessive, mutual obsession
- Mafia-style boss with his bossy li'l assistant
- Major size difference (how will it fit?)
- "Touch him and (then I'll touch you and you'll) die"
- Exorbitant gifts as a love language for an unapologetic sugar baby (just don't call Wolfy daddy)
- Absolutely filthy dirty talk (from both sides this time)
- Praise (for Wolfy) and degradation (for Simon)
- A blowie while wearing a onesie
- Biting, marking & territorial cum play
- Voyeurism + exhibitionism
- LEATHER (especially leather gloves)
- Asphyxiation and hand necklaces
- Primal play/chase
- CNC that includes being overpowered
- Role play and the willing exchange of power (with both men being vers)
- Cozy cockwarming for comfort
- **MAJOR SPIT KINK** (more fluid bonding than degrading - I triple dog dare you to give it a chance)
- SO MUCH TENSION + EDGING (for the reader and the characters)
- Spanking/paddling, sensory deprivation & sensory play (in the bonus epilogue)
- All the stretching, blow jobs, rim jobs, felching, frotting, and dicks in asses because this is an MM romance

Possible triggers (please also check above list):

- Sweary dialogue
- Slutty French and an absolutely bastardized mix of French and British/American English
- Naughty, medium-dark humor
- Cutesy pet names and honorifics (Boss/Sir and his sweet little murder baby cream puff/pet)
- Using religious phrases in an overtly sexual context (oh, my God/Jesus Christ), along with the use of the words slut/brat/whore
- Fear/tears & violence (against others) as foreplay
- A concerning lack of lube (but that's how they like it)
- Morally gray characters
- Psychotic ideation (including from our normie)
- Violent battle scenes with mentions of gore (eg. heads exploding like watermelons and eyes being gouged out - no details, but it happens)
- Superpowered abuse (parental - past, mentioned & on page as adult)
- Restraints (non-sexy kind)
- Threat of forced institutionalization (past, mentioned)
- **SA (on page - brief, mild, and immediately punished in a most satisfying way) - please email the author directly if you would like a heads up of where in the book this occurs**
- A cutthroat, dubious moral code for supes that isn't meant to be understood by normies - "It's how the game is played." *(Please also see the following page for a note on supe identities)*

A NOTE ON SUPERHERO & VILLAIN IDENTITIES

A SUPE'S IDENTITY IS SACRED!

In this world I've created, superheroes and villains are supposed to guard ALL secret identities from normies—including their own, that of their family/clan, and even their enemies.

This is why Vortexio "outing" Xander as a Suarez supervillain in book 1 was a major faux pas, and why Xander and Butch didn't simply tell each other who they were at the start of the book (plus, there wouldn't have been much of a story if they did, hmm?). That being said, Wolfy drags out his secrets for far longer than he needs to—for reasons you'll understand as you read this book. Give our sweet murder baby a break.

And when one supe addresses another as their supe name, that is a not-so-subtle way of making it clear they are considered the enemy at that moment. (Siblings may also do this to show the battle has begun—especially during notoriously cutthroat, annual White Elephant gift exchanges.)

To further clarify:

Captain Masculine = Supe name
Butch Hawthorne = Civilian name (for use around normies)
Butch Holt = Secret identity

Doctor Antihero = Supe name
Xander Marin = Civilian name (for use around normies)
Xander Suarez = Secret identity

The Hand of Death = Supe name
Wolfgang Espanto = Civilian name (for use around normies)
Wolfgang Suarez = Secret identity

STALK C. ROCHELLE

Stalk me in all the places!
(by joining my Clubhouse of Smut on Patreon, my Little Sinners FB Group, and subscribing to my newsletter)

Gloves off, my villainous things

CHAPTER 1
SIMON

"What are your thoughts on blood?"

I dragged my gaze away from the not-at-all-inconspicuous two-way mirror on the opposite wall and returned my dwindling attention to the ancient man sitting across from me.

"Pardon?" I asked, unsure if I'd heard the old geezer correctly.

He coughed wetly, making me grimace. "Blood. Do you have a problem with blood, Mr. Alarie?"

At this point, the lawyer for my soon-to-be-employer had interrogated me for close to an hour. Interviewed, technically, but I'd certainly never suffered through onboarding like this before.

It will be waterboarding next.

To complete the ambience, we were in what was clearly an interrogation room, deep inside the stuffy old Biggs Enterprises building. Before it was seized by the United Super Nations for a private investigation, this was the hub of Big City's police force, led by the hero who truly knew how to fill out a supersuit—Captain Masculine.

I was more of a supervillain fan, personally, and had found myself shamefully glued to the news along with everyone else when the Captain announced his engagement to a mysterious villain by the name of Doctor Antihero.

Americans do excel at trash TV.

However, not even daydreaming about gay supes could make this interview bearable. The endless questions had devolved from mildly unprofessional to borderline illegal, and I'd started to wonder if I was being recruited by the mob.

The thought of evil empires had my mind wandering yet again. There'd been quite a bit of juicy drama late last year surrounding the Biggs conglomerate, specifically about how the superheroes they employed to protect the city were little more than indentured servants. Just how any human could boss around a super-powered being who could crush your head with their fingers was a mystery.

Another mystery was just why I was humoring a job opportunity my notoriously clueless—yet somehow successful—therapist father had secured for me through one of his clients.

It's because this job is your ticket out of here, Simon.

My desire to put Big City far behind me was all-consuming. The only reason I was here in the first place was because of my mother. She'd fallen into one of her nostalgic moods while drunk on brut rosé and suggested I look into an American university for grad school.

Her dream of me rebuilding my relationship with my estranged father was nothing more than that. Two years later, I had nothing to show for my time here besides a master's degree in International Business and more canceled plans than memories with the man who'd given me nothing but the Austrian side of my DNA.

Since I've always used my mother's last name.

Needless to say, it was time to say *au revoir* to this hellscape, with no intention of ever sullying myself on U.S. soil again.

Plastering on my best 'rich idiot on the Riviera' smile, I smoothly countered, "Why do you ask? Does the mysterious 'Mr. S' make a habit of bleeding everywhere? Because if wearing a nursemaid's uniform is to be part of the job description, I'd like to prepare. You know, by making a waxing appointment for my legs before we depart."

My jailer gaped so openly, I feared his dentures might dislodge and fall into his drink. Understandably lost for words, he redirected his cataracts to the lengthy contract spread out between us—perhaps debating if adding a stipend for esthetician appointments would be appropriate.

If it includes waxing my arsehole, my vote is yes.

Before the torture session could resume, the door on my right swung open. Whoever entered was light on their feet and had enough of a chilling effect on the lawyer that I immediately swiveled in my metal chair, eager for any excitement.

It was my turn to gape as my gaze landed on the living, breathing embodiment of tall, dark, and handsome.

Make that tall, morally gray, and fuckable.

If I'm lucky.

The newcomer was dressed in a suit so black it sucked the fluorescent light from the room. A custom-tailored suit—judging by how perfectly it hugged his deliciously intimidating muscles. His skin was a gorgeous golden brown, although his face and neck were sadly the only sections I could see, as he wore leather gloves for some delightfully ominous reason.

His amber eyes were predatorily fixed on my face, and when his hands clasped in front of his no doubt enormous cock with an enticingly leathery creak, I almost swooned.

If my future boss thought he could send in his terrifying bodyguard and accomplish anything other than giving me a raging hard-on, he needed to reassess his methods.

Since red flags are my love language.

"Is there a problem, Randal?" Hot Muscle's gaze shifted to my interrogator while I practically climaxed over the silky smoothness of his voice. "Proceed."

"Y-yes... Sir," the bag of bones across the table stuttered, obviously too old for hard-ons. "Mr. Alarie was just confirming whether blood would be an issue—"

"Not at all," I casually interrupted, keeping my gaze locked on the eye candy. "I love blood. It's so good for the skin. Although, to be honest," I leaned toward my new crush to stage-whisper, "I much prefer a clean kill."

A bored Simon is a dangerous Simon.

I'd been expecting the bodyguard to stare me into the ground, but the corner of his tasty lips twitched as if he were fighting off a smile over my terrible joke.

Smugly pleased, I turned to face Randal-the-lawyer, only to find abject horror on his wrinkly face. Whether his reaction was to me acting like an irreverent twat or that our companion only ever smiled before opening fire, I couldn't be sure.

Either way, I'm having a good time.

"I couldn't agree more."

My attention snapped back to the main attraction, more than ready to drop to my knees and properly pray to this golden god, while he shared his gospel.

"Copious blood is always enjoyable," he continued, quite conversationally, "but there's nothing more satisfying than feeling a man's life slowly leave his body, knowing it was *your* hands that took it from him."

I hoped this interview would never end—not only so I could continue basking in the glow of His Royal Hotness, but because I was so turned on, there was no way I could stand without sharing the news.

But what's an inappropriate boner between coworkers?

My face must have given me away, as the bodyguard smirked, those captivating eyes sliding down my body before he shifted his attention to the lawyer and nodded once.

"V-very good," Randal stammered as he shuffled papers around, sweating profusely for no obvious purpose other than annoying me. "We'll need you to sign these non-disclosure and non-compete agreements, as well as this offer letter stating the basic assistant duties we've discussed, along with your salary…"

It was only thanks to my upper-class upbringing that my eyes didn't pop out of my head and roll away at the number of zeroes printed on the page. Blinking away my shock, I confirmed that my new employer was indeed offering me more money for a temp position than I would have made in five years elsewhere, even with my shiny new MA.

"…and as Mr. S wishes to leave the country by the end of the week," Randal droned on, "you will need to make the necessary arrangements for your current living situation, as well as any pets or other personal relationships—"

"I've been house-sitting anyway," I absently murmured while searching for a pen. "And as I'm neither a dog nor a cat person—and entirely uninterested in personal relationships…"

I trailed off as the mysterious visitor suddenly appeared at my side, maintaining intense eye contact while offering me a pen. He was holding it in a way that ensured our hands had no hope of casually touching, but I instantly forgave him, as he smelled fantastic. Like bergamot and lavender with an undertone of leather that caused a slightly embarrassing moan to escape me.

God, I'm already an absolute slut for this man.

"However." I cleared my throat, snatching the pen and attempting to recover a shred of dignity. "I *do* have a house-plant I'm quite fond of. She's a Venus flytrap named Twoey, and as I've hand-fed her all her life, I fear she won't survive in the care of another."

Especially with how my father kills every plant he touches.

The bodyguard barked a laugh, making me grin in return. Backing away—much to my disappointment—he leveled me with an openly amused look that warmed me all the way down to my curling toes.

"I believe *Mr. S* would make an exception for your plant," he chuckled. "Especially one named after a mean green mother from outer space. Be outside your apartment at 7 am Friday morning so you can be collected for the airport. You *and* Twoey. Now sign the papers, Mr. Alarie," he commanded before sweeping out of the room like some sort of sexy phantom.

Yes, Sir.

That this unidentified stranger apparently knew where I lived was immediately forgotten in light of the fact he was creepy-hot and a fellow *Little Shop of Horrors* fan.

One must have priorities.

Barely bothering to read the fine print, I signed away the next three months of my life, eager to escape this stifling room and begin preparations for my journey.

Which may or may not include a waxing appointment.

Again, priorities.

CHAPTER 2
WOLFGANG

"Did you really need to go in there, Wolfy?"

I frowned as I reentered the observation room to find a pair of cold blue eyes judgmentally focused on me.

Simon's eyes are green. And better.

"Yes, Captain, I did," I calmly replied, turning to face the glass—partly to escape Butch's stare, but more so I could watch *my new assistant* sign the papers Randal prepared for me.

Look at how he holds that pen...

"Why is that?" The hero beside me was relentless, but I'd learned to respect the trait, even if I didn't approve of how it was used in the past.

Interrogating villains in this very room had been one of Butch's many unsavory duties while working as Solomon Biggs' attack dog. While a petty part of me had invited him here to confront his questionable past, I also trusted the hero's judgment about others implicitly.

Unless it's aimed at me.

"Because I needed to see if he would be afraid of me or not," I lied through my teeth, keeping my gaze fixed on Simon and praying Butch would let it go.

Yes, certain humans naturally recoiled in my presence—as if they instinctively *knew* I worked for Death himself—but prior to today, I hadn't given a shit whether my new employee was one of them. My only goal was to pay whatever it took to secure someone intelligent enough to help track down my infamous sister before she did something stupid.

Like force me to kill her.

Simon Alarie was all that and more on paper, and being the son of Xander's therapist gave me a bargaining chip should things go sideways. My reason for being here today had simply been to observe his final interview while Butch peered into his soul to sniff out anything suspicious I may have missed during my background check.

But then Simon had to flash that pretty smile and start roasting our family lawyer in the same way my siblings and I would have... and I simply couldn't resist.

It didn't help that he looked like sin itself—with caramel-colored hair, creamy skin, and pouty lips twisted in a permanent smirk I wanted to see wrapped around my cock. Even his stature was perfect. Despite his big personality—and even bigger set of balls—Simon was a tiny thing. Most normies were shorter than me anyway, but this one barely reached my chest, making him the optimal size to pick up, pin down, and rough up a little.

Play with like a toy.

Bite-sized.

While I knew I was playing with fire, hiring a temptation like him, the idea of letting Simon walk away felt unacceptable. It wasn't like I could touch him anyway—regardless of how little I cared about professionalism—so I assumed once my infatuation died down, I could refocus on business.

As if to test that theory, Simon absently slid the end of the pen into his mouth, deep in thought over his contract. Then, those olive green eyes lifted, somehow finding mine through the glass as he took the pen deeper, hollowing his cheeks around it before slowly dragging it back out over his soft tongue...

This is a terrible idea.

"This isn't a good idea." Butch matched my thoughts so uncannily, I froze.

The Captain can't read minds...

Right?

I had to remind myself that if Butch had psychic abilities, Xanny would too—as his power-sharing *inventus*. And if my brother could dig around in my brain, I would know about it every time the asshole opened his mouth.

Since he has zero filter.

This was more about how goddamn good Captain Masculine was at his job. If I'd been eye-fucking Simon as hard as the rest of me wanted to, then it was no surprise the hero easily picked up on it.

"The only thing that matters is bringing Violentia back to our family—preferably alive," I stated, which was the truth.

She'd disappeared without a trace after I'd framed our mother, Glacial Girl, for the murder of Butch's power-hungry fiancé, setting the stage for a final showdown with the hero's corrupt father, Vortexio. Neither survived, and since Xanny had incapacitated our father, Apocalypto Man, enough for me to kill the supervillain myself, I'd successfully rid my clan of our greatest enemies.

I hope.

I'd spent countless hours since our parents' deaths making deals with their former allies—and disposing of any supes looking for revenge on their behalf. A trail of bodies had been left in my wake, but it was the only way to make my stance clear.

You're either with us… or dead.

There was no way of knowing if Vi was hiding out in mourning or busy plotting my demise, but I had to find her either way. Protecting my siblings—and the wannabe villain beside me—was my top priority.

As our family motto stated, blood was thicker than murder.

My sister was still a Suarez, so it was safe to assume she'd holed up in one of our international properties. Figuring out which one—and reaching her before she hopped to another—would require strategy and cunning. Besides not fully trusting any supes outside of my family, I liked the idea of having a human assistant, as they would have ideas and methods vastly different from my own.

And maybe I also want some normalcy for once.

I hadn't counted on being so drawn to a normie, but something inside of me had already decided Simon was *mine*, even if I couldn't have him. There wasn't much to be done about it besides ignoring the problem.

And pining pathetically.

Tearing my gaze away from my new obsession, I turned to face the supe at my side. "Don't worry about me, Butch. We both know I can't touch him anyway, so it doesn't matter how attractive I may or may not find him—"

"I'm worried about his attraction to *you*," Butch quietly interrupted, impressively standing his ground despite how close we were standing and who I was. "He's clearly the type who goes after what he wants. What if... what if he—you know—makes the first move? The instant he touches you, he'll *die*, Wolfy."

Butch's ridiculous blushing at the vague implication of s-e-x paled in comparison to the absolute *terror* I experienced at his implication. My blood actually ran cold, which was impressive, considering the sheer amount of blood I had on my hands.

This reaction made no sense. I felt nothing every time I took a life—except for one time—but the idea of accidentally killing the man on the other side of the glass made my chest inexplicably ache.

Don't start getting soft now, Wolfy.

You're The Hand of Death.

"Yes, I'm aware my touch is deadly," I snapped, more annoyed with myself than anything. "But I assure you, I'll take the proper precautions."

"Like telling him who you are?" Butch asked, his voice equally hard. "Randal's having him sign an NDA, and the United Super Nations has declared that document legally binding for normies professionally involved with supes, so your identity will be protected."

I sighed heavily, suddenly exhausted. Yes, I could have asked Xander and Butch to assist me with this trip, but they were both needed here. Captain Masculine was the de facto defender of Big City and Xanny was the logical choice to keep our younger brothers in line while I was gone.

As usual, it's on me to handle things.

Despite my endless to-do list, I always had the time to put a sibling in their place—including the fiancé of one. "You know, Captain... you're awfully mouthy for someone who hasn't *officially* joined the Suarez clan yet."

Just as I'd hoped, Butch responded to my vague threat with a Suarez-worthy comeback. "Actually, Xan and I were thinking we'd *both* take his civilian name when we get married. You know, to branch out with our *own* villainous family."

Well played.

"Oh, I do love a brat," I murmured, my gaze drifting back to Simon like a moth to the flame. "Almost as much as I love the adult onesie you had custom-made for me for our Christmas gift exchange this year."

"I had that made for Xander," Butch growled, rapidly losing the upper hand.

"And I highly doubt he wants it back now that I've rubbed my balls all over the inside," I chuckled evilly. "It was so *thoughtful* of you to make it fleece-lined. So cozy."

Butch threw up his hands in defeat. "I can't with this family! It's like you're fueled by torturing each other."

He's not wrong.

I laughed, wishing I could give the poor man an encouraging pat on the back. "You'll get the hang of it eventually, only child. And just for the record—you *will* be taking the Suarez name when you and Xanny tie the knot."

End of discussion.

Butch's golden boy dimples appeared as he failed to contain his grin. "Yes, Daddy."

Oh, hell no.

"That will be all, Captain," I gritted out, unable to contain the full-body shudder that ran through me.

You've won this round.

"Happy to be of service!" He smugly grinned, pulling on his identity-shielding mask so he could fly off to wherever his *actual* 'Daddy' was waiting for him. "But please, let us know if you need our help during your search for Ultra Violent. Hopefully, it won't be to bury a body."

With those annoying—and slightly ominous—parting words, my soon-to-be brother-in-law swiftly departed. Turning back to the glass, I resumed digging *my* grave by secretly coveting the one thing I could never have.

CHAPTER 3
SIMON

As instructed, I was waiting at the curb at 6:55 Friday morning, fully packed and dressed in my favorite black and silver Juicy Couture tracksuit.

Comfort—without sacrificing style—is key when traveling abroad.

Despite my lack of personal and professional commitments, preparing for the journey had made my week busier than usual. After an obligatory phone call to my father—which went straight to voicemail—I'd suffered through countless hours of freshening my wardrobe and having every stray hair on my body styled, plucked, and waxed.

Being this fabulous is truly a full-time job.

Adjusting the strap of the carry-on slung over my shoulder, I glanced down at the small houseplant in my hand, briefly worrying my dream man may have thought I was joking about bringing my Venus flytrap with me.

Or whether he even has the authority to say Twoey can join us.

Before I could wonder where a bodyguard stood in the company hierarchy, I reminded myself that I was being paid a lot of money to not question what was obviously an illegal operation. And that I'd sell my soul to the devil if it got me the hell out of this plebeian country, so it was best to just go along for the ride.

It's not like some superhero is going to swoop in to stop a few humans, anyway.

At exactly 7 am, a Mercedes pulled up with windows as black as the paint job. The driver's side door opened and Hottie McBodyguard appeared in an equally black suit, making me grin like an idiot despite the ungodly hour.

"*Bonjour!*" I sang out, firing up my native French and waggling my fingers in a saucy greeting as he approached. "Aren't you a man of many talents? A chauffeur and the hired muscle. Will you also be my chaperone during our voyage?"

Because the mile high club awaits!

When he nodded—those *lips* of his curling as he fought off another smile at my ridiculousness—I took that as full permission to continue my flirtations.

"How rude of me to not properly introduce myself yet. I'm Simon, and please don't attempt to shorten that in any way unless you aren't expecting me to answer."

I held out my hand the same moment he grabbed two of my many bags, which made for a moment of awkwardness where the poor man looked legitimately conflicted over what to do.

Instead of dropping the bags to shake, he offered me a smile that almost blinded me with perfection before inclining his head. "Simon it is then, although I can't imagine *you* answering to anyone."

He gets me.

"For the right man, I will," I laughed airily, bending to grab another bag. "Especially one as *mysterious* as our employer…"

I trailed off as he sharply shook his head, narrowing his amber eyes on where my hand had wrapped around a luggage handle. Slowly releasing it, I straightened, noticing how he visibly relaxed now that I was no longer threatening to lift a finger.

Oh, he really *gets me.*

Many an ex-boyfriend had whined about how 'high maintenance' I was. If they'd thought their complaints would result in me lowering my standards, they realized their mistake when I promptly threw them back into the swamp whence they came.

High maintenance? More like above your pay grade, darling.

A genuine smile stretched across my face as all *ten* of my bags were loaded into the boot of the car with nary a complaint in sight.

Especially not from the person watching those muscles flex.

"Aren't you going to tell me your name?" I asked, as the boot was somehow shut tight, despite being filled to the brim.

Those arresting amber eyes met mine again as the man in question opened the car door for me. "Wolfgang. But *you* may call me Wolfy."

Oh, I most definitely will.

A comment about howling his name was on the tip of my tongue when I noticed it was the backseat he was ushering me into.

"Oh, come now, Wolfy," I chided. "We're friends, aren't we? Twoey and I are perfectly happy to sit up front with you."

All humor disappeared as what looked like panic flashed over his handsome face. "I'd... prefer you sit in the back. Please."

Okay...

"Well, since you asked so nicely," I cooed, burying my disappointment beneath a flirty smile as I climbed in. It didn't go unnoticed that he also stepped further away from me as I passed, but I assumed it was part of his inconvenient professionalism.

Which only makes me want to cross the line even more.

Despite how irreverently I'd behaved during my final interview with Randal-the-dourpuss, I'd given the utmost attention to the company policies section of the paperwork. This had less to do with me wanting to be a good worker bee and more about confirming whether I'd get spanked in the not-fun way for sleeping with a fellow employee.

Finding no mention of an anti-fraternization policy was a good enough green light for me, but I still wanted to test the waters first. Even though my position was still suspiciously unspecified, the last thing I needed was for the next few months to be awkward.

Time for some reconnaissance.

"So, tell me about the boss-man," I called out as Wolfy pulled into traffic, taking that he hadn't put on any music as an invitation to chat. "Is he strict or easy going? And most importantly, how *obsessed* with me is he going to be?"

Wolfy's eyes snapped to mine in the rearview before returning to the road. "I would say he's somewhere in between, but leaning more toward strict..." He spoke slowly, carefully choosing his words. "He *has* to be in control, because of the severity of his responsibilities."

There was a long enough pause afterward that I feared I'd overstepped, but then Wolfy huffed a laugh. "And I believe he'll be absolutely obsessed with you. How could he not when the word *'juicy'* is printed across your velour-covered ass?"

You devil.

It was impressive that Mr. S had found a male-model who could presumably kill a man with his bare hands and hold his own in a conversation with *me*. While Wolfy had already secured his standing as my first love on this transcontinental adventure, I couldn't wait to meet the evil genius in charge of this operation.

I bet he looks like a cartoon villain.

"So our first stop is Tokyo, hmm?" I murmured, digging around in my carry-on to triple-check that my passport and other essentials were within reach. "My Japanese is a bit rusty, but hopefully I can be of service with how expertly I serve tea."

Wolfy's eyes found mine in the mirror again. "Mr. S speaks eleven languages fluently, including Japanese, but... you're familiar with tea ceremonies?"

I made a non-committal sound, although inwardly I was preening at the chance to share my obscure knowledge. "Yes. My mother went through a Buddhist phase at one point that included silent retreats, *ikebana*, and tea gatherings. Blessedly, she excused me from the first two, but as one can't properly serve tea to an empty house, she liked to practice her *temae* technique with me."

Wolfy was quiet for a few minutes, confirming he was the strong, silent type who liked to think things through properly before opening his mouth.

How perfect can one man be?

"For as many times as I've been to Japan, I've never experienced a tea ceremony," he replied so softly I felt like he was telling me a secret. "We'll have work to do once we're there, but maybe... maybe you could see about finding us a tea house?"

"You're interested in tea?" I asked, delighted by this whimsical turn of events.

My Hottie McZen Master.

He cleared his throat, and I would have given my left nut to see if he was blushing. "It would be a nice change to actually *experience* the country, instead of simply passing through on business. All work and no play makes a dull boy, as they say."

I grinned wildly. "If by 'they' you mean Jack Nicholson in *The Shining* typing up the phrase hundreds of times before attempting to murder his family, I will reserve a tea house forthwith. We can't have you resorting to murder to pass the time while we're abroad."

"Why not both?" he mused, his tone heavy with wide-eyed innocence. "I've heard tea and murder pair well together."

Oh, you and I are going to have some fun.

"*Merde!* Fine!" I shouted in mock exasperation. "I'll find a tea house that specializes in murder. Who knew I was dealing with such a diva?"

Wolfy chuckled as he passed departures and instead pulled up to a guard booth positioned outside the high chain-link fence surrounding the airport.

I sat up straighter as the guard took one—noticeably nervous—look at my chauffeur and hurriedly waved us through. It took my still foggy morning brain another minute to realize we were driving onto the tarmac and toward what appeared to be a private plane.

Sighing in satisfaction, I reclined against the luxury leather, feeling like the luckiest man this side of the Pacific.

As far as I was concerned, I'd already left Big City—and my father—in the dust, with neither to be bothered with ever again. I was about to spend the next dozen hours cozying up with a piping hot, tea-loving murderer, while traveling like the rockstar I was.

They really, really *get me.*

CHAPTER 4
WOLFGANG

I probably should have officially introduced myself to Simon by this point, but I was having far too much fun fulfilling his adorable bodyguard fantasy.

While the NDA fully protected my supe identity, it was liberating to pretend to be someone I wasn't.

To not automatically be feared.

As Simon excitedly banged around in the kitchen area of my family's plane, I settled into my window seat to consider the consequences.

Normies were well aware of supes, and the more notorious ones—like my villainous family—were household names. But they were generally ignorant of the gory details of our lives.

Maybe I could tell him I'm a distant Suarez cousin…

My gaze drifted down to the gloves covering my hands, specially designed by Xander to lessen the effect of my deadly touch on supes. There was no way to stop my powers completely, and with fragile humans, making contact with *any* part of my body would not end well for them—gloves or not.

Fuck.

As much as I hated to admit it, Butch was right. Simon was exactly the type to set his sights on what he wanted and go after it with singular purpose. I wouldn't be the least bit surprised to wake up and find him crawling into bed with me—positioning his lithe body over mine as he slid my aching cock into his *juicy* ass...

Fuck, I'm fucked.

"All right, Wolfy, don't *murder* me, but I took a wild guess how you take your coffee. If I'm right, I get to pick the first in-flight movie. If I'm wrong, you get to put me over your knee and spank me until I cry. Deal?"

I gaped at the man standing over me—although he was so short, I barely had to crane my neck at all. The top of his tracksuit had become partially unzipped, revealing skin beneath that was so soft looking, I had to clench my fists to resist the *very bad* urge to touch him.

He'd look so good with my gloves wrapped around his neck...

Simon cleared his throat, yanking my thoughts away from the dangerous path they were headed down. Not wanting to risk any accidental contact, I canted my chin toward the table in front of me. "You can put the coffee there. I like to wait until after takeoff before consuming anything."

Like fantasies about you.

His face lit up mischievously as he set down the mug, but then his eyes narrowed on the laptop bag I'd purposefully used to occupy the seat next to me.

It's for your own good, normie.

With a huff, he begrudgingly took the hint and flopped into the seat across the aisle. Kicking off his designer sneakers, he returned his focus to me.

"Take a goddamn sip, Wolfy," he adorably bossed. "I refuse to wait until takeoff to know if I *pegged* you right."

A choked sound escaped me at Simon's bold flirtations, even as I simultaneously hoped he never toned it down.

Even once he learns I'm the one signing his exorbitant checks.

I dutifully reached for my coffee as he hummed, thoughtfully tapping his plush lower lip. "Mmm, how silly of me. You're clearly the type of man who prefers to be on top."

I froze with the mug raised to my lips. The truth was, I didn't know *what* I liked with another person, as I couldn't physically be with anyone. But the things I enjoyed *watching* in the darkest corners of this world would probably make Simon question how attractive he thought I was.

If only I could share some of my favorites with him...

Before I could head down yet *another* dangerous road, I caught the scent of chocolate and a hint of vanilla cream swirling around in my premium dark roast.

Perfect.

"Perfect," I sighed, closing my eyes and taking a long sip, moaning in absolute contentment as I swallowed.

You're perfect.

"*Merde!* I think I just got *pregnant* watching you drink that," Simon laughed, fanning himself as the plane taxied. "And it appears I've won our bet—although it would have been a win for me either way."

I laughed as he snatched the remote and began scrolling through the endless choices on the 60-inch screen in front of our lie-flat seats. It was just one of the many features on our Falcon 8X I'd stopped noticing years ago, but witnessing Simon's pure excitement over the luxuries I took for granted made me indescribably happy.

I'm going to spoil his juicy ass on this trip.

Even if I can't touch it.

"Ugh, I already have decision paralysis over the sheer number of choices," he cried, tossing the remote into his lap just as the plane lifted into the sky. "What are *you* in the mood to watch?"

I blinked in surprise. My daily life was focused on nothing but making sure my family was taken care of—and that our enemies were also *taken care of*. Someone asking what *I* wanted was so unheard of, it was almost laughable.

My gaze drifted to where Simon had given Twoey her own seat. "*Little Shop of Horrors* should be on there," I murmured, continuing to sip my exquisitely prepared coffee. "The 1986 version is my favorite."

Simon scoffed good-naturedly. "And the *only* version worth mentioning. Never mind the top tier production and jazzy musical numbers—the casting is a wet dream."

After getting the film started up, he snuggled under the complimentary blanket and turned sideways to face me again. "Favorite character in the movie. Go. Don't think—just say it."

"Steve Martin's sadistic, nitrous oxide-addicted dentist," I replied without hesitation, before frowning and quickly adding, "Minus the abusive boyfriend aspect."

Pain in the bedroom should always be consensual.

"*Putain...*" Simon whispered, drawing my attention back to his gorgeous face.

He didn't elaborate on his reaction, but our gazes remained locked through almost the entire Greek chorus-style opening number—the air between us threatening to burst into flames.

I am so fucking fucked.

My phone loudly dinged, breaking the spell. Partly relieved, but mostly annoyed, I pulled it out of my pocket to see my brother Xander had texted me.

In the Suarez family group chat.

The Mouthy One: *You haven't fucked him yet, have you Wolfy?*

With a sigh, I braced myself for what was coming next.

The Dumb One: *Fucked who? Who's getting the Dick of Death?*

Baltasar has entered the chat.

The Mouthy One: *Wolfy hired a normie brat with a Frenchy-Brit accent to suck his dick.*

The Mouthy One: *I mean... to be his assistant.*

The Dumb One: *Oh, I'm totally sending you normie porn now, you fucking animal [wolf emoji] [tongue emoji] [baguette emoji]*

The Token Hero: *Who added me to this chat?*

The Mouthy One: *I did, sweetheart. You're one of us now.*

The Dumb One: *TRIAL BY FIRE, MOTHERFUCKER!!!*

Thing One *has left the chat.*
Thing Two *has left the chat.*
The Dumb One *added **Thing One** and **Thing Two** to the chat.*

The Dumb One: *Nice try, assholes.*

The Token Hero: *You haven't though... right, Wolfy?*

Sighing again, I shoved my phone deep into my pocket, trying to ignore how much my chest ached to not see **The One With the Biggest Dick** reply and put us all in our place.

A nickname Vi programmed for herself in my contacts, of course.

Being only a year younger than me, Violentia and I had been inseparable practically since birth. She was my first friend, my partner in crime, and the only one I'd ever opened up to about how deeply I despised my powers.

Unless I'm using them to protect the extremely short list of people I care about.

I could have searched for my sister alone, since I had enough allies in each location to keep my enemies in line. But I was concerned that—without needing to put on a brave face for someone else—I would drift dangerously closer to having a nervous breakdown over the situation.

Maybe I should also start seeing Dr. Ownit when I get back...

My gaze drifted to where the therapist's estranged son was watching the movie, only to discover he was watching *me* instead.

How much did he see?!

"Let me guess." Simon smirked, although there was solidarity in his expression. "That was one of your parents texting... or a sibling."

Everything, apparently.

"Siblings—plural—busting my balls in our group chat," I sighed, reaching into my pocket again to silence my phone. "Four younger brothers and one soon-to-be brother-in-law. And one... sister."

I wonder if she's seeing our texts?

Obviously, I'd already threatened my brothers and our **Token Hero** with bodily harm if they shared anything in the group chat that Vi could use against us. Still, I couldn't bring myself to start a new chat without her.

It feels too... final.

"That sounds delightful," Simon drily replied. "I have a couple of half-siblings out there, but we're not close. Here." He reached a demanding hand across the aisle. "Let me see what they wrote. I'm King Ball-Buster. Sic me on 'em."

"No!" I barked, much louder and harsher than I meant to, but rather than looking hurt, Simon's grin only grew.

"Ooooooooh!" he chortled, sitting up and swinging his legs over the side of the chair to face me. "Were the texts about *me?*" He flashed a cheeky grin, his eyes sparkling with mischief while awaiting my reply.

I simply stared at him, my impassive mask firmly in place despite how distracting his fuzzy pink socks were.

They look so soft...

"Is it about *a girrrrrl?*" he sang, dramatically fluttering his long eyelashes.

"No." I grimaced, unable to hide my visceral reaction.

Gross.

"Oh, thank fuck," he huffed a laugh, falling back onto the seat. "I was starting to worry that I was barking up the wrong tree here. But I'm not, am I, Wolfy?"

Simon's green eyes were laser-focused on me, and I couldn't have looked away if I tried.

"No," I answered truthfully.

"And you feel this too, don't you?" He gestured between us, clearly referring to the palpable tension that was making my cock *throb* against my zipper.

I hesitated. While I didn't like the idea of lying to Simon, denying our connection would be the perfect opportunity to shut this down—before he could get hurt.

Before anyone *gets hurt.*

"Yes," I answered, honest yet again.

Idiot.

Before he could pounce, I held up a gloved hand, determined to finally tell him I was his *boss* and that we needed to put a stop to this. "But we *can't,* Simon, because of us working—"

"Pshhh!" The little demon silenced me with a wave of his hand. "We can and we will. End of discussion."

Yes, Sir.

"You're a bossy one, aren't you?" I muttered, so incredibly out of my element, yet beyond enamored with this tiny tyrant.

"I've been called worse." He shrugged, continuing to maintain eye contact long after deadly supes would have backed down. "And you like it."

"Yes. I do," I admitted again, like a fucking fool.

"You like *me*," he continued, absolutely relentless.

"Watch the movie, Simon." I tried to make my voice stern, but couldn't stop the smile twitching my lips.

"Fine," he chuckled, reclining his chair further to settle in. "But don't think you've escaped my clutches, Wolfgang. I'm cracking that hard shell of yours if it's the last thing I do."

Famous last words.

CHAPTER 5
SIMON

I awoke with a start, momentarily confused where I was. My dream had been a chaotic jumble of imagery, with the only memorable bit being the feel of leather gliding over my skin.

One guess who I was dreaming about...

Covertly rolling onto my side, I peeked at my man of mystery across the aisle. Wolfgang had his laptop out, his attention fully focused on the screen as his gloved hands flew over the keys.

Updating his OnlyFans I hope.

It wasn't merely his devastating good looks that made Wolfy so attractive. His wit and humor—not to mention his unending patience with *me*—only added more fascinating layers to this intriguing, leather-wrapped package.

How did this gem end up doing grunt work for Mr. S?

For all her faults, my Parisian mother had passed down an appreciation for the finer things in life—items built to last. While she may not have been referring to *people* when she declared "if it feels cheap, it will look cheap," the statement had imprinted on my brain as a way to categorize men who were only good for a fuck versus those worth my time.

And my traveling companion here appears to be both.

"Are you done spying on me, Simon?" Wolfy murmured, closing his laptop with a definitive click before turning his mesmerizing gaze my way.

His piercing stare may have flustered a lesser man, but for how legitimately intimidating he was, nothing about Wolfy actually frightened me.

He can chase me into the bedroom anytime.

"Let's call it *admiring*," I laughed, sitting up for a languid stretch before noticing we'd begun our descent to Tokyo. "How long was I asleep for?"

"Two hours and thirty-six minutes," he replied—the level of awareness raising his creepy-hot quota by at least a dozen points. "But it's good you rested. Most of our business will be conducted after dark, so you should prepare to become nocturnal."

"Oh, *putain*—thank God!" I gasped, blindly reaching around to locate my trainers. "When you picked me up at the arse crack of dawn, I feared perhaps I'd been hired by a cult of... *morning people.*"

When that earned me the slightest twitch of Wolfy's lips, I powered on. "If night moves are to be our *modus operandi*, why did we catch such an early flight?" I glanced at my phone. "It's only noon, Tokyo time."

Time zone-hopping is enough of an adventure as it is.

Any humor I'd inspired in the man across from me instantly vanished. "Because a daytime meeting was scheduled with some associates, as a courtesy for us visiting their country on… business." Wolfy was watching me closely, perhaps to gauge my reaction to the mafioso implications of his statement.

As if the whole sleep-with-the-fishes vibe isn't making me salivate.

I held his gaze. "And if this meeting doesn't go as planned, I assume that means an after-hours addendum will be in order?"

Something almost like relief passed over his face. "Yes. But either way, you'll be staying behind at the hotel, where it's safe."

The strangest feeling of panic washed over me—not for my safety, but for *his*.

That's… odd.

"Will Mr. S be making an appearance soon?" I casually asked, carefully watching his expression in return. "I'd like to discuss a few details of the job with him."

Like requesting he not endanger the eye candy.

That Wolfy was keeping his expression unreadable made me wonder if he was purposefully creating professional distance between us before our employer showed up.

Perhaps to discourage me from sliding down his cock like a fireman's pole during business hours.

His jaw ticked, confirming my suspicions. "He'll be there when we deplane."

Before I could pry for further intel, we landed, and the pilot rattled off the usual procedures and pleasantries. While reorganizing my carry-on, my gaze caught on Twoey, and I smiled to discover some Good Samaritan had buckled her in while I was sleeping.

That's it. We're getting married.

"Did you *buckle* Twoey into her seat?" I asked, having absolutely zero intention of letting his good deed go unacknowledged.

The slightest hint of color rose to Wolfy's cheeks as he nodded, somehow making him not only hotter, but *adorable* as well. Maintaining this stoic demeanor, he stood and slung his laptop bag over his broad shoulders. The movement caused his impressively unwrinkled suit jacket to open, and I caught sight of something metallic hidden underneath.

Ooh, kinky.

"Is that a knife under your jacket, or are you just happy to see me?" I joked, legitimately curious about *everything* Wolfgang was packing.

He froze before running his gaze over me in an assessing way that made me shiver. "The only knife I carry is strapped to my ankle. I prefer long-range weapons."

I cocked my head. That he'd so readily share this information was interesting, but I assumed he was doing so to make me feel properly protected.

And horny.

"Because you prefer taking down your targets before they can get too close to you? To avoid hand-to-hand combat?" I ventured, wondering just how much spank bank material I could get out of him.

Wolfy's eyes widened as if that were the last thing he'd expected me to say. "No," he replied. "Because once they're within reach, I can easily take them down with no weapons."

CAN HE GET ANY HOTTER?!

As if he knew I was moments away from dragging him to the lavatory, he gestured for me to lead the way off the plane.

I sighed, but obeyed. If we'd been animals, the pheromones pouring off me would have told the wolf at my heels to mount me, stat. As we were nothing but a couple of humans, my Gucci Rush cologne was forced to suffice.

A limo was waiting for us on the tarmac, and the uniformed man standing beside it was obviously just a boring old chauffeur, unlike my multi-talented future husband.

"*Konnichiwa*, Mr. S," The driver bowed deeply before opening the back door.

Time seemed to stand still as I went into auto-pilot—sliding into the empty compartment while realizing exactly *who* I'd spent the last twelve tension-filled hours with.

Instead of following, Wolfy bent his head and peered in at me, looking almost *afraid* of my wrath.

Smart man.

Unsurprisingly, this revelation was *not* a deal-breaker, but the delivery was trash. I wasn't *embarrassed* to have thrown myself at my new employer—since all it meant was that I had excellent taste—but I didn't appreciate being deceived.

What else have I misinterpreted?

Because, if I was going to be honest, the main thing bothering me about this plot twist was whether I'd completely invented the attraction crackling between us.

He seemed like he was enjoying himself as much as I was…

Wasn't he?

Unfortunately, Wolfy had the nerve to clear his throat at that moment, and I exploded.

GENTLEMEN PREFER VILLAINS

"Get your arse in the car, Wolfgang," I hissed, snapping my fingers and pointing at the seat across from me. "Or should I say, *Mr. S*? Assuming that's even your real name."

He pressed his lips together but obediently took the jump seat, choosing the corner farthest away from me—presumably so as not to catch hands.

"Wolfgang Suarez *is* my real name," he carefully replied after the door was closed and the driver had busied himself with collecting our luggage. "And very few people know that."

The last name seemed vaguely familiar, but wasn't ringing any immediate bells. All that meant was that his mafia family had kept their noses clean by using legal businesses as fronts.

Or by paying off law enforcement.

"If you're trying to butter me up with supposed secrets, you'll need to do better than that," I muttered, crossing my arms and staring out the window as the limo jerked into drive. "You lied to me."

"I did no such thing," Wolfy scoffed, his amused tone making me turn my head to better glare at his annoyingly chiseled jawline. "You're the one who assumed I was the right-hand man. I just neither confirmed nor denied."

"It was lying by omission," I sniffed, although he was absolutely correct that I'd made assumptions instead of introductions.

Rude.

Wolfy leaned forward, and for one foolish moment, I thought he might join me on my side of the car—or perhaps pull me into his lap and stick his tongue down my throat.

Either would certainly help smooth things over.

Instead, he gently lifted Twoey from where I'd set her down on the floor, before placing her on the seat beside him and *buckling her in.*

"Bloody hell, Wolfy!" I shouted, flinging my hands into the air in loving exasperation. "How am I supposed to stay pissed off when you do shit like that?"

He's going to be so good with our future children.

Because he was the sweetest maybe murderer ever, he simply shrugged, adorably apologetic.

"Even if you're angry now," he murmured. "I hope you continue to be yourself around me, despite… who I am." Wolfy looked so earnest, I instantly forgave him—for this and all future infractions until the end of time.

Forever and ever, amen.

The limo pulled up to a towering glass building that I immediately recognized as the world-famous Mandarin Grand Hotel. While I was no stranger to traveling in style, *this* was far beyond any benefit I'd enjoyed as the son of a woman who knew how to marry up.

Even if choosing who to procreate with wasn't her strong suit.

I was so busy gawking like a peasant while the bellboy transferred my luggage onto a trolley, I almost missed that Wolfy hadn't joined me on the pavement.

"Wait." I used my body to block the driver before he could close the door. "Where are you going?"

Wolfgang carefully handed Twoey to me before quickly sitting back, out of reach. "I told you, I have a meeting. You'll remain here to go over the files I slipped into your carry-on while you were asleep."

I'll be staying behind at the hotel…

"Where it's safe."

Even when I'd believed Wolfy was an actual bodyguard, I was concerned for his safety. Now that I knew he was just a regular businessman walking into the sort of meeting that required multiple concealed weapons, a protective instinct unlike anything I'd experienced before roared to life.

Randal did not properly address this during orientation!

Wolfy cocked his head, giving me an incredulous look. "Are you... worried about me?"

"Maybe," I huffed, hugging Twoey to my chest for carnivorous comfort. "Just promise me—if it comes down to it—you'll shoot first and ask questions later."

Despite having a Very Important Appointment, Wolfy took the time to slowly drag his gaze over me, his amber eyes darkening as if my suggestion turned him on.

Now, I definitely didn't imagine that.

"I do this all the time, Simon." He smirked, clearly enjoying me fussing over him. "Please don't worry. Order anything you want from room service, but remain inside our suite until I return. I promise, I have the situation well in hand."

CHAPTER 6
WOLFGANG

How did this situation get so out of hand?

I glared down at the steaming piles of bloody meat, wondering why the hell Orochi San would send *normies* to ambush me.

Was this some fucked up version of kamikaze?

It wasn't that I felt bad for the now extremely dead humans. They should have known facing off with me would result in their brains blasting out through their nostrils. I also wasn't concerned about the legal repercussions as a supe who'd just killed a bunch of normies. This was my property and I could claim self-defense.

They just walked into my hands, your honor.

I also wasn't worried that the *tatami* mats in the traditional *minka* we owned outside of Tokyo were now ruined. My cleaners were already on their way, and within an hour, you'd be able to eat off the floor if you chose.

No, what was angering me at the moment—besides a prominent villain I'd respected my entire life betraying me—was that I now had normie gore splattered all over my new Italian suit.

And that Violentia was nowhere to be found.

My sister was long gone by the time I arrived, despite Orochi assuring me she'd been living here for weeks. Overall, my meeting with the yakuza *oyabun* at his Marunouchi high-rise had been civil enough, even with his small army of *kobun* eyeing me like a bomb ready to detonate.

Fair.

As I'd told Simon, this meeting was simply a formal acknowledgment of me operating on another villain's turf—a courtesy call. Orochi had been one of the first of my parents' allies I'd contacted after their deaths, and he'd sworn that the loyalty of his organization would seamlessly transfer to me as the new head of the Suarez clan.

Fucking snake.

Carefully sliding the *shoji* screen open so as not to get blood on the paper, I stepped outside to get some air. The sun was setting over Mount Fuji in the distance, and I allowed myself a moment to enjoy its beauty as I contemplated my next move.

The Suarez way would be to immediately return to Marunouchi and wipe Orochi's entire conglomerate off the face of the earth. But the idea of starting a war sounded exhausting and, more importantly, I didn't *want* to do things the way my parents had.

I'll just have to figure this out on my own.

All at once, I remembered that wasn't exactly true. I had an *assistant* waiting for me back at the Mandarin Grand Hotel—one I'd hired to actually *assist* me. Granted, I wished he'd help by dropping to his knees, but all sexual tension aside, I'd seen Simon's credentials. He was incredibly intelligent—genius level, in fact—and had traveled almost as widely as I had.

And he's not turned off by blood.

Brushing stray bits of brains off my jacket, I returned to my rental car, wishing—not for the first time—that I could fly like my idiot brother. But then I would need to strap on my super-suit, and I preferred to do business in wool, not Lycra.

Although, it is easier to clean...

Soon enough, I was pulling up in front of the Mandarin and tossing my keys to the valet. Mindful to keep my distance from any normies heading out for dinner, I stepped inside the vacant elevator, wondering if Simon had eaten yet as the doors closed and the cab shot skyward.

My siblings were all old enough to feed themselves at this point—and our family cook, Betsy, was tasked with hounding the twins when they became so engrossed in their art they forgot to eat—but my old caretaking habits were hard to break.

Something had rattled to life when Simon reacted to my insistence on loading his luggage into my Mercedes. He *liked* being spoiled. It probably turned him on to be showered with expensive gifts and waited on hand and foot, like a little prince.

Fuck, now I'm hard again.

To be fair, the sight of my wannabe assassins' heads exploding like a bunch of watermelons had gotten me halfway there, but there was just something about this normie that drove me crazy.

Everything, really.

Nodding at the guard I'd stationed outside our door, I slid my keycard into the slot and quietly entered the suite.

Simon wasn't in the common area, although an impressive spread of food covered the table—implying he'd already eaten. I knew I should head straight for the shower and get cleaned up, but the *need* to set eyes on him was all-consuming.

Because he's mine.

Moving with the absolute silence I was known for, I glided toward the bedroom I assumed Simon would claim. It featured a luxurious jacuzzi next to a wall of windows looking out over the city, and for one lecherous moment, I hoped I might catch him using it.

Instead, I found the object of my obsession sprawled on the bed, his pretty green eyes glued to the iPad propped against a pillow, and his hand down his pants.

Stroking himself.

I failed to mask my sharp intake of breath, which brought Simon's gaze snapping to where I lurked in the doorway. True to form, he didn't look embarrassed or guilty to be caught.

"Welcome home, darling," he drawled, adding to his overwhelming attractiveness with a slow, satisfied smile. "How was your day at the office?"

Ripping my gaze away from the now motionless velour bulge, I forced my thoughts away from a fantasy scenario where I *did* come home to Simon every day.

Preferably with less clothing on.

"Eventful," I answered hoarsely. "Watching something good over there?"

He licked his lips. "Quite. I was watching Cillian Murphy's *lips* in *Peaky Blinders*, only to see him kill a man and, well... one thing led to another."

He's killing me.

"Did you eat already?" I blurted out, desperate to redirect the conversation.

He hummed, giving himself a casual pull under his pants, as if I wasn't two seconds away from demanding he remove them so I could watch.

"Mmm, yes, and no," he murmured. "Looking over the thrilling dossier you left behind made me peckish, but then I decided to simply order one of everything out of boredom. Aaaand... maybe also because I was a tad miffed that you'd left me trapped in this tower like a princess."

Fuck, I want to make him my princess.

His honesty made me smile. "You don't have to act out with me, Simon, but if spending my money makes you happy, go ahead. We could stay in this suite for the rest of our lives and not make a dent in what I—"

My words ended with a choked sound as Simon withdrew his hand.

His *gloved* hand.

"What?" He shrugged, although those lips of his were turning up in what I now realized was a signature smirk. "I've recently unlocked a new kink for leather."

Get me the fuck away from this man!

My cock was trying to punch its way out of my pants as I backed into the hallway. "I... need to get cleaned up. I'm covered in..."

47

"Blood?" All humor left Simon's face as he leaped off the bed and advanced on me, much to my terror. "I swear, Wolfy, none of that better be yours."

"It's not," I stammered, continuing my rapid retreat, even as I soaked up his obvious concern like a greedy little sponge. "I just need…"

I need…

Spinning on my heel, I fired up my super speed to flee to my bedroom—closing and locking the door behind me before doing the same with the en suite.

I need to come before I die.

Blasting the shower to the hottest it could go, I frantically tore off my clothing.

He likes leather on his skin.

The sight of my gloves haphazardly tossed on my discarded suit had me gripping the base of my cock in agony.

He wants my *leather on his…*

I stumbled into the massive walk-in shower, not bothering to grab the complimentary body wash for lube before fisting my dick. Dropping my forehead to the tile, I shut my eyes tight, focusing every atom of attention on the exquisite burn of my hand shuttling over my foreskin, squeezing so tightly I saw stars.

That fucking mouth…

That fucking mouth I want to fuck.

My balls drew up tight—all the blood in my body racing south as I imagined Simon kneeling before me. His green eyes locked on mine as I throat-fucked him until he cried.

Fuck, fuck, fuck, fuuuck.

With a pained groan, I unloaded all over the shower wall, milking every drop as my free hand scrabbled against the slippery surface and my knees buckled.

"Simon…" I murmured breathlessly, tilting my head to press a flushed cheek against the cool tile, willing myself to get a grip. "What am I going to do with you?"

I knew it was a terrible idea to hire someone I was this attracted to. In a move so uncharacteristic of my controlled nature, I identified a major distraction to my mission—a temptation to my entire existence—but I didn't eliminate it. Instead, I welcomed it in.

What am I going to do with myself?

Sighing heavily, I washed up and carefully collected my bloody clothing into a dry cleaning bag for the hotel's discreet laundry service.

After dressing in a fresh suit and pulling on my gloves, I stood in front of the mirror for a long moment, eyeing my reflection. I looked almost the same as usual, except for the extremely concerning glint of *excitement* in my eyes.

I can't remember the last time I was excited about anything.

Get a hold of yourself, Wolfy.

Your family's counting on you.

Sliding my practiced mask of impassivity back over my face, I opened my bedroom door, tamped down the anticipation fizzing in my gut, and headed back into the fire.

CHAPTER 7
WOLFGANG

Returning to the common area, I found Simon had also showered and changed into a pair of dark wash skinny jeans and a cropped black T-shirt that said 'Your Dad is My Cardio.'

Jesus...

"I'd say you clean up nice, but you look as fit as usual." There was a hint of lingering concern in his appraisal, but he quickly buried it beneath his signature sass. "Noticeably less tense, however. I wonder why that is..."

He truly is King Ball-Buster.

I dropped into a leather armchair near the floor-to-ceiling windows and huffed a laugh, not even bothering to deny *how* I'd relieved my tension.

My family would love him.

"Murder always leaves me a little... tense." I met his gaze, knowing full well I was playing a dangerous game, but apparently set on this self-destructive spiral. "But so does leather, apparently."

Especially knowing it was wrapped around your cock.

Simon's lips turned up in a smug smile before he abruptly sobered. "Tell me what happened today."

I blinked at him, surprised he wouldn't continue teasing but appreciating the out. "Long story short—I was unsuccessful in locating the target. You read the case file I left for you?"

He nodded and began filling a plate from the copious room service selection. "Yes. Violentia Signesdottir—which is quite a mouthful, and sounds fake, by the way. Age 33, 182 centimeters tall, black hair, medium brown skin, and light brown eyes..." His gaze drifted to me before refocusing on the mountain of sushi he was creating. "And she's apparently wanted for embezzlement. Although I call bullshit, as money is no object to you."

Well, shit.

Despite Simon signing the NDA and being hired to assist me, I'd still been careful about what information I gave him. I used Vi's civilian name on the paperwork, partly because a supe's identity was sacred—legal agreement or not—but also because I didn't want him to know she was related to me. Supes publicly associating with family members out of uniform was frowned upon, but that wasn't the main reason I was keeping this major detail under wraps.

If I ended up bringing my own sister home in a body bag, I didn't know how I'd explain something like that to him.

Or to myself?

"What is it?" Simon was suddenly standing in front of me, so close I could smell the coconut shampoo on his damp hair. "You just went somewhere... your entire demeanor changed."

"I..." I stuttered, thrown off by his astute observation while simultaneously realizing he was handing the sushi to me—

that he'd prepared it for *me*. Accepting the plate, I noticed he'd also added a secondary mountain of wasabi, which happened to be my favorite. "It's just... been a long day."

He pressed his lips together, clearly stopping himself from calling bullshit yet again. "I want to know what happened today, Wolfy. As your *assistant*."

"Only as my *assistant*, hmm?" I teased, although I wasn't joking and apparently enjoyed torturing myself with what I could never have.

Get your shit together.

Simon held my gaze, the pure earnestness in his expression making me dizzy. "I'll be whatever you need me to be if it will help you talk."

Whatever I need?

Again, the idea of someone doing anything for *me* sounded ridiculous. But then my gaze dropped to the sushi on my plate, and my throat became strangely raw.

Desperate to buy myself some time, I picked up the chopsticks and snagged a spicy tuna roll. Adding a healthy dollop of wasabi, I popped it into my mouth, letting the burn clear my sinuses—and my head—as I debated how much to tell my assistant.

Honesty was an extremely important character trait to me, but there were still aspects of my world I was struggling to share. Besides hating the idea of Simon being afraid of me, I didn't want to put him in unnecessary danger by sharing too much information.

Too little *information could also hurt him, Wolfy.*

I was snapped out of my reverie when Simon placed a glass of water on the side table next to me before sinking to the rug at my feet.

Fuck, he looks good down there.

"Start with the meeting," he prompted, impressively determined to keep us on track.

I washed down my sushi and nodded. "Very well. The man I met with today is the boss—the *oyabun*—of one of the largest yakuza families. He told me where to find Violentia, but when I arrived at the location, several of his men were waiting for me instead."

"But you killed them all," Simon whispered, his jaw clenching and his green eyes practically glowing with rage.

For a moment, I feared he was angry with *me*, but then realized he was angry on my behalf.

This is so surreal.

"Yes." I cleared my throat and shifted awkwardly in my chair, careful not to accidentally bump him with my leg.

The desire to touch him, combined with the knowledge of what would happen if I did, was making it hard to concentrate.

"How many men were there, Wolfy?" he gritted out when I buried my feelings beneath more sushi instead of elaborating.

Chewing slowly, I considered how to reply. Casual murder was simply my reality—and the same was true for most supes—but normies typically lacked the stomach for it. Yes, Simon seemed abnormally comfortable with violence, but there would be no rational explanation for what I'd accomplished today.

And exploding heads would probably be a hard limit for him.

I chose my words carefully. "There were eight of them. They jumped me as soon as I walked through the door, but I... took care of the problem."

That should do it.

Simon was gaping at me now. "You killed EIGHT MEN?! *By YOURSELF?!*"

I grimaced. It had actually been *twelve,* but I thought eight sounded more doable by human standards.

"They were extremely easy to kill!" I blurted out, scrambling for anything to not give my supe status away. Not yet. "Which was odd and, frankly, slightly offensive, considering Orochi San knows what I'm capable of."

Hmph.

Simon cocked his head, his fury replaced by a cool calculation Butch would have been proud of. "This *Orochi* didn't send his best men to fight you, even knowing what a badass you are?"

When I nodded, Simon leaped to his feet and raced into his bedroom. Returning with the files I'd left with him earlier, he reclaimed his spot on the rug and pulled out the various international properties we needed to investigate.

"Where were you thinking of traveling to next?" he asked, moving papers around like pawns on a chessboard.

What are you up to down there?

I set aside my plate and leaned forward to better observe. "Probably Thailand, since it's the closest—"

"Wrong!" Simon crowed triumphantly. "I would hazard a guess your Thai colleagues are already well aware of your Japanese dealings and expecting you to arrive on their shores any day now." He froze before warily glancing up at me. "Have you scheduled any further meetings?"

I shook my head. "No. I wanted to see where *you* thought we should go first."

Simon's pale cheeks pinked slightly, and I inwardly sobbed over how I couldn't tackle him to the floor. "Well, I think we should keep your *associates* on their toes. Skip around a bit, since we have the means to fly wherever, whenever. And absolutely *no* meetings."

"No meetings?" I eyed my assistant dubiously, noticing he'd moved Berlin to the front of the line. "It's, uh, considered bad form to enter another supe… *ervisor's* territory on business without permission."

He's going to get us killed.

"Don't care," he stated, before thoughtfully tapping his lower lip. "In fact, I believe that's what your Japanese friend was trying to tell you… with the message he sent."

"Message?" I murmured, fixated on his mouth, wishing I could bite it. "I'm not sure there was any message besides telling me to fuck off."

"Au contraire, mon chéri." He raised a brow in challenge, pairing it with a saucy smirk. "Yakuza believe in a strict code of conduct. You requested the meeting, so Orochi accommodated. He could have taken the opportunity to *politely* tell you to fuck off and leave, but he gave you permission to continue searching for Violentia instead. On paper, you were both following the rules of engagement."

I sat back and considered Simon's words—all of which were true. It was entirely within Orochi's right as clan leader of this territory to forbid me from poking around, but that would have immediately triggered my Spidey sense. No, the *oyabun* graciously gave me permission, even though Vi could have easily gotten to him first, possibly shifting his alliances…

Which would have ended badly had he sent actual supes to ambush me.

"He was warning me of what *could* happen in other countries if I continued following the rules," I huffed as the truth washed over me. "But he also wants to officially stay out of *my* business, so it had to look like business as usual."

A gorgeous smile stretched across Simon's face. "Look at you—beauty *and* brains! You're truly the complete package."

A genuine smile stretched across my face, even as I felt myself *blush* at the praise. Between the mind blowing jerk-off session in the shower, being handed sushi on a platter, and Simon changing *all* the rules on supe engagement, I felt off-kilter, but exhilarated.

Which is terrifying.

In the best way possible.

"It's clear who's the brains of this operation, but that's fine," I chuckled, grabbing my plate and chopsticks again. "I'll let you boss me around, even if your methods go against how it's always been done."

Simon reached forward to steal off my plate, and I instinctively recoiled. Oblivious to the danger of accidental contact, he casually snagged a sushi roll and popped it into his mouth with a cheeky grin.

"How long have you been involved in this world?" he asked, gracefully standing and returning to the makeshift buffet on the table.

I immediately loathed the space between us, but reminded myself to stop being an idiot. "I was born into it," I replied, knowing he meant the criminal underbelly, not the world of supes.

Although it's true in both cases.

He froze with a piece of tempura halfway to his plate. "So you never had a choice." It wasn't a question. "Wolfy, have you ever… talked to anyone about this? I don't mean a therapist necessarily, but a *friend.*"

A friend?

"I used to talk to my sister—when she was still around." It was difficult to keep the bitterness out of my tone. Violentia took my one sounding board with her when she ran off, as if suddenly being the head of our clan wasn't an added burden on top of my cursed powers.

And I still have no idea if she was in Japan at all…

"I see." Simon nodded, refocusing on his grazing and the previous subject. "Do you think Orochi plans to kill us if we don't leave Japan immediately?"

I almost dropped my chopsticks. If I'd thought for a moment Orochi San's *kobun*—the *supe* ones—would show up here, we would've already been on my plane. But part of me had already realized the *oyabun* was giving me the equivalent of a slap on the wrist—even if I needed Simon to help me puzzle through it.

I need him.

But I also can't put him in danger.

My appetite gone, I set aside my plate for good. "No. If he wanted us dead, we would be. But… I should send *you* away, for your own safety. I know you don't consider Big City your home, so my pilot can drop you off anywhere you want."

Even if it kills me.

"How dare you try to get rid of me just as things are getting good!" he gasped, tossing a spring roll at my head, which I easily dodged. "You're stuck with me now, for better or worse, twenty-four seven. On that note, if you think it's safe enough to venture out, how about we go have some fun? I'd like to show you some action."

Yes, please.

His grin turned wicked. "Get your mind out of the gutter, Boss Man. I want us to paint the town red tonight—figuratively speaking—before enjoying the sunrise at the most murderous tea house I could find."

CHAPTER 8
SIMON

It was far too early to be sitting in a fucking tea house, but I supposed I'd done it to myself.

For Wolfy, rather.

It was safe to say I was smitten with this man. Yes, I wished he would take off his trousers already, but in an entirely unexpected turn of events, I found myself *more* interested in removing his mask.

Who are you under there?

I thoroughly enjoyed Tokyo last night, thanks to Wolfy indulging my every whim. When I wanted the most expensive *sake* dirty money could buy, he found it. When I was thirsting for digital blood, he brought me to an exclusive retro *gesen* for rich businessmen and their trophy wives, so he could repeatedly spank my arse in Street Fighter II.

He's the Dhalsim to my Blanka.

In return, I coaxed him into renting a private-room for karaoke—although he sadly refused to duet with me—and dragged him into almost every sex toy shop we passed. To my utter delight and continued sexual frustration, even the most extreme items didn't seem to shock him.

What I wouldn't give to see his private collection.

Most importantly, I ensured we avoided large crowds of people whenever possible, which was a challenge in this city. While I'd never been good at sharing my things, the main reason for this caution was to avoid triggering him.

I didn't think Wolfy had a full-blown phobia, but I noticed how he strongly disliked others being in his personal space. It most likely had something to do with his upbringing, and I was committed to maintaining his comfort at all times.

My precious murder baby.

"You promised me murder with my *matcha*, Simon," Wolfy murmured, his sexy as sin voice extra raspy, thanks to our all-nighter. "But this looks like a regular old tea house to me."

I smirked and surveyed the items spread out before me. Having finished our meal and sweets, we'd moved on to the tea ceremony, and my chance to flex my knowledge. Traditionally, it was performed in silence—which would have helped me concentrate on the intricate process—but I'd never been one to follow the rules.

And I'm certainly not going to stop Wolfy from flirting with me.

Selecting my tools, I added one and a half scoops of *matcha* to his tea bowl before ladling in hot water from the iron pot and slowly pouring it over the powder.

"Well, I *did* debate setting up an elaborate trap for your pleasure," I cooed. "Something similar to that scene in *You Only Live Twice,* where the Spectre assassin creeps around the rafters before dangling a poison-covered rope above a sleeping, kimono-clad Sean Connery. Of course, with how the poison drips down the rope at a snail's pace, you would need to roll directly into the line of fire with your mouth wide open, like Bond's doomed lady love, Aki."

Wolfy was watching me closely as I whisked the powder into a green foam, his searing gaze darkening. "You would poison me?"

The raw *lust* dripping from his tone sent an involuntary shudder down my spine. "Perhaps if you asked nicely, Wolfgang. *Begged*, rather."

I'd always been a shameless flirt—shameless in most everything in life—but this man did something to me that raised the stakes. And I wasn't exactly sure how I felt about it.

He's going to be a tough act to follow once this job is through.

Wolfy briefly closed his eyes and released a slow breath, as if trying to collect himself, before opening them again. He then shifted his gaze to where the *shoji* doors were opened to the garden outside—perfectly framing the sunrise peeking over the treetops.

I was grateful for the opportunity to clear my head by focusing on preparing a bowl of tea for myself before carefully cleaning the utensils.

Don't get attached.

"I once read that 'Teaism is a cult founded upon the adoration of the beautiful among the sordid facts of everyday existence,'" Wolfy suddenly spoke, startling my attention back to him.

After another thoughtful pause, he added, "The idea of finding beauty, even when you're surrounded by absolute shit, really speaks to me."

His breathtaking amber eyes met mine again, and it was all I could do to not crawl into his lap for a cuddle—tea ceremony decorum and loose professionalism be damned.

If ever there was someone who needed a hug…

"I'm sorry," I blurted out, unable to hold it back any longer. When he furrowed his brow, I hurriedly explained. "For whatever happened. You don't have to tell me, but I've noticed you… don't like to be touched…"

I abruptly stopped talking as his criminally handsome face went ashen, realizing I'd majorly overstepped.

Why can't I just shut the fuck up sometimes?

"Thank you," he quietly replied, giving me a tight smile. "I'm sorry, too. Unfortunately, there isn't much to be done about it." His gaze dropped to the tea I'd prepared for him. "But I'll take whatever you can give me."

Like a stray dog eating scraps.

Not trusting myself to speak, I lifted Wolfy's tea bowl and reverently placed it in front of him before placing my hands in my lap. A small—almost shy—smile curled his lips as he lifted the bowl and took three sips, slurping a bit on the last to show good manners.

I love a man who does his homework.

He placed his bowl on the *tatami* and inclined his head in the cutest little bow. That was my cue to pick up my bowl and take a sip.

"*Putain*, this is terrible!" I choked out, placing the bowl as far away from me as possible before glaring at my guest. "Why on earth would you let me drink that?"

Pure mischief danced over his face. "If I had to suffer through it, so did you." When my scowl deepened, he snickered. "You make excellent coffee, however, and that's what matters most."

He's impossible to stay mad at.

I barked a laugh, my sorry attempt at tea already forgotten. "Well, we should plan to pick up some coffee on the way back to the hotel, along with some flies."

"Flies?" Wolfy muttered.

I nodded. "For Twoey! I haven't fed her in months, but the Mandarin keeps its hotel so clean, a fly wouldn't dare enter the premises. Surely a man of your stature would know where to acquire such things at this hour, hmm?"

Wolfy simply smirked before lifting his chopsticks and *snatching a fly out of midair.*

"WHAT THE *FUCK?!*" I shouted, ruining the last shred of Zen we'd attained as my jaw practically dropped to the *tatami.* "Is your... is your secret identity actually Mr. Miyagi?"

"'Man who catch fly with chopstick accomplish anything,'" Wolfy recited before removing the silk handkerchief from his suit pocket to wrap up his kill. "But it was Daniel who caught the fly, not Miyagi."

This man is a treasure.

"What an excellent provider you are for our carnivorous child," I praised, feeling no small amount of satisfaction when he looked slightly embarrassed. "Venus flytraps only need to feed a few times a year, so Twoey will be all set until next quarter."

I was hit with an unexpected wave of *grief* as I realized my contract with Wolfy would be up by then.

Maybe I can convince him to keep me on...

He must have had a similar revelation, as he frowned and began collecting our discarded plates and bowls, even though it was technically my job.

But he looks so good servicing me.

"We should get ourselves to the plane," he murmured distractedly, although he peeked up at me with a twinkle in his eye. "I need to make sure you get your beauty rest before we reach Berlin."

Good man.

CHAPTER 9
SIMON

We chose a few musicals to play during our long flight, and I allowed the sweet melodies of *Sweeney Todd* to lull me to sleep.

It's no surprise Wolfy's a Stephen Sondheim man.

I awoke as we touched down at Brandenburg airport only to discover *someone* had considerately draped me with a brand new, criminally soft blanket while I slept.

I'm so happy I could eat him up.

Rolling onto my side, I found the man responsible for my creature comforts typing away on his laptop—working hard, yet again.

"Do you ever sleep?" I mumbled, noticing he'd showered and changed into a fresh suit during our journey. It was black, per usual, only this time, it was made out of leather.

Is he trying to kill me?

Wolfy glanced over before returning his attention to his screen. "Occasionally. I don't... require as much sleep as others do. Plus, I prefer beds."

I swear, he hands me these openings.

"Such a shame," I drawled, returning my seat to its upright position and carefully folding my new security blankie. "I'd hoped you were the 'rail someone against the wall until they saw the Holy Spirit' type."

That someone being me.

As with every time I said something remotely suggestive—which was often—Wolfy clenched his chiseled jaw and blew out a slow breath, but didn't immediately respond. He didn't look upset or uncomfortable. If anything, he seemed to be reining himself in from having *more* of a reaction to my words.

What would it take to unleash him?

"Watch your mouth, Simon," he finally replied, turning to give me a deliciously threatening stare that had my toes curling in my fuzzy socks. "I was planning to take you to church with me for Sunday Mass…"

My answering grimace inspired a smirk on his devilishly handsome face that was anything but saintly.

"I do hope you're joking, Wolfgang," I huffed. "You must know I would immediately burst into flames upon entering any house of worship…" I trailed off as understanding washed over me. "Hold on a tick. Are you… are you talking about going to Benediktion?!"

Berlin was the clubbing capital of Europe, with Benediktion being the holy grail for dark techno and depraved debauchery. It was nearly 10 pm on a Sunday, but all that meant was the weekly party had been going for forty-eight hours straight already, with at least another twelve to go.

Absolutely no photography was allowed inside, but—rumor had it—the cavernous interior felt like a cathedral to those who entered the sacred space on this day of our Lord. Hence, why the club was often referred to as 'church,' with Sundays being 'Mass.'

The ecstasy and Special K running through their veins probably support the holy visions.

I had no idea how churchlike the club actually was. As it was near impossible to gain entry, I'd never bothered to try. Besides the threat of rejection from the bouncers, the ridiculously long queue had always been enough of a deterrent for me.

Why waste the night when less discerning clubs are available?

When Wolfy nodded to affirm my guess, I squinted at him across the aisle. "I'm not interested in getting all dolled up just to be turned away at the door like common peasants."

He cracked his leather-clad knuckles with a series of satisfying pops. "It won't be a problem, Simon. All *you* need to worry about is looking like a pretty distraction."

Oh.

Well, that *I can do.*

Rising from my seat, I headed past the kitchen and into the bedroom. I had the perfect outfit in mind and didn't mind one bit that my assignment tonight was focused on my appearance alone. Wolfy made it clear he respected my opinion and intelligence, so if my juicy arse could also help him achieve his goals, I was more than happy to assist.

I'm such a team player.

An hour later—freshly showered and immaculately clothed—I took a final twirl in front of the mirror to appreciate the masterpiece I'd created. It was widely known the dress code for Benediktion was 'the less clothing the better,' but I always preferred keeping an air of mystery rather than giving it away for free.

It doesn't mean I can't offer a little tease.

My lips twisted in a smirk as I took in my reflection. The black lace tank and booty shorts were both sheer enough to show off the electrical tape x's hiding my nipples and my satin thong. To top it off, I'd added leather gloves, a jaunty WWII British officer visor cap, and shit-kicker combat boots.

While I knew I'd be turning the heads of every man in the club—including the few claiming to be straight—there was only one whose opinion I cared about.

As I turned to exit the room, my gaze drifted over the bed. The sheets were wrinkled just enough to imply Wolfy *had* snuck back here at some point to rest, which made me uneasy. Yes, he'd mentioned how he preferred sleeping in beds, but I couldn't help wondering if what he truly required was a room where he could lock the door.

Does he not trust me?

The man had obviously endured some sort of trauma that made him averse to touch. Whether it was a one-time incident or years of abuse, I couldn't be sure. But the idea of anyone hurting *my man* made my vague ideations of serial killing drift dangerously close to reality.

Easy, Simon.

A sudden thought made me tense. For as naturally flirty as I was, I respected boundaries and consent. Wolfy hadn't explicitly *told* me to stop coming on to him—and he seemed to enjoy it—but I wondered if I should back off for a bit.

Especially if he feels the need to lock the bedroom door on me...

My mood was sour as I opened the door, but the dulcet tones of Wolfy's voice coming from the main cabin perked me right up.

"You're certain REM will be there tonight?" He was barely speaking above a whisper, so I crept closer, hoping to catch more of his phone conversation.

"Yes, Wolfgang." The unexpected sound of a second man with a thick German accent had me stopping in my tracks. "That *arschgeige* lurks in the 360 Bar almost every weekend. The only reason he hasn't been banned from the club is because of who he works for."

There was a pregnant pause before the mystery guest added, "And tonight should be no different... considering no one was told you'd be in town."

Fuck.

Wolfy sighed, sounding more exasperated than angry. "Mind your own, Erich. I'm simply conducting business differently this time."

Because of me.

"*Krass!*" the German—Erich—chuckled incredulously. "Just because you're the scariest motherfucker around doesn't mean you're invincible, my friend. Those *hands* of yours would be considered an extremely desirable trophy in certain circles—"

Who wants to cut off his hands?!

"Erich, I'd like you to meet my new *civilian* assistant." Wolfy smoothly shut down both the German's morbid train of thought and my panic attack, while also implying he knew I was eavesdropping. "Simon Alarie is helping me on this trip, before the situation escalates."

I took my cue and strutted down the aisle of the plane like it was a Parisian catwalk, knowing full well I looked like sex on a stick. The German gave me a nod of approval that was more friendly than lecherous, but by the time I reached the pair, Wolfy's jaw was practically scraping the carpet.

Looks like I understood the assignment.

Erich barked a laugh. "Careful, Wolfgang. You'll end up catching flies with your mouth hanging open like that."

Wolfy was completely ignoring the other man—too preoccupied with taking in my outfit in a way that suggested he wanted to eat it off of me. As satisfying as it was to affect him so intensely, I still wasn't sure how much he *wanted* to be having this reaction to me. Or how much he'd regret it if things went any further.

I should back off until we can talk about it.

"Yes, *Wolfgang,* there's no need to catch flies," I coolly agreed. "Twoey has been fed and we have business to attend to, hmm?"

Wolfy snapped his mouth shut, his cheeks pinking slightly as his gaze drifted to where he'd buckled my plant into her own seat again—as if to check on her well-being.

It would help if he wasn't so goddamn perfect.

Our guest had been watching our exchange with open amusement, but he took the opportunity to warmly smile and extend his hand to me. "Hallo, Simon. I'm Erich Nachtnebel—one of Wolfy's oldest *civilian* friends and his favorite person to hit the dance floor with whenever he graces our fair city with his infamous presence."

"I don't dance, you *tratschtante,*" Wolfy grouched, fixing the other man with a glare that was truly terrifying. "I simply prefer to avoid the petri dish of Benediktion's main floor, and the 360 Bar is where they stick the B-list DJs like you."

Confirming their best mate status, Erich broadly grinned at the burn. "Calm down, *stinkstiefel*. Nobody wants to see an ogre like you dance, anyway."

I wouldn't be opposed to a horizontal mambo demonstration...

"So who's this REM character?" I casually asked, determined to focus on business instead of how badly I wanted my boss.

Both men visibly froze—implying our target was a Very Bad Man—although only Erich showed any sign of fear. Even more interesting was how the chatty German shut his trap and deferred to Wolfy to answer.

Friends, but with a hierarchy.

"*Remington* is an enforcer for a local... crime family," Wolfy carefully replied, obviously putting it into *Peaky Blinders* terms for my Cillian Murphy-loving heart. "But I simply want to ask him a few questions about that woman we're looking for. Violentia *Signesdottir*..."

Erich glanced at him sharply—almost in disapproval. "And just why are you putting sweet little Simon here in Remington's line of sight? You know what he's capable of—"

"I also know REM's an idiot who can't help running his mouth," Wolfy hissed, his amber eyes flashing dangerously, clearly in need of another hot shower to de-stress. "He'll tell me everything I want to know if he's properly distracted."

Okay, so REM is short for Remington and he's a creepy arsehole. Got it.

The German ran his assessing gaze over me again, although he still looked concerned. "And distracted he will be, with this tasty treat being dangled in front of him…" He trailed off as Wolfy growled low, like a dog protecting his food.

This man is a health hazard!

"*Putain*, Wolfy!" I shouted, clutching my dick in desperation. "I can*not* afford an erection in this outfit. Keep your… *sex noises* to a minimum, or so help me."

Wolfy immediately dropped his gaze to the floor. "Sorry," he whispered, genuinely apologetic.

Again. Perfect.

It was Erich's turn to catch flies, his gaze darting between us with a comical amount of confusion, shock, and awe before he chuckled. "Well, now that I see who wears the *lace* pants in this relationship, let's go to church."

Aiming a secretive smile at Wolfy, Erich clapped me on the back and leaned in close—seemingly for no other reason than to make the other man growl again. "Despite your employer's refusal to have any fun, *you* should fully enjoy Benediktion tonight, Simon. *Da steppt der Bär,* my friends!"

CHAPTER 10
WOLFGANG

Not that I'd doubted his abilities, but Simon had succeeded in his mission to dress for maximum distraction.

Unfortunately, the main person he was distracting was *me*.

Fuck, he's barely left anything to the imagination with those shorts...

The vision of flossing my teeth with Simon's thong was rudely destroyed when REM himself slithered up the industrial staircase leading from the main dance floor to the 360 Bar. The cool blue glow from the area where I lounged harshly illuminated half of his craggy face, and I grimaced as he turned and spotted me.

Truly, the man has no good side.

Even before Xander and Butch exposed the truth, I knew the narrative surrounding heroes and villains was a load of bullshit. Yes, my parents embodied their villainy to the full extent, but they were both terrible people who only cared about getting ahead—never mind how many untimely deaths needed to happen along the way.

Or how they used their own children as murder weapons.

Despite the recent bombshell that we were all genetically the same, it was business as usual on both sides of the divide. Superiority still needed to be asserted and maintained—whether through money or murder—and while some heroes liked to pretend they were the 'good' guys, nature and nurture seemed a better indicator of psychopathy, rather than how someone identified.

We're all just villainous things.

"Well, well, well," REM dramatically sang, folding his massive frame into the neon teal chair near the opposite end of the couch I sat on. "Funny seeing *you* here, since I don't recall Mistress Noir-Rouge mentioning we had any important visitors from Big City. I wonder if *she* knows…"

Continuing with his annoying display, REM slowly pulled out his phone, as if the supervillain who ran Berlin was only a call away for someone like him. In reality, he was a foot soldier—not a clan member by blood—so he wasn't fooling anyone with the overblown bravado.

Especially since he sat as far away from me as possible.

"I'm not here on business, REM," I sighed heavily, sipping my martini and adopting a bored expression. "Erich begged me to come hear his new set, as if all EDM doesn't sound like wannabe Daft Punk monkeys pushing buttons."

REM scowled at the dig to his most favorite thing on earth before trying to use his sleep paralysis powers to get inside my head and retaliate. Unfortunately for this idiot, my youngest brothers were two of the most powerful mind-melters alive, so I had decades of strengthening my mental defenses under my belt.

*He's probably a clueless only child, like our **Token Hero**, Butch.*

Realizing his sorry attempt at dominance wasn't working, REM huffed, the light catching on his gaudy jeweled rings as he dismissively gestured at Erich finishing up his set behind the deck.

Which was actually quite good.

"I don't know why you waste your time associating with *normies*, Wolfgang. Everyone knows they're only good for a fuck. Oh, wait…" He smirked. "You wouldn't know anything about that, now would you?"

I bristled—not from the low blow to my virginity, but to the broad stereotype. True, normies *were* a physically inferior species, most of the time, but I'd met a few worthy of respect.

Or worship…

Like a magnet, my gaze was drawn to where Simon was dancing his perfect ass off among the other sweaty, half-naked bodies on the small dance floor of 360. I'd instructed him to stay there until our target found me, but had already come close to theoretically dragging him out of the overly handsy throng multiple times.

Mine, mine, mine.

"Oh, I might know a thing or two, REM." I allowed a sinister smile to curl my lips, keeping my gaze as soulless as possible as I stared unblinkingly at my fellow villain. "After all, what do I care if they're *dead* when I'm done with them?"

As I'd hoped, pure *disgust*—and a hint of fear—passed over his face in response. While my deadly reputation was wholly deserved, I found it amusing to keep my competition off-balance by adding to my lore with creepy rumors.

It gets boring at the top.

And lonely.

As if he could sense my need for him, Simon suddenly appeared, breathless and glistening with sweat—causing my brain to momentarily short-circuit.

"Whew! I believe I got pregnant *and* picked up a contact high just from dancing with those maniacs. Do you boys mind if I sit here for a minute to rehydrate? I am *thirsty!*" He flopped onto the couch next to me—so close I instinctively slid further away—before cracking open a bottle of water and guzzling it down.

REM had zeroed in on Simon like a predator, but I wasn't behaving much better. My gaze was locked on the way his Adam's apple bobbed with every swallow, imagining it was my cum he was chugging like his life depended on it.

I want to bathe him in it—starting with his insides.

"Oh, pardon! Did I interrupt a top secret conversation? Perhaps a gay tryst negotiation between old friends?" Simon batted his long eyelashes, making my dick twitch. "My name's Charles, but you can call me Chazzy... or Cherry. Since no one's popped mine yet."

Jesus. Fucking. Christ.

REM wasted no time moving in. "Hey there, little Cherry. Why don't you slide down this way and sit by me? Our friend Wolfgang isn't someone you want to get too close to."

It was all I could do to choke down another possessive growl. I *knew* this was part of the game we'd agreed on, but the thought of Simon moving one millimeter toward the slimeball openly leering at him...

Mine.

"Mmm... I think I'll stay right where I am, thank you very much," Simon cooed, scooting closer to me while still being careful not to touch. "*Wolfgang* smells good—like lavender fields in the South of France. Like *home."* He leaned in to take a deep inhale, and I clenched my fists in agony.

This wasn't part of the plan!

Simon lifted his head and gave me a meaningful look before turning to face the other villain. "And I can already tell *you* smell like gin and failure."

He's such a delicious brat.

The sour look on REM's face almost made my assistant's performance worth the torment, but I needed to focus on what intel I could gather while he was distracted. Leaning forward, I made a show of ignoring Simon's antics—as if he truly were a drunken nuisance and not my wildest dream.

"Before you go, Remington…" I smoothly used his full civilian name, just as we would in any normie's presence. "You haven't seen Violentia Signesdottir lately, have you?"

REM cocked his head in interest, although he kept one lecherous eye on *my* Simon. "Is there a problem with Violentia? I thought you two were thick as thieves."

I gritted my teeth. Of course, the low-level asshole was going to drag this out, when a simple yes or no would be the more mature thing to do.

But this is REM we're talking about.

"It's not a topic fit for present company," I drawled, hoping he'd cut to the chase. REM's focus was entirely on Simon now, who had removed his top so he could tie it around his neck like a bandanna.

Like a collar.

My jaw clenched, but I powered on. "Regardless, I *do* need to talk to Violentia, so if you run into her—"

"It's a shame you had a falling out with your *girlfriend*, Wolfgang," REM murmured, making me freeze.

What the fuck is he talking about?

The other villain shrugged nonchalantly, but slyly smiled as he met my gaze. "That's what this is about, right? You had a lover's quarrel with Violentia, and she ran off on you."

Just as I opened my mouth to tell him off, Simon abruptly stood. "As thrilling as sitting here with you two wet blankets has been, I'm going to see about getting my dick sucked in the loo. *Ciao!*"

Ah, fuck.

I could only helplessly watch as Simon stomped away, clearly upset over the bullshit REM had spouted about my relationship with Vi. Circumventing the dance floor, he briskly headed down a side hallway leading to the restrooms, and it was all I could do not to run after him and explain.

For a moment, I wondered if REM had figured out our ruse, but when I met the asshole's gaze again, I found nothing but male posturing.

"Oops, my bad," he snickered, pleased with his cockblocking. "Didn't mean to scare away your next victim. And, no, I haven't seen your psycho sister. Although, on that note, I'm gonna go get my dick wet, too." Standing, REM grotesquely adjusted his no doubt tiny cock and headed back downstairs to the main dance floor—on the hunt for *his* next victim.

Good riddance.

The instant he was out of sight, I was off the couch and down the hallway, intent on finding Simon. Even though we weren't in anything close to a relationship, the thought of him believing I was dragging him around the globe looking for my *ex-girlfriend* made me ill.

When I rounded the corner, I found an obscenely long line to the restrooms, but no sign of Simon. Confused, my gaze drifted beyond the mass of bodies, noticing there was a back stairwell leading down to the main level.

Which was where REM went.

OH MY GOD!

Uncaring who I brushed against, I raced down the hall, practically leaping over normies in my haste and ignoring the stray shouts of pain I left in my wake.

The scene on the first floor was chaotic, with the strobe lights, pulsing beat, and the sheer number of people adding to my growing panic. Luckily, the stairs had dropped me off near another back hallway, so with nothing more than a feeling in my gut, I headed in that direction.

Supes didn't have perfect night vision—unless that was your power—but our eyesight was far better than humans'. Considering the clientele were mostly normies, this area of Benediktion was abnormally dark, aside from the stray emergency exit sign illuminating whoever was fucking nearby.

Where is he?

Something was pulling me onward, and I prayed to whatever god or devil might be listening that I'd find Simon in time.

If he gets hurt, I will kill everyone here.

All at once, I stopped in my tracks, realizing I'd actually *found* him—alive and unharmed.

And in someone else's arms.

My vision tunneled as I took in how *my* Simon was being pressed up against an exit door by a much larger body. The red glow above the pair illuminated how the electrical tape he wore on his chest was now gone, allowing the other man to circle a thumb over Simon's exposed nipple while sucking on his perfect neck.

No…

I bit the inside of my cheek so hard I tasted blood—feeling something break inside me when Simon dropped his head back with a pleasure-filled moan.

Wait.

The expression on Simon's face wasn't one of ecstasy. His gaze was confused—unfocused—and the way his tiny body was limply propped against the door suggested he wasn't totally aware of what was happening.

OH, MY FUCKING GOD!

With murder on my mind, I stalked closer, only to freeze when the light caught on the assaulter's gaudy rings.

REM.

The villain had probably used his sleep paralysis powers on Simon, so he couldn't resist—even after being outright rejected—and bile rose in my throat as I wondered how many others he'd done the same to.

He's a fucking dead man, either way.

My vision went as red as the exit sign when REM's hand trailed down Simon's bare chest and abs, headed for the waistband of his shorts. Touching him everywhere.

Touching what belongs to me.

CHAPTER 11
SIMON

Why can't I move?

I was delirious, trapped in a nightmare and cornered by a monster who was going to eat me alive. Only instead of teeth tearing my flesh, I felt hands burning my skin... touching me where they shouldn't...

Because the only hands I want on me are his.

"Wolfy..." I whimpered, desperate to get my vision to focus and my limbs to work. To escape.

"The fuck did you say—" The monster's snarl turned into a shriek as something bigger and scarier ripped him away from me with an inhuman growl.

No longer being held captive, I fell forward, crying out as my knees hit the cement floor. The pain cut through my unnatural brain fog, and I groggily lifted my head just in time to see two enormous men barrel through the metal exit door so violently the hinges cracked.

HOLY SHIT!!!

People were screaming—and I scrambled to my feet to follow the crowd and run—but then I caught the scent of bergamot and lavender amidst the violence.

Wolfy?

Realizing it was my dream man who'd saved me from a nightmare, I shoved my way outside. I *knew* it was stupid—that I should go find Erich or security instead—but the thought of Wolfy being in danger had me ready to charge into battle.

If he gets hurt, I will kill everyone here!

I bit off more than I could chew as a fresh wave of dizziness sent me to my knees again as soon as I crossed the threshold. Blindly flailing, I grabbed onto the side of a skip bin and hauled myself up before gingerly peering around it.

What I saw made my heart stop.

Wolfy's broad back was to me—his black suit jacket covered in brick dust as he crouched over someone on the ground. Gaping, I took in the partially caved-in wall of a neighboring building, along with the twisted pile of metal that may have once been a chain-link fence.

Did… he do that?

"I told you, I don't know shit about Ultra Violent," Remington—who I now realized was my attacker—was babbling incoherently from where he cowered pathetically, with Wolfy looming over him like a predator.

How does it feel, arsehole?

"I don't give a *fuck* about her right now." Wolfy's normally measured voice was trembling with barely contained rage. "You put your hands on *him*."

"Who?" Remington stuttered. "T-the kid in the club? It's none of your business where I stick my dick, you fucking psycho!"

Wolfy dropped his head back and released a slow breath before returning his gaze to the man at his feet. "You fucked up, REM." His tone was calm again—which was somehow more terrifying than his earlier rage. "Never mind your diseased dick and where you mistakenly *thought* you were going to stick it. You. Touched. Someone who belongs to *me*."

Holy. Fuck.

I felt dizzy again, but for an entirely different reason. Regardless of how staunchly Wolfy resisted our connection, he'd just claimed me as *his*. He said I *belonged to him* after body-slamming my attacker through a metal door into a back alleyway and beating him into submission.

He's never getting rid of me now.

A scream of pure terror snapped my attention back to the panty-melting scene before me. Wolfy had removed his gloves, and Remington—*REM*—was howling as if the grim reaper himself had come for him.

Is he on drugs or something?

"Oh, fuck, oh, fuck, nonononono. I didn't know he was yours. I swear, I thought he was just looking for a good time. Jesus *FUCK*, Wolfgang! Are you really gonna *drain* me over some slutty cocktease?"

Rude.

Accurate, but still rude.

Wolfy lifted a hand, making Remington immediately stop his yammering and start trying to crawl away. "No. I'm not. But I'm going to make sure you never *look* at what's mine again."

Faster than I could register, Wolfy pounced—caging the other man in while he did *something* that had him shrieking in unholy agony. When he rose to his feet again, his hands were dripping with blood and Remington was convulsing on the ground, clutching at his face.

This is pure torture porn.

"Really, Wolfgang?" Erich suddenly appeared at my side, taking in the carnage with a surprising amount of resigned acceptance.

Maybe violence also turns him on...

Wolfy spun to face us, his eyes widening when he discovered me standing there. I couldn't stop staring at his blood-covered hands, which he frantically wiped with his handkerchief before shoving them back inside his gloves.

"Did you..." I swept my gaze over the man groaning on the ground, still absorbing what I'd stumbled upon. "Did you just *gouge out his eyes?* For me?"

"I'm going to make sure you never look at what's mine again."

Clearly misunderstanding the effect this was having on me, Wolfy winced—looking almost ashamed. "He was going to hurt you..."

Because I belong to him.

The reality of the situation suddenly washed over me like a bucket of ice water, causing my adrenaline to plummet and my body to shake.

He was going to hurt me...

Being the size I was, I always tried to be extra vigilant. I never accepted drinks I hadn't watched being made—and rarely wandered off alone—but I'd allowed my emotions to get the better of me. I'd been so blinded by jealousy over whoever

Violentia was to Wolfy, I let down my guard and left myself open to attack.

But then my hero arrived.

Wolfy took a step toward me before stopping in his tracks, his eyes traveling over every inch of me, as if assessing my injuries.

Please come closer.

Touch me, please.

"Can you tell us what happened, Simon?" Erich gently spoke, allowing me to lean on him while he impatiently gestured at Wolfy to remove his suit jacket.

"I-I'm not sure…" I mumbled, still struggling to make sense of it. "All of a sudden, I felt so *tired*… like I could barely keep my eyes open. The next thing I knew, Remington had me pinned against the door. I couldn't move… It felt like I was paralyzed."

Erich swore under his breath. "That *arschloch* must have used his power—"

"He must have *drugged* Simon somehow," Wolfy cut in, fixing Erich with a hard look as he handed his jacket to *him* instead of me before quickly backing away from us again.

"Wolfy…" I took a step toward him with my arms outstretched. While I knew I should respect his boundaries, I legitimately felt as if I would perish if he didn't hold me. "I *need* you."

Please.

He took another step backwards, his expression pained. "I… *can't*, Simon. I'm sorry—"

"Du vollidiot hast es ihm verschwiegen, Wolfgang?" Erich shouted as he yanked me back and wrestled me into Wolfy's jacket. *"Was hast du dir nur dabei gedacht, du verdammter, wichser! Er könnte verletzt werden!"*

Wolfy frantically shook his head at Erich—most likely to shut him up since I understood German well enough to be dangerous.

My Austrian father was good for something.

"Tell me *what?!*" I shouted, nearly imploding with the cocktail of emotions I was feeling. *"C'est des conneries!* What *else* have you *lied* to me about, *boss?*"

Enough of this!

Wolfy flinched, but didn't reply. I opened my mouth to truly give him a piece of my mind when horrible laughter filled the blood-soaked air.

"That he's actually a *monster,*" Remington chuckled low—shakily clambering to his knees and lowering his hands from his battered face. I gaped at the sight of his *empty eye sockets,* but he kept going as if nothing were amiss. "A monster among monsters, and all you've done is sign your fucking death warrant by associating—"

"Don't you *dare* threaten him," Wolfy growled, starting to remove his gloves again for some inexplicable reason.

Some inexplicable, yet incredibly attractive reason...

"I don't *need* to, Suarez!" Remington barked, grinning like a madman and revealing that most of his teeth were missing now as well. "If he doesn't die by your cursed hand, someone from my clan will finish the job. After what you've done to me tonight—*unprovoked*—you'll be lucky if Mistress Noir-Rouge lets either of you live. Oh! And I may have already let her know you were in town…"

Erich swore again as Wolfy fumbled his phone out of his pocket and began texting someone. I noticed the slightest tremor in his hands, even though his voice remained steady as he responded to Remington's not-so-mild threat.

"Unprovoked?" he huffed, stuffing his phone back in his pocket and catching the car keys Erich tossed at him. "It was entirely within my right to protect what's *mine*."

"He's not your *clan*, Wolfgang," Remington taunted, as shouting from inside the club made him turn his sightless eyes toward the busted exit door. "Rules are rules—"

"He's my *inventus*, you piece of shit," Wolfy hissed, which immediately made the other man clamp his mouth shut.

Inventus?

"*Inventus?*" Erich echoed my thoughts, sounding as confused as I was before clearing his throat. "Wolfgang, you and Simon need to leave. Now."

The commotion inside was drawing closer, but Wolfy wasn't done. "That's right, you fucking scumbag. Tell your Mistress *who* you pissed off tonight. She knows I already have one bonded pair in my pocket. What the fuck is Noir-Rouge gonna do against *two?*"

Remington had lowered himself to the ground during this monologue, shaking in terror as he plastered himself to the asphalt like a fresh coat of paint.

I was still racking my brain to figure out what an *inventus* was when Wolfy turned to address me. "Noir-Rouge soldiers are here, Simon. We need to go." When I hesitated, he took a tentative step closer. "Please, *boss*."

Oh, this man.

I huffed a laugh, physically unable to stay mad at him. "Well, since you asked so nicely…"

Drawing Wolfy's fantastic smelling jacket tighter around me, I obediently followed him to Erich's car, realizing a swift getaway was more important than my tender emotions.

It doesn't mean I won't expect something for the pain.

"However," I sweetly cooed as I slid into the passenger seat, "I have a few questions you *will* be answering once we get to whatever five-star resort you're taking me to."

"Yes, boss," my dream man murmured, and I breathed a sigh of relief to see his lips curling up ever so slightly. "I'll tell you everything I can."

CHAPTER 12
WOLFGANG

I hoped Simon would forgive me. Not only for what happened to him at Benediktion, but for how I responded. While I didn't regret taking REM's eyes—he deserved far worse—I prayed I hadn't scarred the normie for life.

He never should have witnessed that...

REM's extremely accurate description of me as 'a monster among monsters' played on an endless loop in my brain as I drove us to our hideout. Simon hadn't *looked* scared when he heard it said, but he could have been dissociating after his traumatic experience.

What if he asks why REM called me that?

"Violentia isn't my girlfriend," I blurted out, desperate to give him something without revealing everything. "Remington was just being an asshole cockblocker after you turned him down. Vi's my *sister*, and she's been missing for months."

And I need to talk to someone about it.

Simon slowly turned in the passenger seat to face me. I'd allowed him to sit up front—even though it was terrifying—

because I couldn't bring myself to disappoint him any more than I already had.

"Thank you for telling me," he quietly replied. "That... makes a lot more sense, and now I feel a bit silly for stomping away." He paused, obviously mulling over my revelation. "Why didn't you include that information in the file you gave me?"

Tell him the truth, Wolfy.

I pulled into the hidden garage at our destination but left Erich's car running while I gathered my courage. Blowing out a slow breath, I finally turned to face the man beside me.

"Because I don't know if she's defected from our family," I carefully spoke, still wanting to keep my monstrous supe qualities to myself. "And I didn't want you to think less of me if I ended up having to... *kill* my own sister..."

Simon slowly nodded, searching my face in the low light from the dashboard, his green eyes piercing my soul. "You don't want to kill her."

It wasn't a question, and for a moment, I was too stunned to speak. That he immediately understood my anguish cracked something open deep inside me—letting in the tiniest glimmer of light.

He sees me.

"No," I breathed out, my shoulders slumping from the weight of carrying it all. "I really fucking don't."

Because it will kill a piece of me as well.

"We're here, then?" Simon peered through the windshield, smoothly changing the subject before I could shatter completely. "This doesn't appear to be the Ritz..."

I chuckled and turned off the car. "It's not, but it was the safest bet. By now, the Noir-Rouge clan will be swarming every hotel in the city looking for us. It's why I also texted our pilot to hop to another airport. Let them think we left Berlin—"

"Won't they know to look at your family's properties?" Simon interrupted, surprising me yet again with how his brain worked.

I'm so thankful to have someone like him around.

"They will," I confirmed, exiting the car and circling to his side to open the door. "But no one knows about this place except me."

Simon nodded and stepped out of the car, holding my jacket closed over his bare chest as he followed me inside. I assumed it was less about modesty and more for warmth and comfort, as I'd caught him sniffing the lapel a few times during the drive.

He said I smelled like home.

I knew he'd only been putting on a show in 360 Bar, but he smelled like heaven to me. Fruity, floral, and spicy, with a hint of vanilla that I assumed came from whatever cologne he wore. But there was a natural undertone that tempted me closer, and I wished I could bury my face against every inch of him—inhale his skin into my lungs until the only thing I ever smelled again was *him.*

"I love what you've done with the place," Simon dryly commented—his sarcasm making me smile as he brought me back to our present location.

The street level first floor we'd entered was barren, but there was a reason for that. "It's an art gallery," I explained. "Or it will be once my brothers graduate."

He glanced at me. "Your brothers are artists?"

I should have kept this intel to myself, since a supe's identity was sacred. This unwritten—but extremely binding—rule included your enemies, but especially applied to your family. That two of the most powerful villains in Big City were attending art school alongside a bunch of normies would be front-page news, but all Gabe and Dre ever wanted was to blend into the background.

Except their art does the exact opposite.

"Yes." I smiled, glancing around and envisioning the space filled with their creations. "The two youngest are twins and aspiring industrial designers. They're finishing up their senior year in college and never wanted to be a part of the... family business."

My smile faded. I'd done my best to keep my parents' attention on me—to offer *my* services whenever they needed to instill terror or eliminate another supe—but the twins had occasionally been dragged into a job. They would be unresponsive for days afterward, and the memories of them as kids, staring at the wall and holding hands while tears ran down their identical faces, still haunted me.

I'll never let that happen again.

"So they plan to move to Berlin after university?" Simon softly spoke. He'd stepped closer—not too close—and lowered his voice, as if coaxing me out of my painful thoughts like an injured animal who'd retreated into a hole.

Another accurate description.

I cleared my throat. "They, um... they don't know about this place yet." I could feel my cheeks heat, and I was thankful that the only light was from the street lamps outside the windows. "I purchased the building as a graduation present..."

Simon huffed a laugh. "Extravagant gifts are your love language, hmm?"

"Only for people I care about," I replied, holding his gaze. "Which is a very short list."

A list you're on now.

He took another discreet sniff of my jacket. "Is the shower upstairs? I need to scrub *eau de fils de pute* off my skin."

Recalling REM's hands on Simon caused a fresh wave of fury and shame to wash over me. If it hadn't been for *me*, that piece of shit wouldn't have targeted my... my...

Fuck, I called him my inventus.

I'd said it in the heat of the moment, so REM would think twice before seeking revenge for my attack. I also trusted the villain was too stupid to challenge the legitimacy of my claim since, for all he knew, Simon was a supe adept at hiding his powers.

And luckily, only Erich openly questioned it.

Normies didn't know what an *inventus* was. Even to supes, it was more urban legend than reality, since so few with the ability to bond survived being preemptively picked off by overly cautious competition.

I'd suspected something related to an *inventus* bond was brewing when Xander started exhibiting powers after decades of nothing. When he idiotically brought Butch to dinner at the Suarez family compound, our mother poked at the hero's leashed powers just enough to alert me to the fact he was a supe—and therefore, a threat.

I'm sure she expected me to take him out while Xanny was away from the table.

Unfortunately for her, my loyalties had already been spoken for. And when Xander solidified his connection with Butch before throwing our father's cryonic power back at him like a fastball, I knew I'd bet on the right horse.

I wasn't only proud of my brother for taking out a legendary villain like Apocalypto Man, or thankful his dormant superpowers had finally come out to play. More than anything, I recognized his bond with Captain Masculine for what it was —a chance for the Suarez clan to be even more formidable and feared than we already were.

It's how the game is played.

Thanks to the hours I'd spent in my family's archives researching the phenomenon, I also knew having an *inventus* was about more than just power-sharing. These pairs—or triads, in rare cases—also possessed deep emotional connections, along with extra murderous levels of protectiveness.

The kind of relationship I can only dream about.

I cleared my throat, realizing Simon was still waiting for directions. "The shower's upstairs, next to the bedroom." I led the way in the unlikely event our location had been compromised. "There are towels in the cabinet and I'll dig up some clothes for—"

"There's no rush on that, as I prefer to sleep naked," Simon brightly replied, blessedly back to his usual antics. "But did you say bed*room*—singular? Are we to have an only-one-bed, forced-proximity situation?"

I stifled a smile as we passed through the singular bedroom in question. "As you can see, there are *two* beds. This place is for twins, remember?"

Simon scoffed behind me. "Or an old married couple from a 1950s sitcom. But we're neither of those things, are we, Wolfy?"

I flicked on the bathroom light and turned to face him, sharply inhaling at what had been illuminated. The sight of Simon standing next to the bed—engulfed in little else but boots, leather gloves, and *my* suit jacket—flipped a primal switch in my brain.

Mine.

I'd hastily called this tiny tyrant my *inventus* to save our skins, even though the bond only ever happened between supes. But there was no denying the ownership I felt.

He's definitely mine.

I knew this was a dangerous game to be playing, but I despised every secret left between us. This connection we shared—whatever you wanted to label it—was impossible to deny.

And I'll take anything I can get from him.

"No. We're not," I confirmed, gesturing for him to approach —knowing he wouldn't touch me. "And we're not just an employer with his employee, either."

Simon smiled as he came to a stop, shrugging off my suit jacket and carefully handing it to me. "Good man," he whispered before entering the bathroom.

He glanced back over his shoulder before shutting the door— but instead of commenting on how I was ogling his lace-covered ass, his expression sobered.

"Will you do something about the separate beds, Wolfy? I promise I'll respect your boundaries, but I just... I need to be as close to you as possible tonight."

I solemnly nodded, even as I broke out in a cold sweat over the idea. In the end, we both knew I'd push the beds together. While I couldn't give Simon everything he wanted—everything we *both* wanted—I'd give him anything I could.

And wish it could be everything.

CHAPTER 13
SIMON

I was shocked to have slept as well as I did, considering what happened at Benediktion. But no monsters pursued me—no nightmares disturbed my slumber—and I peacefully blinked myself awake just as the sun was setting again.

It's the nocturnal life for me.

Even more thrilling than the lack of sunlight was the flawless face I woke up to.

That I'd actually caught Wolfy *sleeping* felt like a gift, and I allowed my gaze to take in the perfect specimen before me. He was lying on his side, his criminally long lashes brushing his cheekbones, and his kissable lips parted slightly as he puffed out adorable little snoozy breaths.

He's simply the cutest, most handsomest eyeball gouger there ever was.

While awake, Wolfy was a fascinating combination of intimidation and mystery—an untouchable yet tempting package of hot sex. But right now, he looked almost... vulnerable.

I want to take care of him.

And fuck him.

But the before and aftercare would be part of the deal.

Despite his own hangups, he'd pushed the beds together as I'd requested. I swore up and down I wouldn't cross the divide, and I'd kept my promise all night—even though I felt almost sick to my stomach with the overwhelming need to touch him.

Maybe I'm coming down with something.

Just as I was enjoying my fiftieth trip down Lecherous Lane, Wolfy startled awake, freezing like a deer in the headlights to find me admiring him from across the way.

"Relax, Sleeping Beauty," I cooed, laughing when he attempted to hide his face in the pillow he'd cuddled with all night. "I would never fondle you while you dozed. Not unless *somnophilia* is one of your many latent kinks..."

Wolfy immediately lifted his head, and I gasped at the dark lust replacing his normally impassive expression.

Oh, he likes that idea, does he?

Just as quickly, his eyes widened, and I watched—fascinated—as an entire gamut of emotions passed over his face. Uncertainty, concern, murderous rage, and shame all had their turn, and it was that last one that spurred me into action.

"Stop that right now, Wolfgang," I scolded, wishing I could slap some sense into him. "None of this is your fault."

"It is, though," he hissed, but I knew his vitriol was squarely aimed at himself. "Erich was right. I never should have put you on Remington's radar."

"No!" I barked, propping myself up on an elbow to better glare at him. "You are *not* responsible for his deplorable actions. If it hadn't been me, that predator would've just targeted someone else."

"But it *was* you," Wolfy growled, his hotness factor skyrocketing the more agitated he became. "And it's my responsibility to protect you. Because you're mi—"

He snapped his mouth shut, cutting himself off before he could finish the sentence, but I knew exactly what he was going to say.

Mine.

That *word* caused something to click into place. Wolfy had swooped in like an angel of death last night, showing Remington in no uncertain terms who I belonged to. He then took me somewhere safe and stepped out of his own comfort zone to push the beds together and provide me with the extra security I needed.

The entire situation could have been much worse, but as long as I was with Wolfy, I knew I would be safe from harm and avenged in the most violent way possible.

Which is why he's my dream man.

Well, that and his latent kinks…

"That's right," I purred, tossing fuel on the fire while wondering if I could finally strike the match. "I am yours. Which means the only man who gets to stalk me down dark hallways is you. Because it should have been *you* pinning me up against that door. It should have been *your* hands on me —touching me everywhere while I was helpless to stop you…"

"Careful, Simon," Wolfy warned, his jaw clenched so tightly I feared he'd chip a tooth. His gloved hand clenched around the pillow—the leathery creak going straight to my balls.

He must know that only encourages me.

"*Putain*, I'm so hard just thinking about it," I kept going—brat that I was—slipping my hand beneath the sheet to find my aching cock.

Wolfy tracked the movement, his gorgeous eyes darkening when I blatantly slid my hand along my shaft.

Luckily, the loose sweatpants I wore allowed full freedom of movement, although I would have preferred to sleep naked. I also would have preferred Wolfy be in less clothing, rather than the fresh suit he'd disappointingly put on after his shower.

I'm going to get this man naked if it's the last thing I do.

For a moment, I wondered if he was horribly scarred under his clothes—if *that* was why he wore gloves all the time. Of course, all that mental picture did was turn me on more, and I had to grip the base of my dick to not spill too soon.

There's still plenty of teasing to do.

"Do you want to know what makes me even harder?" I rasped, edging myself right along with him. "Recalling what you did to Remington last night."

Wolfy's gaze snapped to mine. "You... *enjoyed* seeing that?" he choked out, the look of pure astonishment on his face making me smirk.

"Mmhmm..." I hummed, resuming my strokes and wishing I'd put my leather gloves back on. "When I saw you standing over him with blood dripping from your hands... knowing you did that for me... *fuuuck.*"

With a growl, Wolfy flung his pillow barrier away, prowling close enough that I could have reached out and grabbed him.

But I want it to be on his *terms.*

Unsurprisingly, he didn't touch me, but I was enjoying this game far too much to care.

"You want to see, Wolfy?" I panted, thrusting up into my hand as I increased my pace. "Want to see how fucking hard you make me?"

"Yes," he whispered, barely audible, his eyes wild and locked on the action. "Show me."

Time for a little exposure therapy.

"Pull the sheet down and I'll show you," I taunted, feeling pressure building in my spine.

My gaze drifted from the outline of his enormous cock—visibly straining against his trousers—to his gloved hand as it reached for me. I wiggled closer, praying to every unholy god that the leather would brush against my skin when he moved the sheet.

Almost there...

Then his goddamn phone rang.

Wolfy leaped away from me like I had the plague—his eyes wide and terrified and both hands held up like he was under arrest.

"I am going to *MURDER* whoever that is on the line!" I shouted, already envisioning the possibilities as I squeezed my cock in despair. "And it won't be quick. I will resurrect medieval torture methods for this person. They'll be tarred and feathered and closed up in the Iron Maiden so they can think long and hard about what they've done—"

"Shit," Wolfy quietly swore as he checked the screen before glancing at me apologetically. "Simon, please, just..."

While I would have loved to continue ranting so the offender could hear it, the look of deep concern on Wolfy's face told me this was serious. I obediently quieted down, fully intending on luring him back into my clutches after the call ended.

Yet again, I watched in fascination as Wolfy's expression smoothed out—his entire demeanor morphing into an impenetrable mask as he answered his phone.

Why is that so hot?

"Mistress," he spoke so calmly, it took me a moment to realize *who* was on the other end of the line.

Shit is right.

"Yes, I *was* in Berlin—visiting an acquaintance," Wolfy replied to the head of the Noir-Rouge mafia, sounding like he couldn't be any less interested in the conversation. "But I left soon after I had the displeasure of running into one of *your* men. I'm sure you've heard how disrespectful Remington was to me?"

The size of this man's balls...

My thoughts drifted to dreaming about how large Wolfy's balls *were* when he suddenly tensed.

I held my breath, but Wolfy kept his voice impressively steady as he asked, "What do you mean, you're outside my door?"

No one knows about this location but him...

Wolfy quickly put the call on speaker so he could multitask on his phone. I scooted closer, feeling no small bit of satisfaction when he didn't flinch at my proximity.

We're making progress.

"I'm outside the former Handwerk Galerie." A seductively low female voice with a hint of a French accent drifted up from the speaker as he brought up a security app. "I believe you know the one."

The security camera's live feed flickered on and I froze to see the street view outside—along with an extremely formidable dominatrix.

Smirking at the camera.

Wolfy dropped his head in defeat before bringing the phone to his ear again. "I'll be down in a minute, Sabine."

Wait, what?!

"What?!" I repeated out loud as soon as he ended the call. "Y-you can't go down there. What if she tries to... *stab* you? She looks like the type to wear a garter full of knives. She may even have a few stuffed up her vagina."

Women do love their pockets.

My extremely valid concerns only earned me a humorless chuckle from Wolfy. "If Mistress Noir-Rouge wanted us dead, we'd be buried in a pile of rubble, fifty feet underground. Trust me on that."

He stood and smoothed his gloved hands over his miraculously unwrinkled suit before meeting my gaze again. "However, I didn't follow protocol by letting her know I was in town—"

"Which was *my* fault," I huffed before sliding off the bed. "Therefore, I'm going with you." I shoved my feet into my boots and grabbed the T-shirt Wolfy tried—and failed—to make me wear to bed last night.

The sweatpants were quite enough, thank you.

"Absolutely not!" he hissed, sending me a sexy glare that only made my deflating boner stir to life again. "I refuse to put you in another villain's sights."

I rolled my eyes. "Such a dramatic choice of words. Listen, Wolfgang. I'm not allowing you to walk into danger alone, and that's final."

Wolfy opened and closed his mouth a few times, before rather unwisely choosing to continue arguing. "Simon, this is my life. It's the world I've been actively involved in since I was young. Mistress Noir-Rouge was an associate of my parents, so I've known her since I was born."

"What's the hierarchy here?" I bluntly asked, crossing my arms and jutting out a cheeky hip.

And a cheeky boner, full disclosure.

Wolfy definitely noticed my cheek, but staunchly focused on my question. "Well, my parents are both *dead*, so—"

"So you're head of your family and therefore, at the same level as this Mistress," I deduced. When he nodded, I smoothly added, "So it would be entirely appropriate for your assistant to accompany you to a business meeting. Your *inventus*, too, I gather."

Whatever the hell that is.

Wolfy paled and swallowed thickly—looking exactly as guilty as when I'd discovered he was actually my boss instead of just a Hottie McBodyguard.

But we both know I'm the boss around here.

"It's decided then." I clapped my hands, ready to move things along so we could get back to bed. "Lead the way! I can't wait to meet another one of your old friends."

CHAPTER 14
WOLFGANG

As unpleasant as this conversation with Sabine Noir-Rouge was going to be, I was grateful for the interruption.

My self-control was usually unshakable, but Simon had a pull on me that I was finding harder and harder to resist. I may have looked relaxed on the outside, but it took everything in me to regain the composure I'd lost as I led him downstairs to the street-level gallery.

What the hell was I thinking back there?

I'd been so blinded by lust, I'd come within inches of accidentally killing him. This was a dangerous game for both of us, but especially for the temptation on my heels.

I would never forgive myself if he died by my hand.

Butch was right. Erich was right. Even that idiot REM was right. My conscience was screaming at me to stop playing with fire and just *tell* Simon who I was. He could still work for me, but he'd at least know to keep his distance, and I wouldn't have to worry about what happened upstairs ever happening again.

But fuck, I want it to…

It was incredibly selfish of me to continue down this path knowing how it could end, but I couldn't bring myself to stop. Simon *wanted* me. He wanted *me*. Not just the normie-sanctioned veneer of money and power, but what lay beneath.

What no one ever saw.

Because I'd never shown them.

And because no one's ever cared to look.

But Simon had glimpsed the broken pieces of my violent soul, and instead of running in the opposite direction, he'd willingly beckoned me closer. Of course, he had no idea that death's embrace waited for him in my arms, but I was starting to wonder if he'd care even if he knew.

From what I'd seen, I wouldn't be surprised if he chose to burn with me.

How can I be expected to give up someone like that?

"Please stay here," I murmured, gesturing for Simon to position himself near one of the load-bearing columns dotting the open space. Blessedly, he obeyed without his usual sass.

As much as I love his attitude, now is not the time.

I hadn't been exaggerating when I mentioned Mistress Noir-Rouge—otherwise known as Seisma—could bring the building down around us if she wanted to. She was an extremely powerful supe, capable of manipulating the earth's mantle and entire tectonic plates. I'd once witnessed her create a tidal wave that wiped an entire island off the map, with no survivors.

One of my earliest memories, actually…

"Ah, *mon loup*," the villain at my door cooed when I swung it open, although her broad smile was more like a baring of teeth. She appeared to be alone, but I spotted at least five locations where one of her men could be lurking, waiting to take me out.

But that's not how we play.

With a polite nod, I stepped back and allowed her to enter, knowing better than to flinch when she swept past so close, her leather duster brushed against me.

We were in a pissing contest at this point. Yes, I was in Noir-Rouge's territory—unannounced—but I was her equal, in standing and superpowers. It didn't matter that she'd seen me in diapers. The day my parents died, Sabine owed me the same level of respect she commanded.

As expected, she zeroed in on Simon the instant the door was closed. True to form, he unflinchingly stared back, which—unsurprisingly—made my dick twitch.

He carries himself like a supe.

Sabine made an amused sound in the back of her throat before addressing me alone. "It's such a pleasant surprise to find you in my city, Wolfgang. I wasn't expecting to see your handsome face so soon after Ender and Signe's... *untimely* demise."

"Yes, I've been preoccupied with getting my family's affairs in order," I sighed, absently brushing invisible lint off my suit even as I kept my awareness locked on her. "To lose both of my parents so suddenly was a terrible blow, so I decided a trip abroad was needed—to take my mind off my grief."

I kept my voice steady, with just a hint of sadness, knowing full well she was fishing for proof that I was behind their deaths.

Which I was.

And I'd do it again.

I felt zero remorse for my hand in it—and had been plotting their *untimely* demise for decades. While my strict childhood was fairly standard for any supe born into a high-powered family, I knew for a fact the way my siblings and I were treated was exceptionally harsh. Especially for me.

Some would even call it abusive.

Our value had always been determined by our usefulness—how strong our powers were, plus how willing we were to get our hands bloody for the family. The exception to the rule was Xander. Despite his genius inventions and availability to fuck up normies we supes weren't supposed to touch, my brother's apparent lack of powers made him expendable in our parents' eyes.

Which made them *my enemies.*

From what Xanny told me, Butch experienced a similar upbringing to mine, although the fundamental difference was that *his* parents apparently cared whether he lived or died.

Such a shame Vortexio met his end at the bottom of Dead Man's Ravine.

Along with my mother.

A serene smile stretched across my face at the fond memories. "Sabine, I'd like to introduce you to—"

"Simon Alarie, I know." She advanced on the other man and I stiffened, although all the villain did was extend a hand to him as if expecting him to kiss her rings.

To my surprise, Simon looked at *me,* as if to confirm what would be an appropriate response in this situation.

This has to be an act.

I subtly nodded, and he pinched the tips of her fingers between his own, delivering the limpest shake I'd ever seen.

"Enchanté," he cooed, laying his French accent on thick, which only turned me on even more. "I see my reputation precedes me."

Who is this polite man, and what has he done with Simon?

I should've known better than to believe his attitude would stay under wraps.

"Although, I'm afraid you've interrupted our daily spanking session," he casually added, fluttering his long eyelashes—the epitome of bratty innocence. "So if we could wrap up this social call, Wolfy's arse would appreciate it."

Fuck, he's going to get me hard in front of this woman.

Sabine only threw back her head and cackled. *"Enchantée,* indeed," she hummed before slyly glancing at me. "Although if you were so desperate to experience *la petite mort* at the hands of the French, Wolfgang, I would have been more than happy to demonstrate…"

Shit.

Before I could intervene, Simon growled like a rabid animal, bringing Sabine's smug attention back to him.

"So it *is* true," she murmured, smiling triumphantly and circling Simon like prey while I internally panicked. "You've finally found someone who can… *handle* you."

Shit, shit, shit.

I was in an extremely precarious position. While it was known how insanely protective *inventus* pairs were over each other, they were also supposedly equal in power.

Sabine would rightfully find it unusual that I'd somehow found a previously unknown supe to bond with who also happened to be a perfect match.

Extremely powerful supes—like me, Sabine, and Butch—could lock down our powers to where we could blend in with normies, undetectable by our own kind. She was probably already sending out tendrils of power to push against Simon's barriers—to see if she could coax his powers into surfacing.

Sizing up her potential opponent.

I had to pray that Mistress Noir-Rouge's failure to elicit a response from Simon would be interpreted as proof of his supremacy.

Otherwise, he's as good as dead.

Meanwhile, I had to fucking stand here and watch as the man I was obsessed with was stalked by yet another predator. If I gave any hint that Simon *needed* my protection, the game would be up.

I swear on all that is holy—if she touches him, I will start a war.

"Interesting," she finally murmured, looking begrudgingly impressed. "And here I thought Remington was simply telling stories."

"I would suggest never speaking that name in my presence again, Mistress," I warned, as respectfully as I could, considering how close I was to detonation. "He's lucky I left him alive, considering he touched what's *mine*."

Uncaring that I was laying every card I had on the table—save one—I held Simon's gaze as I made this proclamation, hopefully conveying how desperately I wanted those words to be true.

I wish you could be mine.

Simon's perfect lips curled into a soft smile, his gaze momentarily dropping to trail over me before he sent a judgmental glare Sabine's way.

"Yes, and I, for one, am a bit disappointed that cunt didn't join you here today," he sniffed. "Since he owes *both* of us an apology—preferably while groveling on his knees."

That's it. Now I'm hard again.

Having been involved in this world since I was young, I thought very little could surprise me. But that was until I saw Mistress Sabine Noir-Rouge—*Seisma*—respectfully give Simon space before inclining her head.

"I agree with you completely," she gracefully replied. "But I felt it would be better if you heard it from me."

Simon remained impressively aloof, while my jaw dropped to the floor at this uncharacteristic display of deference.

If only she knew she was apologizing to a normie.

"The Noir-Rouge family may not have the cleanest hands," Sabine continued, awkwardly smoothing hers down the front of her signature corset. "But I apologize for what was done in my city—in *my* name. Consent is of utmost importance to me, and my men know that. Remington attempted to excuse his heinous actions, but luckily, your friend Erich was available to give me the full story of what happened at Benediktion."

When I sharply inhaled, she clarified. "Oh, don't fret, *mon loup*. Your precious DJ is much too talented for me to damage. Thanks to him—and others at the club—I now know that Remington made a habit of assaulting patrons with his... special talents. And as I no longer find these talents useful, I've disposed of their owner."

I would have done worse.

My gaze drifted to Simon again, curious about how he would interpret Sabine's words. He'd *claimed* to enjoy seeing REM's blood on my hands after I made his eyeballs explode, but an execution—sans trial—was a different story.

He didn't disappoint. "Did you at least cut off his dick first? Preferably with a butter knife to drag out the event."

Fuck, can I get any harder?

Mistress Noir-Rouge laughed again, throwing Simon a genuine smile. "What a delightful terror you are—perfect for our Wolfgang." Winking at me, she turned and headed for the door.

"We'll be leaving Berlin today," I called after her, instinctively moving closer to Simon. "Wouldn't want to wear out our welcome."

Especially as this location is apparently compromised.

"You're welcome in my city any time, *mon loup*, as is anyone in your clan," she replied, pausing at the door to face us again. "Although your *sister* might want to steer clear."

I froze. "You've seen Violentia?"

Sabine gave me a tight smile. "No, I haven't. But there are rumors that *someone* is vying for your throne—and all signs point to her, no?"

It felt like being punched in the gut. All this time, I'd been hoping Vi was simply pissed at me for hiding what I knew about Xanny's powers and then aligning with him and Butch to eliminate our parents. Yes, they were *big* secrets, but I had my reasons for keeping them from her.

How could she fucking betray me?

Being the only Suarez daughter, Violentia and our mother had always been close. But my sister *knew* how Glacial Girl and Apocalypto Man treated me—how they sent me into battle in their stead, against much older supes I had no business stepping into the ring with.

And then left me battered and alone afterward to lick my own bloody wounds.

"She would never," I rasped, pure rage setting my veins on fire before ice-cold despair washed it all away.

I'm such a fucking fool.

The Mistress of Berlin hummed thoughtfully as she turned to go. "Perhaps Violentia isn't the one you truly need to worry about. If I were in your shoes, I'd be more concerned about who your sister may be working for."

CHAPTER 15
SIMON

Thanks for murdering my boner, Mistress.

To be fair, I was thankful Noir-Rouge hadn't tried killing us, but the dazed look her bombshell had left on Wolfy's handsome face made me itch to unalive someone.

I'd start with Violentia if it wouldn't make things worse.

Wolfy had confided that the last thing he wanted was to harm his sister, but now it had been all but confirmed she was plotting against him. I couldn't imagine the position that put him in—on top of the existing responsibilities of running his empire. The weight of that would almost be unbearable.

But now he has me to help him carry it.

I straightened my shoulders. Regardless of the extremely blurred lines of our professional relationship, it was my actual job to assist him, so I made an executive decision.

If I can't give my boss a stress-relieving blowie, he'll get the next best thing.

"How about I draw you a bath," I softly spoke, so as not to startle him.

"What?" Wolfy choked out, the surprise in his expression breaking my heart all over again.

"A bath. In the tub," I enunciated. "That way you can relax for a tick while our pilot returns to Brandenburg and I instruct Uber Eats to deliver the fattest bratwurst around. You know, since my attempt at getting my hands on *yours* earlier was so rudely interrupted."

I preened when Wolfy huffed an amused sound. "You really are ridiculous," he chuckled, blessedly released from his dark mood.

"You like it," I teased, smiling up at him.

He gazed down at me with so much intensity, my breath caught. "Yes. I do."

Another moment passed before he huffed again, running a gloved hand through his hair. "You actually remind me of my brother, Xander. Specifically, your lack of filter and general brattiness... although it's far less annoying coming from you."

I smirked, pleased as punch by this overshare. "It's because I'm your favorite."

He nodded, rewarding me with a broad smile, although his eyes still seemed sad.

My poor broken murder baby.

"So, about that bath..." I urged, herding him upstairs the best I could without touching him.

"A shower will be fine, Simon," he murmured, his attention already on his phone. "I'll get the plane back to Berlin and let Erich know where we are..."

This man needs a vacation.

"Well then, at least allow me to *turn on* the shower for you," I sighed, throwing up my hands in exasperation. *"Tu es vraiment emmerdant!* You're such a pain in my arse."

He shot me a cheeky smirk over his shoulder. "But I'm your favorite, too."

I sniffed. "Not at the moment."

Always and forever.

After following Wolfy upstairs, I fulfilled my very important duty of turning the shower knob before leaving him in peace. Despite wishing he'd invited me in to assist with washing his dick, I busied myself with ordering us food and straightening up to prepare for our departure.

My gaze fell on where Wolfy's suit jacket had been thrown across a chair in a surprisingly haphazard manner. It wasn't bothering *me*, but *he* seemed like the type to press his socks, so I took it as just another sign of his splintering mental state.

Wanting him to find nothing but order after his shower, I started to neatly rearrange the jacket when the pocket suddenly vibrated.

Should I?

I was torn. Previous employers had given me *carte blanche* to intercept their incoming calls and messages, but Wolfy and I hadn't discussed that yet.

Then his phone buzzed again—and again—and I decided it must be our pilot or Erich requiring an immediate response.

And if it's neither, I'll immediately avert my eyes.

Just kidding. I'm totally gonna snoop.

The lock screen hadn't activated yet, so when I tapped his phone, I was immediately delivered to a group chat named **The Rabble.**

The Mouthy One: *Word on the street is that Wolfy melted REM's face like the creepy Nazi henchmen in Raiders of the Lost Ark.*

That's... oddly accurate.

The Dumb One: *Holy shit, I would have paid money to see that. REM-job was such a tampon.*

The Token Hero: *Guys, I don't think this is the best place to be discussing things, because of... you know...*

All at once, it clicked that *this* was the infamous group chat with his ball-buster siblings. Wolfy had mentioned one brother having a fiancé, so I assumed the polite voice of reason was him.

The Dumb One: *You're no fun, Cappy [eye roll emoji]*

The Dumb One: *Ok, how's dis... How are things going, Wolfgang? Have you melted the Frenchy-Brit's ass on your dick yet? [peach emoji] [volcano emoji]*

Oh, it's on.

As overjoyed as I was to discover Wolfy had gushed about me to his family, I immediately focused on trolling the trolls.

> ***I have, actually. By the time I was done with him, I could fit three John Holmes dildos in there alongside my cock.***

As expected, the chat went nuclear with simultaneous replies.

The Token Hero: Sugar!

The Dumb One: GYICTXJYRK YOU FUCKIN ANIMAAAAAL!!!!

The Mouthy One: I mean...

The Mouthy One: As long as everyone enjoyed themselves.

Three dots appeared and disappeared from **Thing One** before there was a break in the action.

Thing Two: What's my favorite color, Wolfy?

Ah, we have a detective in our midst.

It didn't take a rocket scientist to figure out this was one-half of the artistic twins.

> **Carnelian red. Like fresh blood that's crusted over just a smidge.**

Thing Two: Poetic, but wrong. Who is this?

The Dumb One: WHOEVER THIS IS I'M GONNA FUCKING POUND YOU INTO THE GROUND IF YOU'VE HURT MY BROTHER.

These Suarez men are so dramatic.

It was all I could do to not simply reply with an eye roll emoji myself.

> **No need to wave your dick around, Baby Hulk. This is Wolfy's assistant/true love/boss bitch, Simon.**

Your brother's currently in the shower having a wank. Would you like to leave a message?

The Mouthy One: *Ok, fuck Kai. Simon's my new bestie.*

The Token Hero: *Hi, Simon. I'm Butch. It's nice to meet you.*

Oh, he's precious.

The Dumb One: *Oh, ok cool. Hey, are you guys still in Berlin? Can you have Wolfy send me a case of Jäger?*

The Token Hero: *Baltasar...*

I can see why he's labeled **The Dumb One.**

It suddenly occurred to me that Violentia might still be a—silent—part of this conversation. A quick glance at the group members confirmed there was a sibling who hadn't yet piped in.

The One With the Biggest Dick.

Oh, no, darling. That's my *title.*

I'm afraid we're already on the plane, bound for Thailand. I've reserved a couple of rocket launchers upon arrival so Wolfy can blow things up and decompress.

Oh! And it looks like we're ready for take-off. Ciao, future brothers-in-law!

Feeling satisfied with my sneaky red herring, I quickly scrolled up to peek at the conversation from a few days prior, extremely chuffed to see it *was* about me, after all.

A fall wedding feels appropriate.

Deciding to save poking through Wolfy's browser history for another day, I minimized the app and slid his phone back into his jacket pocket just as the shower turned off.

My phone dinged to alert me that the food had arrived, so I quickly skipped downstairs to retrieve it. Thinking I might catch Wolfy in a towel, I hustled back as quickly as possible, but he was already dressed when I returned.

I swear, he has super speed.

"Ready for a two-person sausage party?" I sang, shaking the takeout bags enticingly and thankful to receive a smile in return.

He truly is painfully handsome.

"Let's save it for the plane," Wolfy replied, snagging his suit jacket and retrieving his phone from the pocket. "Erich is getting dropped off here any minute to drive us to the airport, but I can tell him to wait downstairs if you'd like to shower first."

"That won't be necessary." I waved a dismissive hand. "I'd rather be reunited with my full wardrobe first, anyway…"

I trailed off as Wolfy's phone rang and he frowned down at it before answering. "Butch? Is everything all right? No, we haven't decided where we're going… Thailand? Who told you—"

Oh…

Wolfy stiffened and slowly turned to face me, his amber eyes narrowing accusingly.

Well, well, well, if it isn't the consequences of my actions?

"Let me call you back," he growled before hanging up on his annoyingly do-gooder brother-in-law.

I immediately addressed the jury. "Your phone started going off, and I feared it was an emergency. The next thing I knew, I was defending *your* honor in **The Rabble** group chat."

Wolfy's eyes had now widened in horror—his face draining of color until he was almost as pale as me. Before I could say more, he'd opened the app and started scrolling, his other hand covering his mouth as he reviewed the damning evidence.

Probably to keep his jaw off the floor.

When he was done, he slid his phone back into his pocket and met my gaze—back to his impenetrable mask.

That's not a good sign.

"Do you have anything else to say?" he asked, the slightly threatening timbre of his voice making my cock stir to life again.

I squirmed, but held his gaze. "Well… I can see why you call the dumb one **The Dumb One**."

Wolfy stared at me another moment before barking a laugh. "You are absolutely fucking ridiculous. But yes, Balty is nowhere near the sharpest tool in the shed. Although, he means well. Most of the time."

"So you're not angry at me?" I tentatively asked. When he shook his head, I bit my lip and peered up at him through my eyelashes. "Not even enough for a mild spanking?"

He cocked an eyebrow. "I thought you told Noir-Rouge *I* was the one getting spanked."

I shrugged. "We can take turns. What if I told you I scrolled up to read more of the group chat?"

Just put me over your knee already.

Wolfy adorably pinked as he returned to frantically scrolling—his blush deepening as he went. When he met my gaze again, he looked sheepish.

"I didn't... hire you to... suck my dick," he mumbled. "Just so you know."

"Well, that's a disappointment!" I snapped good-naturedly. "How else am I supposed to get a performance review?"

He huffed another laugh. "What am I going to do with you, Simon?" His phone vibrated again, and he glanced down at the screen. "Erich's out back. It's time to go."

We didn't even get to christen the bed!

As we headed down the stairs, he murmured, almost hesitantly, "We shouldn't go to Thailand, however. The group chat isn't secure—"

"Yes, I know." I sniffed, offended he'd think so little of me. "I only said it to send your sister on a wild goose chase while we headed elsewhere for some R&R."

Wolfy turned to face me as we reached the door to the garage. "I love the way your mind works," he murmured with a smile that was far more respectful than I would have preferred.

The softness in his expression made me dizzy and produced an odd *pulling* sensation in my chest that felt like butterflies trying to escape.

I'm definitely coming down with something.

"Other parts of me also work quite well," I helpfully quipped. "In case you'd like a demonstration once we arrive."

The heartbreaking sadness returned to his eyes, but he didn't comment on my offer. "Which of my properties are we going to, anyway?"

"None of them," I smirked, excited to treat *him* for once. "We're headed to one of *mine*."

Somewhere no one will know to look.

CHAPTER 16
SIMON

Despite the Valensole fields being a two-and -a-half-hour drive away, the scent of lavender filled my nostrils as soon as we deplaned at the Nice Côte d'Azur Airport.

Or perhaps it's the tease of a man beside me.

That Wolfy smelled like my favorite things on earth—lavender, Earl Grey tea, and bondage—seemed terribly unfair. The compulsion to rub myself on him like a cat was driving me mad. If it wasn't for the mob boss who'd rudely interrupted us earlier, I could have been walking with a limp by now.

Yet, my arse is woefully unmolested.

"I would ask what you're thinking about," Wolfy murmured as he gestured for me to enter the car awaiting us on the tarmac. "But that's probably an invitation for trouble."

"Oh, you know I'll tell you anyway," I primly replied, even as I inwardly jumped for joy that he'd instigated the conversation at all.

Since Benediktion, the walls surrounding Wolfy were cracking. I assumed whatever happened to him in the past made it difficult to open up, but I was determined to draw him out until no barriers were left between us.

I may be a bit obsessed.

It was clear the news about Violentia had devastated him. More than anything, I wished I could give Wolfy a hug and a cuddle, but begrudgingly accepted that any physical contact between us would have to be on *his* terms.

Although, if he could hurry up and touch me already, I'd appreciate it.

So while I—slightly impatiently—waited for my boss to make the first move, I was more than happy to support him in other ways.

As a travel agent and tour guide!

I'd chosen the Provence region as our hideaway for a couple of reasons. Besides Wolfy's family not owning any property in the South of France—making it less likely his sister would find us—the man needed to take a vacation.

So why not bring him to one of my favorite places on earth?

The cliffside mansion we were being driven to belonged to my mother. It originally belonged to an ex-husband of hers, but he'd given it to her to apologize for cheating with both the maid and the pool boy.

At the same time.

Because she had standards, my mother promptly filed for divorce and took the bastard to court for every penny their prenup allowed. The poor sod was so beaten down by the end of the ordeal, he didn't dare ask for the property back.

She probably would have taken his balls if he had.

"I was thinking about how good you smell," I finally replied, meeting *my* future husband's gaze. "Good enough to eat."

As usual, he clenched his jaw and released a slow breath, but then surprised me with his reply. "You smell nice as well. Also edible."

Sir.

I fluttered my eyelashes. "Oh, that's probably my cologne, combined with the undertone of *je ne sais COCK* I was born with."

He huffed a laugh, firmly my number one fan. "Well, I have no idea what I smell like to you. I don't wear cologne."

"Excuse me?" I choked out. "You're telling me you *naturally* smell like hot sex in a wet dream?"

Wolfy cleared his throat, looking adorably flustered. "I thought you said I smelled like... home."

My sweet man.

"Both," I laughed. "You smell like the lavender fields near my grandparents' house just north of here. It's where I spent many formative summers of my life."

I sighed fondly before choosing a wicked path. "It's also where I lost my virginity—face down in a patch of lavender with the taste of bergamot on my tongue, while some punk in a leather jacket plowed me into the dirt."

As I'd hoped, Wolfy's amber eyes flashed gold, his already orgasm-inducing voice becoming even more growly. "This is a dangerous game you're playing, Simon."

Don't I know it!

Our banter tapered off as we ascended the narrow drive. Wolfy gazed out the window, taking in the panoramic view of

Villefranche-sur-Mer far below. The port was aglow—still bustling with trade despite the late hour—and I couldn't wait for him to see the deep blue Mediterranean in the light of day.

Assuming we night owls get out of bed in time...

We rolled to a stop and Wolfy turned to face me, his expression suddenly unreadable. "Wait here."

"What?" I hissed, caught off guard by his change in demeanor.

He opened the door and exited the car in one fluid motion. Still confused, I gaped as he accessed sexy phantom mode—soundlessly gliding over the gravel to reach the ground-level door.

The caretaker had left the modern, glassed-in building lit up for our arrival, so I was blessed with an unobstructed view of Wolfy checking every room. His hand remained inside his jacket the entire time—no doubt wrapped around his not-so-secret enormous weapon.

I hope I get to see him maim someone again.

To say I was turned on by the time he returned would be an understatement. In fact, I was so hard, I feared for the integrity of my trousers. Still, I obediently waited for my bags to be unloaded and for the car to drive away before following Wolfy back inside.

"*Will* you be able to relax while we're here, Wolfgang?" I chuckled, noticing him warily eyeing the floor-to-ceiling windows. "Would it help if I told you the glass was bulletproof?"

"Not really," he muttered before meeting my gaze. "I just refuse to let anything happen to you again."

Because I'm his.

"And it won't," I soothed, placing Twoey where she would receive enough light come morning. Pointing to the bags I wanted Wolfy to collect for me, I grabbed my carry-on and led the way down the hall to the master bedroom.

"I now understand why you told me to stay within your sights at the club," I chattered on, loving the feel of him at my back. "So I promise not to wander off in the future. On that note... I assume we'll be sharing a bed from now on? You know, so you can keep an eye on me. All. Night. Long."

Wolfy set down my bags and eyed the king bed with the same trepidation he'd given the windows. "Simon... we can't. *I* can't."

And I can't take it anymore!

"But why not?" I huffed, plowing ahead despite knowing I should let it go. "If you'll just *tell* me what happened to you... then maybe I could help you work through your aversion to being touched."

Please let me in.

Let me take care of you.

"What happened to me..." he slowly repeated, his brows furrowing until suddenly, his eyes widened. "No, Simon, nothing happened to me—not like that. I'm just... I was just *born* like this."

Oh, no...

"*Putain!*" I cursed, clutching the front of my velour top and taking a step away from him. "Are you asexual? Or demi? I'm so sorry, Wolfy. All this time, I assumed you were attracted to me, but holding back for external reasons... Fuck. I've only been adding to your discomfort, haven't I?"

Wolfy was vehemently shaking his head before I'd even finished, stalking toward me until the back of my thighs were pressed against the bed.

"Simon, I want you so bad I can fucking taste it," he hissed—looming over me in a way that illustrated just how much bigger he was. "But I can't, because... I don't want to *hurt* you."

Does he not realize who he's dealing with at this point?

I swallowed thickly, drunk on the scent of him. "Would it help if I told you I like it very, very rough?"

He choked on a pained laugh. "No. All that does is make me want to do very, very bad things to you."

The desire flowing through me was scalding my veins. "I want you to," I rasped, tilting my head, desperate for his lips on mine. "You can do anything you want to me. Touch me, *please...*"

I had never begged a day in my life, for anyone or anything, but Wolfy made me feral. The raw *need* I was feeling was almost suffocating. I wanted to tear off his clothes—rip open his skin—whatever it took to become one with each other.

Make me yours.

"I can't," he whispered, gritting his teeth. "Because I'm a monster."

Incensed by his crude and inaccurate self-assessment, I opened my mouth to protest. My words died on my lips the instant he gingerly pinched the slider on my top between two fingers before slowly unzipping it—the sound of the metal teeth opening making my dick throb.

"But maybe…" he continued, his arresting amber eyes locked on my bare chest as he stepped back to admire his work. "Maybe I could watch instead."

CHAPTER 17
WOLFGANG

Yet again, I knew this was a terrible idea. But I couldn't stop.

Show me.

Unsurprisingly, Simon was game. "All right," he breathily replied, tossing his bag onto the bed and shrugging off the top of his tracksuit. "I can give you a show. Why don't you pull up a chair?"

With pleasure.

I'd already seen him shirtless—when he almost refused to sleep in any clothes at all in Berlin—but nothing compared to watching Simon strip for me.

He was lithe but fit, with the perfect amount of definition beneath his creamy skin. The tempting V of his lower abdomen was a beacon, drawing my gaze downward to what I really wanted to see.

Show me everything.

I grabbed the vanity chair and placed it at the foot of the bed. Removing my suit jacket, I slung it over the back before taking a seat, spreading my legs wide to accommodate my aching cock.

Simon had already kicked off his shoes and fuzzy socks, but the bottom half of his tracksuit was still on as he climbed onto the bed. Kneeling in front of the headboard, he leaned back against it before teasingly running his palm over the bulge in his velour pants.

"You want to see, don't you, Wolfy?" He smirked and licked his pouty lips. "You want to see the cock that belongs to you?"

Fucking hell.

I couldn't stop the possessive rumble in my chest. Every inch of Simon belonged to me—including his cock—and if he didn't present it to me in the next five seconds, I was going to detonate.

"Show me," I growled. "Show me what's mine."

Simon's eyelids fluttered closed on a contented sigh as he thrust upward into his hand. "Mmm, I like the sound of that… being yours. However"—his eyes snapped open again—"you didn't say *please.*"

Fuck, I wish I could spank his ass.

"Please, Simon," I gritted out, more than happy to beg for this man. "Please show me your cock."

Continuing to misbehave, he countered. "I want to see more of *you* in return. It doesn't seem fair that I'm showing so much skin while you're not."

Two can play this game.

With a smirk of my own, I unbuttoned the top two buttons on my dress shirt before undoing my cuffs and rolling up my sleeves.

"Bordel de merde!" Simon exclaimed, grabbing his dick as he dropped onto his heels. "For fuck's sake, Wolfy, not the fore-

arms. Have mercy!"

I fought back my smile, instead leaning back in my chair and fixing him with an icy stare. "I'm still waiting."

Simon narrowed his pretty green eyes before his gaze drifted to the spilled contents of his carry-on. "As you wish. But first, I need some protection…"

Before I could insist he get on with it, Simon grabbed a leather glove, slipping it onto his right hand just as he pulled his pants down his thighs with the other.

Oh, fuck…

I could only helplessly watch as his gorgeous cock sprang free of its confines. Being European, he was uncut—like a villain—and perfectly straight, with a juicy head peeking out of his foreskin that I could only dream of wrapping my lips around.

The perfect toy.

He was also larger than I expected—given his size—although nowhere near as big as me.

I bet he'd fit me like a glove.

"That's better," he moaned, fisting himself *with his gloved hand* for a rough stroke along his full length.

"*Fuck,*" I choked out, grinding the heel of my palm over my cock—desperate for relief while also not wanting to immediately blow.

"Don't you dare!" Simon snapped, pointing an accusing finger at my crotch. "You want to look but not touch? That means you don't touch *yourself* either."

Fucking motherfucking hell.

"You're so bossy," I grumbled, even as I obediently moved my hands to the arms of the chair.

"You like it," he murmured, leaning back against the headboard for leverage as he began to stroke. "You want me to own you."

White-hot lust shot down my spine at the thought of Simon topping me from the bottom, but I kept my face neutral. "Maybe. Maybe I want to own you, too."

I want us to own each other.

"Tell me how," Simon panted, thrusting up into his gloved hand, his every stroke matching the pulsing in my cock. "Tell me how you'd fuck me."

This is torture.

Gripping the arms of the chair so tightly my knuckles turned white, I locked my gaze on his hand as he worked himself.

"I'm waiting," he snapped, although the slight waver in his voice told me he was already skirting the edge. "Shall I ring Pierre? See if he's still in the area and available to fuck me in a field of flowers again?"

Naughty boy.

There were only two ways this current situation could end. As much as I wanted our relationship to evolve into more—including me fucking him senseless—I needed to choose the path where Simon could still walk away.

He *thought* he wanted to play with me, but even without the death sentence, the reality of who I was and what I enjoyed would be enough to send anyone in their right mind running.

Time to show you how I'd play.

"You want to know how *I'd* fuck you, Simon?" I kept my voice steady and cold, even as my cock throbbed to its own heartbeat. "First, I'd put you on your stomach and tie your wrists behind your back. I'd probably use zip ties. Something you couldn't escape from. Something that would hurt. You'd keep your legs crossed—keeping yourself nice and tight for me—so when I forced my way in, you'd feel. Every. Fucking. Inch."

"*Merde*," he gasped, reaching his free hand over his shoulder to grasp the headboard, digging his nails into the wood. "No lube for me, Wolfy?"

"No," I replied, noticing how slick his glove was with the precum pouring out of his tip. "The only lube you'd get is the spit you leave on my cock mixed with the spit I put in your hole."

"Oh, my God, *ohmyfuckinggod*, keep going," he harshly chanted, thrusting frantically. "Tell me how you'd ruin me."

He's perfect.

Willfully forgetting the point of this game, I began subtly thrusting as well, just enough to feel the burn of the fabric against the sensitive head of my cock.

"Then I'd fuck you mercilessly," I continued. "Hard and fast with my hand so tight around your throat, you'd start to lose consciousness. But I wouldn't stop until you'd painted the bed—over and over. Not until the mattress was *soaked* with your cum."

"And my tears," he croaked, his eyes rolling back in his head as his movements became erratic. "I'd cry and beg you to stop."

So fucking perfect.

"That's right." My lips curled in an evil grin, too far gone to not finish what we'd started. "But no matter how much you cried and begged, I wouldn't stop until *I* was done. Because by the time I filled you up—by the time your ass was raw and overflowing with my cum—you'd know better than to say the name of another man you've fucked ever again."

"*Yes, yes, ohfuckyes!*" Simon cried out, dropping his head back as thick ropes began jetting out of his cock, coating his chest and abs.

And his glove.

That did it. Just the sight of Simon's cum decorating the leather finished me off. I gritted my teeth and dug my nails into the chair, releasing a single grunt as I released in my pants.

Well, shit.

This wasn't what I'd had in mind, but the dizzying euphoria that swept through me as we came together was painfully sweet.

Oblivious to the mess I'd made of myself, Simon lifted his head, blinking his eyes in dazed silence for a moment before reaching for a tissue.

"Don't," I snarled.

Mine.

Ignoring my discomfort, I rose from my chair and climbed onto the bed. Prowling forward, I stopped in front of Simon and meaningfully nodded at his gloved hand.

Feed it to me.

With wide eyes, he lifted his hand, offering it as if I were a dog getting a treat.

Accurate.

I leaned forward and tentatively touched the tip of my tongue to the leather. Simon hissed, and I froze, but his outburst wasn't from pain. His expression held so much bald hunger, I moaned.

He likes it.

Keeping my gaze on his face, I ran my tongue down one gloved finger, then the next, careful not to apply too much pressure. The salty taste of him had my cock stirring to life again, but I focused on my task, intent on collecting every drop of his cum.

Because every drop belonged to me.

All fucking mine.

"*Putain*, Wolfy," he whispered, shuddering as he watched me lick him clean. "You're gonna fucking kill me."

Not if I can help it.

Simon was my perfect match in every way, but that didn't change the fact nothing could ever come of this.

Nothing good, anyway.

Knowing what needed to happen, I slid off the bed, collected my suit jacket, and returned the chair to the vanity before facing him again.

It's now or never.

The next words out of my mouth broke something inside of me. "I'm going to clean up now. Then I'm going to take the bedroom next to you—which is where I'll be sleeping while we're here. And tomorrow, I'm going to explain exactly why this can't ever happen again."

Just walk away.

Then I turned my back on the hurt on Simon's perfect face—pain *I'd* put there—and strode from the room, loathing myself with every ounce of my damaged soul.

CHAPTER 18
WOLFGANG

An unfamiliar woman was in the kitchen the next morning.

No, not completely unfamiliar.

"*Bonjour,*" she hummed flirtatiously, fluttering long eyelashes over olive green eyes while daintily sipping what appeared to be a mimosa. "Are you the new caretaker?"

"*Maman?*" Simon padded in from his *separate* bedroom, looking achingly edible in tiny sleep shorts and a cropped top.

No, Wolfy.

Bad.

"That depends," I smoothly replied, intent on charming Simon's mother so she wouldn't boot me out at her son's command. "Is there something you need taken care of?"

Besides the one person I want *to take care of.*

"This is my *boss*, mother," Simon sourly interjected, and I couldn't help noticing the extra bite he added to that statement.

Like mother, like son—she soldiered on, undeterred. *"Très merveilleux!* Is this your first time on the Riviera? *Mon vilain!"* She impatiently gestured at Simon, and I smiled at how perfect the nickname was. "We must show the *monsieur* around Provence. Would you enjoy that, Mr..."

"Espanto." I gave her my civilian name, trying to catch Simon's eye, but being pointedly ignored. "And a tour sounds wonderful, but please forgive me if I don't shake hands."

"Or kiss," Simon warned as his mother advanced, no doubt ready to give me the classic French greeting.

I want to kiss every inch of him.

That Simon was still protecting my personal space—even after I'd walked out on him—warmed my shattered heart. I may have looked unruffled this morning, but internally, I was a fucking wreck.

I'd tossed and turned all night, and it wasn't because I was forcing myself off my usual nocturnal schedule for this equally forced vacation.

It was because I could *feel* the presence of the man in the bedroom beside mine—as if we were connected by an invisible thread.

How will I ever know peace?

For the most part, I accepted my limitations—that I'd never be able to hug or punch my siblings—but not being able to touch *Simon* was pure hell.

Especially now that I've tasted him...

What happened between us last night left me harder than I'd ever been, even after I'd come in my pants like a teenager. But instead of fucking my fist in the shower again, I'd blasted the cold water until I was shivering—like a monk practicing self-flagellation as discipline.

And while I'd slept alone my entire life, I suddenly couldn't stand the sight of the empty bed I found waiting for me. I *wanted* Simon next to me. I wanted his beautiful face to be the first thing I saw the next morning, and every time I woke up after that.

I wanted, I wanted, I *wanted.*

But since I couldn't fucking have what I wanted, I at least needed to make things right. My plan had been to tell Simon about my supe identity over coffee—to explain how my deadly powers were the reason we couldn't be together, despite how badly I wished things could be different.

How badly I want everything *with him.*

It was a cruel twist of fate to meet someone so perfect for me, who clearly desired me just as much. But it was even more insulting to be cockblocked by his *mother* just as I was about to smooth things over.

Play nice, Wolfy.

"I think we should take *Mr. Espanto* to the lavender fields near *grand-maman* and *grand-papa's* cottage," Simon piped up, busying himself with the instant coffee maker. "I have such precious memories of the area, I can almost *feel* them—deep in my guts."

So this is how it's going to be today.

The object of my obsession finally made eye contact as he handed me a steaming mug. "I've prepared your coffee, *boss,* exactly how you take it—with extra vanilla and a touch of arsenic."

"Simon." I kept my voice low, when all I wanted was to beg. "May I have a word with you? In private?"

"No, you may not!" he sang, already showing me his back—and his juicy ass—to work on his coffee. "I wouldn't want to be rude to our surprise guest. What *are* you doing here, anyway, mother? Did husband-number-whatever not work out?"

His mother tittered a laugh, clearly unoffended by his attitude. "Giovanni is well, thank you for asking. He's still on the yacht, losing obscene amounts of money in a silly poker game. Since we were docked here in Villefranche, I figured I'd check on the house before heading to my favorite vineyard to stock up on supplies."

Simon made a disgruntled sound. "Yes, we shan't risk you running out of alcohol. Heaven knows, you haven't been sober since you were pregnant with me."

"Darling, I doubt I was sober even then," she chuckled before blasting me with a beaming smile. "Shall we call a car for the day, Mr. Espanto?"

"Only if you allow me to treat you to brunch at the winery," I smoothly countered. "And tell me your name."

Simon audibly rolled his eyes as his mother preened. "Oh, how rude of me! I'm Claire, but everyone calls me Bunny."

The perfect prey.

I grinned broadly, doing my best to keep the display non-threatening. "Bunny it is, then. You may call me"—I glanced at Simon to find him watching our exchange with a frown—"Wolfgang."

He visibly relaxed before haughtily lifting his chin. "Fine. I'll dust off my little sailor boy outfit, since it's perfect for this traveling circus. That is... assuming I'm invited along?"

"Of course, you're invited, *mon vilain!* Don't be silly," Bunny tsked. "When the wine is poured, it must be drunk!"

No truer words were ever spoken.

An hour and a half—and what felt like a lifetime of small talk—later, the three of us were seated on the terrace of Château Scélérat, admiring the view.

Or, in my case, the petulant company.

My gaze drifted to Simon yet again as I took a sip of my rosé. He'd barely spoken a word since handing me my coffee—not in the car, or since we'd arrived at the vineyard for brunch.

Unable to stand the distance between us any longer, I released a tendril of power, wrapping it around him like a caress. It was a stupid thing to do—the equivalent of sending up a Bat Signal to any supes lurking nearby—but I *needed* to connect with him somehow.

Even if he won't feel it.

"What are you doing?" he hissed, making me freeze and interrupting his mother's latest monologue on the current market for sailboats.

What?

"What do you mean?" I replied impassively, even as I hurriedly retracted my power and locked it down tight.

Simon gave an exaggerated shudder. "I don't know. You were staring at me so intensely I *felt* it. That wannabe evil villain friend of yours, Noir-Rouge, gave me the same heebie-jeebies when she invaded my personal space in Berlin. Clearly, you both studied at the same school for creeps."

That's... not possible.

The waiter appeared, arranging our scrambled eggs with truffle oil, bacon and cheddar quiche, and flaugnarde with pears on the cast iron table as I eyed my assistant with newfound wariness.

Simon was a normie. I'd checked his background extensively before having Randal bring him in for an interview. I'd had Captain Masculine himself stare at the man for over an hour, accessing whatever witchy inquisitor powers the hero used when sniffing out his enemies.

And with all the time we'd spent together—with how I'd *slept next to him,* even just for a night—I surely would have noticed anything amiss.

Right?!

"So, how did you two meet?" Bunny asked, dabbing her coral-painted lips with a linen napkin.

It was the first time the woman had asked me a question since getting my name, and I could only assume it was so she could eat.

And drink.

"I hired Simon to help me catalog my international properties," I calmly replied, even as my heart pounded in my chest over the revelation that her son could somehow *feel* my power. "He'll also be assisting with expanding my business operations on a global scale."

"Oh?" His mother perked up at the scent of money. "And what is your business, Wolfgang?"

I grinned wolfishly. "Plastic surgery."

Simon snorted a laugh, but immediately covered it up with a cough and a scowl. "Don't forget to tell her about the Lasik.

Wolfy has developed a revolutionary method, mother! It's almost like he's removing your old, tired eyeballs altogether before replacing them with shiny new ones. If he feels like it."

At least he's talking to me.

Kind of.

Bunny bobbed her bleached-blonde head with interest. "*Magnifique!* I've always had endless respect for doctors and others in the medical profession. True miracle workers, just like your father, Simon."

This time, Simon didn't even attempt to stifle his disbelief. "*Tais-toi!* Franz Ownit is a low-rent therapist with a Gmail address who never moved past the swinging sixties motto of 'free love for everyone.' For everyone except his own son, that is."

He abruptly quieted, focusing his gaze on the flaugnarde and his anger on mashing the dessert into a pulp.

You're still mine.

Bunny sighed in commiseration, although her next words were careless. "Yes, Franz never seemed too keen on claiming you as his."

I'm not above murdering this woman.

Simon snapped his gaze to his mother's with an incredulous huff. "Well, he can take a number, as that seems to be the theme of the day."

Ouch.

I asked the waiter to bring me the check, not batting an eye when Bunny added a case of house wine to the tab.

Simon rose from the table as the dishes were cleared—wandering away to stare out over the seemingly endless rows of grapevines. The sky was hazy, casting a golden light that made everything seem both everlasting and painfully insubstantial.

Just like Simon and me.

I quickly pulled out my phone to snap a few photos, telling myself it was to share the scenery with the two artists in my family who'd appreciate the quality of light, and *not* because Simon looked like a backlit angel.

Whatever helps you sleep at night, Wolfy.

Or not.

"I trust you'll clean up whatever mess you've made here?" Bunny's normally airy voice had gone impressively hard.

My gaze snapped to hers, finding an unexpectedly shrewd woman staring back at me, sizing me up.

And clearly, well aware that I've hurt her son.

"I'll try my best," I replied, meaning every word.

She nodded once before gracefully standing. "See that you do, or you'll be dealing with me in a far less social situation. Never underestimate an Alarie, Wolfgang."

The smile that curled my lips was genuine. "I wouldn't dream of it."

Of course, I'd initially done my homework on Simon's parents as well before hiring him, and there was one piece of information I'd found confusing, especially compared to how supes operated.

Squaring my shoulders, I dared to ask this slightly terrifying woman to clarify. "Why do you and Simon use your maiden name?"

Bunny breezily laughed, effortlessly transitioning back to idle chatter. "I never take my husband's name. And you should know, I've taught my son that most men are easily replaced."

"Some aren't," I murmured, my gaze drifting to where Simon was walking toward us, glowing in the sunlight while my heart hammered in my chest.

Fuck, I might be in love.

"What are you two old biddies gossiping about?" he grumped, eyeing us suspiciously.

His mother laughed again, ruffling his hair in an easy show of affection that made my jaw clench. "Oh, we were simply discussing what a catch you are… and how I need to get back to the yacht before Giovanni forgets I exist and I'm forced to remarry all over again."

With those closing words, Claire 'Bunny' Alarie marched away on towering heels, leaving someone *else* to carry her purchases.

Of course, that someone would be me.

"Should I assume you'll be my new step-father by the end of the month?" Simon sniffed as I lifted his mother's fresh case of wine.

"It was a close call," I hummed, thrilled he was speaking to me again. "But I told her I only have eyes for younger men with severe attitude problems and bottles of arsenic in their pockets."

My victory was short-lived, as Simon cocked an eyebrow to coolly assess me. "Such pretty words. Unfortunately, *this* rightfully disgruntled younger man requires more than pretty words to make amends. Let's drop the elder gold digger off at the docks so you can wave that platinum card of yours around in the downtown shops. Show me how *sorry* you are by buying me anything my black heart desires."

Yes, boss.

Using every ounce of willpower not to get a boner in front of Simon's mother, I eagerly followed my tiny tyrant to the waiting car.

I would gladly buy him anything he wanted. Simon would be *dripping* in jewels by the end of the day—not only because I enjoyed spoiling him, but because it would soften the blow for the bombshell I still needed to drop later.

Whatever it takes to make things right.

CHAPTER 19
SIMON

To say Wolfy looked out of place as we wandered *les petites rues* of Villefranche would be an understatement.

While the man wore a black suit better than anyone I'd met, the ridiculous sight of him lurking like Death itself amongst the sunrise parfait paint jobs of the harborside buildings almost made me forgive him.

Almost.

I didn't think I'd ever been as angry with someone as I was with him. And that I *cared* enough to be angry at all only made me angrier.

Stupid, perfect man.

After brunch at the Château, we'd deposited my mother back at her latest husband's yacht, where she threw Wolfy a meaningful look I pointedly ignored. Then she'd made things worse by whispering her version of Waspy wisdom in my ear while we kissed goodbye.

"If a man ever looked at *me* the way Wolfgang looks at *you*, I'd never bother signing another prenup."

Carve it on my tombstone, Bunny.

Relationship advice from *my mother* was the last thing I needed. She was also three sheets to the wind by that point, so for all I knew, she'd mistaken the nearby street lamp for my employer.

Because, in the end, that was all Wolfy was—the man who signed my checks while I drooled over him like a pathetic dog.

"And I'm no one's dog," I muttered as we reached the last shop on our current street.

"What?" Wolfy asked as I spun on my heel and prepared to return to go back the way we came. Unfortunately, his enormous sexy frame was blocking my path, even sexier for being laden with my many purchases.

Stupid, sexy, sugar daddy.

"I said I'm tired of being fucked around!" I snapped, unconcerned with the scandalized gasps of passing heiresses. "There's no bloody good reason for you to be behaving this way. I don't appreciate being strung along and lied to—especially not when I've repeatedly thrown myself at your feet like a common peasant."

Further proving how annoyingly perfect he was, Wolfy didn't match my energy. Instead, he patiently waited for me to finish my rant before calmly replying.

"I haven't lied to you, Simon, but I *have* kept some very important information to myself... because I didn't want to scare you away. That was incredibly selfish of me, and I'm sorry my actions have hurt you. We can't have this discussion in public, but as soon as we return to the house, I will tell you *everything* you want to know. I promise."

His smooth voice faltered a bit at the end—his impassive mask slipping to show the vulnerable man beneath—and it was at this terrible moment I realized I'd fallen in love.

I hate him so much.

"That depends." I straightened my shoulders and lifted my chin to glare up at him. "Are you simply planning on giving me a laundry list of reasons we can't be together?"

He sighed, pressing his lips into a thin line and nodding once.

That's it then.

"Very well." I smiled coldly. "Let's return to the house now. That way, *you* can pack your bags, get back on your shiny plane, and fly the hell out of my life. I'm done, Wolfgang. With this job, this situation, and you."

I didn't know what I'd expected. More of his infuriating calm, or perhaps for him to finally raise his voice. Instead, Wolfy dropped the bags he'd been carrying and advanced on me so quickly, I barely saw him move.

How the fu...

"No," he growled menacingly, the rumbling sound sending a shot of lust down my spine. "You're not going anywhere. I'm going to tell you what you need to know, and then we'll adjust accordingly before continuing to search for Violentia. And once your three-month contract with me is done, you'll stay on as my assistant—indefinitely—because there's no way in *hell* I am letting you go now."

The audacity!

"*ARE YOU MAD?!*" I shouted, welcoming the drama—bathing myself in the scandal we were causing in this sleepy town. "You think you're going to lock me up like a princess and *force* me to continue working for you? *Have we met?!*"

I stepped forward and jabbed my finger at his broad chest, but Wolfy leaped away before I could make contact.

"And there it is." I laughed bitterly, feeling traitorous tears prick my eyelids. "No matter what you have to tell me, it doesn't change the fact that the very *thought* of my touch makes you recoil in horror."

The look on Wolfy's face was anguished, but just as he opened his mouth to speak, we were interrupted.

Because, of course, we were.

"Well, this is something I never thought I'd see. Wolfgang *Espanto*, whipped by a civilian."

Blinded by rage, I spun on the source of the booming voice, coming face to face with a man even bigger than the one I was scolding. He was devastatingly handsome, his mahogany skin shining in the Mediterranean sun, muscles rippling as he crossed his enormous arms over his 'The Riviera Makes Me Wet' tank top.

Normally, I'd appreciate the humor.

But not today.

"Now is *not* the time, Zion," Wolfy gritted out, *his* delicious muscles practically vibrating as his gloved hands clenched into fists.

"Oh, I wouldn't say that," the man—Zion—joyfully replied, his accent placing him as an idiotic American as well. "It actually looks like I arrived just in time to stop you from doing something stupid. Since, you know, we're *in public*. Among *civilians*."

Enough of this.

"What is this 'civilian' nonsense? You're not military," I huffed, throwing my hands in the air, beyond exasperated with these muscled mafiosos who kept multiplying. "Who *is* this, Wolfgang? Another one of your unsavory associates? Am I to be chased down the Rue Obscure and assaulted before you swoop in and save me like a *hero* again?"

Wolfy glanced to where I was pointing, his eyes flaring with interest at the sight of the famous medieval street-turned-tunnel, disappearing into the dark.

Don't you dare distract me right now!

"Is *that* what happened with Rem…ington?" Zion cautiously asked, all humor gone as his gaze flitted between the two of us. "You were defending your…"

"Assistant," I coldly interrupted. "*Ex*-assistant, if you want to get technical. Although Wolfgang also claims I'm his *inventus*, whatever the fuck that is."

"Simon…" Wolfy warned, but it was too late.

"Hohoho! Wolfgang, you sly fucking dog," Zion chuckled, back to his jovial state. "I swear, there's something in the water out there in Big City. Your entire family are some of the luckiest motherfuckers I've ever met."

Wolfy had apparently reached his limit. "It wasn't *luck* when Baltasar wiped the field with you during the Supremacy Championships two years ago," he hissed, glaring daggers at the other man.

"Oh, is that how it went down?" Zion coldly replied, taking a threatening step forward, irrationally angry over what sounded like a football match.

Although I know firsthand how riled up my countrymen get over football.

The air felt like it was rippling between us, accompanied by a buzzing in my ears and an odd *pulling* sensation concentrated in my chest. It was similar to what I'd experienced when Mistress Noir-Rouge had circled me—and that Wolfy had mimicked at brunch—only this time, I felt compelled to *defend* Wolfgang against this enormous man.

Maybe I'm *the one on drugs.*

"Enough!" I croaked, suddenly nauseous. "Wolfy, I-I need to get back to the house... I'm feeling faint..."

"Fuck," Wolfy swore, deep concern lining his face, although he stopped short of moving closer.

"Of course, you wouldn't even attempt to offer me a shoulder," I weakly murmured, my own slumping in defeat.

All fury had left my body, along with my energy, so I didn't protest when the mysterious footballer, Zion, gently led me to a nearby bench facing the water instead.

Wolfy growled at the contact, but Zion only glared at him in return. "Does he not know who you are, Wolfgang?"

Why should I when everyone else does?

"Just mind your own, Zion," Wolfy growled, his eyes already on his phone. "I need to get a taxi for my..."

Say I'm yours.

Zion sighed heavily before pointing up the street. "The taxi station is just beyond Chapelle Saint-Pierre—"

"Stay here with Simon," Wolfy ordered. "If he's gone or harmed in any way when I get back, I'll rip your fucking spine out through your throat."

"Wolfgang!" I spun around to scold, but he'd somehow already disappeared.

That man needs a good spanking!

"I am dreadfully sorry for his behavior," I muttered. "It's like dealing with a feral animal who happens to know how to wear a suit."

Zion barked a laugh before worriedly glancing toward the chapel, as if Wolfy might suddenly appear and follow through on his graphic threat. "That is... an extremely accurate description of Wolfgang, but he's actually being fairly well-behaved. For him."

"But you were just trying to help," I sighed, feeling more tired than I had in my entire life. "After going out of your way to come say hello."

He grimaced. "To be honest, I mostly came over here to give him shit about carrying your shopping bags like a butler. But now, I'm deeply regretting not just keeping my ass parked on the beach with my family where it belonged."

Zion shaded his eyes and peered across the bay. I followed his gaze, squinting at the ant-sized people littering the sand.

How did he even spot us over here?

"Why won't he just tell me the truth?" I huffed in exasperation, more to myself than the man standing guard over me.

"I am *not* getting in the middle of this mess," Zion chuckled humorlessly. "But I will say this. My partner was... an *outsider*, like you. She knew nothing about this world until we met and, well, it wasn't an easy conversation—explaining who I was. And that's without the extra... challenges *you're* dealing with here."

He awkwardly cleared his throat and glanced warily down the street again before standing a little straighter. "However things shake out, please just give my man Wolfgang a break. He's a good guy under that feral exterior. I think."

The problem is, I think so too.

I nodded stiffly, too emotionally wrung out to give him a proper reply.

Just then, a taxi rolled to a stop on the curb, and Wolfy leaped out of the backseat before loading my bags into the boot. Zion walked me to the car before nodding his goodbye to the other man.

"Can we give you a ride?" Wolfy asked, although his gaze was locked on me—assessing my state.

Zion waved him off. "Nah. I'm gonna swim back. Maybe start some rumors among the locals about a sea monster. Be well, Simon. Don't let this maniac boss you around too much."

He can surely try.

Wolfy huffed a sad laugh before gesturing for me to slide into the backseat. I did, but peeked around him to watch Zion dive into the Mediterranean and start swimming toward the far-off beach, just like he'd said.

I think he's the maniac around here.

The silence was thick on the ride back to the cliff house. Once we arrived, I walked inside without a word, leaving Wolfy to carry in all the purchases I didn't even want anymore.

I just want him.

While I knew what Wolfy had to tell me was important, I was dreading hearing it—especially as it sounded like he'd already decided we couldn't be together.

He doesn't want to 'hurt' me.

How cliché.

Wolfy set down the last bag in the entryway before straightening and cautiously facing me. "Simon—"

"I'm going to lie down for a bit," I interrupted, already backing away from him. "There's no way I can handle whatever it is you're going to say right now."

He nodded, dropping his gaze to the floor. "Whatever you need."

Oh, please.

I couldn't stop the scoff that escaped me. "Well, I know what I *need,* but you've made it clear I can't have it. So I guess it's *not* 'whatever I need,' hmm?"

Wolfy's eyes snapped to mine. The pure sorrow in their amber depths almost had me closing the distance between us so I could wrap myself around him—boundaries be damned.

Almost.

"I'm so sorry, Simon," he whispered with a shaky breath. "I wish things could be different."

"Me too," I replied, holding his gaze for a moment before turning my back on him—just like he'd done to me last night—and walking away.

CHAPTER 20
SIMON

I couldn't sleep—not with all the dark thoughts swirling in my head. After falling into more shame spirals than I cared to admit, I finally threw off the covers and got out of bed.

Might as well get this over with.

I already knew Wolfy was going to end things before they had the chance to begin, but I couldn't imagine how he expected me to continue working for him. Neither of us seemed able to resist the other, and I was uninterested in the constant rotation of brief satisfaction and crushing rejection this toxic arrangement would bring.

Both of us deserve better than that.

At least I could stay here in Villefranche after he left, proactively sending out resumes instead of wallowing. Best-case scenario, I'd find work in Paris, but I was open to a variety of locations, as long as I understood the language.

Because the miscommunication trope is getting old.

"I didn't call you back because I was a little busy handling family business." Wolfy's voice had taken on the unfairly hot growl he got whenever he was angry, and I had to mentally scold my burgeoning boner as I crept down the hallway toward the sound. "And last I checked, I don't answer to you, *Captain.*"

Captain?

Maybe they are *military…*

Reaching the common area, I found Wolfy in the kitchen with his mobile pressed to his ear. His back was to me as he stared down into the sink, and I could *feel* the rage radiating off him as if it were my own.

I need to go to him.

Yet again, the overwhelming urge to *touch him* permeated my brain. Whereas before I'd tamped it down—out of respect for his boundaries—I no longer found myself able to resist the pull.

"Yes, I *understand* the implications of our property in Thailand being bombed, especially as Simon only mentioned it in our group chat. No. No, I do *not* think you should go there."

Wolfy dropped his head forward, running his unusually *bare* hand over his neck as he listened to whatever this 'Captain' had to say.

Mesmerized by the scandalous sight of his skin, I marveled over how unblemished it was—not covered in scars, as I'd suspected.

So why does he wear the gloves?

"I SAID NO!" he shouted, pounding his fist on the counter and making me freeze only a step away from him. "I am the head of this fucking household and I *forbid you* from going after her… Because you'll fucking *TORCH* her on sight, that's why! And tell Xanny to shut the fuck up in the background!"

Mon chou…

Suddenly, *my* needs seemed rather small and selfish compared to the immeasurable weight this man carried on his shoulders. All I'd cared about was getting my hands on Wolfy's dick. Meanwhile, he was running an empire and trying to bring back his sister—alive.

He needs someone to be there for him.

He needs me.

Raising my hand, I slowly reached for his broad back, intent on showing Wolfy I was here—in any way he needed. I would listen to what he had to say, and we'd figure it out from there, because I realized I'd rather cut out my heart than leave him.

"Wolfy," I murmured the instant my fingertips touched the wool of his suit.

I'm here.

Faster than I could blink, he'd spun and wrapped his bare hand around my throat, instantly cutting off my airways. I choked on a gasp as a blast of *something* shot through my system, burning me up from the inside out.

PUTAIN!

Wolfy's eyes had gone almost completely black—like an animal response—but the amber quickly returned as they widened in horror.

"No," he croaked, instantly releasing me and letting my limp body fall to the floor. "Please, no..."

And that was the last thing I registered before everything went dark.

CHAPTER 21
SIMON

After what felt like years later, I cracked open my eyelids, but all I could see was a blinding white light.

Am I... dead?

Surely I was destined to go in the other direction...

Everything vaguely hurt, but the pain seemed to be concentrated at the back of my head—as if I'd hit it against something. My mouth was bone-dry, and I was having so much difficulty moving my limbs, I wondered if I'd been tied down.

I wouldn't be opposed to Wolfy restraining me.

My eyes flew wide open at the memory of what had happened—how touching Wolfy ended with me cracking my head on the tiles. That's when I realized the heavenly light hovering overhead was nothing more than the kitchen pendant lamp.

Why would he leave me lying on the floor?

An unfamiliar voice caught my attention. "Just start at the beginning, with as many details as you can remember. Then we'll have Randal file an official report to notify next of kin before we wipe the scene."

Who the fuck is that?

Needing to focus my effort on confronting whoever was in *my* house, I attempted to roll over. It took a few tries as my limbs were behaving like wet spaghetti, but I eventually flopped onto my stomach and got my forearms under me.

Lifting my head, I blearily looked around. Unfortunately, the kitchen island was obscuring my view of the living room, but I immediately spotted Wolfy.

And he looked *terrible.*

The man of my dreams was slumped in a chair, leaning forward with his face buried in his hands. His normally slicked back hair was a mess—as if he'd been running his hands through it—and even his impeccable suit looked wrinkled.

WHO DID THIS TO HIM?!

"Sweetheart, now might not be the time for *Blade Runner* Butch to make an appearance. Wolfy's... he's a little upset about... uh, accidentally killing his boyfriend."

Boyfriend?

"I'm just doing my job, Xan. I *told* Wolfy to tell Simon who he was, specifically so we wouldn't end up in this situation—tasked with burying a body."

Oh no!

Wolfy thinks I'm dead.

But they called me his boyfriend!

Wait...

Enraged at this turn of events, I clawed my way up to my knees. Steadying myself against the island, I willed the world to stop spinning long enough for me to put these fools in their place.

"If you *putains de connards* think you're dumping me in an unmarked grave—"

My words ended with a yelp when a bloody *fireball* shot over my head, making me hit the deck as something exploded behind me.

WHAT THE FUCK?!

"Jesus fucking *CHRIST*, baby!" the second mystery guest bellowed. "This is what I'm talking about with the *Blade Runner* shit. Chill!"

"He surprised me—cheez-its! Uh, sorry about your microwave and... exterior wall. We'll get that taken care of. You okay, little buddy?"

A pair of shiny black boots appeared in my line of sight, and I tentatively raised my head.

My mouth dropped open as I was greeted with the sight of a brick house of a man—his pretty blue eyes sparkling above a pair of dimples adorning a broad smile that almost blinded me with its perfection.

He was also wearing some *very* form-fitting—and familiar—Lycra that left little to the imagination.

At least he seems proportional.

"Why the hell are you dressed like Captain Masculine?" I croaked, in desperate need of some water.

And a Xanax.

Pretty boy-next-door blinked down at me before his eyes narrowed and he turned partway to face the living room. This allowed me to glimpse the *other* visitor, who resembled Wolfy too closely not to be one of his siblings. *He* was wearing a Doctor Antihero costume for some ungodly reason.

"Do you dress like this often?" I huffed, wondering if I'd hit my head harder than I thought. "Or are the outfits some sort of *sex thing* with you two?"

Wannabe Masculine blushed a deep scarlet while Wolfy's brother grinned mischievously. "Yes, and *yessss*. But only if he begs."

"Simon..." The only voice I cared about cut through the chatter, drawing my attention past the others.

To *him*.

Wolfy had risen from the chair, still uncharacteristically disheveled, as he stared at me with wide eyes. "I thought I killed you," he whispered, his expression so devastated I immediately scrambled to my feet.

"It was an accident, Wolfy," I soothed, taking a step closer. "I'm all right—"

"Don't!" he shouted, putting the chair between us before hurriedly backing away. "Please, just... let Butch and Xander take you away from here. Away from *me.*"

What?!

He turned and disappeared down the hallway—unnaturally fast—leaving me standing in the rubble.

With **The Rabble**.

The one who *had* to be Butch cleared his throat and shot Xander a pointed look before nodding in the direction his brother had fled.

"What the fuck am *I* gonna do?" **The Mouthy One** looked at his significant other like he had three heads. "It's not like I can give him a *hug* or anything."

Enough of this.

"Well, then *I* will!" I yelled, *needing* to go to my…

My…

Whatever he is, he's mine.

"Oh, no you don't." Butch grabbed my shoulder and held me in place with his ridiculously muscular fingers. "You and I are going to talk while *Xan comforts his brother.*" When the other man only stared, he added, "Just use some of the communication tools we've learned in therapy."

When Xander *still* made no move to obey, Butch dropped his voice low. "If you take care of this, I'll do *the thing.* You know… with the fried chicken…"

Those were the magic words, apparently. Wolfy's brother sprang into action, racing down the hall as he called over his shoulder. "Get ready, baby—I'm gonna slather you in hot sauce tonight!"

These two are wild.

Butch cleared his throat again before blinding me with another dimpled smile and gesturing toward the couch. "Please, sit."

I begrudgingly dropped onto a cushion as he took the chair Wolfy had occupied. "So, it's clear you haven't been told everything you need to know… about *us.*"

"What about *you?*" I sniffed. "I only care about Wolfy."

I *knew* I was being salty, but it wasn't every day you were electrocuted half to death only to have a pair of unhinged sex cosplayers shoot a Roman candle into your kitchen.

Or whatever happened back there.

Butch simply stared at me for a minute, his eyes roaming over my face as the rest of him stayed unnervingly still. "So, you apparently heard of Captain Masculine during your time in Big City, huh, Simon?"

I scoffed, annoyed by the direction the conversation was abruptly taking. "Well, yes, considering every idiot within city limits is ridiculously obsessed with the meathead... case in point." I dismissively gestured at his costume, as finely made as it was.

His dimples popped out as he stifled a smile. Then he raised a hand, and I could only gape as a real-life *ball of fire* appeared in his palm.

Bordel de merde...

I'd never understood the concept of the world tipping on its axis until this very moment, but here we were. I had to actually grip the edge of the sofa to avoid tumbling off and bashing my skull again.

But... he looks like a human.

An enormous, extremely fit, ridiculously attractive human...

If the man seated before me was *The* Defender of Big City, then quite a few unexplained occurrences with Wolfy were making a hell of a lot more sense.

Clearly, I was too busy being blinded by all those delicious red flags.

"Sorry again about your kitchen." He hurriedly extinguished his magical flame, his cheeks pinking as if he were embarrassed about showing off. "I'm Butch Holt, although

Hawthorne is the civilian name I use around normies... uh, *humans*. And yes, all those 'adoring idiots' know me best as Captain Masculine."

*Or **The Token Hero** in the group chat.*

The... family group chat...

Eyeing me carefully, Butch continued, "My fiancé is Doctor Antihero—known as Xander Marin to most normies—although he's the third born in the supervillain Suarez clan. Have you heard of them?"

Of *course*, I knew of the infamous Suarez clan. Everybody in Big City did. According to the gossip rags, it was the unprecedented—and terrifying—marriage of the now-deceased Apocalypto Man and Glacial Girl that prompted the USN to require extra powerful supes to be registered at birth.

Like Wolfy and his siblings...

"Well, at least he gave me his real name," I absently murmured, realizing I simply hadn't put two and two together when he broke the news upon our arrival in Japan. "Although, that was more about making amends for letting me believe he was nothing but the company muscle."

When he's actually the first born Suarez supervillain...

Otherwise known as The Hand of Death.

Again... not a deal-breaker.

Butch softly smiled. "That says a lot about how much he trusts you. Our real names are not given to normies lightly, even with an NDA. But he *should* have told you his supe identity—if only so you'd know to keep your distance."

But I don't want *to keep my distance.*

The superhero's smile faded, his gaze flickering to my swollen and no doubt battered-looking throat with predatory focus. "So he really *grabbed* you, huh?" he murmured. "And you survived..."

All at once, I felt that all too familiar invasive sensation that made my skin crawl—and I realized just how many pushy supes I'd come in contact with over the past several days.

Time to show them who's boss.

"Stop that this instant!" I barked. "I've had quite enough of being poked and prodded with superpowered woo-woo, thank you very much. I don't know what you weirdos think you're going to find by *probing* me, but it's making my balls tingle—and not in a good way!"

Captain Masculine's baby blues widened in surprise at my outburst just as Doctor Antihero reappeared from the hallway.

"Welp," Xander began with a grimace, which did not bode well. "He's shut down completely at this point. More than usual, I mean." He brightened, throwing a sly, sidelong glance at his man. "However, he *has* dressed himself in a certain White Elephant gift that seems to be helping him chill out..."

Butch dropped his head back and loudly sighed as he rose to his feet. "Whyyyy does he still have that? It was supposed to be *your* gift."

Xander batted his eyelashes, and I immediately recognized a fellow brat when I saw one. "Sweetheart, you can't possibly expect me to take away his full-body ThunderShirt! Our boy's like a skittish animal right now."

That's it. I'm going in.

"Right!" I stood and briskly clapped my hands. "Thank you both for your service today. Between incinerating my mother's property and threatening to bury my body, you've been most helpful. You may go now, but *I* will be staying here. Regardless of what Wolfy thinks is best for me, he needs his *inventus*."

Both men gaped at me this time. Unsurprisingly, it was **The Mouthy One** who spoke first.

"How can you be Wolfy's *inventus*?!" Xander sputtered. "You're just a..." His familiar amber eyes flitted to the other supe. "Isn't he?"

Butch shrugged—looking far less confident than before—which distracted me just long enough for Xander to *yank out a few strands of my hair*.

"*Casse-toi!*" I yelled, clutching my head and glaring daggers. "You have officially worn out your welcome. *SHOO!*"

Xander snickered, producing a specimen container from his pocket like some sort of mad scientist. "I'll be testing this back at the lab, thank *you* very much. Speaking of which..." He turned to face Butch. "The Observatoire Oceanologique is located in Villefranche. Besides their renowned research on cell biology, I wanna check out the optical sensors they've developed for marine observation. Maybe buy a few—or all of them. Can we make a pit stop before we fly home, baby?"

Fly...

Does he mean that literally?

When Butch simply stared at him with a glazed expression that matched my own, Xander added, "I'll make it worth your while... with that thing *you* like..."

Instead of verbally elaborating, Doctor Antihero snapped his fingers and pointed at his shiny black boots.

"Yes, Daddy," Captain Masculine breathily whispered, his entire face going slack and dreamy.

Well, I've learned quite a bit here today.

As if suddenly remembering they had an audience, Butch snapped out of his subspace—turning bright red and clearing his throat before yanking on his head-covering superhero mask.

"It was nice to meet you in person, Simon," he stiffly addressed me in his now distorted voice. "And I'm glad Wolfgang didn't actually… *kill* you."

"Samesies," Xander agreed while pulling on his own mask, not embarrassed in the least over their various displays of kinky fuckery. "Now go take care of your *inventus*. We'd all appreciate it if you'd show Wolfy what he's been missing all these years. Maybe it will make him *less* of an uptight prick."

I sniffed, unimpressed with the insinuation—although fully intending to suck Wolfy's soul out through his cock. "Don't hold your breath for a regime overhaul. I'd suggest bracing yourselves for *two* unholy terrors running this family once I'm done."

I always wanted to be a mafia queen.

With an imaginary hair flip over my shoulder, I spun on my heel and headed down the hallway, leaving my future brothers-in-law blushing and cackling behind me.

Now, to finally get my hands on Mr. Tall, Morally Gray, and Fuckable.

CHAPTER 22
WOLFGANG

I killed Simon.

I watched him die...

While I knew it was a cowardly move to hide in the bedroom until Xanny and Butch flew Simon out of here, I was in no state to say goodbye.

He died, he died, he died.

Xander had tried his best to bully me out of my self-loathing, but all I could focus on was the visual loop of my hand wrapping around Simon's throat. The way I drained the life from his body—his olive green eyes widening as his pale skin bleached color—was something I'd never forget.

Along with the vow I made long ago to never kill someone I cared about again.

Promises, promises...

I wasn't usually so jumpy, but our earlier run-in with Zion had left me on edge. Thanks to *another* superhero then aggravating me over the phone, by the time I realized someone had crept up on me, it was too late.

This is why I can't have nice things.

I'd instantly released Simon once I recognized who he was, but didn't want to make things worse by grabbing him. So I watched helplessly as he fell backward and hit the tiled floor with a sickening crack.

What was he trying to accomplish, anyway?

The bigger question was how he'd survived my touch. A small part of me wondered if this meant he was immune to my powers, but I tamped it right the fuck down.

I wasn't willing to risk whether he'd return from the dead a second time. The best thing for *Simon* was to be taken away from me—where I couldn't break him any further.

"What *are* you wearing?"

My head snapped up at the sound of Simon's voice, and I gaped to see him standing in the bedroom doorway like a linen-clad apparition.

Only he could make a sailor boy outfit look good.

Although, I'm one to talk about ridiculous outfits…

"Um…" I stuttered, glancing down at the fleece-lined adult onesie I was wearing. The one I won, fair and square, during the Suarez family's annual White Elephant gift exchange.

The one with 'Captain Masculine's Favorite Brat' printed across the chest.

Well, the situation can't get any worse.

"Butch had it made for Xanny last Christmas, but brought it to our notoriously cutthroat gift exchange because he didn't understand the rules. I ended up winning it…" I trailed off as I spied the others flying off through the glass wall. "Why are you not going with them?"

"You're not truly a brat, though," Simon mused, ignoring my question completely as he took a step toward the chair I was sitting in. "Because there's only room for one brat in this relationship."

"Simon," I tried to make my voice stern, even as I clenched my bare fists to stop from reaching for him.

This is not good.

Since I'd *thought* he was leaving, I'd prepared myself for an evening of doing nothing but watching *Little Shop of Horrors* on repeat while eating as much imported Cherry Garcia ice cream as inhumanly possible.

Which is better done without gloves…

But here he remained—apparently intent on torturing me forever with his irresistible presence.

"Your brother Xander is obviously a brat as well, although my *favorite* discovery of the day was that Big City's savior just wants to be a good boy for his Daddy…" Simon continued musing while slowly moving closer, as if I were a wild animal he was trying to corner.

Accurate.

I cleared my throat, my heart rate kicking up a notch as my gaze traveled over all the exposed skin his adorable little outfit was blessing me with.

"Yes, well, they can keep the Daddy kink," I gruffly replied. "Because it's not one of mine."

I have enough as it is…

He hummed thoughtfully, continuing to approach until he was standing only a few feet in front of me. "Me neither, so that works out. In fact"—another step closer—"I can't wait to learn every one of yours."

"Simon!" I huffed as he got uncomfortably close. "Do you have a death wish or something? I fucking *killed* you out there! I-I can't go through that again... I can't..."

My breathing turned into harsh pants as my vision blurred and my palms grew sweaty. The idea of Simon convulsing in my hold again had me panicking. All I could think about was getting a locked door—or a continent—between us until he learned some goddamned self-preservation.

Then I felt a *hand* on my cheek.

"Mon chou," Simon soothed, placing *his other hand* on my other cheek after *climbing into my lap.* "Look! I'm touching you now and am still very much alive." He gave a saucy wiggle, making me instantly harden beneath him. "And it appears you're alive as well."

My entire body was *shuddering* from the foreign sensations. His cool hands cupping my face—nails scratching through my stubble—and his perfect ass grazing my cock, with only this stupid onesie and his tiny linen shorts as separation.

I'm gonna fucking pass out.

"And you *didn't* kill me earlier," he continued, correctly assuming I was beyond speech at this point. "You gave me a severe hand necklace—which I would have greatly enjoyed under different circumstances—before letting me crack my head on the tile."

When I winced, he smiled, brushing my hair off my sweaty forehead, causing an undignified whimper to escape me.

Jesus, what's gonna happen when he touches my dick?

The cock in question gave an eager kick at the thought, and Simon purred in satisfaction. "Oh, I simply cannot wait to hear what noises you make—what I can get you to sound like, just for me."

Before I could reply, he leaned down and pressed his lips to mine.

Holy. Fuck.

Simon's lips were just as soft as I'd imagined they would be, and when his wet tongue insistently nudged along the seam of my mouth, I groaned and blissfully opened for him.

It felt as if my own powers had been turned inward, as if pieces of my soul were being drained out of my body and siphoned into his, leaving pure euphoria behind.

He chuckled against my mouth as I moaned. The feel of his tongue tangling with mine—of his *saliva* mixing with mine—made goosebumps break out over my skin.

His skin…

I'd flung my hands out of the way as soon as he'd appeared on my lap, but now I tentatively placed them on the sides of his slender neck.

Another shudder passed through me as I traced my thumbs along his jawline and teased the hair at his nape. His hair was so fucking soft—so unlike the coarse texture of mine—and the skin that was available to me even softer.

At this moment, I no longer cared about my missing sister or the mysterious nemesis plotting against me. All I wanted to do was explore every inch of the man before me.

Every inch of what's mine.

"Mmm…" Simon hummed again before lifting his head and gazing down at me. "I like your hands on me—on my neck." His voice dropped an octave, turning even more seductive than it already was. "Did you leave marks from when you choked me earlier?"

He tilted his head back, giving me an unobstructed view of the angry-looking bruises now decorating his pale skin in mottled shades of purple and green.

Fuck, that's hot.

As much as the marks turned me on, I wasn't sure how *he* felt about them. "Yes," I answered honestly, incredibly conflicted over what I was seeing. "You look like someone much bigger and stronger tried to kill you."

He smirked, peering at me through heavy lids. "But do I look pretty?"

Fuck me.

"Yes," I gritted out, shaking again—although this time it was with the effort it took to restrain myself. "You look so fucking pretty. I want to mark you up everywhere until there isn't an inch of you I've left untouched. I want to make you cry while I do it, so you look even prettier."

I want to destroy you.

"Because I'm yours, and you want everyone to know it—including me," he replied matter-of-factly, completely and perfectly unfazed by the shit coming out of my mouth.

I slowly nodded, surprised I didn't immediately pounce. Never in my wildest, darkest dreams did I think I'd be able to touch another person like this—let alone someone I was so insanely attracted to.

My animalistic nature wanted to throw him to the ground and fuck him like I'd been dying to since we met, but I also wanted to savor the moment.

Ignoring my baser instincts for the time being, I concentrated on running my hands all over him, amazed that I *could*.

Simon patiently let me explore, keeping *his* hands on my face the entire time—grounding me.

Never let me go.

"So you've never..." he gently began, before plowing ahead. "You've never been touched by anyone before?"

I blinked at him. It would have made so much more sense to point out that *I'd* never touched anyone else, so I had no clue where he was going with this.

"Well," I carefully replied, trailing my fingertips down his sides, noticing where he was ticklish. "I had a nanny once. A lesser supe named Martha. Unfortunately for her, she was there when my powers manifested, holding me in her lap as she read me a bedtime story. It was the only kill I ever regretted."

I paused before haltingly adding, "As you could imagine, no one *chose* to touch me ever again."

Simon clenched his jaw, his pretty green eyes filling up with tears. As much as I wanted to see him cry in different circumstances, this raw display sent my protective instincts into overdrive.

"They... left you alone?" he hissed. "A fucking *CHILD?!*"

He's upset for *me?*

That his intense anger was on my behalf was doing all sorts of things to me—and my cock. Simon may have been five feet nothing, but even I wouldn't want to be on the receiving end of this beautiful rage.

Fuck, he'd make such a good villain.

"There was nothing to be done about it," I replied, caressing my way down his back until I found the strip of bare skin between his shirt and shorts. "Besides a one-time murder attempt fueled by petty jealousy, I never truly *wanted* to kill my siblings, so I was always careful to avoid contact. I could probably briefly touch them now—with how powerful they all are—but I'd rather not risk it."

"What about your *parents?*" Simon spat out the word—his unfiltered hatred lighting me up.

I nodded slowly, understanding that the ruthless way supes operated would seem harsh to a normie, even without the layers of abuse.

But he's in my world now, for better or worse.

"We were all raised to believe supes couldn't kill their parents, but it was hard to gauge the truth of that rumor, since mine weren't exactly the nurturing types to offer hugs, anyway."

He cocked his head, his gaze missing nothing as calculation dominated his expression again. "Is it true? That supes can't kill their parents?"

I couldn't stop my lips from twisting into a smirk. "No. It's not."

Because he was perfect—because he was absolutely the only man for me—Simon's tasty lips curled in a matching grin before he bent to kiss me again.

"Well, it sounds like everyone got what they deserved," he murmured, gliding his fingers along my jaw, making my eyelids flutter. "Including *you*—because I'm going to fucking spoil you, Wolfy."

Yes, please.

"I thought that was my job," I choked out as Simon moved in a way that dragged his ass over my cock—and dragged another groan from my chest.

He smirked as he continued sliding down my body, taking the zipper of my ridiculous onesie with him as he went. His lips brushed over my skin as it became exposed—my collarbone followed by my chest—each moment of contact sending jolts of pleasure shooting through my veins.

Keep going...

Please...

"Oh, I won't stop you from spending exorbitant amounts of money on me," he laughed, pausing to flick his tongue over my nipple, making me hiss. "But what *I* plan to do is ensure every one of your first times is as magical as possible. Since I'm going to be your first *and* your last."

Simon stopped what he was doing to intently meet my gaze—pointedly conveying the unspoken threat of his words.

My perfect, tiny tyrant.

I smiled as best I could, considering my nerves were on fire. "That's right," I growled, just as crazy and possessive over this normie as he was for me. "Just like no one else gets to touch *you* ever again—except me."

All mine.

He rewarded me with a villainous smile before continuing his —and my zipper's—torturous trajectory south.

"Very good, Wolfy," he praised, pausing with the zipper at my abs, centimeters above my leaking crown. "Now, how about I swallow your cock?"

CHAPTER 23
WOLFGANG

How will I survive this?

It seemed almost ridiculous now that I'd been so concerned about *Simon* dying. If anyone was in danger of having their head explode, it was me.

He's going to touch my cock.

HE'S GOING TO SUCK MY COCK!

While I was technically a virgin, I was by no means a blushing innocent. But it was one thing to fuck a Fleshlight and another to have the living, breathing object of my obsession kneeling before me, eyeing my weeping cock like it was a juicy steak.

"Look at you," Simon cooed, releasing the onesie zipper at my ankle and sitting back on his heels to admire me. "You're even bigger than I imagined."

Besides the obvious ego boost his words gave me, I found myself conflicted once again. The idea of forcing my way inside him—his mouth or his ass—made a fresh burst of precum drip down my shaft, but I also didn't want to cause *unenjoyable* discomfort.

Pain in the bedroom should always be consensual.

"Simon," I tried—and failed—to keep my tone even. "You don't… have to take all of me if you don't want to. I'll enjoy anything—"

"Pardon?" he scoffed, eyes flashing as he glared up at me. "I can and I *will* swallow your beautiful cock, Wolfy. In fact, I'm going to devour every thick inch of you until I feel you in my guts. Same goes for when I ride you later, but first things first."

Whatever you say, boss.

His hungry gaze fell to my cock again, and he lightly traced a finger along a throbbing vein while I shuddered in agony.

"My only concern is that I'm a bit parched from my near-death experience." He smirked and licked his lips. "So this won't be as *sloppy* as I would've preferred. However—"

Oh, I can help with that.

Leaning forward, I roughly gripped his chin. "Open your mouth," I growled.

Simon didn't argue or question my request. Instead, he dutifully opened wide, like a sinner accepting communion, exposing that soft pink tunnel that was calling to my cock.

Get me in there.

Giving him plenty of time to reconsider, I gathered the saliva in my mouth and allowed it to slowly drip down into his.

Of course, he didn't even flinch. The instant the thread hit his tongue, his eyes rolled back in his head, and I almost came from connecting with him in this way.

From claiming him.

"Merci," he mumbled, fluttering his eyelashes coquettishly as I released him.

Then he lowered his mouth over my cock.

"Fuuuuck," I gasped, gripping the arms of my chair as my vision practically whited out.

Simon hadn't been exaggerating when he said he could handle all of me. Like some sort of demonic vacuum, he sucked me down, flexing his tongue against my shaft as he forced me deeper into the wet, heavenly heat of his throat.

I will not survive this.

He hummed as I bottomed out—sending a shockwave of vibrations straight to my soul. Then his throat constricted so tightly around me, I wondered if I'd ever be able to pull myself free.

Not that I'd mind being stuck here forever.

As if he hadn't just swallowed half his body weight, Simon casually dragged himself off my full length with an audible pop.

"I almost forgot." He gazed up at me earnestly. "You need a safe word."

"No, I don't," I hurriedly replied, frantically reaching for him —intent on pulling him back to me. "I really fucking don't."

He gracefully evaded me, clasping both his hands around my girth and working *our combined saliva* along my shaft—no doubt to shut me up.

Well-played.

"You *do*, Wolfy," he chuckled, twisting his hands in a way that pulled a pathetic whimper from my throat. "Because while you may want to *try* everything, it doesn't mean you'll *like* everything."

"I disagree," I choked out, mindlessly thrusting into his hands, my gaze locked on the wet mess covering my cock. "I'm going to fucking *love* everything you do. Because it's you."

Simon froze, snapping my attention to his face. He stared back at me—wide-eyed and uncharacteristically speechless—and, for a moment, I feared I'd overstepped.

Maybe he only wants this thing between us to be physical…

The realization I wanted so much more—with *him*—slammed into me the same moment that a slight blush crept over Simon's delicate cheekbones.

"And I know I'm going to *love* everything you do. Because it's *you*," he whispered back, using his thumb to trace the V under my crown. "But I want to do this *right*. And that involves consent from both of us, especially considering what sort of things I suspect we're both into."

"What's your safe word?" I asked, knowing it was better to just do what Simon said.

Because he's the boss.

"Polyester," he replied. "And if my mouth is otherwise engaged, I'll pinch you a few times, or punch you, if need be."

"I might be into that," I warned, sliding my hand into his soft hair. "The idea of you trying to fight me off turns me on way more than it probably should."

Might as well be honest.

Simon held my gaze as a filthy smirk stretched across his beautiful face. "Oh, you and I are going to have some fun.

Let's say your safe word is *Daddy* for now, since we both know you won't call me that. Even though I own you."

Is that so?

I roughly yanked him closer in response, effortlessly holding him in place over my dick.

It would be so easy to just take control.

Unbothered by my dominant display, Simon only chuckled, his voice turning deliciously breathy as lust took over. "Is this what you want, Wolfy? You want to hold me captive so you can throat fuck me until I cry?"

Fucking hell.

"Yes," I rasped, wiping the mix of saliva and precum from my crown over his lips while my grip on his hair tightened. "I want your tears all over my cock."

I want to make you cry.

"Well, then," he murmured, moving my other hand to his hair as well. "You'd better treat me like the wanton whore I am."

Without waiting for me to reply, he swallowed me down again in one smooth motion, gagging around me as his nose hit my groin.

"Fuck," I cursed on an exhale as he bobbed his head. "Do you know how long I've wanted to fuck this mouth? Since the first time I heard you running it during your final interview. If I'd known I could touch you then, I would have told everyone to get the hell out so I could bend you over the table and fuck you until the only words coming out were slutty French nonsense."

When he came up for air again, I moaned at the sight of two tears traveling down his face.

"You want slutty French, Wolfy?" he panted, flicking his tongue over my slit. *"Plus fort, s'il te plaît."*

"So polite," I chuckled, collecting his tears on my thumb before popping it into his mouth to suck clean. "You want me to fuck you harder? You want your throat to be raw by the time I'm done with you?"

"Oui," he gasped, reaching up to scratch his nails over my abs, continuing his path south until his palms rested on my thighs. "I want you to use me. *S'il te plaît,* Wolfy. Make me yours."

Fucking fucking hell.

I had no doubt Simon knew exactly what he was doing with his choice of words, but the idea of unloading on or inside him—of claiming him as *mine*—made me go fucking feral.

Burying my hands in his hair, I abruptly shoved his face down on my cock, relishing his muffled yelp. Holding his lips flush against my groin, I waited for him to tap out—or pass out—but Simon only dug his nails into my thigh with one hand while dropping the other to slip inside his shorts.

He is such a whore…

My whore.

"Is your needy cock feeling neglected?" I huffed, yanking him upright so he could gasp in a breath and I could have a look at him.

His swollen lips were trembling—eyes narrowed and tears freely streaming down his face—and I'd never seen anything more beautiful in my entire life.

I'm in danger.

"Tu me rends fou," he hissed, the vehemence in his tone driving *me* insane. "What I *need* is to make you come."

"Come here," I growled, releasing his hair and hauling him back into my lap. "Get your cock out and your mouth on mine."

"Who's bossy now?" he murmured against my lips, although he wiggled out of his linen shorts so there was no longer any separation between us.

"Spit," I commanded, holding out my palm expectantly.

He momentarily broke our kiss to obey, and I gripped both our cocks in my hand before giving us a rough pull.

Holy fuuuuck.

The feel of Simon's skin on mine was already exquisite, but the slide of his foreskin against mine was a religious experience.

"Merde!" he gasped, dropping his head back and giving me a perfect view of the bruises I'd left on his neck. "Wolfy... I-I'm so close. I'm about to come all over your adorable little onesie."

What a delicious brat.

"Show me," I snarled, beyond ready to be covered in him. "Fuck yourself with my fist. Make us both come."

Dropping his forehead to mine, Simon rode me hard, fucking into my fist like a man possessed, dragging his length against mine until I was seeing stars.

"You're mine too, you know," he growled, staring into my eyes with an intensity that felt electric. "In case there was any doubt. You belong to me and only me."

"Yes," I rasped, too close to the edge to put him in his place, and not caring to, anyway. Everything he was saying was true, and I'd be a fool to deny any of it.

I belong to you.

"Say it," Simon hissed, burying his hand in my hair and tilting my head backward so he could glare down at me. "Swear that you're mine."

My free hand fell to cup his ass, fingers digging into his flesh as I encouraged him to go faster. Harder. Needing to come like I needed air. Needing to claim him—and be claimed—in every way possible.

"I swear it," I choked out, groaning as ropes of cum began shooting out of me, coating my hand, my abs, and our cocks.

Marking us both.

"You sound so sweet when you come for me," Simon murmured. Lowering his mouth to mine, he bit my bottom lip so hard I tasted blood—prolonging my orgasm until I thought I might pass out.

His thrusts grew erratic as he joined me in release before collapsing onto my chest with a satisfied groan.

"Mmm... how was that, *mon chou?*" he asked, gently kissing my neck, making me shiver.

I almost laughed. There weren't words in any of the various languages we both spoke to describe what I'd just experienced.

"It was a good start," I teased, smiling when he lifted his head to scowl at me. "I might require more of a demonstration before I can give a full performance review."

"Challenge accepted," he haughtily sniffed, sliding off my lap and pulling his shirt over his head before carelessly tossing it aside. "But first, let's get dolled up so you can take me out for dinner. I'm only a helpless *normie*. I need to maintain my strength."

You are more powerful than you think.

I chuckled. Spending money on Simon only turned me on, so if he was trying to momentarily cool things down at an expensive restaurant, then he needed to re-examine his strategy.

Although he probably knows exactly what he's doing.

CHAPTER 24
SIMON

What am I doing?

It was so unlike me to be this enamored with any one person, but here I was, not only staking *my* claim on Wolfy—an actual *superhuman*—but insisting he do the same for me.

But I was already fully on board this crazy train before I knew who he was.

"It's not every day I get to have dinner with a real live action hero," I teased, helping myself to a bite of scallop carpaccio with citrus. "Or gobble his dick."

Wolfy paused with a lobster ravioli halfway to his mouth, and I felt no small amount of satisfaction to spy the slight blush I lived for.

"I'm not a *hero*, Simon. Not even close," he gruffly replied before popping the ravioli in his mouth to avoid saying more.

Since I know all his tells by now.

I'd long suspected this was a divisive topic behind the scenes, but that only made me *more* determined to pry the tea out of my newly unmasked superman.

"Perhaps not on paper…" I mused. "I never understood what the difference was between heroes and villains, and based on the ones I've met so far, it doesn't appear that being 'good' or 'evil' has anything to do with what you're classified as. And let's not forget *who* swooped in and saved me at Benediktion —like a *hero*." I sent my protector a meaningful look. "So it sounds like semantics to me."

Wolfy was eerily still, his head cocked—like a predator—and I suddenly realized the way he *moved* should have given away his true nature before now.

But, apparently, we 'normies' were blissfully ignorant. While aware of supes—and rapt with attention when a battle was on the news—we saw little of them in our day-to-day lives.

Or so we thought.

I now understood just how adept supes were at blending in with the rest of us—like an invasive species that evolved to mimic its neighbors.

How deliciously creepy.

"That's… very observant of you." Wolfy leaned across the restaurant booth and lowered his voice, clearly ready to spill the juicy details. "I also always suspected the differences were bullshit, and Butch and Xander recently uncovered proof that it's all politics. So-called 'heroes' are the ones who willingly signed their loyalties over to humans, while 'villains' refused. That's it. The USN is working to expose the major players in this scheme, but the paper trail extends far beyond Big City, so it will take time."

He sat back and gave me a hard look that only made me harder. "And I shouldn't need to mention that this intel is classified."

I smirked as I stole a ravioli from Wolfy's plate, pleased when our hands brushed. "Look at you! Finally realizing that sharing pertinent information with your *assistant* will allow me to actually *assist* you with running your empire."

Wolfy grimaced, looking adorably scolded. "I know, and… I'm sorry I kept things from you, even after you signed the NDA."

"I know," I soothed, reaching across the table to place my much smaller hand on top of his gloved one. "Although I wish you'd told me who you were from the start."

You don't need to hide from me anymore.

Wolfy's amber eyes were fixed on our joined hands—his expression holding such open wonder, I wanted to climb beneath the table and remind him how I could touch him *everywhere* now.

"I didn't want you to be afraid of me," he whispered, snapping his gaze to mine. "You need to understand… even extremely powerful supes are terrified of me, and rightfully so. I can strip them of their powers and drain their life force until all that's left is an empty husk. And with lesser supes or humans? Let's just say what my touch does to them is not pretty."

"Pretty, like when you popped REM's eyeballs on *my* behalf?" I innocently blinked at him. "That was sexy as fuck."

The reminder of my bloodthirstiness had Wolfy's gaze darkening, but then the waiter appeared to replace the appetizers with our entrées.

Food first, Simon—then fucking.

Giving the unsuspecting man a winning smile, I nodded in approval at the John Dory filet with scalloped potatoes and roasted butternut squash for Wolfy and foie gras-stuffed quail with herbed polenta and a port sauce for me.

A simple meal.

We enjoyed our food in amicable silence for a few minutes before Wolfy chuckled softly. "As much as you claimed to tolerate blood from the start, I did *not* expect you to be so comfortable with the... casual maiming and murder that comes with the supe territory."

Time for you to learn some intel about me.

Clearing my throat, I set down my silverware and squared my shoulders. "I'm not... *right* in the head, Wolfy—at least not according to medical professionals. My own father psychoanalyzed me when I was young. The only reason I wasn't institutionalized was because my mother refused to sign off on the diagnosis."

Seeing Wolfy's look of horror, I offered him a small smile. "Not that Bunny would have recognized the signs, since most of the rich assholes she associates with could easily be psychopaths."

"Nothing is *wrong* with you. You're fucking perfect," Wolfy hissed, looking ready to unalive anyone who thought otherwise, which turned me on immensely.

Case in point.

"Yes—to *you*," I chuckled softly, reaching to give his hand a squeeze again. "But most humans do not find a murderous personality attractive. Unless it's a fictional book boyfriend in a dark mafia romance, that is."

He cocked his head again, his eyes lighting up with interest. "Have you ever killed anyone?"

Ooh, let the foreplay begin!

"No." I lightly laughed, releasing him so I could enjoy another bite of quail. "Although there have been some much deserved close calls. I don't know if you've noticed, but I'm built on the smaller side—"

"Again. Perfect," Wolfy growled, gaze roaming over me in a way that had me—and my cock—sitting up straighter.

I licked my lips, not at all mad that the man sitting across from me was three times my size. "Well, I suppose I could be an ambush predator, like my favorite villain—The Hand of Death."

Wolfy rolled his eyes. "I doubt I'm anyone's favorite."

Excuse me?

I scoffed. "Do you honestly not know what a legend you are? *Your* trading card is one of the most sought after in certain dark corners of the internet."

He gaped at me. "I have a *trading card?* I thought that was just a cheesy tourist souvenir Biggs Enterprises did for heroes like Captain Masculine."

This is adorable.

"Yes, my villainous thing—you do." I cackled. "And it's one I've been dying to get my hands on for years, mostly because of what you're wearing on the front…"

"Oh, no," he croaked.

"…your *supersuit*," I cooed, already scheming about when I'd get the chance to peel it off him. "Matte black—big surprise—and so deliciously form-fitting."

Again, the slightest blush appeared, and I wondered if my scary supervillain had a praise kink.

We must make a point to explore that one.

"I don't wear it much... anymore..." he trailed off, and I instinctively knew the conversation was headed somewhere unpleasant.

"Why not?" I gently asked, hoping Wolfy wasn't about to shovel more food into his mouth to avoid answering.

He cleared his throat and shifted in his seat. "I really only wore it for... when my parents sent me to take out their adversaries for them."

My heart dropped into my stomach, along with the foie gras. I may not have been a cape chaser, but I knew Apocalypto Man and Glacial Girl were in a league of their own—with only the most powerful supes able to face them on the battlefield and survive.

And they treated their son as infantry.

"How old were you when they started doing that?" I gritted out, already bracing for the answer.

Wolfy sighed, knowing better than to evade the question. "I was twelve the first time. It did not go well, and I... almost didn't make it out alive."

My vision went red, coloring everything around me in a blood-soaked haze. All I could see was a vision of me somehow resurrecting Wolfy's supervillain parents just so I could re-murder them repeatedly.

However they died, it wasn't painful enough.

"Simon." Wolfy's smooth voice cut through my imaginary killing spree, and I returned to the present to find him tightly gripping my hand. "Do that again."

I blinked at him, confused. "Do *what* again?"

His amber eyes searched my face, although he looked more intrigued than concerned. "I don't know. I felt a... *pull* on my powers, and I think it came from you."

I practically fell out of my seat. "Pardon? I-I wouldn't even know how to do that. I'm just a human."

"Are you sure about that?" Wolfy blurted out, his expression heartbreakingly hopeful.

What else would I be?!

Yes, I'd somehow survived The Hand of Death, but that didn't necessarily mean anything. It could simply be a glitch in my DNA, or that I'd spent enough time with Wolfy to adapt to his deadly hotness.

"I'm fairly certain I don't have special powers, Wolfy." I smiled sweetly, while feeling terrible for disappointing him. "Besides deepthroating and being a shameless size queen, of course. Perhaps you could try *probing* me again?"

When Wolfy simply gaped at me, I clarified, "Whatever you were trying to do to me at the Château. Mistress Noir-Rouge did something similar at the art gallery and Butch tried it as well earlier today. It's a bit creepy, to be honest, but I don't mind it coming from *you*."

"I'm surprised you could feel that," Wolfy mused, still eyeing me with interest. "It's a fairly regular occurrence between supes—something we do to size up potential opponents—but it's usually too subtle for normies to pick up on. Where it gets tricky is that high-level supes can lock down their powers enough to be undetectable, even when 'probed.'"

Something wasn't adding up. "So Noir-Rouge wanted to measure her dick against mine, and Butch was probably trying to figure out how I survived your touch... but why you, Wolfy? Why would *you* be sizing me up?"

I'm no threat to you.

He winced, looking almost embarrassed. "I wasn't. I-I just wanted to touch you in any way I could. It was a compulsion—an *urge* I couldn't ignore—but I shouldn't have done it without your permission."

Oh, when will you learn?

"What other *urges* do you have when it comes to me?" I whispered.

Wolfy froze. "What do you mean?"

Let's play.

I smirked and rose from my seat before grabbing my coat. "How about you pay the bill while I get a head start? If you manage to track me down, you can explore some of those big, bad urges of yours."

Wolfy's pupils were as blown out as when he accidentally attacked me in the kitchen, making me shiver in anticipation of our game.

"Go ahead and run, Simon," he growled low, briefly nodding at the waiter across the room to bring the check. "You'll never get away from me."

CHAPTER 25
SIMON

My heartbeat was pounding in my ears as I fled the restaurant. All previous concerns over whether I was jumping into things too quickly evaporated as an overwhelming sense of *rightness* took over.

Wolfy was it for me. It didn't matter that he was a legendary, universally feared 'villain,' while I was simply an extra fabulous human who'd tripped and fallen onto a supercharged dick.

Not everyone can be this lucky.

Despite our differences, we were perfectly matched. And right now, we were about to play a game we'd *both* enjoy.

One where he's the predator.

And I'm the prey.

Wrapping my cropped suede coat more tightly around myself, I passed a couple out for the evening, smirking at their obliviousness to my filthy fun.

I was so engrossed in how scandalous I was being, I didn't notice the eerie quiet that had fallen over the docks. Only moments ago, the strip had been bustling with people, but suddenly, I found myself completely alone.

That's... odd.

Warily glancing over my shoulder, I witnessed the streetlight outside the restaurant flicker and die—followed by the next closest one, and the next.

And the next.

Oh, my God.

Anticipation gripped me, made even more delightful by not knowing if it was actually Wolfy causing the phenomenon.

It's just like being a victim in a horror movie!

Spurred on by the thought of getting impaled on Wolfy's meat hook, I picked up the pace, spontaneously veering down the nearest side street.

Which happened to be the Rue Obscure.

This walled passageway had originally been a route for soldiers to travel from the seafront to the village, but in the centuries since, development above had created a tunnel. The original rough-hewn walls remained, with only various alcoves and locked doorways breaking up the monotonous stone.

The occasional hanging lantern added to the spooky ambience, with only the rare barred window or accidental skylight allowing dim moonlight to filter in.

A perfect location for murder...

...of my arsehole.

I made it about halfway through when a lantern behind me abruptly shattered, inspiring me to squeal in surprise and break into a full run.

Okay, but what if that's not Wolfy?!

To add to my belated concern, every remaining lantern extinguished simultaneously, leaving the deserted tunnel in near darkness.

Before I could call for help, I was swept off my feet and slammed into the nearest door so forcefully it knocked the breath from my lungs. It was so similar to what happened at Benediktion that my entire body began shuddering uncontrollably.

Oh, fuck.

Until I smelled bergamot, lavender, and leather—instantly calming me.

I'm safe.

A growl, too primal to be human, rumbled out of him as he lowered his mouth to my neck. I whimpered as my already bruised skin was sucked into his mouth, teeth dragging over the tender surface until I was writhing in his hold.

"Wolfy..." The needy moan that escaped me was borderline embarrassing, especially with how it echoed in the tunnel. "Please..."

What exactly I was begging for was unclear. Obviously, I wanted *him*—his perfect cock, especially—but the entirety of what I desperately needed at this moment was more complex than that.

By the time Wolfy was done with me, I no longer wanted to know where I ended and he began. I wanted him to claim me so thoroughly that I'd never be able to erase the memory of his hands on me, of the feel of his leather on my skin, or the sensation of him filling me to the point of pain.

I want him to consume me.

"Please," I repeated, attempting to rub myself on him even though I could barely move.

Wolfy didn't answer with words. Instead, he grabbed the neck of my designer T-shirt and ripped it down the middle, exposing my chest to him. His thumb found my nipple, the leather-covered digit absently circling the sensitive peak as he continued tormenting my neck.

All at once, I realized he was mimicking what REM had done to me at Benediktion. Whether it was to erase my unwanted memories with this desired situation, or to reclaim me for himself, I couldn't be sure. But I didn't want this encounter to stop where that night had ended.

"More," I commanded, threading my hands through his thick hair and giving an insistent tug. "Make me forget about everyone else who's ever touched what's *yours*."

Who says I can't play dirty?

As expected, Wolfy responded with the possessive response I was hoping for. He growled again as his hand dropped to the waistband of my shorts, expertly flicking open the hook before sliding inside.

Then he froze.

And I smirked.

"Find something you like?" I purred, inwardly wiggling with glee over my surprise.

"*Fuck*, Simon," he rasped, finally breaking character as he quickly withdrew his hand.

He rustled in the dark for a moment before slipping his hand back into my shorts. My moan mirrored his as I realized he'd removed his glove so he could better feel what I'd worn for him.

Satin. Bikini. Briefs.

Only the best for my murder baby.

"Jesus, *fuck,*" he cursed again, caressing my satin-clad balls before loosely wrapping his fist around my length and giving me a slow stroke. "And they're… fucking *pink.* Jesus."

I choked on my surprise. "You can *see* in here? I can barely make out an inch in front of my face."

He chuckled before easefully picking me up and setting me down on a nearby window ledge. "Yes, I can see well enough. Just like I can smell the cum I left on your skin."

That statement has no business being as hot as it is.

Yes, I'd purposely skipped a shower before we left the house, but that was more because *I* liked the idea of going to a fancy dinner filthy and debauched. Now that I knew Wolfy had super-senses, I would be sure to use that intel to my advantage in the future.

Since he clearly has the upper hand, otherwise.

I leaned back against the iron bars as he pulled off my shorts completely. "So I suppose I never stood a chance with our little game of chase, hmm?"

He chuckled again. "Nope. But I *loved* watching you run from me."

There was that L-word again, and even though it wasn't directed *at* me, it was doing traitorous things to my insides.

"Stop," he commanded.

For a moment, I panicked, thinking mind-reading might be one of his powers. But then his hand closed over mine—stopping me from pulling down my briefs.

"These stay on," Wolfy clarified, ghosting a finger down my shaft, making my cock twitch against the satin. "I want you to come inside them before giving them to me."

No, no, nooooo…

"*C'est des conneries,*" I cried, realizing my dream man *didn't* plan on fucking me in a medieval tunnel in the South of France. "If you insist on torturing me just so you can get a filthy keepsake, Wolfgang, then you'd better give me the orgasm of my life."

Wolfy huffed a laugh as he stepped back. "I'll do my best," he replied as I heard the distinctive click of a lube bottle being opened in the dark.

At least he came prepared.

To torture me and ruin my dreams.

I yelped as my legs were suddenly tossed over his forearms and I was forced to grab the bars behind my head for leverage.

"What are you—" I began, but my words ended with a strangled sound as Wolfy cupped my arse with his hand, slipping inside my briefs before gliding his lubed finger over my hole.

His lubed *gloved* finger.

Oh, my God.

Ohmyfuckinggodddd.

"Mmm…" he hummed, moving his bare hand to torment my trapped cock once again. "You look so good like this. Held captive and wrapped up like a pretty present. A gift just for me."

I *was* immobilized, but still attempted to rub against my jailer, desperate for him to enter me. "Just for you… until some drunks wander this way with their mobile torches on. Do you think they'll enjoy the sight of my cock encased in satin? Will they stop and enjoy the show?"

With a snarl, Wolfy forced his finger into my hole, almost making me come just from the feel of leather skating over my p-spot. Without giving me a moment to recover, he stuffed another finger inside, using his free hand to wrench my briefs upwards—trapping my cock and balls in a satin prison.

Merde!

"You saw what happened when someone thought they could look at you. What happened when they thought they could touch what's mine," he hissed, fucking my ass with his fingers, psychotically slow. "And you liked it. You love how goddamn crazy you make me. How I'll spill blood for you. I bet you'd enjoy watching me do it, too. You'd come so fucking hard just from watching me kill, knowing it was all for you."

The animalistic sounds I was making would have kept anyone in their right mind from entering the Rue Obscure, but I was lost in his arms. Even if he didn't have me trapped, I wouldn't have been able to escape.

Wouldn't have *wanted* to.

Using the bars behind me as leverage, I rode him as best I could, but Wolfy was unquestionably the one in control. All I could do was sweat and moan as he increased his pace—pounding his fingers into me as he continued holding my throbbing cock captive.

He truly is a villain!

I needed to come. I needed to come more than I needed my next breath. My hips bucked as I pathetically tried to rub myself against my briefs, sobbing in despair at the lack of friction the satin provided.

"S'il te plaît!" I gasped, feeling frustrated tears rolling down my face—knowing my anguish was only turning him on more. "I want to *come* for you, Wolfy. Please let me come in my little pink panties so you can rub them all over your handsome face the next time you have a wank."

Wolfy instantly released the pressure on my cock, wrapping his free hand around the back of my neck as he hauled me closer.

"You delicious little thing," he chuckled against my mouth, licking away the tears that had gathered on my lips. "I *love* how bratty you are."

That did it. That fucking L-word booted me—howling—off the cliff. Wolfy crashed his lips to mine as I came, massaging my gland with his *gloved fingers* until my throat was hoarse from sobbing against his smirking, perfect mouth.

I'm so in love with this man, it makes me sick.

He held me through my aftershocks before withdrawing his hand and gently removing my soaked briefs. More mysterious rustling occurred before he gently lifted me off the ledge, helped me back into my shorts, and guided me out of the Rue Obscure with his freakishly hot night vision.

While buttoning my coat over my bare chest, I noticed the new pink pocket square adorning Wolfy's suit jacket.

"How fashionable," I cooed, reaching up to give the soggy material a little flick. "And I *love* the new cologne. Is that *eau de cum* I smell?"

Wolfy's lips twisted in an amused smile, and I couldn't hold mine back either—especially when he took my hand in his and pulled me down the once-again crowded street.

"C'mon, you tiny tyrant," he teased, giving my hand an adorable squeeze. "Let's find a dark corner in a bar somewhere, so you can put that bratty mouth to good use before we head home for the night."

Biting my tongue to stop myself from pointing out I already *was* home, I let Wolfy pull me along, determined to show this amazing man just how *good* my bratty mouth could be.

CHAPTER 26
WOLFGANG

"Love is for the weak, Wolfy, and falling for a normie *is a liability."*

"Just think about how easily he could be killed, hmm?"

"Watch how easily I could do it…"

My mother's voice echoed in my head as I sat up in bed with a startled gasp, desperately patting the bed next to me, gripped with terror.

WHERE IS HE?!

"Hey, hey, shhh… you're fine, *mon chou*. Everything's fine."

My body instantly relaxed at the sound of Simon's groggy voice, and I laid back down just as he turned on the bedside light.

Because he can't see in the dark.

It was wild to be sleeping next to *anyone,* but especially a normie, of all people.

A very fragile, easily killed normie…

"Simon." I flipped over and grabbed him, pulling him into my arms faster than he expected, based on his surprised squeak. "We need to make sure you're able to protect yourself. In case... well, you're not... I just... I just need you to be ready."

I can't lose you.

He rolled his eyes, but then tempered it with a quick kiss to the tip of my nose. "It's four in the morning, Wolfgang. But I promise, once it's a reasonable hour again, I shall call Mr. Miyagi personally to see if he's taking new students. Wax on, wax off."

It was my turn to roll my eyes, only I couldn't resist kissing the bratty mouth I was obsessed with.

Simon had indeed demonstrated how talented his mouth was last night, kneeling beneath a dirty table at the only dive bar we could find. My eyes had remained locked on his pretty green ones as I unloaded down his throat, shuddering through that odd *pull* on my powers I often felt around him.

Which doesn't make any sense.

I'd done enough research on the *inventus* bond to know what my powers were *trying* to do. Unfortunately, with nothing on the other end to connect with, this natural compulsion was only making me more possessive, more determined to claim him some other way.

And more determined to protect him.

"Have you ever fired a gun?" I blurted out, accidentally waking Simon again just as he was drifting off.

He snuggled closer, his hand traveling down my bare chest and abs to where my cock had already taken notice of his proximity. "If you're trying to get me on your dick again, all you have to do is ask. But yes, I've fired a gun once or twice."

I trailed my hands down his bare back and ass, still marveling over the foreign texture of someone else's skin under my fingertips.

This is heaven.

"I'll teach you how to use mine..." My words ended with a groan as he ran a finger over my slit. "I would just feel better knowing you had a weapon at your disposal that can kill supes."

That got his attention. "Your gun can kill supes?" He tried to sit up, but I yanked him back down, pointedly placing his hand on my cock again.

Where it belongs.

"Well, yeah," I murmured, kissing him some more because I couldn't get enough. "I don't need any weapons against humans since I can explode their heads like watermelons."

Unsurprisingly, Simon's cock jumped against my thigh at the mention of gory violence.

We should fuck while watching something bloody.

We should do nothing but fuck...

Needing to claim him again, I rolled Simon onto his back and covered his much smaller body with my own. Nestling my cock between his ass and the mattress, I kissed and bit his battered neck, determined that my marks become a permanent feature on his skin.

"Hold on a tick," he laughed, playfully pushing me off. *"You're* the one who started this very urgent conversation in the middle of the night. I want to know more about your gun. How does it kill supes?"

I obediently sat back on my heels, although I couldn't stop myself from subtly dragging my length along his crack, chasing the sensation I needed to survive.

Fuck, I need to come again...

...I need to come all over him.

"Focus, you sex maniac," he huffed, flicking my nipple to get my attention. "I won't give up until I know."

I huffed. "It's the bullets. Xanny infuses the gunpowder with my DNA. So when the bullet enters another supe's body—assuming their suits and skin can be penetrated—it drains them from the inside out. The knife I wear was forged in a similar way, but I rarely use it."

Simon's expression grew thoughtful. "Your brother is the mad scientist of the family, hmm? I wonder if he'll find anything interesting when he tests the hair he rudely yanked from my head."

Excuse me?!

"He did *what?*" I sputtered, my thoughts skirting toward murderous before I reminded myself this behavior tracked.

Xander thinking he could treat a normie like a lab rat was unsurprising, and his idiot fiancé wasn't much better. Butch was lucky I'd been shell-shocked by Simon's unexpected resurrection yesterday. Otherwise, I would have sent the hero into a power-drained time-out again for throwing a fireball anywhere near my...

I wish he could truly be mine.

"Ooh, I take it back. Now I'm *definitely* in the mood." Simon snickered, pulling me back down on top of him. "You must know your angry voice is boner-inducing, right?"

I was more than happy to be distracted from thinking about my annoying family. Refocusing on using Simon's juicy ass like a cock sleeve, I devoured his lips, losing myself in the sensations.

In *him*.

I couldn't decide which was better—my sensitive crown skipping over his twitching hole, or our warm, wet tongues tangling with each other. Simon moaned through it all, regardless, which only made me want to claim every uninhibited inch of him.

Patience, Wolfy.

While I was dying to feel Simon's tight hole strangling my cock, I also wanted to savor each new experience as it happened. After being deprived of this level of intimacy my entire life, I was determined to enjoy every milestone to the fullest extent.

Especially with him.

Simon's cock jumped between us, and suddenly, it felt imperative that I get my mouth on it—that I learned how he felt sliding over my tongue.

What he tastes like…

No longer bothering to hide my super speed, I slid down Simon's lithe body and tossed his legs over my shoulders before he even realized what was happening.

"Wolfy!" he gasped, burying his hands in my hair as I wrapped my lips around his crown. *"Oui, suce-moi la bite.* Devour me. That's it, yessss…"

Simon's 'slutty' French, combined with his praise and the salty flavor bursting on my tongue, had me moaning around him as if *I* were the one receiving pleasure.

Give me more.

I didn't know what the fuck I was doing, but it wasn't dampening my enthusiasm in the least. Mimicking what I liked, I circled his plump head with my tongue—tracing the V before flicking the tip over his slit and greedily drinking every drop of precum that spurted out in response.

Popping off, I licked my way down his shaft, teasing his retracted foreskin and gently sucking his balls into my mouth until he was sobbing.

"*Putain!*" Simon whimpered, yanking on my hair to try pulling me back onto his weeping cock. "Wolfy, I'm so close already. Please, please, pleeeease… put me back in your mouth. *S'il te plaît!*"

Since he looked so cute thrashing on the bed, I took pity on him. Repositioning myself, I swallowed him down until my lips were flush with his groin, relishing the strangled sound he made as I contracted my throat around his swollen cock.

Simon *tried* to control the action by thrusting into my mouth, but I was having none of it. Placing my arm across his abs, I held my brat in place as I bobbed my head, loving how desperate I was making him.

The pull on my powers returned, and I noticed Simon clutching his chest as well. For a moment, I pretended he was my *inventus*—that the bond between us was real—even if he was most likely just responding to his pounding heartbeat.

I can't help wishing it was more.

Regardless, I felt like a god when his cock began pulsing after only a few minutes—rewarding me with a mouthful of his heady flavor.

And I know exactly where I'm putting this.

Pulling myself off his cock, I clamped my mouth shut and rose to my knees before flipping Simon onto his belly. Spreading him open, I took a moment to admire the puckered hole I *would* be ruining eventually before carefully parting my lips.

The mixture of come and saliva threaded downward from my mouth, coating his crack to create the perfect channel for me to fuck.

Sliding my throbbing cock into the silky, wet mess, I closed his juicy cheeks around me and began to thrust.

His ass jiggled enticingly as I dug my fingers into his flesh hard enough to bruise. My eyes rolled back in my head every time my crown hammered over his hole, which only encouraged the babbling and writhing occurring beneath me.

"Oh, *merde*, oh *fuck*, Wolfy!" Simon gasped, clawing at the rumpled bed sheets as he seized up. "I'm gonna... I'm fucking coming again... *Putain!*"

"Give it to me," I growled.

Give me what's mine.

The feel of his needy hole twitching as he came all over the bedspread had me instantly spilling—coating him in return until I thought I might pass out.

Mine, mine, mine.

I collapsed onto the bed beside him, my insatiable compulsion to claim him slightly lessened.

For now.

Simon weakly turned his head to face me, looking gorgeously disheveled and only seconds away from sleep as his eyes drifted closed.

Of course, his *mouth* wasn't yet ready for bed. "I'm simply going to sleep in this mess like the heathen I am," he murmured. "I'll worry about scraping it off tomorrow..."

Unfortunately, the thought of him washing me away made my possessiveness roar to life again.

I'm going to go mad at this rate.

"No," I growled, dragging my hand through the cum I'd left on his lower back, collecting it to massage over his hole. "You won't be showering until *after* we've driven out to the lavender field where you lost your virginity to that fuckhead, Pierre. By the time I'm done with you, the only cock you'll remember is mine."

Simon hummed weakly, cracking open an eye to peer at me. "Honestly, I don't even remember if his name *was* Pierre or not. He was easily forgettable and already forgotten. But I do *love* how crazy I make you..."

His reply soothed my pacing beast, even as I wished he'd used certain words in that sentence *slightly* differently. But I also knew I needed to chill the fuck out.

Simon was just a normie—and one who'd proclaimed he was uninterested in personal relationships—so I couldn't expect the same intensity of emotion I was irrationally feeling.

But I'll still take whatever I can get.

"That's good to hear," I softly replied, not wanting to startle him awake again but needing to make something clear. "Since you're never getting away from me."

Because he was the perfect man for me, Simon rallied to add a mild threat of his own. "Likewise. Mark my words, Wolfgang. If you ever try to escape me, I will hunt you down."

"Noted, boss," I murmured, feeling my heart sing as I reached to turn off the bedside light before settling in next to him again.

It didn't matter that we couldn't connect on a supe level. Simon was the closest thing to an *inventus* I'd ever had, and the only way I was letting him go was over my dead body.

And maybe not even then.

My eyelids grew heavy as I finally surrendered to sleep, and I prayed the ghost of my mother wasn't waiting in my dreams to show me my worst nightmare.

CHAPTER 27
WOLFGANG

"I hate to be *that* person, but I assume we'll eventually need to get back to work, hmm?"

Simon's voice cut through my sunbaked daze the same instant I felt a splash of chlorinated water hit my bare chest.

Sliding my sunglasses to the top of my head, I did my best to glare down the lounge chair to where my smirking assistant peered over the edge of the cliff house's infinity pool.

Even though it only encourages him.

Which then only encourages me.

Another splash had me out of my chair and striding closer, enjoying the feel of the sun on my bare shoulders. For obvious reasons, I had no interest in the crowded beach of Villefranche-sur-Mer, and with no one but Simon around, I could comfortably strip down.

We both begrudgingly agreed to not walk around completely naked—despite the privacy of our location. This was less about our comfort levels with each other and more to do with the threat of nosey younger brothers or gold-digging mothers stopping by unannounced.

Neither would surprise me.

I lowered myself to sit on the edge of the pool where Simon had been lazily paddling around for at least an hour, wearing the tiniest swimsuit known to man.

Hot pink, of course.

True to form, he didn't try to swim away to avoid punishment. Instead, he boldly glided closer, standing between my legs and smoothing his palms up and down my shins—warming me more than the sun.

I loved how freely—and often—Simon touched me, and how he patiently allowed me to do the same to him. Even though he struck me as a fiercely independent individual, I had to trust I wasn't constantly invading his personal space by behaving like a stage five clinger.

I'm sure he'd let me know if he didn't like it.

"Would it sound terrible if I said I never wanted to work again?" I chuckled, although I was only half-joking.

I just want to be with you.

Simon continued to slide his hands up my legs until he reached my thighs, causing goosebumps to appear on my skin. He'd already commented on my natural lack of body hair, which I explained was fairly common among supes.

Probably for reasons of aerodynamics.

This led to an entire afternoon of rapid-fire questions where Simon grilled me on every piece of supe trivia he could come up with. By the time he was done, I was exhausted, and he was enough of an expert to be a supe himself.

Or a supervillain's assistant.

"No, it doesn't sound terrible," he laughed airily. "You sound like most people who have to work for a living. Except *you* have more money than God, Wolfy, so you don't." His expression grew serious. "What do you *want* to do?"

"I *have* to find Violentia," I sighed, knowing full well retirement wasn't ever going to be an option—unless I was killed. "She's a loose end and a potential threat to my family."

Which includes you.

"So why not let your famous brother-in-law take care of the problem for you?" Simon shrugged. "He's certainly the trigger-happy type—"

"Because Captain Masculine has killed enough supposed *villains!*" I barked, harsher than I meant to.

Before I could apologize for my tone, Simon pushed away from the edge and reached his arms up, beckoning me to join him. "Come here, *mon chou.*"

He'd called me that a few times now, and while I secretly loved having a nickname that wasn't meant to instill terror, I was confused by his choice of endearments.

"Do I *look* like a cabbage to you, Simon?" I huffed, but it was all for show as I eagerly slid into the pool to join him.

He beamed triumphantly, immediately wrapping himself around me like a monkey in a tree.

"A very grumpy one, yes," he gaily replied. "But you're a man of many languages. Surely you're aware that calling someone *mon chou* in French is similar to 'sweetheart' or 'darling?' And while it *technically* translates to 'my cabbage,' I prefer to think of you as *choux à la crème*—a sweet little cream puff."

I don't know if that's any better.

But I still love it.

I cleared my throat, deciding to give this tiny tyrant more random intel. "I'm not... actually fluent in French. Since Spanish is my second language, and they're so similar, I never bothered learning it."

Simon scoffed in mock outrage. "Excuse you, Sir? Why are you not speaking slutty Spanish to me in bed, then? I demand a refund!"

Beyond enamored, I rolled my eyes and carried him to the end of the pool shaded by an oversized canopy.

Since he hasn't reapplied sunscreen for three hours and twenty-one minutes.

"Because I don't speak Spanish unless I have to," I haltingly explained, willingly handing him even more ammunition. "It... reminds me too much of my father."

He eyed me for a moment, his expression thoughtful. "You truly hated your parents."

It wasn't a question, and there was zero judgment in his statement, but I still felt the need to explain. "They weren't good people, Simon. I've met countless villains in my life—including a few dozen legendary ones—but my parents were two of the most evil."

Simon's plush lips pressed into a thin line. "But no heroes, hmm?" When I furrowed my brow, he continued. "You mentioned how this supe distinction was bullshit politics, yet you're still speaking of villains as if they're expected to be naturally evil—and of yourself as if you could never be heroic."

Well, shit.

"I guess old habits die hard," I admitted. "Especially when you're known as one of the most dangerous villains—from one of the most notoriously ruthless families."

"That may be so," he interrupted. "But that's not who you *are*. Yes, you are quite adept at exploding heads and creeping around in the shadows like a sexy phantom, but I've seen the *real you*, and it's not at all frightening."

And that *is somehow more terrifying.*

I nodded, desperate to redirect the conversation before I did something ridiculous.

Like propose.

"You've definitely seen a side of me I don't show many people, including my own family," I carefully spoke. "But my reputation has allowed me to protect my siblings, even with our parents no longer in the picture. My transition to head of household has gone a lot smoother than others have. If I was *less* frightening, older clan leaders—like Noir-Rouge or Orochi—may have swept in to either wipe out my house completely or absorb us as soldiers into their clan."

And the only thing stopping that from happening still… is me.

Simon brushed away a strand of hair that had fallen over my forehead before depositing a soft kiss on my lips. "Don't forget, you now have *me* to help you, and I'm even scarier than you are."

He's not wrong.

I quickly ran a hand over my face to disguise any traitorous tears with pool water before gazing over the edge of the cliff to the town far below.

Simon's original question still stood. As much as putting myself on a permanent vacation with this man sounded like heaven, I wanted—*needed*—to find Violentia.

Along with whoever she's working for.

"Tell me about your siblings." Simon casually switched gears, although I suspected it wasn't casual at all. "Obviously, I've met **The Mouthy One** with his **Token Hero**. Are your other brothers all breathtakingly beautiful buff supermodels with luscious golden brown skin and gem-like amber eyes, like you?"

To my horror, my cheeks heated, and I prayed the extra sun I'd soaked up today would disguise my embarrassment.

I knew I was conventionally attractive, but no supes had ever dared *flirt* with me before, unless it was done to show their dominance. My beauty was poisonous—an exotic flower you observed from a safe distance away.

Look, but never touch.

"Well." I cleared my throat, suddenly more than happy to talk about my family. "We're all fairly tall—like most supes. Balty and the twins have a slightly lighter skin tone, and Gabe and Dre inherited our mother's blue eyes. Xanny, Vi, and I look the most alike. That's how we divided ourselves to play, too, growing up—big versus little kids—but there's also a big age gap between Xanny and Balty. Vi was always the one I was closest to…"

I hadn't meant to share so much, but Simon was just so easy to talk to—and I hadn't casually chatted with anyone in so long.

And never like this.

Whereas Violentia was my go-to sounding board, her dramatic responses usually only riled me up more. But Simon had the uncanny ability to pinpoint the source of my anxiety and subtly distract me from it with an adjacent topic that still allowed me to vent.

He *should be the therapist.*

"What's Violentia like?" he asked. I tensed—already beginning to shut down until he cupped my face in his hands. "I don't mean as our *target*, Wolfy. I want to know what she's like *as your sister.*"

"Okay…" I nodded, debating what to tell him.

How about the truth?

"She doesn't give a fuck," I laughed, surprised by how easily I could talk about her, after all. "Xanny's like that too, but his behavior is more of an act to shut others out. Vi honestly couldn't give two shits what anyone else thinks of her, and she will make sure you *know* how little your opinion matters."

"Sounds like my kind of person." Simon smiled softly. "Go on."

He wasn't asking for anything specific, but I realized intel about my sister's powers would be useful for him to know.

Not that I want him anywhere near her.

"There's a common misconception among normies that supes are just killing machines, but most of us are completely lucid while fighting, even those that shift into other forms." I chewed my lip, knowing this wouldn't paint my sister in a good light. "Vi is different, though. She goes into a trance—almost like an Old Norse berserker—while anything becomes a weapon in her hands. "

Simon nodded. "So she makes the perfect killing machine, especially for someone else controlling the reins."

Why are you so perfect?

The tension I'd been holding on to instantly evaporated. "Yes, exactly. Even when she's not engaged in battle, Vi is extremely impulsive. She doesn't think things through before acting. That's why I need to find her—to *talk* to her—and figure out what's going on."

My voice was breathless as the rest came out in a rush. "I can't help thinking she just made a rash decision with... *whoever* she joined up with. That she's riding the adrenaline high of our chase, but not thinking of the consequences. I-I can't... *kill* her over that."

I can't...

Simon's soft lips pressed to mine, halting my downward spiral and giving me something to hold on to—infusing me with calm.

"And that's why her supe name is Ultra Violent, correct?" He lifted his head to better look at me, and I realized how close I was allowing this normie to get to me.

He's not just any normie.

I debated how to reply. Simon had either overheard Vi's supe name during my confrontation with REM—or was simply putting two and two together now that he knew who *I* was.

But rules are rules.

"I'm sorry, Simon," I croaked, hating *any* secrets left between us. "A supe's identity is sacred. The only way I could reveal a family member's identity is if—"

"If I'm part of your clan," he sighed, his face falling as he wiggled out of my arms to put space between us. "And that will never happen since I'm not like you."

"Simon..." I reached for him, feeling that *pull* between us intensify to the point of pain. "That's not... I would love nothing more to—"

Because my family was the worst, *someone* chose that moment to call—with the ringtone telling me it was the line we reserved for emergencies only.

If only I could kill them all.

"I have to get that," I murmured, my heart breaking when Simon turned his back to me as I climbed out of the pool.

My thoughts turned even more murderous when I saw it was *Balty* calling, since what he considered an 'emergency' could very well be that he was out of beer.

"What?" I snapped, not even bothering to say hello as I answered my phone.

"Um..." His idiotic voice grated on my last nerve. "I don't know how else to say this, but... father's missing from his grave."

CHAPTER 28
SIMON

What was I expecting—a marriage proposal?

I had to turn away from Wolfy so he wouldn't see the fucking *tears* that were stinging the corners of my eyes.

Don't get attached to a superhuman, Simon.

I'd gotten so caught up in the excitement of finding out who Wolfy was, I hadn't considered how me being a normie might be a deal-breaker for *him*.

Even if he enjoyed temporarily slumming on this side of the tracks, there was no future here. While we still didn't know *why* Wolfy could touch me, it didn't mean I was special, and it certainly didn't mean we were compatible. His supervillain family would always come first.

And I can never be one of them.

"What do you *mean*, father's missing?" Wolfy growled in anger, which only pissed me off more because of how hot he sounded. "I put him in that grave myself."

Oh, no…

Immediately understanding the severity of the situation, I dried my eyes and scrambled out of the pool so quickly, I scraped my knee.

As if he could *smell* my blood—and for all I knew, he could—Wolfy spun to face me, zeroing in on my injury like it personally offended him.

"Are the twins in the dorms? Make sure they stay there and put Betsy up in a hotel." Wolfy barked instructions into his phone as he roughly grabbed my biceps and yanked me into the house.

"Ouch!" I snapped, more dramatically than was warranted, but I was already feeling salty. "I'm still wet and don't appreciate being handled like—"

"I don't fucking care!" Wolfy shouted, and for a moment, I thought he was daring to speak to *me* like that.

I'll put him in a grave myself!

"I don't *know*, Balty!" he continued yelling at **The Dumb One** as he dragged me into the bathroom and forcefully sat me down on the closed toilet. "Get a hotel room for yourself or go find a cape chaser to fuck for a few days—I don't give a shit. And keep trying to get a hold of Xanny or Butch. They're probably just buried in each other's asses at thirty-thousand feet."

Well... that's a visual.

Wolfy abruptly ended his call and tossed his phone on the vanity before draping a plush bath towel over my shoulders. I attempted to catch his eye as I dried off, but he was wholly focused on rummaging around in the medicine cabinet, refusing to look at me.

Shutting me out.

Not trusting myself to speak, I mutely watched as he kneeled and carefully applied antibiotic ointment to my injury before unwrapping a bright pink Band-Aid.

The sight of his enormous hands—hands that could so easily *kill*—being so gentle with me made my bottom lip tremble. Then, the thought of how he'd probably never had anyone bandage *his* knee before caused tears to blur my vision.

And *then* my heart was thoroughly shattered when he smoothed the plaster over my scrape and sealed it with a goddamn *kiss*.

"Bloody hell, Wolfy!" I exclaimed, not for the first time. "How do you expect me to stay pissed off when you do shit like *that?*"

He finally met my gaze, his expression holding so much anguish, I reminded myself he was preemptively excused from all offenses until the end of time.

"Please don't be angry with me," he whispered, barely audible. "I *need* you."

Mon chou...

I ran my fingers down his temples, tracing his jawline before tilting his chin so I could deliver a kiss.

"Tell me what happened," I gently, but firmly, commanded.

He nodded, working his jaw. "Baltasar returned home after a night out and noticed the empty... grave behind our house." Wolfy paused, eyeing me carefully before elaborating. "My family has a compound outside the city limits. The twins prefer to stay on campus, and Xanny's had his own apartment for years, but the rest of us live there full-time. It's fortified and hidden somewhere no one outside our family can find it."

Which means I'll never see it.

Burying my misguided disappointment about the future, I simply focused on the present facts. "And your father was buried on the premises."

Wolfy's gaze held mine as he gripped my thighs so tightly, I knew there would be bruises. "Yes. I buried him there like a war prize, after I... *Fuck,* Simon. What if I *didn't* actually kill him? I thought I drained him completely, but he's fucking Apocalypto Man! One of his goddamn powers is cryogenic freezing. Oh, my God... he's gonna fucking kill us all..."

I knew a panic attack when I saw one. Wolfy was shuddering violently, and before he laid his head down in my lap, I glimpsed pure terror on his face. Not for himself, but for his family.

For those he loves.

How this man could see himself as nothing more than a stereotypical villain was beyond me, but I knew he wasn't thinking clearly at the moment.

Let me handle this for you.

"What did the grave *look* like?" I calmly asked.

"What?" he rasped, lifting his head to glance up at me.

I gently scratched my nails through the hair at the nape of his neck. "Did it look like he was dug up, or did he claw his way out?" I clarified.

Wolfy froze. "I-I don't know..."

Of course, **The Dumb One** *would leave out that very important detail.*

With a sigh, I grabbed his phone and texted Baltasar directly to demand he send photos of the gravesite. Apparently, a life or death situation instilled *some* sense into his oafish head, as he replied immediately with half a dozen photos.

I perused the selection before tilting the phone so Wolfy could see. "Someone else dug him up," I stated.

Someone who knew he was buried there.

He snatched the phone from me and flipped through the images himself before releasing a shaky breath and nodding in agreement.

"Okay," Wolfy said, almost to himself, although I noticed his breathing was returning to normal. "We can work with this. Even if my father *did* somehow survive, he's obviously not back to full power... or else Balty would no longer have been around to call me..."

The way his voice cracked broke my heart. Wolfy *tried* to behave as if his siblings did nothing but annoy him, but I knew he would burn down the world for them.

*Even **The Dumb One**.*

"Are there any supe laws against patricide?" I asked, my brain already whirring with probabilities. He shook his head, and I recalled him mentioning the belief that supes *couldn't* kill their parents.

A rumor most likely created to keep the youths in line.

"What about stealing corpses, or trespassing, or clan members conspiring against the clan leader?" I continued, racking my brain for anything we could pin on his sister and her accomplices.

Wolfy chewed his bottom lip, but he'd settled enough to consider my words. "It's not *illegal* to kill or overthrow the head of your clan, but it is deeply frowned upon without just cause. That's one reason why I didn't tell most of my siblings about my plans for our parents ahead of time. I only involved Xanny and Butch because having their combined power behind me outweighed the risks of them turning on me."

But what if they've changed their minds?

I didn't wish to add to his stress, but we needed to examine every angle. "You don't... think *they* might have had anything to do with this, do you?"

He huffed a soft laugh, which was a good sign. "You know how you keep saying *I'm* the hero in villain's clothing? Well, Xanny creates anti-pollution inventions and rescues sea turtles in his spare time. Butch can barely swear, and is now protecting Big City pro bono—simply because he enjoys... *helping people.*"

Wolfy shuddered dramatically at the end of his rant, which told me it was safe to make a joke. "Gentlemen in the streets, freaks in the sheets, hmm?" I ventured.

He smiled—wider this time—before standing and offering me his hand. "Gentlemen prefer villains, don't they, Simon?"

Absolutely.

I tossed my towel aside and allowed him to guide me out of the bathroom and down the hall. Upon arriving in the main living area, Wolfy wrapped me in a fluffy blanket and made me sit on the couch while he put the kettle on for some Earl Grey.

My favorite.

"Don't you think *I* should be the one coddling you?" I called out, beyond pleased he ignored the new microwave in favor of making tea correctly.

"I *like* taking care of you, Simon," he murmured, his gaze fixed on the flames under the kettle. "It relieves my tension."

Yes, I will *be taking this opening.*

"You know, Wolfgang," I threw off the blanket and languidly stretched across the couch, "there are other ways to relieve tension that make tea and murder look tame."

He shot me a heated look, those gorgeous eyes of his roaming over me like a caress. "I don't think that would be a good idea right now. I'm already holding back my full strength with you in bed, and I don't feel… stable at the moment."

Ooh, kinky.

"Don't threaten me with a good time!" I laughed. "Maybe I *want* to see you Hulk out."

The full-bodied laugh that came from Wolfy warmed every inch of me. I decided it didn't matter if he ever put a ring on this normie finger. I would always be *his*—if only to hear him laugh like that again.

"Yeah, I noticed you called Balty 'Baby Hulk' in the group chat," Wolfy snickered as the kettle began to sing. "Please do that as often as possible. He'll hate it because it's so accurate."

You devil.

"Is that a clue?" I eagerly leaped to my feet and joined him on the other side of the kitchen island. "Are you breaking supe law to tell me about your sibling's powers?"

Wolfy rolled his eyes good-naturedly. "I wouldn't say it's against the *law* to share intel about another supe's powers, but it *is* extremely bad manners."

I snorted, balancing on my tippy toes to reach a pair of mugs. Of course, I fell short, so the much taller man in the room retrieved them for me.

Husband material.

"We couldn't have that, could we?" I teased. "Above all else, villains must be well-mannered."

My words ended with a laugh as Wolfy snatched me up and sat me on the counter. "Yes," he smirked before giving me a kiss with an extra bite. "But the best part of being a villain is that we've never been beholden to humans. We do whatever the hell we want. Make our own rules."

His comment inspired an idea. "Is there any sort of… governing body for supes, or is it truly survival of the fittest among your kind?"

Wolfy thoughtfully steeped my tea before handing me the 'Dock Me in Villefranche' mug I'd had custom-made.

"It's mostly martial law and dubious moral code," he finally replied. "But there *is* a governing body for when a rogue supe needs to be dealt with. Their stance is generally objective, but where the humans at the USN conduct fair and balanced trials, this supe-run collective usually backs the sovereignty of individual clans."

A smirk curled my lip. "And the sovereignty of your clans is determined by the head of the household."

Wolfy sipped his tea, his addicting scent only intensified by our steaming beverages. "Yes. My word is technically law in the Suarez house." He took another sip before adding, "Even if you're the boss of me."

He's impossible to stay mad at.

I couldn't contain the smile that stretched across my face. "Well then, it sounds like we need to pay the powers that be a visit to see if they'll address the threat to *our* sovereignty."

He bent down to kiss me again, the taste of bergamot on his lips making me salivate. "Sounds like a plan, boss. Let's fly to Switzerland."

CHAPTER 29
SIMON

My undergrad studies were in international relations and diplomacy, so it was fascinating to discover a governing body for supes existed at all, let alone in a notoriously neutral country like Switzerland.

Learning that untouchable heroes and villains were 'just like us' while still operating under a wildly disparate moral code was giving me life.

Along with all sorts of ideas.

I wonder if they host old-fashioned executions?

As I'd confessed to Wolfy during our recent date night, I wasn't like other boys. I didn't mean this flippantly. There were actually core aspects of my personality that didn't fit the social norms. Traits *I'd* internalized as a negative until recently.

For more years than I cared to admit, I believed my father's wary disinterest represented how *all* my relationships in life would be. But all it took was spending a fair share of my time online—and at choice parties in certain scenes—to realize there were others like me.

Well, mostly like me…

I now knew that *kink* wasn't something to be ashamed of—that as long as it was practiced in a safe, sane, and consensual manner, I could freely explore. The *other* thoughts occasionally drifting through my head, however, were unacceptable in any scene.

At least in human ones.

After my father's attempt to institutionalize me, I was smart enough to bury my darker fantasies, but meeting Wolfy had brought it all rushing back to the surface. And now that my hidden desires had been uncorked, there was no way I'd be able to stuff them back into the bottle again.

I want to watch him kill.

Maybe I could even help…

As if he could sense my bloodlust, my morally gray dream man magically appeared in our Geneva hotel room's dressing room doorway, tucking his phone back into his jacket pocket.

His TUXEDO jacket.

"*Merde…*" I drawled, lecherously drinking him in. Despite Wolfy wearing a boner-inducing suit every day of the week, the sight of him in a *tux* was beyond my wildest, dirtiest dreams.

Unable to resist getting my hands on him, I sauntered over. "You look positively edible," I cooed, running a finger along the satin lapel. "Although, are you feeling feverish? I see you're wearing a *white* dress shirt and a navy bow tie! I didn't think you were physically capable of donning anything that wasn't as pitch-black as my heart…"

His tasty lips twitched in amusement, although the look in his eyes was pure hunger as he appraised *my* outfit in return.

"I decided to live a little," he responded, showcasing that delightfully dry humor of his. "Although, I see *you're* going the all-black route tonight. Perhaps we're both a little sick?"

I certainly hope so.

An uncharacteristic wave of nerves suddenly hit, and I quickly turned back to the mirror to busy myself with adjusting the lapel of my slim-fit suit jacket. The deep V of the neckline was echoed in the sheer black shirt I wore beneath, and—as I'd hoped—the generous peek at my bare chest seemed to have caught Wolfy's eye.

"I assume my ensemble is appropriate for tonight's prestigious event?" I haughtily asked, although I didn't actually care.

Yes, we were in Geneva to appeal to a council of powerful supes, but The Hand of Death's reputation spoke for itself. I could wear Trash Bag Couture, but as long as I was on *his* arm, they'd pay me respect.

But I still care if Wolfy *likes what he sees.*

"The way you look in this suit…" he murmured, looming over me from behind most deliciously. "With so much skin on display…"

With a gloved hand, Wolfy gently lifted my chin, surveying the bruises he'd put there in the mirror's reflection. He frowned—presumably because my marks were already fading—before releasing me and using both hands to pull open my shirt and jacket.

He silently stared at my exposed chest for a full minute—his jaw working, as if he were debating whether he should share his thoughts.

He definitely should.

"Go on." I turned to face him, thirsty for proof that he was made for me. "Tell me what the sight of my skin does to you."

Wolfy released a growl that made every inch of me stand at attention. "It makes me want to…" His gaze briefly flickered to mine as he swallowed hard, before refocusing on my chest. "I *need* to show everyone you belong to me by marking you up some more."

I felt dizzy. Since our conversation in the pool, I hadn't allowed myself to even humor the thought that I was special to Wolfy—or special at all. I'd assumed my immunity to his powers was simply one more flaw in my DNA, but this man was looking at me like I was one in a million.

It's too good to be true.

"You want others to know you're stuck with me, hmm?" I teased, attempting to keep my tone light. "Not that I'm simply the one lucky normie you've found who can survive your magic fingers?"

Wolfy's gaze snapped to mine, astonishment and fury on his perfect face. "Is that what you think?" he scoffed. "That I only want you because I can touch you?!"

I couldn't be sure if he had purposefully raised his voice, but the confusing cocktail of horniness and insecurity I was experiencing was making my cock throb and my chest ache.

"Simon," he growled, herding me backward until I was pressed against the wall. "I was already *obsessed* with you back when I thought I had no hope of ever feeling your skin on mine. I was ready to claim you from day one—if only in a limited way—but now that I can have *all* of you? Goddamn right, I want everyone to know you're mine. That way, if they dare touch you, they'll know what's coming to them."

Swoon!

My heart was pounding so intensely, it felt as if it were trying to leap out of my chest and into his. "You say such sweet things—"

"Are you all right?" Wolfy interrupted, his gaze flitting back and forth between my face and the hand I'd placed over my heart. "Why are you rubbing your chest?"

I almost laughed at the urgency in his tone. "It's just a pesky human reaction, Wolfgang. We're not built for this level of excitement, but I'll be fine in a moment."

He nodded, looking strangely disappointed by my answer. "Very well. Let's go over things again before we head out."

I nodded pleasantly, even though we'd been over the game plan twenty times already. But I also knew Wolfy mistakenly blamed himself for what happened at Benediktion, so if it eased his worry to *over* prepare, I supported that.

Plus, I enjoy him fussing over me.

Wolfy eyed me as he spoke, carefully monitoring my reaction. "There will be other heavy hitters in attendance tonight besides the council, but this is an inarguably neutral zone. We might get some big talk thrown our way—a dick measuring contest or two—but no supe would dare attack us on the premises."

I nodded to show I'd understood. "But once we leave the event?"

He pressed his lips into a thin line. "We're fair game. On that note, I want you in my sight at all times—preferably at my side. We will have allies tonight, and I've heard word has spread about my supposed *inventus* status, so I'd be surprised if anyone tried anything. But I still don't want to risk it. I can't... risk *you*."

I felt that alarming *pull* in my chest again, but I had no intention of concerning Wolfy with the news.

Although I expect him *to spill every piece of intel.*

"Are you finally going to tell me what an *inventus* is?" I huffed. "Especially as I'll be *pretending* to be yours tonight."

He sharply inhaled, and I froze, wondering if I'd overstepped. But then I spied something like sorrow on his handsome face before he buried it beneath business.

"An *inventus* is an equally powerful supe who can connect their powers with yours to form a bonded pair. Xander and Butch are an example of this, with their formidable abilities shared and amplified between them. It's about more than just power, however. The bond creates a deep emotional connection with fiercely protective instincts. Almost like... murderous soulmates."

I want that.

With him.

He drifted off for a moment before clearing his throat and refocusing. "You'll probably feel more of that... *probing* tonight—from rival supes—but it's nothing you need to worry about. When another supe doesn't feel you respond, they'll simply assume you're able to keep your powers locked down, like I can. This will confirm our claim, because if you were my *inventus*, you'd naturally be as powerful as me."

If.

Because I never can be.

A traitorous sniffle escaped as my mouth ran away from me. "So it's just for show, is it? Since I can never actually be your *inventus*. Because I'm not like you."

Faster than I could register, Wolfy cupped my face in his hands—forcing me to look at him. "Simon. It's *killing me* to not be able to bond with you, but it doesn't change how I feel. As far as I'm concerned, you *are* my *inventus*, because you're everything I've ever wanted. You are *mine*. Now, can I please put a fresh mark on you before I fucking explode?"

My heart stopped beating this time as the enormity of his words washed over me. Wolfy saw me as the equivalent of a supe soulmate, despite me being nothing but his normie assistant—and he wanted everyone to know it.

His unfiltered proclamation was startling but also validating. In the end, I didn't need a witchy bond to know how I felt about Wolfy either, even if I wasn't quite mature enough to declare my devotion as openly as he had.

This is an age-gap relationship, after all.

"Well, since you put it that way," I laughed, holding my jacket and shirt open for him—offering my unblemished chest for his abuse.

Mark me up, murder baby.

With a growl so low it sounded like a purr, Wolfy lowered his mouth to the area directly above my heart—gathering me into his arms to press tightly against him. I gasped as he sucked my skin into his mouth, scraping his teeth over my flesh so roughly, I knew it would be tender for days.

Make me yours.

I closed my eyes with a groan, letting my sexy psychopath do his primal marking thing.

The sensations coursing through me were unreal. I'd always had a penchant for pain, but this felt as if my soul was being pulled out of my body and combined with his, before being reinserted as something different.

Something new.

What I was meant to be.

Even if I could never fully fit into his world, I was Wolfy's, and he was mine—and nothing in my entire existence had ever felt so right.

And anyone who tries to come between us will get what's coming to them.

CHAPTER 30
WOLFGANG

I hadn't attended a council soirée in Geneva since my parents died, and it didn't take long to remember why I avoided these events like the plague.

From the instant Simon and I entered the ornate grand ballroom of the Palais de la souveraineté, I felt multiple sets of eyes upon us. The longer we made the rounds, checking in with various allies and potential enemies, the more I was convinced we were being stalked.

This wasn't surprising, as most supes behaved like predators, but I wasn't anyone's prey.

And neither is Simon.

Of course, I was still terrified of anything happening to him, but I had to trust that my wrath—and his mystique—would be enough to keep the lions at bay.

At least until I can figure out who's plotting against us.

"Ah, Wolfgang. I heard I might find you lurking here tonight."

And so it begins.

Conjuring as serene an expression as I could manage, I turned to face the statuesque superhero addressing me.

Dahlia Salah, otherwise known as Atmosphera, could control the weather and air pressure so effortlessly, she made Butch's dead dad look like a weakling. While she was one of my contemporaries, her hero status—and piss poor attitude—had me avoiding her as much as possible.

"Greetings, Dahlia," I murmured, noticing Simon stiffen at the familiarity. "I just can't seem to get a moment's peace from your family, can I?"

Thanks to her preppy East Coast upbringing, she produced a sound that was both derisive and elegant. "Yes, my brother told me he found you wandering the streets of Villefranche—*shopping*, of all things. Even more surprising was that Zion seemed to think you'd joined him in answering to a... *normie*."

Someone needs to turn that lizard into a pair of boots.

Zion was absolutely right that I answered to Simon, but intel like that could be seen as a weapon to other supes.

Or a weakness.

Clearly choosing the second option, Dahlia gave an exaggerated shudder and fixed her dark brown eyes on the man at my side. If she'd hoped to insult or intimidate Simon with her display of disgust, she was in for a surprise.

True to form, he immediately blasted her with a sunny smile, his tone dripping with sarcasm. "*Oui!* Meeting Zion was an absolute delight. He told me all about his *wife*... specifically about how much you adored her."

Well-played, brat.

It was all I could do not to laugh at how affronted Dahlia looked. "Who said she was his *wife?!*" she hissed, lightning dramatically flashing in her eyes. "If I were head of our household, I would never have allowed—"

"But you're not," I smoothly interrupted her tantrum, reminding her of the hierarchy here. "Not like I am."

Dahlia immediately settled, wisely realizing causing a scene at a council event wasn't the best idea.

Especially since I outrank her now.

Because it was Dahlia, however, she couldn't let it go completely. "What is this, Wolfgang? A political statement? Is shacking up with a *powerless normie* supposed to prove that we're all just—"

For the second time in possibly her entire existence, Dahlia Salah stopped talking—her mouth dropping open at the sight of Simon casually slipping his arm through mine.

Touching The Hand of Death.

"Oh, how rude of me not to introduce myself," he breezily spoke, matching her lofty air. "My name's Simon, but *you* may call me Mr. Alarie. Or better yet, simply refer to me as *yes, Sir, sorry, Sir.*"

Fuck me, he's perfect.

The sight of this pompous hero recoiling from Simon's tiny outstretched hand almost had me whisking him away to the nearest supply closet—propriety be damned.

"Forgive me if I don't... shake hands," Dahlia sniffed, although she was finally eyeing Simon with the respect he deserved.

She'd walked into this confrontation thinking she only needed to scare away a normie, but now didn't know *what* she was dealing with. If Zion ran his mouth about our encounter in Villefranche, then Dahlia had also heard the *inventus* rumor, which meant she was now probably assuming Simon could drain her dry if he chose to.

And something tells me he would.

Dahlia accepted a flute of champagne from a passing server—probably to regain her composure. I nodded at Simon, but he shook his head at the offer, his gaze unwaveringly fixed on his opponent.

A true villain.

"How *lucky* can one man be?" Dahlia abruptly continued, the calculation in her expression telling me trouble was brewing. "You've somehow found your own *inventus,* after already having one pair in the family. And let's not forget how *both* Apocalypto Man and Glacial Girl recently died—seamlessly setting you up to take over the clan…"

Simon tightened his grip on my arm, but I didn't skip a beat. "Perhaps we should all have a moment of silence for the late Vortexio. It's thanks to *him* that Captain Masculine was born and that both my parents met their untimely ends. Such a shame to lose *three* legends all at once."

The smile she gave me was brittle. "Yes. Tragic. Lucky for *you*—dead men tell no tales. I sure hope no one goes digging…"

"*What?*" I snapped, momentarily losing my cool.

I swear, if someone in her clan stole my father's body…

"How does it feel having a purebred *hero* in the family, Wolfgang?" Dahlia cooed, on a roll now that she'd struck a nerve. "I bet the copious villain blood on Captain Masculine's righteous hands just *kills* you—"

"If you're lucky, you might find your own villainous match someday," Simon coolly interrupted, protectively placing his much smaller body between us. "A more powerful family like Wolfgang's might feel charitable enough to take you in like a mangy stray."

Dahlia's silver evening gown flapped around her mahogany skin as a sudden gust of wind snaked through the ballroom. The few supes in attendance who *hadn't* already been staring at us since we arrived—or since Simon had cozied up to my side—were now rapt with attention.

They can look all they want.

As long as they don't touch.

Further proving he had the biggest set of balls in the room, Simon gleefully continued, "I'm sure at least one of the Suarez brothers has yet to discover the wonderful world of dick. Perhaps joining *our* illustrious clan could be your chance to truly make something of yourself."

"I. Am. Not. A. Villain." Dahlia had gone into full Atmosphera mode. She was levitating off the marble floor—her brown eyes glowing electric blue as the crystal chandeliers flickered and swayed high above.

Several supes were hurrying for the door, and I spied a familiar council member briskly walking our way, flanked by security.

Oops.

"Oh, darling," Simon tsked, somehow not showing a trace of fear in the face of this threatening show of power. "Haven't you heard? Heroes and villains are all the same."

Careful, Simon.

It was my turn to step forward, deftly maneuvering Simon behind me as I faced off with the hero.

"Do I need to take my gloves off, Atmosphera?" I calmly asked. "Or will you behave for my *inventus?*"

Dahlia's brow furrowed, the brewing storm immediately subsiding as her high heels landed on the marble floor with an echoing clack.

"Why would *you* let someone like *him* hold equal authority to you?" she scoffed, her incredulity erasing any remaining rage. "You're the goddamn Hand of Death, Wolfgang."

My lip curled into a sinister smile. There was no way to explain the sway this man had over me, especially to someone as set in their ways as Dahlia Salah.

Simon was both the grounding force *and* the pin pulled from the grenade. He allowed me to simply exist—apart from my deadly reputation—while encouraging me to fully embrace every dark and depraved desire that came along with an existence such as mine.

He'd accepted all of me.

So, therefore, he owns every piece.

"What can I say?" I shrugged nonchalantly, just as security reached us. "We do things differently in my family."

Dahlia nodded, deep in thought and completely unconcerned that she was being forcefully escorted away. I had no doubt her famous parents would pull enough strings—and grease enough palms—to get their hotheaded daughter out of trouble.

Since heroes *get away with everything.*

"Well, this was a delightful surprise," the gray-haired villain who'd arrived with security chuckled warmly. "Out of all the members of your family, Wolfgang, I wouldn't have bet on *you* to cause a scene at one of my soirées."

Luca Meier was the infamous Kinetic Assassin, with unrivaled abilities in telekinesis and mind control. He'd personally trained Violentia and me—and eventually, the twins—although I suspected the only reason I was originally invited along was because of how much of a fanboy I was.

Who wouldn't want to hang out with a real-life Gambit?

He was one of the oldest supes still alive—probably thanks to the fact he was no longer active in battle—although he looked much younger than he was.

Superior genes will do that for you.

I cleared my throat, determined to stay focused on why we were here. "Yes, Luca... and the Suarez most likely to cause a public disturbance is the one I need to discuss with the council. Preferably in private. Preferably as soon as possible."

Luca solemnly nodded. "I'd heard rumors I hoped were idle gossip, and it saddens me to learn otherwise. The council is meeting tomorrow afternoon at my residence, and both of you would be welcome to drop by. You and your..."

He shifted his focus to Simon, who was still carrying himself like a supe with zero fucks to give. My mentor stared at him for a long moment—apparently choosing to energetically size up my faux *inventus* instead of offering introductions.

Typical.

Simon sharply inhaled and clutched his chest, making me growl and Luca grin broadly. "How interesting..." he mused, completely ignoring my reaction. "I'll see you both tomorrow, but in the meantime, watch your backs. You're not the only wolves in attendance tonight."

With that slightly ominous—but unsurprising—warning, Luca turned on his heel and left Simon and me to see ourselves out.

"Ready to go?" I whispered, trying to keep my voice low while discreetly checking him for injuries.

Simon looked a little dazed but nodded, so I began guiding him toward the exit and our waiting car. Along the way, I met the gaze of every supe we passed, making sure they saw death waiting for them in my eyes should they make a move.

The instant our driver closed the door, I pulled Simon into my lap, instinctively placing a hand over the mark I'd left on his chest as we drove away.

He'd impressively held his own in the face of both Atmosphera's meltdown and the Kinetic Assassin doing… whatever it was he did—but it was a *lot* for a human to handle.

"Are you all right? Luca Meier is a friend, so I don't believe he was trying to hurt you… but none of us are used to dealing with normies. Was he too rough with his power? What do you need right now?"

Simon laughed, and I immediately relaxed. "Stop fussing, Wolfgang. He did the usual invasive power probing, only it felt *different* this time. More intense, somehow…"

He placed his hand over mine and leaned in to kiss me. The instant our lips met, I felt a wave of calm wash over me—along with the now familiar pull on my power, trying in vain to connect with his.

I also really, *really* wanted to fuck.

"Mmm…" Simon hummed against my mouth as the car rolled to a stop. "Is that a special supe-killing gun in your pocket, or are you just happy to see me?"

"Both," I growled, clawing at his clothes, needing his skin on mine.

Needing to claim him.

He pulled back to better look at me. "Well, it's a good thing we're going back to the hotel—"

The unmistakable sound of a gun being cocked interrupted Simon's sentence, followed by the snarl of an unfamiliar voice from the front seat.

"Neither of you are going anywhere."

CHAPTER 31
WOLFGANG

Amateur.

I was so focused on getting us out of the venue—and back to the hotel—I hadn't even noticed our driver had been swapped out. And because of *my* inattentiveness, the man who meant everything to me was now in danger.

Because the gun is aimed at him.

Simon was frozen in my lap, his gaze fixed on mine and his gorgeous face impressively devoid of fear. Not for the first time, I wished for the mind speak abilities the twins possessed, so I could tell him everything would be okay.

I'll keep you safe.

As if he *could* hear my thoughts, the tiniest smile curled the corner of his perfect lips, and I experienced the strangest feeling of reassurance in return.

I nodded imperceptibly, hoping he'd somehow understand that shit was about to get real, and—most importantly—to *stay down* once I attacked.

Because this wannabe assassin is a dead man.

Vowing to apologize later, I roughly shoved Simon to the floor and launched myself at the flimsy plastic partition separating the driver from us. The hitman shrieked in surprise, but I'd already taken him through the windshield and onto the glass covered pavement by the time he fully registered what was happening.

It's just another day at the office for me.

Rising to stand, I brushed debris off my tux, noticing we'd been driven to a vacant lot behind a warehouse during the time I'd idiotically stopped paying attention to my surroundings.

Fucking amateur.

Glaring down at the lesser supe groaning at my feet, I frowned to realize I didn't recognize my prey. His power levels were low enough that he was practically a normie, which had me wondering why *he'd* be sent to face off with *me*.

Was this another message?

"Who FUCKING sent you?!" I hissed, beyond done with this game of cat and mouse we were playing.

The unknown supe was shuddering in pain from the few milliseconds I'd handled him, but he kept his mouth shut while fixing his gaze on my hands.

So he knows who I am…

To my immense satisfaction, his cowering increased—simply from the weight of my stare. And now that I was circling him, toying with my gloves, he was giving me what I needed to make this fucked up situation worthwhile.

The sweet taste of terror.

"P-please… I wasn't sent to k-kill you," he babbled, prostrating himself on the ground—as if there was any mercy to be found. "She told me all I needed to do was aim a gun at the h-human and you'd come crawling back, begging for forgiveness."

Crawling back to who?!

None of this made any sense. Yes, Violentia was my equal in power, but I now outranked her as head of our clan, so if anything, *she* answered to *me*.

Why would Vi think I owe her subservience?

"Are you going to tell us who this mysterious *she* is, random henchman?" Simon appeared beside me, casually poking a toe at the discarded gun that had his name on it. "Or are we wasting our time keeping you alive?"

A strange calm washed over the supe—similar to the trance gazelles fall under when captured in the lion's jaw. "I'd rather *you* killed me than she did," he croaked.

With pleasure.

"May I help?

I froze with my gloved hand only inches away from contact, unsure if I'd heard Simon correctly.

"You want to... *kill* someone with me?" I carefully asked, my heart pounding in my chest.

Please say yes.

Simon's expression held an intoxicating mix of uncharacteristic shyness and bald hunger as he replied. "Yes, I do... If that's all right?"

We are totally fucking after this.

It was all I could do to maintain my icy demeanor, to ensure *our* victim's last moments were as terrifying as possible. "Of course it's all right. Come here."

Licking his lips in anticipation, Simon stepped closer, and I immediately pulled him into my arms, breathing in the scent of everything he was.

"Do you want to make it last, or do you want a dramatic explosion?" I brushed a strand of caramel hair off his forehead, relishing the whimper from the man at our feet in response to my sweet words.

"Maybe a bit of both," Simon breathed, his pupils so blown out there was barely any green left. "But I want a front-row seat."

Anything you say, boss.

I crouched in front of the 'random henchman' before indicating that Simon should join me. He eagerly kneeled at my side, placing one hand on my thigh to steady himself.

My *inner* thigh.

Smirking at his unapologetic flirting, I held up my right hand. "Take this off for me."

Simon released a shaky breath, removing my glove and nestling closer, plastering his entire front to my side. I blew out a breath of my own when I felt how hard he was, knowing this foreplay was turning me on just as much as him.

"All right, Wolfy," he purred in my ear, sliding his hand down to grip my aching cock through my tuxedo pants. "Show me what happens to those who try to come between us."

"You two are fucking sick," the soon-to-be dead man spat, apparently finding his balls just in time to lose them.

Simon hummed in agreement, although his focus was on kissing my neck. "Yes, we are. And as soon as The Hand of Death explodes your head like a watermelon, we're going back to our hotel room to fuck with your blood still on our skin."

His dirty talk is immaculate.

Tamping down the urge to explode this asshole's head immediately so we could race to the hotel, I hovered my hand near his jaw, mimicking a caress.

"You were dead the instant you pointed a gun at my *inventus*," I growled, feeling Simon's hand tighten on my cock at my use of the term.

Because that's what he is to me.

"She promised me power," the supe rasped, suddenly talkative. "Since I'd never have it otherwise."

Something about his words gave me pause, but Simon was right. It would be a waste of time to torture intel out of this fool. Whoever he was working for had brainwashed him and was frightening enough to inspire his loyalty until the end.

How dare *someone be scarier than me!*

The supe cried out as my hand wrapped around his throat, although the noise quickly devolved into a gurgle. Blood began pouring out of his mouth, nose, ears, and eyes as I sucked him dry from the inside out, slowly and painfully.

"*Fuck*," Simon whispered, removing his hand from my cock—much to my dismay. "Can I touch him too?"

I didn't like the idea of this piece of shit getting to experience Simon's touch at all, but the raw lust in his tone had me nodding, anyway.

We both know I'll give him anything he wants.

The instant Simon placed his hand on the man's sunken cheek, my power surged, violently ripping out what was left of his life force and resulting in the gory, wet explosion we'd been waiting for.

I guess I got a little too excited...

Simon froze—his expression shocked and his gaze flickering between his blood-soaked hand and what remained of the unfortunate supe at our feet.

With a sinking feeling, I realized the *fantasy* of killing might have been more palatable than the act itself for him. While Simon was impressively nonchalant about blood and violence for a normie, *this* may have been a hard limit.

And I may have just irreversibly traumatized him.

What have I done?

CHAPTER 32
WOLFGANG

"Simon..." I softly spoke, hurriedly stuffing my bloody hand back into my glove. "I can clean this up if you want to wait in the car—"

I barely finished my sentence before he was on me—knocking me onto my back and crashing his lips to mine. His ass was grinding over my dick while his hands tore at the buttons of my ruined dress shirt, spreading more blood around as he frantically worked to get my clothes off.

"Wolfy," he gasped between breathless kisses. *"Je te veux!* Please... *please*, fuck me. *Baise-moi fort. Baise-moi à mort!"*

I love his slutty French.

While I had no intention of 'fucking him to death,' *hard* I could do.

But maybe not right next to the corpse...

Securely wrapping Simon's legs around me, I rose to my feet and carried him to the wrecked limo—continuing to devour his mouth the entire time. He'd left the back door open, but I still had to briefly break our connection to deposit him on the seat before sliding in after him.

"Take off your clothes," he commanded the instant I sat down, making my cock jump in response.

I also love it when he orders me around.

"Yes, boss," I murmured, quickly loosening my bow tie and unbuttoning my shirt the rest of the way before shrugging it off, along with my jacket.

He did the same, and I became momentarily distracted by the perfection of his naked, blood-spattered body.

I hadn't been kidding when I told Xander that Butch had too many muscles for me. Most supes did. When I watched porn —which was often—I always went for the videos featuring men built like Simon. Lean and fit but delicate-looking, with an ass I wanted to sink my teeth into.

I'll have to do that sometime...

"See something you like?" he teased, reaching into his pile of discarded clothing to grab his leather gloves and slide them over his bloody hands.

Jesus, fuck.

"I want you to leave yours on as well," he added, his gaze locked on where I was wrestling my cock out before I came in my pants again.

"Yes, boss," I repeated, so ready to be inside him, I could *taste* it.

He didn't wait for my pants to come off completely before straddling me, leaning down for another sloppy kiss. I groaned against his mouth as his shaft slid against mine, mindlessly obsessed with how slippery both areas were.

Pressure was already building in my spine—threatening to blow—and I quickly gripped the base of my dick to slow it down.

"No," Simon batted my gloved hand away before replacing it with his. "Only I get to touch this. It's mine."

Yes, it is.

"I need to get you ready for me," I choked out as he gave me an unlubricated stroke that deliciously bordered on pain.

Shoving two fingers into Simon's mouth, I let him soak the leather with saliva before reaching around and smearing it over his hole.

We both groaned as I entered him—two knuckles deep—and the way his ass tightly clenched around the intrusion made me dizzy.

How the fuck am I going to fit?

"I'm so ready for you," he panted, riding my fingers as I stretched him, seemingly uncaring about the lack of lube. "I was ready from the moment you burst into that interrogation room, trying your hardest to look intimidating. That didn't quite work out as planned, hmm?"

Laughing, I pulled him down for another kiss, remembering how delightfully ridiculous he'd been during his final interview. "I wasn't trying to intimidate you. I just couldn't stand having a wall between us any longer."

I already knew you were the one.

He smirked as he pulled back, giving me another rough stroke. "Just like you're about to shove this fat cock in my tight little hole without a condom?"

Oh, shit.

Supes didn't catch or carry normie STDs, but condoms were so far off my radar, they were practically on another planet. While I wanted Simon to be comfortable, the thought of 'shoving my fat cock in his tight little hole' completely bare was now making me *feral*.

I fucking need it...

Luckily, my tiny tyrant decided for me, placing his gloved hand on my chest and solemnly holding my gaze.

"I also can't abide the thought of anything between us," he whispered. "Now help me get *you* ready so you can fill me up."

Unsurprisingly on the same wavelength, Simon and I both tilted our faces, allowing our saliva to thread downward and coat my throbbing cock.

It's a wonder I haven't come already.

"I never thought I'd have a spit kink, but here we are," Simon mused, pumping me in his fist a few times, combining our saliva into one glorious wet mess. "Shall I be expecting you to spit on my face next?"

"Not unless you want it," I gasped, mindlessly thrusting, delirious with the need to get inside him. "For me, it's less about degradation and more about wanting to connect with you—claim you however I can. And I want you to do the same with me."

I want us to live inside each other.

Simon's gaze snapped to mine. "You want *me* to claim you?"

When I nodded, he adjusted his position, raising himself enough to rub the sensitive head of my cock over his hole. "What about *this*, Wolfy? Would you let me fuck *your* tight hole as well?"

"Of course," I gasped, groaning as he lowered himself just enough to swallow up my crown, nearly blinding me with sensation. "I want to do everything."

Simon's outer ring was constricting so tightly around me, my soul was in danger of leaving my body. The need to move—to pound into him—was barely restrained by the knowledge he needed to adjust.

"Because you want to experience everything?" he asked, the slight waver in his voice almost making me come.

"Yes. With *you*," I clarified, spitting in my palm and fisting his cock, loving how his pretty eyelashes fluttered at the added stimulation. "But also because you're the boss of me."

And you already own me completely.

The tiniest wrinkle formed between his brow as he released a breathy laugh and rested his forehead against mine. "You keep calling me that. If *I'm* the boss, Wolfy, what does that make *you*?"

That was simultaneously the easiest and hardest question I'd ever had to answer.

Besides begrudgingly obeying my parents' commands while they were still alive, I'd otherwise been my own master— allowed to run wild and dominate anyone I saw fit.

Because they preferred me unleashed.

It was unsurprising that someone like Dahlia Salah would see answering to anyone we didn't *have* to as a negative. She'd been raised similarly, so of course she'd believe giving up control was incompatible with the natural superiority we were both born into.

But what the hero didn't understand was there was a sort of freedom that came with trusting someone so completely you would give them your heart—your very life—for safekeeping.

In only a short time, Simon had become that someone for me —had become my everything.

I would obey his commands without question and eliminate anyone he wanted me to. His enemies were my enemies, and I would place myself in harm's way if it meant keeping him safe. Simon Alarie could cover me with bites and bruises, put me on a leash, and lock me in a cage. He could do absolutely anything he wanted to me and I would thank him for it.

Just for the privilege of being his.

Swallowing hard, I bravely met his gaze. "I'm your *dog*," I rasped, allowing the freedom of that statement to wash over me like fresh rain. "I'm yours."

I knew I was giving him a power over me that went well beyond anything my parents had possessed. Power I'd never willingly given before, because I'd never trusted anyone enough to receive it.

But as Simon's gaze softened—as he guided me the rest of the way inside him—I knew I'd made the right choice.

"*Mon chou*," he murmured as I clenched my jaw and struggled not to lose my shit. "I hope you know I'm yours as well."

Much to my horror, a single tear escaped at his words before traitorously trailing down my cheek.

What is wrong with me?

I couldn't be sure if my reaction was because of my confession or his, or both mixing with the overwhelming cocktail of emotions and sensations I was feeling, but it didn't matter, anyway. With absolutely zero hesitation, Simon leaned down and licked the evidence away—naturally providing all the care I'd always needed but never received.

"There you go," he crooned, smoothing my hair back into place. "Now let's fuck like two animals after a kill."

Abso-fucking-lutely.

With a growl, I grabbed his waist with both hands, lifting his lean body just enough to slam home again. He shouted in pleasure, wrapping both hands around my throat the best he could as I got to work.

"Is this what you want, Wolfy?" he gasped, his voice catching with each violent thrust. "You want me to collar you like a dog? Claim you as mine? Make you beg in the bedroom before I set you loose on our enemies?"

Fuck. Yes.

"That's all I fucking want," I snarled, groaning when he applied heady pressure to my pulse points. "Now jack yourself until you paint my chest. I want to be covered in you."

"Putain..." he moaned, spitting in one hand and moving it to his cock, fucking his fist like his life depended on it. "I can't wait to see my cum decorating your beautiful skin while yours drips out of me. Fill me up, Wolfy. Fucking *breed* me."

Jesus fuck, this man's mouth.

As much as I wanted to keep the dirty talk going, I could barely form thoughts anymore, let alone words. I'd expected having Simon wrapped around me would be better than any cock sleeve ever created, but *this* was beyond anything I could have imagined.

Tight, hot perfection.

He was *strangling* me at both ends, and even though his hand was way too small to truly choke me out, the slight deprivation of air was sending jolts of pleasure rocketing along my spine.

I slid both hands down to grip his juicy ass—enjoying the way his thick flesh rippled with every slap of his skin against mine. The heat of him, the slutty sounds he was making as he neared oblivion, the way it felt like my powers were burrowing even deeper than my cock—desperate to connect, even though I technically couldn't...

He's mine anyway.

"*Plus fort, plus vite,* yes, yes, fuck. *C'est bon!* So fucking good, Wolfy! Harder, harder... tear me in half!"

Simon bounced on my dick, his head thrown back in ecstasy as he matched my borderline violent thrusts.

I wonder how rough I could get with him.

My ravenous gaze was everywhere—on the bruises still visible on the slim column of his neck, on his abs constricting as he moved, on the blood sprayed on his face and forearms, and his gloved hand frantically fucking his cock like he'd die if he didn't come.

I gave his ass a sharp smack, causing him to cry out and half-collapse in my arms as thick ropes of cum shot out of his cock to spray my chest.

Marking me as his.

The feel of his hot slickness on my skin combined with being claimed in such a primal way sent me over the edge. I came with a possessive howl that echoed off the empty warehouse outside—one that let anyone nearby, everyone in this entire fucking city, know that absolutely nothing would ever come between us.

Because he's mine.

Forever.

CHAPTER 33
SIMON

"Are these council types going to care if I leave my sunnies on inside? It's far too early for me to face the day…"

Never mind that it's 2 pm.

To my credit, it had been a long night. We'd eventually rang for a car to collect us from the scene of the crime, but only after making ourselves presentable. This process started with me licking my cum off Wolfy's chest. Then he returned the favor by flipping me onto my back on the bench seat so he could enjoy the overflow from my ass—bringing me to orgasm again with just his tongue.

Such a chore.

Our insatiable hunger for each other only continued back at our hotel. After ordering one of everything from room service, we passed the time by showering together so Wolfy could face fuck me against the tile. He later confessed he'd had this exact fantasy while jerking off in the shower on our first night in Tokyo.

I knew it!

We'd fucked again—and again—but mostly, we stayed awake until the early morning hours simply talking. We swapped stories about our families and childhoods, and while some of what Wolfy shared made me murderously angry, it also helped me better understand the man I was endlessly fascinated with.

Enamored with.

Okay, madly in love with.

Wolfgang tore his gaze from the actual Vermeer hanging in the sitting room of Luca Meier's Geneva residence to shoot me an amused glance. After taking in my aforementioned sunglasses, he slowly dragged his gaze over my bright orange loose-knit polo and 80s-style pleated trousers.

With Italian loafers—sans socks, naturally.

"I like how you dress," he replied, meeting my gaze again with renewed heat. "In fact, I'd like to take you shopping again."

"*Behave*, Sir!" I good-naturedly scolded. "I'm trying to exude professionalism while *you're* trying to give me a boner."

He chuckled, moving closer until he loomed over me, enveloping me in his signature sexy scent. "If I was trying to turn you on, I'd say something like… *Simon, I'm going to spend so much fucking money on you, my financial advisors will think I've either been kidnapped or killed.*"

Swoon!

"And your sunglasses are fine," he added, planting an incredibly endearing kiss on the top of my head. "They'll add to your mystique. Maybe the council will even assume you have lasers shooting out of your eyeballs, like that one guy in the X-Men."

I rolled my decidedly non-laser eyeballs. "You mean Cyclops? On that note, *are* there real-life versions of the X-Men running around? Did *you* train at Xavier Institute like a good little mutant student?"

"Wolfgang actually trained with me, although there was little I could teach him that he didn't instinctively know."

We turned to find Luca Meier standing in the doorway with a warm smile that was firmly aimed at Wolfy. "A natural born assassin."

So proud!

True to form, adorable color rose to Wolfy's cheeks as he swiftly redirected the conversation. "I realize I failed to introduce you to each other last night. Luca Meier was a colleague of my parents and a mentor to me and my siblings. Simon Alarie has been invaluable in assisting me during our search. He's also my…"

Pausing, he looked down at me with so much raw emotion on his handsome face, my knees almost buckled.

He doesn't even have to say it.

I knew exactly what I was to Wolfy. Between his confessions last night and our murderous foreplay followed by the main event, I felt every bit his—

"Inventus?" Luca interjected, fixing Wolfy with an expectant look.

Wolfy simply stared back, and I realized he respected this man too much to lie to him.

"That's the rumor," I cheerfully piped in before staging my own redirection. "Is the council ready to see us now?"

Luca instantly sobered. "I was sent to tell you the council is unable to come to an agreement on your… situation." His gaze flitted between the two of us. "Because of the players involved."

Wolfy sighed heavily, although he didn't look surprised. "Because of my parents."

A statement, not a question.

Luca nodded slowly, his lips pressed into a thin line. "Wolfgang, you *know* some of my contemporaries already refuse to align with you—or accept you as head of the Suarez clan—because of how Ender and Signe died."

"So that's why the council won't offer us aid?" I scoffed. "Because two dusty old villains got taken out?"

I knew full well Wolfy killed his father and set up his mother to battle Butch's father to the death. From what he'd told me, they'd both deserved far worse for how they'd treated him and his siblings.

Mostly him.

Luca thoughtfully gazed at me a moment before seeming to reach a decision. "We found a zip drive on the body of the hitman sent to replace your driver last night—"

"Fucking *amateur.*" Wolfy dropped his face into his hands with a groan of despair.

I could only gape at his unusual display of emotion. Yes, *I'd* grown accustomed to seeing Wolfy without his mask of impassivity, but he usually kept his cool around other supes.

He must truly trust this man.

Reaching into his pocket, Luca removed what looked like a small remote, before nodding toward a framed flatscreen discreetly hung on the wall among the priceless art. I moved closer to Wolfy, wanting to be within arm's reach for whatever awaited us.

The screen flickered on to reveal a massive, hulking supe wrapped in blood red Lycra, seated on a chair in a barren room, staring at the camera with predatory focus.

Apocalypto Man.

Wolfy sharply inhaled, freezing like a deer in the headlights as all color drained from his face. It was startling to see such a badass be truly *afraid*.

But I'm not.

Granted, I only knew of Apocalypto Man from legend, whereas Wolfy had experienced his reign of terror firsthand—along with the abuse he suffered at home.

Regardless, fear was an unfamiliar emotion for me. While I'd been told this defect would get me in trouble someday, right now, I only cared about somehow transferring my natural calm to the man beside me.

I'll take care of you.

As if he could hear my thoughts, Wolfy visibly relaxed, offering me a tentative smile before bravely returning his attention to the screen.

"Ready?" Luca asked, and when Wolfy nodded once, he pressed play.

"Mi lobo." A heavily accented voice boomed from the speakers. *"You have brought shame on our household. You gravely disrespected the very supervillains who brought you into this world by plotting to overthrow them, and now you've wrongfully taken their place. Vengeance is coming, and no one will be spared. You will watch everyone you care about die before being brought to your knees."*

Then the video cut out.

Dramatic much?

Wolfy apparently didn't share my unimpressed outlook as he frantically texted on his phone, cursing under his breath.

Probably telling his siblings to seek cover.

"Was there anything else on the driver?" I turned to Luca, determined to stay calm and get the facts. "A camera or other recording device?"

He shook his head. "No. The supe was simply a vessel to deliver this video."

An unwitting messenger, no doubt.

"Play it again," I commanded, and Luca obeyed as I stepped closer to the flatscreen.

There it is.

The clue was in the presentation. While many supes—like Captain Masculine—had head-coverings that only left their mouths visible, Apocalypto Man's face was completely obscured by his indigenous death god mask.

It could be anyone under there.

Or a corpse.

"Are there supes who can mimic voices?" I asked, continuing to direct my questions to Luca so Wolfy could handle logistics.

"Yes," Luca replied, an almost *proud* smile twitching his lips. "Although it's considered a fairly weak superpower. If that was your claim to fame, you'd need to look for other ways to increase your standing."

Like by becoming a minion for a more powerful supe.

"Yes." I nodded as the pieces fell into place. "Our doomed assassin referenced a 'she' who'd promised him power if he pointed a gun at my head. Perhaps he answers to Violentia?"

Wolfy frowned, tearing his gaze away from his phone to rejoin the conversation. "That doesn't sound like something my sister would say. She's more puppet than mastermind and needs a puppeteer pulling the strings. Mistress Noir-Rouge mentioned we should be more concerned about *who* Vi's working for..."

"Which could be anyone!" I threw my hands into the air. "It could be Noir-Rouge herself, trying to throw us off the trail. It could be that Storm-wannabe who confronted us at the event last night."

"It could be a council member," Luca quietly added. "I believe whoever planted the video on your victim may have wanted the *council* to see it—to cast further doubt on your claim as Suarez clan leader."

How dare they!

Wolfy briefly closed his eyes, taking a steadying breath before opening them again. "I can't believe I didn't search the body, Luca... and that I didn't notice the driver had been swapped out—"

"You've been distracted," Luca calmly replied, with a pointed glance my way.

Excuse—

"...by something *good*," he added. "Something you—more than anyone—deserve."

That's better.

When all Wolfy did was swallow thickly, Luca continued. "I am sorry I couldn't save you and your siblings from the conditions you grew up in. But we all know Signe and Ender never would have allowed that much collective power to slip from their grasp."

"It's all right, Luca," Wolfy gruffly replied, clearly wanting to sweep the topic back under the rug. "I survived."

"I know you did," the older supe powered on, rightfully making Wolfy *hear* what he had to say. "I know what you endured, simply so your siblings wouldn't have to. And then you took on the weight of becoming head of your household, fully knowing the risks…"

And he says he's no hero.

"All I've done is put my siblings in danger by making new enemies," Wolfy whispered, once again showing his concern lay with his family first.

Luca waved a hand dismissively. "Bah! I've lost track of how many supes want to eliminate me. It's all part of the game. If we no longer had any enemies, it would mean we were dead."

That's the spirit!

When Wolfy cracked a smile at the inspirational quip, Luca solemnly added, "Even though we were considered allies, I was *thankful* when your parents died. Their existence was a constant threat, not just to other supes but to humanity. You're a good man, Wolfgang—a far better person than either of them were—and I can think of no one better to lead your clan."

Wolfy was quiet, his gaze fixed on the floor as he absorbed his mentor's words. My heart broke for him—for everything he'd been through.

For how different his life could have been.

Wanting to give my man a minute to regain his composure, I drew Luca's attention back to me. "So what does it mean for us, if the council is at a stalemate over the situation?"

The supe gave me a tight smile. "It means you're on your own, but also that you won't get any trouble from Geneva. This video may have given the more rigid council members ammunition, but only because they were already threatened by Wolfgang's ascension to clan leader."

"What do you suggest we do?" Wolfy asked.

Luca smiled broadly. "Continue to shake things up. Show them how clans don't have to be run like dictatorships. How an *inventus* bond,"—he gestured between the two of us—"can be used as more than just a weapon."

Wolfy sighed. "Luca, you know I can't bond with Simon."

The older supe scoffed. "Don't be so sure…"

What is he talking about?

Noticing my confusion, Luca turned and blasted me with a jolt of pure power that electrified me from the inside out.

Fils de pute!

I gasped at the intrusion, but just as quickly as Luca's power flowed into me, it was *pushed* out again—as if by an invisible hand.

"What the FUCK did you just do to him?!" Wolfy shouted, shoving me behind him so he could place himself between me and his mentor.

Luca threw his head back and laughed. "Nothing he can't handle, Wolfgang. Your *normie* just shut down my display of dominance like a seasoned supe."

What?!

"But I don't have any powers!" I sputtered, elbowing my way around Wolfy's massive form and back into the conversation.

The elder supe shrugged, but I caught a smug smile on his face before he spun on his heel and strode from the room.

"You do now," he called over his shoulders. "Thanks to your *inventus.*"

CHAPTER 34
SIMON

I barely recalled leaving the home of Wolfy's mentor or the car ride back to the hotel. All I could focus on—obsess over—was Luca's revelation that I'd somehow bonded to Wolfy and absorbed his powers.

It's not possible.

I'm only human.

My thoughts were spinning, reexamining every interaction I'd had with Wolfy since we'd met, attempting to pinpoint the moment it happened.

Yes, I'd felt a pull towards Wolfy the instant I laid eyes on him, but I'd chalked that up to his incredible hotness. He *had* mentioned it was strange how I could feel the power 'probing' from other supes, but I'd assumed it simply meant I was overly sensitive to such things.

Which doesn't make me *a supe.*

Then I recalled how both Noir-Rouge and Luca had seemed intrigued after they tested me—and the latter's blatant challenge had produced some sort of natural defense response…

But that couldn't have come from me.

Right?

My thoughts drifted to the unexplained sensations I'd experienced over the past several days and how they'd been growing in intensity. The ache in my chest, the need to *touch* Wolfy, the way my soul felt like it was molding to his when he left a bite mark over my heart.

How that hitman's head exploded as soon as I touched him...

"Simon." Wolfy's smooth voice cut through my impending panic, and I snapped back to the present.

He was seated on the couch in our suite, gazing up at me in concern as I listlessly stood before him.

My gaze swept over the room. I'd booked us the executive penthouse at the trendy Geneva D Hotel, mostly because the famous interior designer was French. The mix of masculine blacks and grays—with the occasional splash of a blood red accent—spoke to me on an aesthetic level.

Is that why *blood doesn't bother me?*

"What do you need right now, Simon?"

Again, Wolfy brought me back to earth, and I focused on his familiar face. He was so attractive it almost hurt to look at him, and as we simply stared at each other in silence, I felt that insistent *pull* I'd previously thought meant nothing.

But apparently, it means everything.

I sniffled pathetically, not knowing how to articulate my needs but wanting to give him a reply. "I-it's just... a lot to process."

He softly smiled. "I know, boss. Come here."

Wolfy opened his arms, but I sank to the plush rug at his feet instead. He automatically spread his legs so I could nestle between them and lay my head on his thigh, feeling an instant calm simply from being near him.

This.

This is what I need.

"May I…?" He tentatively placed his enormous hand on the top of my head, adorably new to the world of physical comfort.

I hummed in affirmation, cuddling closer until all I could smell was *him*. Bergamot, lavender, and hottie man musk with a side of leather.

My favorite things.

We sat like this for a few minutes, with Wolfy gently carding his fingers through my hair while I tried to get my face as close as possible to his cock without ruining the moment.

Priorities.

Wolfy finally cleared his throat. "Would it help if I called Xander and asked him some questions? He obviously has experience with this whole *inventus* thing, and maybe he's tested the hair he collected from you… It's okay if you'd rather I don't—"

"No! I mean, *yes!* Please, call him." I briefly raised my head to glance up at him, beyond grateful for the suggestion. "He might have some insight into *whatever* the hell I am."

"Simon…" Wolfy began, his expression pained.

It seemed he thought better of whatever he'd been about to say, as he pulled his phone out of his pocket and brought it to his ear instead of completing the sentiment.

I blew out a relieved breath. While I wouldn't have minded a platitude about my identity crisis, I wasn't sure I was ready to talk about it yet.

First, the facts.

Xander took a few rings to answer, but as soon as he did, he launched into what sounded like breathless chatter. Wolfy looked unsurprised, and I realized he'd probably purposely *not* put the call on speaker, so I wouldn't be directly subjected to **The Mouthy One**.

This man is a natural caretaker.

The monologue finally ceased, and Wolfy took his opening. "The council is playing Switzerland, thanks to old loyalties to mother and father. It didn't help that *someone* also sent a video of Apocalypto Man threatening me and our clan because of this alleged coup."

Xander squawked something, followed by a rustling sound and a second voice joining the conversation.

Wolfy patiently waited before speaking again. "Hi, Butch. Yes, it *looked* like Ender, but he was in full gear—including his Supay mask. As *Simon* pointed out, it could have been an illusion created by a lesser supe with mimic abilities." He paused before adding, "If Apocalypto Man *was* back at full strength, we'd all be dead already. Just in case, we need to come up with a game plan. I... I don't want anyone to get hurt."

I glanced sharply at him again. It didn't surprise me he was sharing intel with Xander and Butch—they were our not-so-secret weapon, after all. But the raw emotion in his voice struck me as unusual.

He's letting down his guard...

Not only had he shown uncertainty and frustration in front of Luca, but he was allowing his family to *see* that he was worried. That he needed their help.

While this warmed my heart on one level, I noticed there was a small part of me that didn't like it one bit. A possessive, covetous part. A part that didn't want my *inventus* showing any weakness to others.

What the fuck is wrong with me?

As if he could sense my heart rate ratcheting up several notches, Wolfy slid his hand down to cup my jaw as he continued his conversation.

"Yeah, he's good." He began absently running the pad of his thumb over my bottom lip. "We've just had an... *exciting* past twenty-four hours."

Since we met, really.

"So..." He awkwardly cleared his throat, shifting in his seat and accidentally bumping me closer to his cock—not that I was complaining. "When did you two *know* you had the *inventus* bond? Did it happen all at once, or..."

Wolfy trailed off to listen to what sounded like both Xander and Butch talking over each other. He was so intent on their reply, he'd left his thumb simply resting on my lip—half nudging its way inside my mouth.

So I popped it the rest of the way in.

And audibly moaned.

It wasn't a conscious decision, but the instant my lips closed around his thumb, the tension I'd been holding onto lessened exponentially. Wolfy's gaze snapped to mine, and the combination of lust and something much deeper in his expression made me dizzy.

Flattening his phone against his chest so not to be overheard, he quietly asked, "Does that help? Having something to suck on?"

When I could only dreamily nod, he licked his lips and pointedly glanced at his crotch. "Then let me give you what you need, boss."

Oh, fuck, yes.

He withdrew his thumb and undid his belt buckle while casually bringing the phone back to his ear. "What was that last part? You cut out for a second."

My eyes were locked on his hand as he deftly unbuttoned and unzipped his trousers before pulling out his cock. Much to my satisfaction, it was already thickening—the gorgeous veins inviting me to trace them with my tongue—but right now, I simply wanted to hold him in my mouth.

I need it.

After wrestling himself free, Wolfy gently ran his crown over my lips, his gaze fixed on my face as an undeniable *something* passed between us.

Because we're connected now.

I opened my mouth, but Wolfy pressed his hard length flat against his thigh, forcing me to lay down my head again to chase my prize.

Once I was comfortably situated, he fed me his cock—slowly and lovingly—just enough so I could close my lips around him without straining my jaw.

Perfect.

My eyelids fluttered closed as I surrendered to the feel of his velvety skin on my tongue, the salty precum teasing my tastebuds, his comforting scent, and the rhythmic way I was lazily sucking on my new favorite toy.

This is what I needed.

Him.

Wolfy blew out a slow breath and returned to petting my hair, providing so much comfort I thought my black heart would burst.

"I could have done without *those* details, Xanny, but yes, that all sounds... familiar." Wolfy was dutifully absorbing the information he was receiving, even as I could sense him still keeping an eye on me.

Ever the protector.

"Well, we saw Luca Meier yesterday and being the goddamn Yoda that he is, he decided to see what Simon would do if energetically provoked. Wanna guess what happened?" Wolfy chuckled as excited chatter erupted on the other end of the line. "Yup," he replied, popping the P and sounding pleased as punch. "Looks like I have an *inventus*, too."

There was more babbling on the other end before Wolfy cut in. "We're not sure... Did you test the hair you *ripped* from my *inventus'* head, Xanny?"

The background noise abruptly quieted, and I briefly cracked open an eye to find Wolfy carefully observing me. "Interesting," he murmured, shifting his hand to wrap it around the back of my neck, as if worried I might bolt.

Not a chance.

I was so relaxed, an army of supes could have burst through the door and I wouldn't have moved a muscle. If I'd known a cock could be used as a self-soothing pacifier, I may have cared more in the past about keeping the same man around for longer than one night.

Maybe.

Probably not.

Wolfy grunted in disapproval, and my eyes flew open again. "That's... unexpected. Do you think the USN might have a wider variety of samples? Maybe from the original scientific study with whatshisname... Your mother's *inventus*, Butch—the one who died at your father's hand. Iron Axe."

That made me tense up. The thought of losing Wolfy—of him *dying*—had me simultaneously spiraling and readying for battle.

How did Smoldering Siren not burn down the entire world when that happened?

Because he was the hottest stalker there was, Wolfy immediately zeroed in on my anxiety. "I need to go. But keep me posted and I'll do the same."

He quickly hung up and set aside his phone, returning his undivided attention to me. "You good down there, boss?"

I smiled around him, which made him smile in return. Once again, I was absolutely blinded by how handsome he was.

And he's mine.

"You sure look good," he murmured, his gaze darkening although he didn't attempt to turn this cockwarming experiment into anything other than it was.

When I continued to stare up at him expectantly, he nodded. "Well, the... *good news* is that you are at least part human, but Xanny hasn't pinpointed the rest of your DNA. Yet."

I furrowed my brow, wondering why Wolfy would think me being part human was the goal.

Wouldn't he prefer I was a supe?

Unfortunately, I lacked the desire to give up my toy long enough to ask. My eyelids were growing heavy, so I allowed myself to fully relax, lulled to sleep by Wolfy's gentle petting and the natural comfort he provided.

"There you go," I heard him murmur as I drifted off. "Just let me take care of things for you."

CHAPTER 35
WOLFGANG

Simon passed out for an hour—*with my cock in his mouth*—but besides checking a few times to make sure he was still breathing, I did my best to focus on business.

Even if it was a special kind of torture.

I received an anonymous email—sent by Luca, no doubt—listing every supe on the council either on the fence or flat-out opposed to my claim as the Suarez clan leader.

A true Jedi he is.

After forwarding this shit list to Baltasar so he could dig up dirt, I focused on the maintenance of my allies and potential allies.

I replied to various emails from fellow clan leaders—and my black market business partners—before assigning fresh foot soldiers to surveillance duty on these same contacts. Then, I scheduled trusted security and drivers for our future stops, vowing to *pay better goddamn attention* before getting into a car next time.

All the above were signed, sealed, and delivered with vague promises of painful death should anyone betray us.

Standard supe communication.

Then I instructed our family lawyer, Randal, to send something legal sounding and mildly threatening to Dahlia Salah's parents. Something that suggested their daughter's disrespectful behavior at last night's council event could be ignored if they aligned their powerful house with mine.

Even if they are a clan of heroes.

What if Simon's a hero?

I huffed, reminding myself that, thanks to Xander and Butch, the USN had already conducted a new study to prove there were zero physiological differences between heroes and villains.

Except heroes being stupid enough to sign their life away to normie politicians.

With these findings, the USN's Deputy Secretary-General, Sylvano Ricci, was now working on reversing the age-old bans on interspecies marriage. Obviously, the first order of business was to allow heroes and villains to wed, since the reasons for banning it were null and void.

And since Big City's savior is already picking out wedding dresses.

And cribs.

I snorted at the thought of a terrified Xanny holding a baby, although we all knew he'd cave to whatever his *other* baby wanted.

It doesn't seem so funny now, does it, Wolfy?

My gaze drifted to the bedroom where my *inventus* was fast asleep. As much as I would have loved for my dick to live inside Simon forever, I hadn't wanted him to develop a sore neck. So I'd begrudgingly woken him up just long enough to help him into a velour tracksuit and fuzzy socks before patting him on his juicy ass and sending him off to bed.

I wish I could make this easier for him...

Simon had obviously suffered a shock over the bombshell Luca dropped on us, and I could understand his reaction on a basic level. When I'd discovered I could actually *touch* someone—not just anyone, but *him*—I'd been so overwhelmed, I almost passed out.

The way he swallowed my cock might have helped with that.

What still needed to be addressed was how *Simon* felt about learning he'd somehow absorbed my powers—that he was more than just a human.

Personally, I was ecstatic. I was so fucking overjoyed I wanted to shout it from the rooftops and celebrate by buying my *inventus* his own private island before fucking until we both couldn't move. But the last thing I wanted to do was make things worse—or pressure him into feeling a certain way—by displaying too *much* outward excitement.

Simon was still processing the situation, turning the facts over in that big brain of his. He'd eventually have no problem telling me exactly what was on his mind—but only when he was good and ready.

So I just need to be patient.

Unfortunately, I couldn't ignore the dread building in my gut. I was an expert at keeping my cool in life or death situations, but I couldn't help worrying that Simon shutting down meant something far worse than a temporary identity crisis.

For all I knew, he was freaking out over being energetically locked in to a lifelong commitment he may not have even wanted. Yes, he'd claimed me as *his*—and said he was *mine* in return—but words were nothing when compared to the permanence of an *inventus* bond.

And I don't think it can be severed without one of us dying...

Unable to stay away any longer, I set aside my laptop and silently stalked to the bedroom. Stopping in the doorway, I allowed my gaze to roam over Simon's sleeping form, noticing how all my uncertainty vanished the instant I laid eyes on him.

Mine.

He was facing me, curled up under the cashmere travel blanket I'd bought for him. His dark eyelashes were resting against his high cheekbones, his fashionably messy hair in disarray, and I couldn't stop from focusing on the way his plush lips were slightly parted as he slept.

It would be so easy to just slide my dick back in there.

Now is not the time, Wolfy.

As tempting as it was, I shook the lecherous thought from my head. However, I *did* make a mental note to ask Simon if he'd be opposed to waking up choking on cock.

I sure wouldn't be.

Interestingly, I no longer felt the blinding *need* to claim him. This supported Luca's theory that Simon and I had successfully bonded, but I still wasn't sure when it happened. Xander and Butch both seemed to think their bond solidified the day they escaped from father's workshop, but also mentioned how they'd felt *pulled* toward each other before then.

When they still thought the other was a normie.

While it was technically still illegal for supes and normies to get married, extramarital fucking was oddly absent from the decree. Most high-ranking supes saw it as beneath them anyway, but others—like Balty—enjoyed tempting 'cape chasers' into bed with vague allusions to their supe status.

But we all know he's not the sharpest tool in the shed.

Xander had fucked nothing but normies before Butch—which I only knew because he never shut up about it—but that was more because no self-respecting supe would touch a supposedly powerless one.

I bet they're all kicking themselves now.

Xanny's Uno reverse powers had simply been dormant and were primarily defensive—when he wasn't accessing Butch's offensive ones, that is.

I wonder…

Pulling out my phone, I shot off a quick text to Luca, asking what Simon's powers had *felt* like when he tested them earlier today.

I wonder if he tossed Luca's power back at him.

While I waited for his reply, I sent a text to Gabe and Dre with photos of the impressive art Luca had hanging in his home.

I can't wait to give the twins their gallery when they graduate.

The Swiss Sensei: *It was your power alone that I felt. But Simon wielded it like a natural.*

Well, there goes my theory.

It shouldn't have surprised me he wasn't the same as Xander, especially as Xanny had confirmed Simon possessed normie DNA.

But what else is he made of?

Xander said the unknown DNA didn't match any supe samples he had on hand. *Why* my brother had these samples at all was beyond me, but he'd always been the 'mad scientist' of our family, puttering around in the secret lair he thought none of us knew about.

Oops.

I smirked as I thought of how *all* my brothers were now packed into Xanny's waterfront warehouse for safety reasons. How everyone being underfoot while he tried to work was probably driving him insane.

Welcome to my life.

My gaze drifted past my *inventus* to the other living thing in my care during our travels. Twoey was on the bedside table, next to the untouched glass of water I'd left earlier, and I recalled how Simon had mentioned his fondness for her during his final interview.

How he was completely uninterested in any other personal relationships...

Swallowing down the panic rising in my throat again, I made an executive decision to leave Twoey on the plane from now on—in case shit really hit the fan.

Since Simon would murder me if anything happened to her.

I knew the gossip mill was already buzzing about the mysterious *inventus* of Wolfgang Suarez. An unknown supe who could somehow stand against the awesome power of Atmosphera *and* touch The Hand of Death—while living to tell the tale.

Except for when I killed him the first time...

Yes, Simon's biggest complaint from that day had been his mild concussion from hitting the kitchen tile, but I'd *seen* his face before he fell. And just like the countless others who'd met their death at my hand, the light dimming from his eyes was unmistakable.

I definitely killed him.

But how did he come back?

I'd been too traumatized at the time to analyze it, but that Simon did *not* explode on contact should have given away his non-normie status. Only supes could handle more than a casual brush with me, and only the most powerful—like Butch—could survive me draining enough power to knock them out cold.

And Simon doesn't strike me as particularly powerful.

I couldn't forget how he'd been helpless to stop a far less formidable supe like REM from using his sleep paralysis abilities on him. Simon might be resilient, but he wasn't invincible.

He may not even have powers of his own.

This is bad.

Going with my gut, I texted Luca again.

> **Have you ever heard of a truly powerless supe?**

My tension returned as I once again awaited my mentor's reply. Simon was in *everyone's* sight now, and if he wasn't able to defend himself properly, he would be in constant danger at every turn.

And what if I'm not there to save him the next time?

The Swiss Sensei: *Only in relation to ancient legends. On that note... seeing your father dressed as the Incan god of death* *reminded me of an old acquaintance of mine. An anthropologist working in Argentina.*

The Swiss Sensei: *While he's a normie, he's wise to the ways of supes. He may have the answers you seek. I'll get you in touch with each other.*

The Swiss Sensei: *Not literally, of course.*

Even Luca's attempt at humor couldn't lessen the *terror* I felt at the idea of setting foot in my father's homeland.

Of taking Simon there.

Before I could spiral, my phone buzzed again.

Thing Two: *I can feel you stressing from here, Wolfy. You good?*

I covered my mouth to mask my horrified gasp. I couldn't be sure if Gabriel could literally sense my anxiety—which wouldn't surprise me—or if he was simply interpreting my random texting of priceless art as the jittery distraction it was. Either way, one thing was abundantly clear.

I'm losing my edge.

The fuck-up with the driver had only been the latest example of how I was slipping. The more my obsession grew with Simon, the less attention I was paying to my surroundings, which was extremely dangerous and irresponsible on my part.

Especially when so many others rely on me.

"Wolfy…" Simon's groggy voice brought my attention back to him. He was still asleep, but his brow was furrowed, obviously in the throes of a bad dream. "Please don't go."

Fuck.

Is everyone a psychic now?

Moving as carefully as possible, I sat on the bed and lightly ran a finger along Simon's jaw, sighing in relief when his expression smoothed out once again.

"I won't, boss," I murmured, my heart beating in time with his. "Not unless I have to."

CHAPTER 36
SIMON

I was trapped in another nightmare.

This time, an icy wind tore over my exposed skin as I crossed a frozen tundra. It was night—endless night—and my pathetic normie eyesight meant I was practically blind.

I need to find him...

A dim light up ahead was my only beacon, and I somehow *knew* Wolfy was being held captive there. But for every step forward I took, the wind pushed me back, until it seemed I would never reach my destination.

Then the screaming began.

"Wolfy!" I shouted, sitting bolt upright, desperate to reach him—to *kill* whoever was hurting him.

To replace his screaming with theirs.

"Jesus!" Wolfy exclaimed, nearly knocking his coffee onto his laptop.

Regardless of how I'd strangely startled him, he was crouched beside my lie-flat seat in an instant. I groggily took in my surroundings while he rubbed my back, remembering we were now en route to Argentina for some mysterious reason.

Even though his family doesn't own property there...

"I-I dreamed you were in danger," I mumbled, blinking rapidly as I struggled to remember the details. "And I couldn't get to you..."

Wolfy's jaw clenched, but he didn't reply. Instead, he stood and lifted me from my seat—security blanket and all—before carrying me to his.

After getting me settled in his lap, Wolfy returned to the email he'd been working on, caging me in with his tree trunk arms so he could type. As he made no move to hide the screen, naturally, I snooped.

This is me we're talking about.

I snorted in amusement at what I found. "Are you... *tattling* to Dahlia's parents about how horribly she behaved at the council event?"

A smirk twitches Wolfy's lips. "I'm using the incident as leverage, yes. The Salah family rules the East Coast the same way my clan does in the West. Despite being heroes, I think they'd make excellent business partners, especially as their hands are far from clean."

I squinted at the screen. "Negotiations look a bit tense. It appears someone from their camp is threatening dismemberment."

Wolfy made a noncommittal noise before typing out a chilly reminder that his hands were just as deadly off his body as when still attached.

"This is a fairly typical exchange," he explained, pressing send on the most lawsuit-worthy work email I'd ever seen. "It purges the instinctual need for violence from our systems so we can get down to business."

"Sounds fun," I chuckled, feeling the last remnants of my nightmare evaporate, thanks to his proximity. "Perhaps that's an administrative task I could assist you with in the future?"

In our *future.*

Wolfy gazed down at me intently. "You'd excel at threatening emails, boss. I actually think you'd make a better clan leader than me, to be honest."

There was something in his tone that didn't sit well with me, so I was careful with my reply. "But I'd rather do it together, as co-leaders. That is... *if* it's all right for a bastard half-human to hold such a position."

Is that *what's troubling him?*

He sighed and closed his laptop before shifting, so I was curled up against his chest. "As I'm sure you've noticed, many heroes and villains see humans as an inferior species. But I'm not one of them."

Because you've also been ostracized.

I scratched my fingernail through the stubble on his jaw—fascinated that he even *had* stubble considering how enviably hairless his body was.

What I wouldn't give to never see hot wax again.

At least, not in that *context...*

"Erich is just a normie, right?" I asked, loving how easily Wolfy talked to me now—that there were no more secrets between us. "How did you two even meet? Certainly it wasn't from all the clubbing you do."

Wolfy chuckled before delivering a quick kiss. "I actually do enjoy his music, but could do without the club scene. So many people packed into small spaces makes it difficult to relax." He chewed on his bottom lip, as if suddenly unsure about sharing more of his story.

Sweet murder baby…

"You *know* you can tell me everything," I reminded him. "I'm *yours.*"

Swallowing thickly, he nodded and continued. "Erich and I met when I…"

He blew out a slow breath, and I braced for the worst. I had no idea where he was going with this story, but he seemed hesitant to tell me.

Please don't be a forbidden romance.

"…When I accidentally saved his life."

"Mon chou!" I cackled, almost falling off his lap from the look of abject *shame* on his face. *"Très merveilleux!* How delightfully nefarious of you."

Truly, I love this man.

Wolfy pinked, but gritted his teeth and soldiered on with the rest of his tale. "I was in Berlin on business and ended up drunk and pissed off, needing to… kill someone."

He paused and searched my face—as if he would find anything but raw lust over this sweet pillow talk he was providing.

"Keep going," I whispered, ignoring the throbbing in my cock in favor of being a good listener.

A smile curled his lip. "I stumbled upon a back alley mugging. Four normies had a fifth on the ground, viciously kicking the body even though he wasn't even attempting to fight back. There was so much blood, I assumed he was already dead, but all I cared about was that I'd found four perfect targets for my rage."

"The man on the ground was Erich?" I asked, and Wolfy nodded.

"Yes," he replied, still looking adorably conflicted over his accidental act of heroism. "Once I was done with his attackers, I turned to find Erich had sat up. He'd not only survived, but seen everything. He'd seen my powers in action and *me*—unmasked. I debated just taking out the witness, but then he politely thanked me and asked if I'd call him an ambulance."

I laughed again. "That is the most perfectly stoic *German* thing I've ever heard. I assume you happily helped out your new bestie?"

Wolfy was smiling now as well. "I did, but left the scene of the crime before the authorities could arrive. The next day, I scoured the news for any claims of a vigilante supe, but found nothing. Still, I tracked down which hospital Erich had been brought to—"

"To check on his well-being?" I teased, knowing full well that wasn't the reason.

He didn't want to leave a loose end undone.

Or unthreatened.

My murderous cream puff rolled his eyes. "I needed to make sure he wouldn't talk, so I brought an NDA and an offer to join my payroll."

I was *dying* to point out that Erich was most likely not given the option to refuse Wolfy's gracious 'offer' as he lay bruised and beaten in his hospital bed.

And that they both clearly got a friendship out of the arrangement.

"It's actually illegal for supes to kill normies without direct provocation," Wolfy added, bringing me back to the conversation.

I furrowed my brow. "But... doesn't Captain Masculine kill the occasional normie? When he's out protecting Big City?"

Wolfy's smile vanished, and I knew I'd struck a nerve. "Yes. Butch has also killed plenty of villains in the past, mostly for no other reason than their bullshit villain status. However, since his actions were sanctioned by the city, he was never held accountable."

I caressed soothing circles over Wolfy's heart, silently encouraging him to release every grievance he'd ever locked away.

Let me carry this with you.

"But *I'd* kept track of his kills. Every. Single. One," he growled, his amber eyes flashing gold. "And had planned to hold him accountable myself one day. Then I learned Butch's parents had contracted him into indentured servitude with Biggs Enterprises before he was born, and he'd been too trusting to ever question his assignments. So I let the idiot live."

Laughing again, I clambered into an upright position, straddling him so I could grin directly into his handsome face. "Is *that* why he's still alive? Not because he's your brother's *inventus* and true love? Or that he's earned his place as another Suarez sibling under your protection?"

Wolfy grumbled the same way a *dog* would, which only brought up delicious memories of him telling me he was exactly that.

My dog.

I began mindlessly grinding in Wolfy's lap, incredibly turned on by everything he was. "I'm on your payroll too," I gasped, feeling his cock thickening against mine through our clothing. "And last I checked your schedule, you could block out some time now to treat me like the whore I am."

"Jesus, fuck, Simon," Wolfy groaned, sliding his bare hands inside my trackies to grip my equally bare ass. "You know I can't say no to you."

Yes, I know.

I hummed in satisfaction, kissing my way down his neck so I could give him some proper love bites. "Don't try to fight it, Boss Man. Your only job right now is to ruin my tight hole with your fat cock."

With an animalistic growl that may have scared someone who gave a fuck, Wolfy rose from his seat and wrapped me around him like a squirrel in a tree.

Appropriate, since I'm after those nuts.

I tightened my grip on my big, scary prize as he stalked down the aisle toward the bedroom—incredibly pleased to have inspired this well-deserved work break.

Mile High Club, here we come!

CHAPTER 37
WOLFGANG

Never mind that I had countless unanswered emails, or that we were headed deep into the jungles of my greatest trauma—I couldn't concentrate on anything that wasn't Simon. All I cared about was getting his skin on mine.

This is very, very bad.

Continuing to pointedly ignore my inner voice of reason and responsibilities, I strode into the bedroom and tossed Simon onto the bed. His gasp turned into a squeak of surprise as I pounced, trapping his body beneath mine and ripping the top of his tracksuit in my haste to remove it.

"I'll buy you twenty more," I rasped in response to the disgruntled noise he made.

His protests died completely as I brought my mouth to his nipple, licking and pulling on the sensitive peak until he was sobbing. Ignoring his attempts to push me lower, I simply moved to the other one to continue my torment.

"Wolfy, Wolfy, *pleeeeease…*" he whined, tossing his head from side to side and thrashing in my hold as best he could.

Which isn't much.

Similar to when I stalked him in the Rue Obscure, having Simon at my mercy was kicking my predatory instincts into overdrive. This desire to dominate someone too small to fight me off was nothing new, but even if I'd been able to get my hands on a normie who fit the size requirements, I would have been hesitant to explore my fantasies.

In case I went too far.

Since I couldn't touch anyone anyway, I'd simply resigned myself to watching others enjoy my darkest dreams, assuming I'd never get to experience them firsthand. But knowing Simon *enjoyed* being my prey gave me all the permission I needed.

Even if permission *is not exactly what I want...*

Momentarily ceasing my torture, I brought my hand to Simon's throat—firmly holding him in place while I ghosted my lips over his.

"If you're going to beg," I growled. "Beg me to *stop.*"

He froze with his pillowy lips parted and his pretty green eyes wide with shock, so I loosened my hold just enough to let him reply.

Do you want to play with me?

A brief flash of lust passed over his face before he transformed his expression into one so tearful and terrified, I almost came in my pants again.

"P-please," he whimpered, his bottom lip trembling with his shaky breath. "Please, let me go."

Such a perfect little toy.

With a satisfied hum, I moved my face back to his chest, abandoning his abused nipples in favor of leaving a trail of painful bites on nearly every inch of his pale skin. His sweat tasted like champagne, and the way he struggled against me had me ravenous as his spicy, floral scent clouded my thoughts.

And my judgment.

I kept one hand on his throat while I marked him up, giving him just enough air to call out his safe word, if he needed to.

Although I doubt he'll use it.

Drifting my other hand over his abs, I purposefully avoided his cock and grabbed his balls instead—roughly tugging and fondling them through the velour while he involuntarily bucked.

"Stop!" he cried out, and I greedily fed on the way his voice cracked. "Don't… don't touch me there!"

I am going to make him come so hard for this performance.

"You like it," I chuckled darkly, sliding a finger along his hole—teasing him through the fabric. "I can hear how much you want my thick cock tearing up your tiny hole."

"No…" he pleaded. "Please don't shove your fat, beautiful cock in my tiny slutty hole. Don't do anything like that!"

Such a brat.

Biting back the laugh threatening to escape, I sat up and tore off his pants, smirking in satisfaction when his fuzzy socks stayed on.

So soft and pretty.

Just like him.

"I think you're lying," I murmured, releasing his neck so I could press his thighs against his chest. "Now hold yourself open for me, and I'll try my best not to kill you."

"Putain!" he gasped as his cock jumped and released a burst of sticky precum onto his abs, making my mouth water. "Not the death threats! Play *fair*, Wolfy."

Despite his glare, Simon dutifully held his thighs in place, gloriously spreading himself wide—showing me everything.

Showing me how he was made for me.

Ignoring the blinding need to bury my dick inside him, I used my thumbs to gently spread open his hole, noticing how pink and tender it was.

"Are you still sore?" I asked, deeply conflicted over what I wanted the answer to be.

Please say yes.

"Yes," Simon answered breathlessly, knowing exactly what I needed to hear. "I might cry when you force your way in there."

Promise?

Releasing a slow breath, I left my aching cock trapped against my zipper and I settled between his legs.

"Don't move," I snarled up at him, with my mouth centimeters from contact. "If you touch your cock, I won't let you come until we land. But if you ride my tongue like a good little whore, I'll fuck you until you cry."

Then I spit on his hole before spearing him with my tongue.

Simon tightened around me, so hot and helpless, I couldn't stop from attempting to devour him from the inside out.

"Fuck, yes, Wolfy!" he moaned, riding my tongue, exactly like the whore he was. "I mean, nooooo... No, please stop licking me there, you big, scary, terrible man."

He's so fucking ridiculous.

Despite his bratting, Simon wanted to play this dangerous game just as much as I did. And while I thrived on him having the upper hand in life, at this moment, I wanted to bring him to heel.

I want to taste his fear.

In an instant, I was looming over him again, my hand so tight around his throat, I knew he'd have fresh bruises when I was done.

"Do you still want this, Simon?" I removed all emotion from my voice, pushing four fingers into his ass and smirking as he legitimately fought to breathe. "You want to play with a supervillain, knowing I could snap your neck like a twig? That I could literally fuck you in half, like a knife slicing through raw, bloody meat? Is that how you want to come?"

I didn't need to ask. Simon's eyes rolled back in his head, his ass gripping my fingers like a vise the more I threatened him. Shockwaves of pleasure coursed through his body—pleasure I could feel like my own—and his mouth opened in a silent scream as copious amounts of cum sprayed from his cock to cover his chest and abs.

Beautiful.

Releasing his neck again, I allowed him a single ragged breath before I withdrew my fingers and flipped him onto his stomach.

"Stop…" he hopelessly whimpered, adorably boneless as I lifted his hips, positioning him how I wanted.

A beautiful toy for me to fuck.

Keeping my gaze fixed on Simon's ass, I finally freed my cock. Then I swiped my hand through the mess he'd made before generously coating both my throbbing length and his needy, twitching hole.

"Are you ready to cry for me?" I asked, notching my crown against his opening.

"Yes," he choked out, no longer playing the brat—no longer playing at all. Surrendering to me completely. "Please, make it hurt."

Anything you want.

Firmly gripping my *inventus* around the waist, I slammed into him in one violent thrust. He weakly wailed, clawing at the sheets, his ass clamping around me as I fought to not immediately unload inside him.

Reaching beneath him, I gave his still sensitive cock a brutal stroke, feeling a villainous grin stretch across my face as he tried in vain to bat my hand away before collapsing onto the bed.

"Is my tiny tyrant too exhausted to fight?" I teased, hauling him up by the throat so his back was flush against my chest. "I guess that means I'll have to treat you like a pretty little cock sleeve."

Simon hummed a delirious sound as his head lolled against my chest, but his safe word was still nowhere to be found.

Sitting back on my heels, I began snapping my hips, fucking up into him—hard and fast and rough—my only goal being to use him until I came.

I need to fill him up.

I need to make him cry.

I need him to be mine forever.

Knowing I was close, I slid my hands under his thighs to spread him wider, hammering up into him with borderline dangerous force. I still had enough sense to hold back my full strength, but I was absolutely *feral* over how limp his body had gone.

This is a dangerous game.

"Wolfy." Simon weakly raised his arms overhead, draping them around my neck as he murmured, "I love... I love how you fuck me."

My rhythm momentarily faltered as I briefly thought he'd said something else.

Fuck.

I want him to love me.

Simon was already my *inventus,* and we'd thoroughly claimed each other in countless ways, but *love* was the highest form of affection among normies.

And if what I'm feeling isn't love, I don't know what is.

"Mon chou..." Simon choked out, and I peered down to discover tears streaming down his face.

"I've got you, boss," I murmured, holding him tightly against me as I shuddered, filling his tight, perfectly ruined ass with my cum.

My mind was blessedly blank, except for him—my only thoughts on claiming him over and over. I wasn't thinking about my missing sister challenging my throne, my terrifying father being back from the grave, or the countless enemies lurking in the shadows. Nor was I worried about my brothers back home being in grave danger because of me.

The only thing that mattered was Simon.

A dangerous game indeed.

CHAPTER 38
SIMON

Wolfy was oddly quiet as we prepared to deplane in Argentina.

It wasn't his usual facade, where he wore an impassive mask while calmly strategizing beneath. This was an uneasy quiet, and I somehow knew he was silently panicking over something.

I hope it's not because of me.

As far as I was concerned, everything we'd experienced together had been incredible—including our consensual non-con in the back of the plane. Even my near-death experience on the kitchen floor in Villefranche was now a fond memory, if only because it proved Wolfy could touch me.

The only thing I was still working through was discovering part of my DNA was something 'other'—something supposedly inhuman.

And something not matching any other supes.

Wolfy had tentatively shared Xander's findings so far, which were annoyingly inconclusive. He and Butch were apparently going to dig around in the United Super Nations for more samples and get back to us. But as of now, I was still a mystery.

What captured my attention the most was how Wolfy delivered this news in a strangely neutral tone, as if not wanting me to know how he felt about it.

Personally, I was pissed off, but not because I wasn't totally human. No, what was truly bothering me was that now I felt an overwhelming need to solve this puzzle, if only to figure out where I fit with my dream man and his family.

Assuming he wants me to fit.

Otherwise, I couldn't be arsed to meet my biological father—whoever the deadbeat was. I'd never fully believed Franz Ownit was my blood relative, but he'd been the only name my mother ever offered.

Lord knows who else she was sleeping with at the time.

While lacking a father figure hadn't been ideal, mother dearest had always looked after me well enough—in the half-inebriated, *blasé* way of hers that taught me independence at a young age.

"I'd like to talk to Bunny," I blurted out as Wolfy shrugged his suit jacket back on.

Him choosing to remove the jacket in private—and therefore reveal his tantalizing supe-killing gun and holster in the process—was yet another example of Wolfy letting down his guard with me.

Which I love.

I also loved how he let me touch his big gun while I rode his even bigger cock back in Geneva.

So much to love with this man.

"What would you like to talk to your mother about?" Wolfy tried to act casual, but I spied uncertainty in his expression before he buried it.

You can't hide from me anymore.

Leaving Twoey behind—as instructed—I slung my carry-on over my shoulder, but made no move to exit the plane.

"I'm curious if she has any idea *who* my real father is," I airily replied, closely watching his reaction across the aisle. "Or *what*."

He flinched, and I immediately realized how dismissive my comment could have come across.

He's not a what…

"Wolfy," I took a step closer. "I didn't mean—"

"No, it makes sense," he brusquely replied, alarmingly *stepping away from me* before indicating I should exit the plane. "Your mother might have some leads for you."

What about for us?

With a sigh, I obediently headed down the aisle, if only because some random anthropologist friend of Luca Meier's was apparently waiting for us outside.

"Buenos días, Mr. Espanto!" the middle-aged man standing on the tarmac called out as we descended the stairs. He was notably cheerful, despite the bright sunlight, and that he was dressed head to toe in safari *khaki.*

No one better think I'm going spelunking.

Not in this wardrobe.

I heard Wolfy sharply inhale before he replied, *"buenos días"* in an accent so smooth, I almost evaporated.

He is definitely bringing that slutty Spanish into the bed...

Suddenly recalling how Wolfy strongly disliked speaking his father's native tongue, I tamped down my horny thoughts and quickly interjected.

"Hiiii!" I raised a hand and waved it obnoxiously, bringing our guide's attention to me. *"No habla español,* soooo... English?"

It was all an act for Wolfy's benefit, of course. I was actually fluent in Spanish, as anyone who studied international business should be.

But Indiana Jones here doesn't need to know that.

As expected, Mr. Khaki's already wide smile only widened. "No problem! Is this your first time in Argentina, Mr....?"

"Alarie, but you may call me Simon." I smiled genuinely in return, as the man's good cheer *was* infectious. "And no, I've never visited your fair country before. I'm looking forward to seeing the sights."

Then I stuck out my hand for him to shake.

"Simon!" Wolfy barked, but before I could register what the issue was, the anthropologist placed his hand in mine.

And nobody died.

"Dr. Lorenzo Torres-Maldonado," he cheerfully quipped, vigorously shaking my hand, while Wolfy looked about ready for a heart attack.

What is his prob—

Ohhhh...

All at once, I realized, as Wolfy's *inventus*, I was also expected to explode normies' heads like watermelons.

That would have been awkward.

For some horribly morbid reason, our new friend surviving made my stomach drop.

What if I don't share his Hand of Death powers?

Luca Meier had declared me Wolfy's *inventus,* but didn't explain how he knew. True, he never shook my hand, but that may have been more of a safety precaution rather than proof of my deadliness.

After what Wolfy told me about how Xander and Butch fully bonded, I'd assumed our connection had solidified the night of the council event—possibly the moment I touched our would-be assassin. But now, I was questioning everything.

Maybe I'm not truly his inventus *after all...*

Oblivious to my inner turmoil, Lorenzo continued prattling, "But that's a mouthful, no? So you can call me Doc. Come! Let me share my research before sharing the best places for lunch. I hope you enjoy meat!"

Not even my building insecurities could stop me from taking *that* opening. "I love meat," I cooed. "Especially sausages."

I shot a cheeky glance Wolfy's way as we followed Doc to his Jeep, only half-listening as the anthropologist babbled about chorizo and something called an *asado*.

Sounds like a sausage party to me.

Instead of appreciating my joke, Wolfy's amber eyes were worriedly roaming over me. I wished we were alone so I could reassure him—promise I was still *his*, even without the bond.

But how can I reassure myself?

I didn't have to spiral for long, because as soon as we started driving away, I felt Wolfy's powers reaching for me from the backseat.

Now that I knew what the invasive sensation was—and that it was courtesy of the man I wanted probing me anyway—I could relax and let myself fully experience it.

And it was *fantastic*.

It was as if the very *essence* of Wolfy was filling me up—his scent, his taste, the way his skin felt under my fingers, and how his cock felt inside me. It was *him* but somehow also *me*, and I never, ever wanted it to stop.

I want us to live inside each other.

Turning in the passenger seat, I faced the back where Wolfy was seated. He was still eyeing me with concern, and I realized he was waiting for confirmation that I could feel him.

Not entirely sure what I was doing, I concentrated on gathering up the newfound energy flowing through me and did my best to funnel it back toward him. To my satisfaction, Wolfy hissed and clutched his chest, confirming he'd felt *something*.

"Did I do it right?" I murmured, finding this entire creepy exchange endearing as fuck.

It's like sexting through vibes alone.

"I... don't know," he whispered, still looking far too puzzled for my liking.

"Well," I sniffed haughtily. "I'm still yours either way."

And that's that.

"All right, lovebirds," Doc chuckled warmly, and I recalled Wolfy mentioning he was accustomed to the ways of supes.

"Luca mentioned you're interested in the earliest legends about your kind?"

Pardon?

I narrowed my eyes at a Wolfy—as this was news to me—but his attention was now firmly on the man driving his Jeep over rough terrain.

"Yes," Wolfy eagerly replied. "Anything to understand where our powers come from, and… how they're shared… or not."

What the hell is going on?

All Wolfy had told me about this detour was that Luca's colleague wanted to meet us—that he might have useful intel. I'd assumed it had something to do with our ongoing search for Violentia, but now I realized *I* was the focus of this jungle jaunt.

Our connection, rather.

Our accidental *connection.*

Doc quietly chewed his lip for a good minute before he spoke again. "I have a hypothesis I've been working on… one I can openly discuss now that people are finally realizing heroes and villains are the same."

When he caught me staring, he grimaced. "Before, it was too risky to talk about. Too many politicians involved with too much to lose. I didn't want to end up disappearing into the jungle for good."

As if on cue, the sunlight abruptly cut out as we entered the thick canopy of the Argentinian rainforest.

I don't even want to think about the spiders lurking here.

"Go on," Wolfy urged with a startling level of intensity.

Doc nodded, his eyes fixed on the makeshift jungle road. "I may have discovered why marriage between supes and normies is forbidden."

My heart panged. I wasn't aware normie-supe marriages were illegal. That particular social issue had never crossed my mind before. This was partly because I never thought I had a chance with a hottie supe, but also because I'd never been the marrying type.

But a lot has changed as of late.

"And what have you discovered?" I asked, knowing the waver in my voice was giving my anxiety away, but far too invested in the answer to care.

What if this is the confirmation Wolfy needs to end things?

Doc parked the Jeep next to an ominously dark cave draped in vines that I would never have considered entering if it weren't for current circumstances.

Then the anthropologist turned to me with what I already knew was an uncharacteristically serious expression. "I think you should come inside and see for yourself."

CHAPTER 39
WOLFGANG

I kept my eyes trained on Simon as we entered the cave—watching his expression, his gestures, every move.

Watching *him*.

I trusted Luca Meier implicitly, and therefore, trusted my mentor's belief that Dr. Lorenzo Torres-Maldonado's research would tell us more about who Simon was.

Or what, as he said.

Whatever we learned here today wouldn't change how I felt about him. I was all in—completely lost for this tiny tyrant—but I had to admit something was… *off* about our connection. And it was my duty as head of household to know the facts.

Especially as he'll be joining my clan, regardless.

Simon's reaction to learning that marriage between our kinds was illegal surprised me. I hadn't thought he cared about such things, but if he wanted a wedding, he'd get one—regardless of who I needed to threaten to make it happen.

Maybe we'll discover a loophole here today…

I was doing everything I could to focus on the purpose of this visit. Unfortunately, my already tenuous stress levels were rapidly rising in response to the anxiety I could feel rolling off of Simon.

He was clearly muscling his way through this uncomfortable journey of self-discovery. And while I was excited to learn more about my *inventus*, I couldn't ignore how agitated I was already, simply from being so deep in the jungle. In Argentina.

The origin of my nightmares.

I wanted to continue giving Simon space to work through things, but my current concern for him was merging with my memories, causing my protective instincts to go haywire.

"Are you all right, boss?" I quietly asked, taking his hand in mine as we followed the anthropologist's flashlight deeper into the cave complex.

"That remains to be seen," he snipped, although I didn't take his tone personally.

Instead, I squeezed his hand, hoping the contact was as soothing for him as it was for me. Rallying false calm, I did my best to project the emotion into him, to allow him to siphon it and take what he needed.

I'll give you anything.

"Ah! Here we are!" Lorenzo—Doc—called out, as oblivious to the drama surrounding him as Xander became when deep in a project.

Xanny would be salivating over this right now.

The narrow passageway we'd been traveling down had opened up into a small cavern. With how close to the cave entrance it was—and how worn the walls were—I assumed humans had inhabited it at some point.

This was confirmed as Lorenzo approached the far wall and aimed his flashlight at the stone, revealing what looked like prehistoric cave paintings.

Simon dragged me closer—his curiosity eclipsing the dark mood he'd been under. Of course, I allowed it, although I didn't understand what some archaic art was going to tell us.

Archeological sites like this were nothing new in Argentina. The famous *Cueva de las Manos*—the Cave of Hands—featured some of the oldest examples of early hunter-gatherers visually recording their world. Besides the hundreds of stenciled hands, there were portraits of people and the animals they ate, in styles ranging from naturalistic to abstract. Art of the everyday.

But that's not what this is.

I could only gape at the paintings covering the wall, dumbfounded by what I was seeing. This was nothing like the mosaic of humanity found in *Cueva de las Manos,* or the usual depictions of pre-Columbian life.

Here, humanlike figures were running away from, and fighting against, an army of invaders—so numerous, they obliterated the sky itself. The enemy looked humanoid as well, except for how much *larger* they were… and for the tails, horns, wings, fangs, and claws.

What. The. Fuck?

The shocking discovery before me was what Dr. Lorenzo Torres-Maldonado had been studying in secret—what he'd been too nervous to talk about before the fall of Biggs Enterprises. It was unprecedented and fantastical, like something out of a sci-fi monster movie.

It looked like the End of Days.

Yet… we're still here.

"*Merde…* When did *this* happen?" Simon whispered, cuddling into my side for comfort—which comforted me as well.

Doc shook his head, his eyes roaming over the art in wonder, even though he'd gazed upon it countless times. "Long before recorded history. And if this *was* ever recorded elsewhere, I would bet those records have been destroyed."

Except for these paintings.

"What *exactly* are we looking at?" I carefully asked, even though something deep inside me already knew the answer.

Human history…

The anthropologist warily swept his gaze over us—probably gauging whether we could handle the truth.

Or what we might do with it.

"I firmly believe," he haltingly began, although he seemed to gather his courage as he continued. "What these paintings show is the moment when supes became the dominant species on earth."

My history.

Of whatever I am…

"Fuck," I breathed, not sure what else to say about this damning evidence.

Of course, Simon was looking with a more critical eye. "But who are these *creatures*? Supes don't have tails or claws…"

Lorenzo and I exchanged a look. "Actually." I cleared my throat, thinking of a certain meddling hero we'd stumbled upon in Villefranche. "Some do."

I'm guessing Zion doesn't have a trading card floating around the internet.

Simon kept going, his signature sass rising to the surface. "Are you suggesting all supes started as *that*"—he stabbed a finger toward the army of beasts—"but then somehow became as hot as Wolfgang?!"

The anthropologist's lip twitched as he nodded in affirmation. "Yes. Think of them as *conquerors* who figured out how to eventually resemble the species they'd conquered—at least in superficial ways."

Holy fucking fuck.

"So this is about..." Simon began.

"...evolution," I concluded, feeling like I'd been punched in the gut.

From a young age, every supe—no matter how powerful—was taught that normies were lower life forms at the bottom of the food chain. Supes were simply faster, stronger, more highly evolved.

Better.

And that was before our superpowers even came into play.

The supremacy of your clan was prized above all else. So, of course, you wouldn't want to dilute the waters by marrying or—heaven forbid—reproducing with lesser beings.

Assuming we could even reproduce with each other.

Marriage contracts between powerful supe families were a fairly recent practice, and now I wondered if the purpose went beyond ensuring your clan produced the best heirs.

What if the plan was to conquer the human race once again?

I think I'm going to be sick.

"Breathe, *mon chou*," Simon soothed, gazing up at me while rubbing my arm. "Who cares if you're descended from terrifying otherworldly creatures who flew in eons ago to take over like an invasive species."

Doc cleared his throat, his gaze traveling over Simon in a strangely assessing way. Before I could get possessive about how this normie was looking at what was *mine*, Simon took over.

"How many people know about this?" he asked, his calm and businesslike tone only proving how excellent of an assistant he was.

What an excellent clan leader he'd make.

"Very few," Doc replied, smiling in visible relief. "Besides my trusted team, Luca Meier, two other council members vetted by him, and the current Deputy Secretary-General of the United Super Nations. In fact, Sylvano Ricci's father started the USN in part because of these findings."

Preparing for the fallout on both sides in case it was ever brought to light.

The anthropologist's smile faltered. "I've been told there was a… security breach from within the original archeological dig's team—about seventy-five years ago. Some well-connected humans learned of this moment in history and used the evidence to blackmail modern supes."

I huffed, imagining the audacity of that conversation. These paintings were exactly the type of ammunition powerful normies would use to rile up the masses—to make all supes out to be the enemy. The only issue was there'd be no way humans would ever win in a war against us…

Especially if heroes and villains worked together.

My heart stopped as the missing puzzle pieces fell into place.

"The contracts with cities..." I murmured. "I'd always wondered how they convinced supes to sign their rights away to less powerful humans."

Lorenzo beamed like a proud professor. "And now you know! Politicians and the corporations they associated with cornered specific supes who they knew were more interested in keeping the peace than in starting a war."

"And that's how the concept of 'heroes' was born," I sighed, running a hand down my face—simultaneously exhausted and motivated.

I was already scheming on how to send this man as many resources as he needed to protect this cave, when a stray thought made me frown.

"Why share this with *us?* Is it because Luca told you about my family's archives? I would happily preserve photographs of these paintings in our collection, for the record."

The anthropologist swallowed nervously, his gaze darting between Simon and me again. "I would greatly appreciate that, but... that's not why your friend Luca thought I should meet both of you."

Both of us...

"Tell us what you know, *Doc,*" Simon gritted out, entering full tiny tyrant mode as I braced myself for what was coming.

Because something tells me it's not good.

With a sigh, Lorenzo took a step backward, repositioning his flashlight on an area of the wall his body had been blocking.

My blood ran cold. Instead of the crude sketches of horrifying invaders, this section showed a detailed portrait of a single monster's face. It was a face I knew well—from my nightmares but also my memories—a face that had been turned into a weapon to instill fear in all who witnessed it.

Supay, the Incan god of death.

And the mask of Apocalypto Man.

Lorenzo was watching me closely as he explained. "These original invaders were monstrous, but somewhere along the line, they started to... resemble the humans who'd survived. We suspect this was done through mimicry, along with crossbreeding."

"With humans," Simon rasped, his previous bravado vanishing as he shrank against me.

I wrapped an arm around his shoulders as the anthropologist continued, "Yes, although nowadays—at least, with modern supes—the preference seems to be on only breeding with other supes."

Something about his choice of wording caught my eye. "You said 'modern supes' as if there are other kinds..."

This time, Dr. Lorenzo Torres-Maldonado's focus fell on Simon alone, and I realized he was looking at him the same way Xander observed a fascinating specimen.

Oh, fuck.

I frantically shook my head, but Lorenzo was already pointing at the man at my side—the man who'd become a vital piece of my damaged soul.

The man I loved.

"Supes with a DNA sequence close to the original invaders still exist," he calmly stated, as if my entire world wasn't crumbling to dust. "And when this ancient bloodline reproduces with a human, they create a supe that *appears* to be powerless... until they've found a host to mimic."

CHAPTER 40
WOLFGANG

"No!" I barked, unwilling to accept what he was saying. "Simon is my *inventus*. He's not some... *parasite!*"

Simon made a strangled sound and pushed me away with a surprising amount of strength. I tried to grab his arm, but he moved out of reach and ran down the darkened passageway, intent on escaping what we'd just learned.

On escaping me.

"I-I'm sorry," Lorenzo stuttered. "I didn't mean..."

With a snarl, I took off after my runaway *inventus*, wondering how the fuck he could navigate the pitch-black tunnel at all.

You know why he can, Wolfy.

Because you *can.*

My heart was pounding, threatening to beat right out of my chest, as unwanted memories washed over me. Memories of the last time I ran through the caves and jungles of Argentina —scared and alone.

"If you can survive the night, you've earned your right to be my son."

Even after all this time, my father's voice still sent terror shooting down my spine.

"You'll have a two-hour head start. After that, I'm coming for you, lobo."

I was only eight years old, but already knew I was an anomaly. All supes were born with power, but most had to hone it as they matured, until they were a deadly force ready for battle. Mine seemed fully formed since the fateful day it manifested, and my parents had been steadily testing me ever since, eager to find out just how powerful their not-so-secret weapon was.

After my nanny, Martha's death, a steady stream of supes were kidnapped and delivered to Apocalypto Man's workshop of horrors beneath the Suarez compound. Each time, I was ordered to drain them — to test how fast I could do it based on how powerful my victims were.

The occasional human was brought in as well, but we quickly learned they were no match for me.
It didn't matter that I wanted no part in this senseless murder. My parents made it clear. Either I killed who they wanted me to, or I was of no use to them and this family.

You're either with us, or dead.

After years of these tests at home, it was time to see if I could hold my own in the field against one of the most powerful villains alive.

Apocalypto Man.

"Listo o no, lobo. Run."

"*Putain!* Ow! Are you trying to squash me, Wolfgang—like the fucking *parasite* I am?"

Snapping back to the present, I realized I'd tackled Simon outside the cave entrance and was now pinning him against the ground while growling like a wild beast.

I can't let him get away.

He's mine

Mine, mine, mine.

"Wolfy..." he hissed, somehow wiggling around enough to face me. "Why are you not letting me get up? I wasn't even running!"

"Run, Wolfgang."

"I can't lose you," I gasped, panic clawing its way out of me like a rabid animal trying to escape. "Not here. Not in *this* fucking jungle, of all places."

Simon scoffed—unbothered, as usual, by my possessive display. "If you believe for one minute that I am willingly existing in this spider-infested locale, or that I would travel *farther* into this humid hellscape..."

He trailed off and peered up at me—his annoyance replaced by deep concern. "Are you... are you all right?"

"No. I'm not." Tears blurred my vision as I buried my face in Simon's neck. "I hate this country. I hate it so fucking much, just like I hate my father and I hate what he did to me here."

So. Much. Hate.

I knew I sounded weak, but couldn't find it in myself to care. Watching Simon disappear into the darkness of the cave—knowing the horrors I'd endured here in the dead of night—had broken something inside me.

I can't lose the one good thing I have.

He stilled. "Was this one of those... *tests* you hinted at... that your parents put you through when you were young?"

I could only murmur in agreement as I raggedly inhaled, greedily breathing in his scent.

I can't, I can't, I can't.

"Shhh... *mon chou*," he soothed, comforting me when I should have been doing the same for him. "You're still here. Whatever that fucked up trial was, you must have conquered it. Because you're here. With me."

I'm here.

With him.

"I did," I whispered against Simon's skin, allowing his words to sink into my bones and chase away any lingering terror. "I was eight when my father tested me in this jungle. He chased me down and tried to kill me, but somehow, I gained the upper hand. I not only survived—I felt like a god."

Until he beat me within an inch of my life.

He let me live, however, and it only occurred to me years later that it must have been because I'd come close to finishing him. Despite the supposed caveat that supes *couldn't* kill their parents.

So, of course, he'd choose to keep me alive.

As a weapon.

The sound of someone awkwardly clearing their throat behind us had me spinning—ready to defend my *inventus* from any threat.

If I can even call him that anymore...

Dr. Lorenzo Torres-Maldonado was hovering nearby with a sheepish expression on his face. "Please forgive me for upsetting you, Simon. For upsetting both of you. I've worked on this research for so long, I hadn't considered how much of a shock it might be for someone with your background to hear it for the first time. It may not mean much, but it is an honor to finally meet a human with ancient supe DNA."

Now that he was no longer trapped beneath me, Simon rose to his feet and haughtily brushed forest debris off his velour tracksuit.

"Well, I'm thrilled to have been the pinnacle of your scientific career, even if you unceremoniously ripped the rug out from under me. The truth is, I've long suspected something was *off* with my genetic makeup—so it's refreshing to have confirmation. Refreshing like a big bucket of ice water."

When Lorenzo gratefully smiled, Simon added, "I do wish you hadn't destroyed my dreams of being Wolfy's *inventus,* however..."

The anthropologist cocked his head. "Yes, I believe I've heard supes mention that word before. *Inventus.* What does it mean?"

"It's a rare connection between equally powerful supes where they can access each other's powers," Simon explained as we all climbed into Lorenzo's Jeep. "Complete with the common side effect of wanting to unalive anyone who looks at them funny."

He delivered this last part with a cheeky glance to where I sat in the backseat, and my tension unwound to know we were okay.

Still connected in all the ways that matter.

"Hmm..." Lorenzo hummed thoughtfully. "To be honest, *that* sounds a lot like a parasitic relationship—from both sides."

He has a point.

An idea surfaced, and I pulled out my phone to send Xander a text.

> *Have you tested Simon's DNA sample against yours and Butch's yet?*

Since *science* was the subject, he responded almost immediately.

The Mouthy One: *Not yet, but I will now. What's up?*

> *A lot. I'm going to get you in contact with a new friend and his research. Keep your conversations encrypted.*

The Mouthy One: *Aye-aye, Capitán.*

Tucking away my phone again, I addressed the man behind the wheel. "Lorenzo—*Doc*—I'd like to connect you with my brother, Xander. He's a scientist and has been testing Simon's DNA against that of other supes. Coincidentally, he's also one half of a confirmed *inventus* bond, which could prove useful to your research."

Catching him glance at me in the rearview mirror, I smoothly continued, "My offer still stands to preserve records of the cave paintings in my family's secure archives. Xander will contact you shortly through an encrypted method, so you can safely share what you have on file. I will also assign full-time guards to be stationed outside the cave—to ensure no further security breaches occur."

Simon shot me a good-natured eye roll while Lorenzo sputtered in disbelief. "Y-yes... of course! That all sounds incredible. Thank you for the generous offer, Mr. Espanto!"

It wasn't optional, but sure.

Knowing I had the anthropologist firmly on the hook, I reeled him in. "This project will now be fully funded by me, so anything you need, just ask. And with that, I will require the names of everyone currently involved, as well as anyone associated in the past—including the original archeological team."

We're gonna catch ourselves a rat.

Naturally, Lorenzo saw nothing but good intentions in my 'generous offer.' He unquestionably agreed to all my terms before babbling excitedly about his research during the entire drive back to our plane.

Simon politely nodded and hummed along, with his eyes either on the man next to him or straight ahead. But I *felt* his power—whether borrowed or not, I didn't care—nudging against mine like a loving caress. Telling me that, no matter what, this connection we had was *real*.

And I will do whatever it takes to protect it.

CHAPTER 41
SIMON

I was surprisingly calm by the time we reached our hotel in Buenos Aires, especially considering I'd recently learned I was possibly not only half-supe but half-parasitic scrounger as well.

It's true that I enjoy spending other people's money.

But Wolfy likes it.

Acknowledging my unapologetically gold-digging ways had me recalling how I'd wanted to put my mother on the spot over my mistaken parentage.

Let's see what Bunny knows.

Clearing my throat, I glanced up at Wolfy as the door to the Presidential Suite shut behind us. "I'd like to talk—"

"To your mother, yes," Wolfy effortlessly completed my thought, although he looked uncharacteristically nervous over the idea.

"Is that all right?" I hesitantly asked, unsure how *he* was processing this new information.

While Wolfy liked to say *I* was the boss, I much preferred the scenario where we made executive decisions together.

A true partnership.

He huffed a laugh, unpacking his laptop and setting it up at the desk. "Of course, Simon. I want to figure out what's going on here as much as you do. Although, you should know… nothing could change how I feel about you."

My heart pounded in my chest so intensely, I barely heard my own whispered reply. "Oh? And how do you feel?"

Wolfy turned to face me, gazing deep into my eyes with so much emotion, I felt it in my soul. "Like I'm hopelessly, madly in love with my *inventus.*"

Merde…

I was utterly speechless. Wolfy was far from the first man who'd professed his love for me, but never had those words resonated like *this*. And never had I felt the same.

So why can't I say it in return?

Wolfy deserved to hear how hopelessly, madly in love *I* was as well. That I'd never felt so cared for—or *seen*—as I did with him. But for some emotionally stunted reason, I couldn't seem to get my foolish mouth to say what I knew to be true in my formerly cold, black heart.

I truly love him so much it makes me sick.

Because he was the perfect man for me, Wolfy didn't even seem upset by my lack of reply. "But to be completely honest," he smoothly continued—as if the conversation hadn't just taken an epic turn. "Bunny scares the shit out of me."

I barked a laugh, grateful for the out. "She *does* have that effect on men with obscene amounts of money. Perhaps she's a supervillain as well..."

He cocked his head as he sat in front of the laptop and invitingly patted his thigh. "Do you think your *mother* might be the one with supe DNA? Are we barking up the wrong tree here?"

My faithful dog.

I perched on his lap and opened up FaceTime, pleased to see my account info and contacts were already there waiting for me.

Top tier stalker vibes.

"I don't believe so," I replied as we waited for my mother to pick up. "Let's be honest. If Bunny Alarie was actually a supervillain, she would have conquered the world by now."

Wolfy chuckled and placed a sweet kiss on the back of my neck, although I noticed he remained half-hidden behind me as the call connected.

"Mon vilain! Très merveilleux... WHAT THE HELL HAPPENED TO YOUR NECK?!"

Oops.

I forgot about all the bruises and love bites.

"Oh, calm down, *Maman!*" I gaily laughed, my evil grin only widening as I added, *"Wolfgang* is to blame, but I assure you, it was *mostly* consensual."

"You fucking brat," Wolfy hissed into my neck as he burrowed deeper, like the scared little murder cabbage he was.

Surely this *will get me the spanking I deserve, no?*

Bunny sighed and took a steadying sip of her mimosa. It might have been breakfast where she was, or not. I didn't bother to calculate the time difference, as the drink was a favorite of hers, no matter the time of day.

"Very well." She waved a freshly manicured hand. "What do I owe the pleasure of this social call? Do you have news—an engagement, perhaps?"

She just wants to analyze the size of my rock.

"Even better!" I chirped, wiggling a bit in villainous excitement. "I recently learned half of my DNA isn't human. Would you know anything about that?"

Wolfy's grip on my waist tightened, and I felt him finally dare to peer around me, most likely to watch my mother's reaction.

Bunny didn't disappoint. First, she froze in place for so long I feared there was a faulty connection. Then she *set aside her drink* and nervously dabbed at her lips with a monogrammed handkerchief.

Oh, she knows something, all right.

"I'm not... entirely certain Franz Ownit is your father," she finally replied.

Well, color me surprised.

I scoffed. "Yes, we gathered that. Any idea *who* the mystery man might be? Shall we dust off your Rolodex, or carbon date the notches on your bedpost for clues?"

Accustomed to my crass commentary, my mother simply rolled her eyes. "I have my suspicions, but even *if* he's still living in Big City, he may be difficult to find. Not only was he notoriously secretive, I'm not entirely sure he gave me his real name when we were being... intimate."

Gross.

I sighed heavily. "All right. What *can* you tell us about Bachelor Number Whatever?"

Bunny shrugged nonchalantly and raised her mimosa to her lacquered lips once again. "He was an artist—a sculptor—and he was..." She fixed her unwavering stare on the enormous man still trying in vain to be invisible. "Whatever *Wolfgang* is."

"He's not a *what!*" I shouted as I felt Wolfy tense beneath me. "He's my..."

My...

My everything.

"I know, *mon vilain*," she gently replied, her gaze softening as it returned to my face. "I simply wanted you to know that I understand *why* you have feelings for him. You've always been different—*special*—and now you've found someone perfect for you."

To my horror, I felt *tears* threatening to make an appearance, but luckily—or unluckily, for Wolfy—Bunny's attention fell to him again.

"That being said, if anything happens to my son *besides* the bruises and bites you heathens apparently enjoy, I *will* find you. Am I understood, Mr. Espanto?"

Wolfy's phone buzzed in his pocket, but he took the time to solemnly reply, "Yes, ma'am. Simon is the most precious gift I've ever received, and I would rather put myself in harm's way than let anything happen to him."

Swoon!

My mother nodded in approval before launching into the update on her life I hadn't asked for. I tried my best to follow along, but became distracted when Wolfy sharply inhaled.

I twisted in his lap to find him staring down at his phone with a look of alarm. Before I could properly snoop, he slid me off his lap and onto the chair before swiftly stalking into the bedroom and shutting the door behind him.

Without sharing the tea.

Rude.

Confident I could get him to spill the details later, I dutifully resumed listening to my mother prattle on about the upcoming shows she was attending for Paris Fashion Week.

When she finally took a breath, I wrapped things up, eager to join my *inventus* in the bedroom.

To see what upset him... obviously.

"I'm coming in!" I sang out, already shrugging off my top as I strode toward the bedroom. "I'm simply *ravenous* for some of that famous Argentinian meat. Then we can both get some dinner afterward."

I smirked as I opened the door to find Wolfy had ended his phone conversation and was already removing his suit.

Good man.

"Simon," he growled in that mildly threatening tone of his that made my toes curl in my fuzzy socks. "I need you."

"Oh, I like that," I purred, kicking off my trainers and removing the rest of my clothes as well. "I like you needy."

The feeling is mutual.

I ogled him as he sat on the bed, gloriously naked, like a marble statue come to life. Giving my hard cock a rough stroke, I noticed Wolfy looked equally ready in that regard, although he was gripping the comforter on either side of him, as if he were *nervous*.

That can't be right.

"Tell me what you need, Wolfy," I softly spoke, somehow knowing I needed to approach him—*this*—carefully.

What could be bothering him?

He swallowed hard, but held my gaze. "I want… I *need* you to top me, Simon. *Please.*"

CHAPTER 42
SIMON

For the second time in under an hour, I was momentarily lost for words.

I assumed Wolfy was upset over whatever news he'd received via text, but instead of taking out his agitation on my —very willing—arse, he was offering me *his*.

And asking so politely, too!

Unfortunately, he misinterpreted my shock for hesitation. "I don't know if you've ever…" Wolfy grimaced and averted his gorgeous eyes. "Or if you even *want* to."

"Wolfgang!" I scolded, stomping over with my dick in hand. "First of all, yes, I *have* topped before. Only a couple of times, since men can get dodgy over being skewered by someone smaller than them."

They don't know what they're missing.

A smile twisted his tasty lips as he bravely looked at me again. "But more importantly," I cooed, draping my arms around his neck so I could lick my way into his mouth. "Yes. So much fucking yes. I would *kill* to get my tongue and cock inside that perfect peach."

Just as I'd hoped, Wolfy adorably blushed at the praise. "Your... *tongue?*" he choked out, apparently only feeling so courageous.

Did you forget who you were dealing with?

"I consider it my *amuse-bouche*, before the main course," I darkly chuckled. "Now, get on your hands and knees and feed it to me."

Because he was the perfect pet, Wolfy instantly obeyed, turning and climbing onto the bed. I groaned at the sight—not only because his arse truly was perfect—but because this immeasurably powerful supe was letting me have my way with him.

It's because he trusts *you, Simon.*

The realization made traitorous tears sting my eyelids again, but I buried my reaction beneath the raw lust blanketing my heavier emotions.

We'll just sweep those pesky feelings aside for now.

"So pretty," I murmured, appreciatively running my hands over his muscular globes. "Has anyone ever told you how pretty you are, Wolfy?"

"Never," he whispered, lowering his head to his forearms—offering himself up to me like a gourmet meal. "Say it again."

I'll tell you every day of your life.

"Pretty, perfect, custom-made for me in every way," I earnestly recited before kneeling on the leather bench at the foot of the bed and swiping my tongue up his crack. "And tasty as fuck."

"Jesus *Christ!*" Wolfy barked, flinching at the novel sensation. "Oh, my fucking *God*, Simon."

I'm just getting started.

"Relax, *mon chou*," I purred. "Let your *boss* get this *tight* hole ready for my cock."

Coating my finger in saliva—since that's how we liked to play—I gently circled his rim, already feral from the whimpers he was trying to hide.

But you can't hide from me.

"Please, boss," he finally rasped, pushing his arse backward, silently begging along with the words he couldn't contain. "I *need* to feel you inside me at least once."

Something about his phrasing made me pause, but I was quickly distracted by the way his hole was twitching, trying to swallow up my finger with every pass.

"My pleasure," I murmured, slowly plunging my finger inside him, relishing how he tightened at the intrusion.

"Holy, *fuuuuuck*," Wolfy groaned, uncharacteristically—and deliciously—vocal.

Nothing like a little hand to gland combat to inspire a battle cry.

I slid another finger in, alternating between stretching him and massaging his p-spot until he seemed ready to detonate.

Time for the fireworks.

Lowering my face again, I licked and nibbled around his rim, continuing to milk his gland, torturously slow. I didn't stop until he was sobbing, and only then did I replace my fingers with my tongue, spearing him as deeply as I could while wrapping my hand around his thick, throbbing cock.

I was already addicted to the way Wolfy smelled, but his *taste* was lighting my veins on fire. Musky and sweet and so fucking raw, he'd have to beat me away with a stick to make me give up this feast.

Speaking of which...

I tightened my hold on his cock, matching the rhythm of his thrusts while using my thumb to trace the V underneath his sensitive crown on every upstroke.

"Fuck, Simon," he gasped. "Fuck, fuck, *fuck.*"

Oh, we'll get there.

Deciding I needed to *see* Wolfy fall apart, I pulled back and replaced my mouth with my other hand—easily sliding three fingers in.

"Does that feel good, *mon chou?*" I crooned. "You're opening up so beautifully, thanks to all this *spit* that I'm shoving into your greedy little hole."

"Oh, fuuuuck." He shivered, so close I could practically taste his release.

"I know you want to come for me," I continued, relentless in every way as I fucked him at both ends. "You want to show me how *pretty* you look while soaking these three hundred thread count bamboo sheets?"

I know exactly how you like it.

Whatever Wolfy said next was lost in a strangled shout as he violently shuddered, releasing rope after rope of cum onto the expensive sheets beneath him.

Such a good pet.

"On your back," I commanded, using his spent cum to lube myself up, knowing he liked it as filthy as me. "I'm *dying* to own you."

"You already do," he rasped as he flipped over and hustled his muscles up the bed. Propping his upper half against the headboard, he planted his feet on the bed and spread himself wide. "And you always will, no matter what."

There was something like *sadness* in Wolfy's tone, and I wondered if he was still worried I might run away after all I'd learned today.

Not a chance.

"And *you* own every piece of me as well," I reassured him, crawling up his enormous body, licking away any stray drops of cum as I went. "Not even death could take you away from me."

"Promise?" he whispered, so low I almost missed it

Lining myself up, I placed my hands on his enormous pecs and gazed down at him. "Promise," I replied, with the seriousness of a solemn vow. "I'm quite good at cheating death, you know."

His expression darkened, but I was already sliding my way in with a contented sigh that turned into a groan—burrowing as deep as I could get.

Claiming what's mine.

"Jesus, *fuck,*" he choked out, his amber eyes unfocused as I bottomed out.

Très bon.

Wolfy felt like silk wrapped around my cock and combined with how worked up I already was, I knew I wouldn't last long. Dropping my forehead to his, I dug my nails into his delicious chest, focusing all my energy into holding off the orgasm I already sensed dancing along my spine.

"Do you think you can come again, Wolfy?" I whispered as I began a slow rhythm. "I want to watch you spill all over these hot muscles."

"Definitely," he growled. Palming my ass with both hands, he forced me to increase my speed—topping me from the bottom, which I didn't mind one bit. "I want to come for you."

"Make sure my name is on your lips when you do." I panted as I edged closer to oblivion. "And keep your eyes on me."

"Yes, boss," he replied, somehow picking up the pace even more—fucking himself with my cock like I was a toy.

Putain!

The noises we both were making sounded inhuman, but I was too far gone to care. I was lost—utterly and completely gone to whatever primal, animal need this was to mark and claim and *fuck* what belonged to me.

Mine, mine, all fucking mine.

"Simon…" Wolfy groaned in the sexiest voice known to man. "Oh, fuck! *Siiiimon…*"

"That's it," I coaxed, fucking him like some sort of unhinged machine, my gaze flickering between his bouncing cock and his gorgeous face. "Give it to me."

Give me what's mine.

With a groan that reverberated in my bones, Wolfy came again, his hole clamping around me so tightly it sucked the orgasm right out of me.

I collapsed onto the sticky mess of his chest as I came, shuddering while I emptied everything I had inside him—claiming him as mine all over again.

'Til death do us part.

We lay like that for a few minutes until I wearily lifted my head to smile stupidly at him.

"How was that?" I asked, unable to keep the swagger from my tone.

He smirked, brushing my sweaty hair out of my face. "You've displayed a solid work ethic. I'll be giving you top scores on your performance review."

This. Man.

Wolfy's gaze grew serious—wistful, even. "I love you, Simon. Not just as my *inventus*, but *you*."

I swallowed hard, struck dumb yet again. "I…"

What is wrong with me?

He smiled softly before delivering an even softer kiss. "I know, boss. Now let's get cleaned up, order a ridiculous amount of room service, and fuck again before sleeping naked—skin to skin."

"Sounds like a plan," I replied, although I made no move to leave our sticky nest just yet.

While I was grateful Wolfy didn't pressure me into telling him how I felt, I was still frustrated with myself for being unable to, for some ungodly reason.

There's always tomorrow, Simon.

CHAPTER 43
WOLFGANG

Cold.

Pain.

Make it stop.

Please…

CHAPTER 44
SIMON

I awoke to the sight of a gorgeous face with familiar amber eyes staring at me from across the room.

But it wasn't the face I was expecting.

"Fils de pute!" I exclaimed, clutching the sheet to my chest as I abruptly sat up in bed. "Who the fu—"

"Rise and shine, Frenchy!" Hottie McMystery Man sang out, rising from his chair and clapping his hands together like some sort of sporty coach. "Big bro says it's time to pack it up and ship out."

Of course, it's another Suarez brother.

The Dumb One, *if I had to guess.*

"Baltasar, I assume?" I sweetly cooed as he nodded enthusiastically. "To what do we owe the pleasure of this intrusive yet invigorating wake up call? And where *is* Wolfy? Don't tell me he's already *working* on his laptop out there…"

I trailed off as the look on Baltasar's face morphed from cheerful to confused—which was probably closer to his natural state. "Uhhh… he didn't tell you?"

My skin prickled, chest tightening as that strange *pulling* sensation I now knew was the parasitic *inventus* bond stretched outward—searching for the connection it wanted.

But coming up empty.

"Tell me *what?*" I gritted out, already knowing in my heart that, whatever it was, it was *bad*.

I can't feel him anywhere....

Now Baltasar looked downright nervous. "I was told to take you back to Big City, so we can keep you safe while Wolfy... handles some things."

Oh, no, he didn't.

"*C'est des conneries...*" Feeling around for my discarded trackies, I pulled them on beneath the covers before rising from the bed. "Enough of this smoke and mirrors bullshit. You will tell me what's going on and where Wolfy went or so help me, I will destroy you."

Baltasar's face lit up as a dimpled, boyish grin stretched across his annoyingly familiar face. "And just what are *you* gonna do, little guy? I could pin you down with my pinky finger."

Oh, it's on.

I had absolutely no patience for male posturing—ever, really—and especially not under the current circumstances.

"Careful, Balty," I growled, stalking closer and cracking my knuckles as I advanced. "You must be aware I'm 'big bro's' *inventus*, right? That means I not only share Wolfy's rule over this family, but his *powers* as well. Rest assured, you don't want to mess with me on either aspect."

Balty's slightly lighter golden brown skin paled further still. "Jesus, chill," he huffed, his machismo faltering. "You're as scary as he is."

"Scarier," I confirmed. "Now tell me what I want to know, Baby Hulk, before I drain you into submission."

His eyes narrowed at the threat—or perhaps, his new pet name—but then he nodded like the good little himbo he was. "Ok. So, I don't know exactly where Wolfy went, but it's wherever Vi is."

My blood ran cold. "He figured out where to find Violentia?"

Why wouldn't he tell me?

All at once, I recalled the text Wolfy received while we were chatting with my mother. Moving past Balty, I strode into the common area, both relieved and concerned to find Wolfy's laptop where we'd last used it.

It can't be good that he purposefully left it behind.

Sitting at the desk, I used the fingerprint access he'd given me to log on before digging around to find his Messages app.

"Whoa," Baltasar scoffed as he lumbered over. "He actually lets you touch his laptop?"

"Well, he lets me touch his *cock,* so, yes," I hissed, amused to see him both recoil *and* drag his gaze over me in response. "I told you, Balty, I'm your new mafia queen."

Don't test me.

"Clearly," he muttered, but otherwise kept his big, dumb mouth shut.

He's smarter than he looks.

Barely.

I made a noise of triumph as I found the text Wolfy had received yesterday in a separate group chat he'd created with **Thing One** and **Thing Two**. It simply urged Wolfy to call them, which it appeared he did a minute later.

Time to meet the twins.

I hit FaceTime and impatiently waited for one or both to pick up, all the while ready to crawl out of my skin with worry over my true love.

What if I never get the chance to tell him how I feel?!

Unsurprisingly, they were together when **Thing Two** answered the call, gazing at me expectantly with their creepily identical, unnervingly attractive faces.

I swear, this family is entirely made up of super models.

Wolfy and I are going to have such beautiful children...

Focus, Simon!

"Hello, *normie*," one twin calmly spoke while the other continued staring at me, his cold blue eyes unblinking.

Thank fuck they don't speak as one.

"Hey, losers," Baltasar bent down, crowding my personal space in order to fit his oafish body into the frame and wave.

Without hesitating, I whipped around and stabbed my finger into his broad chest, somehow releasing just enough of Wolfy's power to give him a dick-shrinking electrical shock.

"MOTHERFUCKER!" Balty roared, stumbling backward until he was a respectful distance away again.

I warned you.

An almost unbearable pressure immediately invaded my mind, threatening to send me toppling out of the chair and to my knees.

Unruly brats—all of them!

With a growl, I spun back around to face the screen, finding the twins murderously glaring at me as they attempted to melt my brain from six thousand miles away.

And that's why they're the infamous duo, Shock and Awe.

"Get the *FUCK* out of my head!" I snarled, somehow slamming shut a mental steel door and throwing away the key.

Their identical expressions changed to surprise and begrudging respect, while I continued to glare.

"Fair enough. What can we do for you, Simon?" the chatty one casually spoke a moment later, as if nothing were amiss.

No wonder Wolfy's exhausted all the time.

"Where is my *inventus?*" I growled, uninterested in playing games while we continued to lose precious time.

The twins paused, their gazes growing distant. At first, I wondered if they were mentally checking Wolfy's location before realizing it was something far less useful.

"None of that!" I barked. "None of this witchy-woo telepathy with each other—not when *your brother* is in danger!"

Like a light switch being flipped, the twins snapped out of their daze to stare at me in confusion.

"What do you mean, Wolfy's in danger?" the *other* twin spoke this time, and by the shocked look on the first one's face, this was a rarity.

I huffed, beyond done with how *everyone* in this family perceived Wolfgang.

Am I the only one who truly sees him?

I stood so I could properly glare down at the screen, ready to give these fools a piece of my mind.

"This *will* come as a surprise, since you're all apparently more than happy to stick your heads in the sand, but Wolfy is not invincible. I'm sure it's extremely difficult to capture him, and he *is* a legitimate badass, but he just willingly put himself in harm's way—to spare the rest of us. Just like he's been doing *his entire life.* Are you aware that your father chased him through these jungles before the four of us were even born? Tried to kill his own child, just to see what he was made of? And that's only one horror story of many he's told me."

Tears of anger and frustration were streaming down my face, mixing with the overwhelming *sorrow* I felt for Wolfy—for all he'd endured alone.

He's not alone anymore.

"Do you know how tirelessly he's worked to ensure none of you suffer like he did?" I continued, not satisfied until everyone involved in this conversation was as emotionally decimated as me. "Not to mention the countless ways he keeps this family business running, despite the *daily* threats I'm sure none of you know anything about. But you're all content to let him martyr himself, instead of fighting to save the man who does *nothing* but spend every waking minute worrying about and protecting the rest of you?"

"Father tried to… *kill* him?" Baltasar croaked, although judging by the wariness in his expression, the revelation tracked.

"Yes," I hissed, shifting my body so I could scold everyone equally. "And as you know, he's supposedly back from the dead, although proof of that remains to be seen. But that's not all. The grueling trials your parents put Wolfy through pale in comparison to the battles they made him fight as their proxy. I may not be as formidable as any of you, but *if* your parents were still alive, I would—"

My words died on my lips. Wolfy had been adamant from the start that he didn't want to kill his sister—that she was just the berserker puppet of whoever was pulling the strings. Mistress Noir-Rouge hinted that Violentia was working for someone far more threatening, and the hitman we'd killed behind the warehouse referenced a 'she' who'd promised him power.

Apocalypto Man was nothing but a distraction.

"Did any of you ever... *see* your mother's dead body?" I asked, already dreading the answer.

"Fuck," Baltasar eloquently replied after a long pause, giving me all the confirmation I needed of who the Big Bad was in this situation.

I briefly closed my eyes and blew out a slow breath. If *I'd* been in charge, Glacial Girl never would have slipped through the cracks. However, I also knew firsthand just how much was on Wolfy's shoulders. There was probably a good reason no one in the family went looking for the body. Or, perhaps, someone simply made a mistake.

These supes are more human than they realize.

Opening my eyes, I found the twins frozen in place again, but this time, they weren't communicating with each other. They were simply staring expectantly—waiting for me to give them their marching orders.

As Wolfy's inventus.

"All right." I straightened my shoulders before pointing at the talkative twin. "**Thing One**, I need you to contact Butch and

Xander and have them organize a search for your mother's body before going after Wolfy."

"On it, boss." He gave me a smirk that—paired with the nickname—made my heart squeeze painfully in my chest. "Although, I'm **Thing Two**, and my name's Gabe."

"And I'm Dre." The quiet one shyly smiled. "Wolfy's in Iceland. We briefly got a read on Violentia at mother's childhood home."

Good man.

I turned to direct the full force of my authority on **The Dumb One**. "Guess what *you're* doing, Balty?"

He sighed and ran a huge hand down his face. "I'm taking you to Iceland, even though Wolfy will literally drain me over it."

"Drained if you do, drained if you don't!" I sang, waggling my fingers to remind him I was the Hand of Death's tiny tyrant. "You supes answer to *me* now."

CHAPTER 45
SIMON

"Your mother grew up above a flower shop?" I suspiciously eyed the quaint but boarded up business across the street, wishing I was in a better mood to appreciate that it was called Blómaggedon.

Which had better not be a Doomsday omen, or so help me.

We'd only recently arrived in Siglufjörður, the northernmost city on the mainland, but after staking out the shop for an hour with no sign of life coming from inside, I was antsy. It had taken us almost a full day to fly here—since Wolfy disappeared with the private jet—and that I couldn't *feel* him the instant we landed did not bode well.

Please be alive in there.

"Yeah," Baltasar replied, his normally vacant gaze impressively focused on our target. "But, now that I think about it, we didn't have any houseplants growing up. On that note..." He shot me a dopey sidelong glance. "I always wondered if Wolfy could touch plants and animals. If his hand *thingie* was just for killing people."

"I..." I stuttered, thrown off by the trajectory of his thoughts—despite being nonstop subjected to Balty's chaos for the past twenty-four hours. "He handled Twoey plenty of times with no adverse effects."

Twoey misses her murder daddy.

Baltasar hummed thoughtfully. "Maybe the reason he can touch *you* is that you're part plant."

I CAN'T TAKE THIS ANYMORE!

"All right, that's it." I sprang to my feet, ready to run into the line of fire to escape Deep Thoughts with **The Dumb One**. "I'm going in."

"Uh, don't you think we should wait for the others?" Baltasar mumbled. "I mean, I've seen our mother when she's angry and *woooooo…*"

I sighed in resignation. It was the smartest thing he'd said since we'd met. Butch and Xander *were* on their way—flying themselves across the goddamn ocean—and we'd agreed to wait until they arrived to make a move.

They would have been here already, but first needed to stop by Dead Man's Ravine to oversee the crew dredging the river.

While the half-frozen body of Vortexio had been found downriver a few days after the original battle, the lack of evidence for Glacial Girl's demise didn't ring any alarm bells. Wolfy had simply believed she'd dematerialized—become one with the ice she used to kill Butch's father—and the reason he believed it was because someone told him that's what happened.

His *sister*.

Apparently, Violentia had briefly disappeared when things came to head between the Suarez and Holt clans. But then she waltzed through the front door of the family compound a few days later, as if she'd only been away on one of her usual benders. This was when she and Wolfy discussed the epic showdown between Vortexio and their mother, and Vi had planted the seed that Glacial Girl was truly dead before disappearing for good.

Just another distraction.

I didn't care how much control their mother had over her. Violentia had some serious groveling to do before being allowed back into this family.

Assuming she doesn't meet an untimely end during whatever boss battle awaits us.

That would be a shame.

I'd just lowered myself to the floor again—to pass the time dreaming of revenge—when I felt an abrupt tug on my *inventus* bond. It wasn't the usual pull either, where either Wolfy or I were trying to connect, or simply remind the other we were there. This was a sharp and cutting sensation, flavored with so much pain, I cried out as I clutched my chest.

MERDE!

Baltasar reacted by wrapping his muscular arms around me, as if to stop me from falling to my not-death, from my oh-so-precarious, seated position on the floor.

Truly, this man has no sense of self-preservation.

"Oh shit! I shouldn't have touched you. Wait... so, you *don't* just automatically zap people? Can you actually turn your Hand of Death powers off and on? That's pretty cool. I always wondered if Wolfy could—"

"Wolfy's being tortured in there, you imbecile!" I gasped. "I'm going in, with or without you."

I punctuated my point with a demonstration of how well I could control my powers by shaking Baltasar off with another electrical shock. I considered it an act of mercy, as it would've ended much worse for him had Wolfy seen his brother touching me.

"But..." **The Dumb One** unwisely began, but I aggressively shushed him until he realized I wasn't playing.

Yes, the logical part of me *knew* I was epitomizing the 'too stupid to live' trope by charging into battle. Facing off against the legendary Glacial Girl and her unhinged marionette—especially as little more than a normie with magic fingers—was inarguably unwise. But I also knew I couldn't simply sit here while the love of my life endured unspeakable pain.

Not when I'm close enough to get my hands on him.

"Let's fucking do this!" Baltasar rallied, abruptly leaping to his feet and performing what looked like pre-workout stretches.

I couldn't be sure if it was more muscle-bound posturing or if this was what Baby Hulk actually did before battle, but I didn't care, because we were actually *doing this*.

Let's go!

I rose to stand, doing a few lunges of my own while formulating a plan. Since Blómaggedon was a commercial space, I assumed there was an exit or loading dock in the back we could infiltrate. Even a fire escape to the apartment above could work, as long as it got us inside the building.

Our secret weapon would have to be the element of surprise. The instant Glacial Girl knew her location was compromised, she could disappear with Wolfgang to any of the family's international properties.

And then this entire adventure would start all over again.

"All right, Balty." I puffed out a breath and faced the Suarez I had on hand. "We're going to going sneak around back and—"

"DESTROY EVERYTHING!!!" Baltasar inhumanly roared, and I could only watch in horror as he quite literally Hulked out.

His already ridiculous muscles expanded—like balloons being rapidly inflated—his clothing falling away like shreds of tissue paper as he grew to fill the small space we were hiding in.

Just before his oversized head could comically pop out of the chimney, Balty grabbed me in one hand like a more fabulous Fay Wray while punching his way out of the building with the other.

This was not the plan!

Luckily, Dingus Kong set me down on the street outside before pulverizing the front of the doomed Blómaggedon. Locals were screaming and running in all directions, so I averted my eyes from my twenty-foot-tall future brother-in-law's *very* proportionate cock and took off running down the alleyway alongside the flower shop.

May as well use the destruction as a distraction.

The back door was bolted shut, but there was a rickety wooden fire escape leading to an apartment above.

Unfortunately, the ladder was too high for me to reach, but then another hit from the supervillain officially known as Blunt Force knocked it to ground level for me.

Thanks, Baby Hulk!

I easefully clambered up the fire escape with what felt like record speed, pleased that all my vanity trips to the gym had paid off. Plastering myself to the timber-framed wall to stay out of sight, I cautiously peeked in the nearest window, finding a bedroom that looked lived in but was currently empty.

Grabbing a discarded terracotta pot from the sill, I waited for the next Hulk smash from Balty to toss it through the glass. Then I carefully slipped through the window and tiptoed across the bedroom, noticing my footsteps were oddly silent despite the glass littering the floor.

Another borrowed Wolfy power, perhaps?

Being a parasite is fun!

A sweep of the apartment revealed no lurking or captive supes, so I cautiously snuck downstairs, almost losing my footing each time the building shook.

"Baltasar Suarez!" a deep but feminine voice scolded. "Do I need to put you on ice until you calm down?"

"LET WOLFY GO!" Baby Hulk roared petulantly, and I continued to take advantage of his overgrown idiocy to reach the ground level undetected.

The back rooms of Blómaggedon were a wreck—independent of whatever damage Baltasar had wrought. It smelled moldy, with broken plant pots and random floral supplies haphazardly strewn about the suspiciously damp floor while a nearby electrical subpanel sent out tiny sparks.

That's a bit… concerning.

More determined than ever to rescue Wolfy from this volatile situation, I peered through the empty refrigerated coolers to spy on the scene up front.

My breath caught as I spotted my *inventus* tied to a chair, although exactly what was holding him in place was unclear through the double panes of filthy glass. I could see enough to know he was injured—judging by his slumped posture and what looked like blood pooling below his bound wrists.

I will kill them all.

His suit jacket had been removed—along with his sexy supe-killing gun and holster—but, as usual, the rest of his clothing looked impeccable.

Only my man could look this fit in such dire circumstances.

A young woman who looked too similar to Wolfy to be anyone other than Violentia was standing near him, although her attention was on the family drama unfolding across the room. Baltasar was still in Blunt Force mode, roaring into his mother's face. The infamous Glacial Girl was inexplicably dressed in her silver and white Lycra—although her head-covering mask was absent—and looked about two seconds away from putting her son in a time-out.

This family is so weird.

Assured that Baby Hulk wasn't in immediate danger, I began army crawling toward the doorway closest to Wolfy, desperately trying to come up with a solid rescue plan.

Yes, I had *some* powers—thanks to Wolfy—but I didn't know exactly what that entailed, or how to wield them properly. Seeing my *inventus* in peril was making me see red, but I was coherent enough to know I wasn't enough of a threat to these formidable supes.

But they *don't know that…*

Just as I was considering going full berserker, something looming amongst the plant pots caught my eye.

SomeONE.

Apocalypto Man was calmly seated in the corner, predatorily still behind his infamous mask as he watched me slink across the grimy floor.

Putain de bordel de merde…

I'm fucked.

CHAPTER 46
WOLFGANG

Being who I was—what I was created to be—meant that Death and I were well-acquainted. I'd watched the light leave another's eyes countless times, and while I'd come close to dying against particularly powerful supes before, I'd never *wished* for it like this before.

Please… make it stop.

The pain I was in was excruciating—pure ice in my veins—and I blamed myself for not being better prepared to face my mother.

I've truly lost my edge.

Glacial Girl had caught me off guard while we were in negotiations, brutally attacking with the full force of her powers until I was just shy of broken. Then she'd secured me to this chair with icy cuffs—the jagged edges of her creations tearing into my frostbitten skin every time I moved.

She was slowly freezing me from the inside out—punishing her oldest son for daring to claim his birthright without her permission.

For daring to make this family about something other than hatred and murder.

That she'd attacked me during a ceasefire was damning enough to get the council involved, but I doubted she'd let me live to tell the tale. Despite being my parents' favorite weapon, even I knew when I'd officially outlived my usefulness.

Because no one will dare challenge her again after she kills The Hand of Death.

In hindsight, none of her behavior was surprising, but some small part of me had stupidly hoped we could work out a compromise. Even if she felt she had to kill me to prove her supremacy, I *needed* to ensure my brothers would be spared before we battled.

Along with my inventus.

That Balty had shown up in Siglufjörður as Blunt Force did not bode well. However, as there was no sign of Simon, I had to trust my idiot brother had still managed to get him to safety first, like I'd instructed.

I hope.

Not for the first time, I inwardly berated myself for not confirming my mother's death—for *trusting* Violentia's tainted word that she was gone.

"How *could* you, Vi?" I quietly hissed as my helpless rage got the better of me. "We were a *team,* and you knew what they did to me when we were kids. You fucking *knew.*"

Violentia kept her gaze fixed on our mother and Balty. She showed no sign that she'd heard me, or that she was anything other than the brainwashed puppet she'd presented herself as since I arrived.

Are you still in there at all, Vi?

Realizing it was pointless to continue, I choked back everything I wanted to say to her, especially as there was still one Suarez nearby who was possibly watching me.

It hurt like hell to move, but I cautiously peered around Vi to the back room, where our *father* silently lorded over the scene in his full Apocalypto Man gear. I still couldn't be sure if he was actually under there—or alive at all—but hadn't dared to use my powers to 'probe' him and check.

I miss Simon's ridiculous way of speaking.

I just miss him.

And I hope he forgives me someday.

As if summoned by my depthless love, *Simon* suddenly appeared in my line of vision, wearing a signature velour tracksuit that was uncharacteristically filthy.

While facing off against Apocalypto Man.

Oh, my God!

I thought walking away from Simon as he slept—after giving him every piece of myself I could to remember me by—was the hardest thing I'd ever done. But watching my *inventus* face off with my father while being helpless to save him was so much worse.

The last thing I wanted to do was confirm any rumors my mother and sister might have heard about me. So I'd tamped down our bond since I arrived in Iceland, but it immediately flared to life at the sight of him—desperate to connect and give him a fighting chance.

Even if he has no hope of defeating my father.

"Vi, I'm *sorry*, okay?" I babbled, frantic to keep what limited awareness she had on *me* and not on the rogue half-normie in the next room. "I should have told you about my plans to take over the clan. I... I just didn't want you to be held responsible if anything went wrong."

It was the truth, and I only now realized I'd never bothered explaining it to her. Violentia was my partner in villainy, and not only because we were often assigned to jobs together. She was my sounding board, the yin to my yang—and I usually told her everything.

Just not this.

When she'd briefly disappeared after Harold Holt outed Butch and Xander's relationship to the masses on TV, I'd only been mildly concerned. If Vi had publicly reappeared at our mother's side, alliances would have been clear. But Glacial Girl showed up alone at Dead Man's Ravine for a showdown with Vortexio, and my sister stumbled home a day later with an alibi, so I never saw the connection.

Even when Violentia disappeared for good, I'd foolishly hoped for the best. Never in a million years would I have expected my sister to choose our terrible mother over me.

But I broke her trust first.

My gaze was riveted to the tense stand-off between Simon and Apocalypto Man, and for one horrific moment, I feared my father had already cryogenically frozen him.

Run, boss.

Please, just run.

Being *Simon*, of course, he didn't run. Instead, he took a bold step—not *away* from the powerful supervillain, but *toward* him.

What the fuck are you doing?!

"What the fuck is he doing?" Violentia echoed my thoughts, sounding oddly coherent as she finally spotted the tiny tyrant in the back room.

Before she could react—or alert our mother—Simon confidently strode to Apocalypto Man's chair, reached up, and *removed his mask.*

The BALLS on this man...

He must have somehow figured out it was safe while I was having a mini heart attack, as his actions only revealed that our father was as dead as I'd left him.

Thank. Fuck.

"Hey, you! What the *hell* are you do—" Violentia's shout turned into a shriek as she ducked, barely avoiding getting smacked in the face by the Supay mask Simon tossed at her like a demonic frisbee.

"What the *hell* is right!" he barked, tossing random debris aside while strutting into the room like he wasn't five feet nothing. "Did we not learn *anything* from the death of Smoldering Siren's *inventus*, hmm? If the council had known about Vortexio's hand in that, he would have been burned at the stake."

I could only gape, unsure *where* Simon was going with his monologue, but riveted all the same.

"But times were different then," he continued, sweeping his gaze over the legendary supervillains in the room as if they were nothing but cosplayers. "Nowadays, the council wishes to be informed of any plots against another's *inventus*. So you should rightfully assume they are well aware of the unsanctioned hostage situation happening here."

You crazy, ridiculous, ballsy, wonderful man.

I'd assumed Simon had been too out of it at the time to pay much attention to my call with Xander and Butch. However, he'd apparently been aware enough to pick up on the intel about Siren's doomed *inventus,* and squirrel it away for future use.

But that was Simon for you—always ten steps ahead of everyone else, including me.

And now I know why he carries himself like a supe.

"*You* have an *inventus?*" Violentia hissed, making direct eye contact with me for the first time since I'd last seen her months ago.

It was interesting she hadn't heard the news, but also highly possible that our mother was purposefully keeping her in the dark.

The better to control her.

Ignoring Vi's question, I refocused on sending my *inventus* the power he'd need to fight. Unfortunately, I'd lost so much blood, I was struggling to connect with him. Simon and I would have to physically *touch* to power-share at this point, and there was no way my mother would allow that if she knew the truth.

Sorry, boss—change of plans.

"Why the fuck would I have a *normie* for an *inventus?*" I huffed, already despising what I knew I had to do. "This is the random *assistant* I hired to find you, Vi—to bring you home."

"You've... been trying to bring me home?" Violentia murmured, looking weirdly confused by the concept.

What the fuck else would I be doing?

Apparently done with humoring her son's misguided rescue attempt, my mother casually flicked her wrist, trapping Baltasar within a cage of ice on the far side of the room before facing the newest attraction.

"How sweet, Wolfgang! You finally have a groupie," she called over, looking as unruffled as expected by Simon's sudden appearance and council-related threats. "Does your *assistant* know one touch from you will kill him?"

With that single question, my mother unwittingly showed her hand. By bringing Simon to the council soirée in Geneva, I'd not only publicly revealed my *inventus,* but showed that he could, in fact, safely touch me. That no supes in attendance—or on the council—had alerted her to this intel told me Glacial Girl had no allies.

At least, none worth worrying about.

Even though it broke something inside me, I shot a disgusted look at the love of my life before answering my mother. "You know I wouldn't tell a worthless *normie* my secrets—especially not a fucking cape chaser like him."

"What d-do you mean?" Simon's bravado evaporated, leaving behind a fragile young man who looked like the rug had been ripped out from under him yet again.

I'm so sorry for this, boss.

"Exactly what I fucking said," I scoffed. "I hired you—temporarily—to help me find Violentia. She's been found, so your assistance is no longer needed."

Even though I need you like oxygen.

"I… I thought we had something *special,* Wolfgang," he sniffled, and my heart officially shattered from the pure anguish in his expression. Pain I'd put there. "You told me I was your *inventus*... your soul mate."

You are.

Sliding on my usual mask of impassivity—the mask *Simon* alone had taught me how to remove—I glanced at Vi. "Fuck, he's annoying. Maybe I *should* touch him... put us *all* out of our misery."

Violentia stared down at me with a practiced mask of her own, and for a moment, I feared I'd shown my hand to the enemy as well.

Last chance, sis.

Something almost recognizable flickered to life in her amber eyes before she looked at our mother. "You know, I haven't watched a good normie death in a while. Not since Xanny shacked up with a *hero.*"

She punctuated her statement by spitting on the damp floor, which sparked on contact, for some reason.

That's... weird.

My concerns about the building's electrical system vanished as my mother excitedly clapped her hands together. "Ooh, yes! A tiny thing like him should explode nicely. You know what to do, Vi-Vi."

Like the good little puppet she was, Violentia immediately grabbed Simon, yanking his arms behind his back and digging her long black nails into his flesh so deeply, he cried out.

Stop touching my things!

A low growl escaped me before I could swallow it down. Thanks to Balty pounding against his icy prison, my mother seemed to have missed the outburst, but Vi's attention snapped to my face before a slow, villainous smile spread across hers.

The moment of truth.

Violentia held my gaze, and I prayed to any god or devil who would listen that *my sister*—not Ultra Violent—would be the one to come out and play.

Because, right now, I need my family.

"So you think you're worthy of being The Hand of Death's *inventus*?" Vi hissed in Simon's ear as she roughly dragged him toward me. "What could *you* possibly give *him* to match his formidable power?"

"Love," Simon quietly replied, his gaze locked on mine and holding so much sorrow, I considered tearing my hands off just to wrap my arms around him.

He'd probably swoon over a bloody gesture like that.

I wanted to remind him I loved him back—that I would love him until, and beyond, my dying day—but I needed to see this charade through.

Just until we can touch.

My sister made a derisive sound in her throat. "How pathetically *human*. Let's see if your precious *love* can save the day…" With barely any effort, Vi lifted Simon's tiny frame and tossed him into my lap.

And then the worst moment of my life repeated itself.

The instant Simon touched me, he stiffened, his face draining of color and pretty green eyes rolling into the back of his head as the life left his body.

"No," I whispered, straining against the jagged ice of my restraints as he slid off my lap, momentarily blinded by the pain.

Nonononoonoooo…

The next thing I knew, Simon was lying motionless at my feet, with one hand loosely resting on my ankle.

Please, no.

CHAPTER 47
WOLFGANG

"Well, shit," Vi muttered as she grimaced down at Simon's crumpled form, confirming that she *had* been counting on a different outcome.

Which is cold comfort at the moment.

"Oh, that was marvelous!" Mother chortled as Balty roared and rattled his cage, before her brow furrowed. "But why didn't he explode? Don't tell me you've lost your *touch*, Wolfgang?"

I was vengeance. I could feel the figurative wings of my ancestors unfurling beneath my skin—my fangs and claws lengthening as I prepared to tear this woman to shreds.

I won't be satisfied until I'm bathing in Glacial Girl's blood.

Before I could attack, I felt movement against my ankle—a featherlight touch as Simon began covertly sliding his hand up my pant leg.

Oh, thank fuck, he's alive!

But what the hell is he doing?

No one else seemed to notice he'd survived, and when I felt his delicate fingers wrap around the DNA-infused knife I kept hidden there, I realized he'd outsmarted everyone yet again.

I am going to make him come so hard for this performance.

"Well, Mother," I growled, keeping her attention on me. "You've been icing me for hours. That tends to put a damper on one's powers."

She waved a dismissive hand. "So dramatic. You behave as though your life was so rough when, in reality, your father and I gave you everything you wanted."

And nothing I needed.

"Wait…" I interrupted her delusions to peer down at Simon with a dramatically confused expression. "I don't… I don't think we're dealing with just a normie here."

That got her attention. My mother was a classist to the bone, so a *human* manifesting as a worthy opponent would be seen as a personal insult.

Just imagine how she'd handle learning our origin story.

"Let me see," she huffed, shoving her way past Violentia to reach Simon.

Crouching next to his tiny body, she unceremoniously rolled him over—which gave Simon the opportunity to stab my knife through Glacial Girl's boot and directly into her femoral vein.

"YOU LITTLE SHIT!" she screeched, landing on her ass in a way that would have been hilarious were I not still worried about Simon's safety.

While she was too strong of a supe to be taken down by a single shot of my power—especially as she yanked out the knife immediately—the blow had been enough to make *her* powers falter.

The instant the icy cuffs binding my wrists melted, I snatched Simon and sprinted for the gaping hole Balty had created in the building. I could see my brother successfully punching his way to freedom, and had to trust that he could get out of there on his own.

Because now that Simon's back in my arms, I'm never letting him go again.

A wall of solid ice materialized to block our escape just as my mother's signature evil villain cackle filled the ruined space.

I turned to face the threat, releasing Simon only so I could shove him behind me. He clung to my shirt, pressing his face against my back through the fabric and inhaling greedily—as if he'd been *starved* for me.

The feeling is mutual, boss.

Glacial Girl had ascended a pile of rubble—all the better to glare down her nose at us, like a haughty queen.

"Leaving so soon, Wolfy?" she crooned, although I noticed she seemed shaky on her perch. "It's impolite not to introduce your own mother to your secret *inventus*, hmm?"

"He's no secret," I laughed, feeling fresh power flow through my veins as our connection restored itself. "Simon and I were the talk of the town at the last council event in Geneva. Funny how the news didn't find its way to you…"

Her icy gaze narrowed, but it was Violentia who spoke first.

"You lied to me," she hissed, her vitriol firmly aimed at our mother. "You told me the council unanimously supported you in the fight to reclaim your throne. And you said Wolfy planned to kill the rest of us so no one else in the family could challenge him…"

What the fuck?

"Excuse me?!" Simon shouted, appearing beside me to boldly glare at Glacial Girl. "How dare you turn the sweet, caring child you were given into a monster—through years of abuse and damaging rumors—simply for your own benefit. And *you.*" He pointed an accusing finger at Vi. "You should have fucking known better than to believe that shit."

I placed my hand on Simon's shoulder, preparing to shield him again should Violentia attack. There was a high probability she would, considering my sister was infamous for her violent temper and complete lack of self-control.

Traits I could only ever vicariously enjoy through her.

To my astonishment, Vi submissively dropped her gaze. "You're right," she murmured. "I should have known better, because I know *Wolfy* better than that. I'm… sorry." She lifted her gaze to mine again. "I'm so fucking sorry."

I blinked in surprise. Yes, my sister was the closest thing I had to a friend before Simon barreled into my life, but I'd *never* seen her stand down to anyone other than our parents and the equally powerful supes they demanded we show respect to.

Tiny tyrant, indeed.

"Enough of this!" Glacial Girl barked, casually flicking her wrist to entrap Vi in a solid ice prison as well—although it seemed less substantial than usual. "I didn't raise you brats to *like* each other. *Every* supe is the enemy until proven otherwise. Your family only gets a pass if they prove useful."

What a horrible mentality to live by.

"Maybe for you," I growled, the protective instincts I had for my siblings going haywire. "Imagine how much more powerful our clan could have been if we were united by *trust* instead of *fear*."

It was almost humorous how genuinely *puzzled* by my suggestion my mother looked, but before she could reply, Simon cut in again.

"Oh, but the infamous Glacial Girl could never have allowed that!" He laughed airily. "Because then her children would have realized how much more impressive than her they were. Why, I'd wager *you* have more power in a single finger than your mother does, Wolfy. Which means… so do I."

And with that, Simon raised his middle finger and blew my mother a kiss.

I'm keeping him forever.

"HOW DARE YOU!" Glacial Girl roared—the air inside the flower shop growing frigid as she stomped her way off her dais of debris to join us peasants on the disgustingly damp floor once again. "I don't care what drunken supe fucked your whore of a mother. No normie speaks to me that way!"

"HOW DARE YOU CALL MY FATHER A DRUNK!" Simon shouted back, although he was practically dancing with glee.

I hope you have a plan here, boss.

Besides going out with a bang.

Both Baltasar and Violentia were making headway on busting out of their respective cages, but I worried neither would free themselves in time to join forces with us.

And the only reason we haven't been caged is because Mother enjoys toying with her food.

While I may have been able to take down the indomitable Glacial Girl with an ambush, I was currently at a disadvantage, even with my *inventus* by my side.

Just as I began to worry Simon's lack of fear was about to get us killed, I noticed something strange. As my mother pulsed with power—liquid ice forming at her fingertips, blanketing the surrounding air in a deadly mist—*sparks* crackled at her feet.

That doesn't usually happen.

Following the source, my gaze drifted in the direction Simon had first appeared from, only to notice the thick electrical wire he'd casually tossed aside as he entered the room.

A live wire.

You delicious little brat.

I knew enough about how my mother's powers operated to recognize the moment she was about to strike. Waiting until the cloud of moisture she'd gathered reached its peak, I yelled for both my siblings to stay back from the ice walls surrounding them before jumping onto a nearby pile of wooden siding with Simon in tow.

My mother's screams rattled what remained of the building as her body was racked with an obscene amount of voltage. Simon cackled at the display, and I couldn't help wondering if the inspiration for this booby trap had come from the demise of a certain 'mean green mother from outer space' in *Little Shop of Horrors*.

Glacial Girl had no idea who she was messing with.

Unfortunately, my mother successfully stopped the current flowing through her by vaporizing the moisture she'd released. Straightening to her full height—noticeably shaky—she zeroed in on us with murder in her eyes.

Looks like it's time to play.

Sliding off the table, I faced the woman who'd taught me how powerful a weapon *fear* was—especially when used against someone weaker than you. Without her icy powers, we were on a level playing field, because with hand-to-hand combat, well…

Let's just say I have the upper Hand.

"How did I know it would come to this?" my mother sneered, apparently uninterested in making amends, even on her deathbed. "That my oldest child would become so drunk on the promise of power, he plotted against his own parents, just so he could steal their throne."

I scoffed. "Is that really what you believe? I assure you, mother, the last thing I've wanted is more power, because all it's ever meant is more blood on my hands. Just because I was a good little killer didn't mean I always *enjoyed* doing it. I would be more than happy to never kill again."

A disgruntled sound had me glancing sideways to find Simon looking displeased with that proclamation.

He really is a natural born clan leader.

"Well, maybe for the occasional date night," I amended.

"Good man," Simon cooed. "Now proceed with making this ice queen pay for everything she did to you."

Yes, boss.

A blast of firepower suddenly rocked the building, instantly melting the thick ice walling us in. Then, a single beam of sunlight illuminated a hero gliding to land in our midst—bathed in a heavenly, golden glow as if he truly were the chosen one of our time.

Barf.

"Looks like I arrived just in time!" Captain Masculine cheerfully announced, which sounded a lot like one of his canned greetings from back in his TV days.

He probably doesn't know how to turn the hero thing off.

"And me! Jesus CHRIST, baby, we can't keep flying over the ocean like this. My *enormous* cock wasn't made for that level of wind speed. Maybe you should check to make sure I didn't break something important…"

Hello, Xander.

Butch awkwardly cleared his throat, and I would've bet money he was blushing scarlet underneath his headgear. "Okay… what do we have here?" He quickly scanned the room. "Three rescues and two prisoners?"

"We don't need rescuing, *baby*," Simon grumbled, hopping off the table to join me. "Wolfy was just about to make his mother's head explode like a watermelon, and Violentia appears to be on our side again… I suppose."

I couldn't help noticing he didn't seem overly pleased with that statement, but the fact he made it—for *me*—warmed my heart all the same.

My inventus.

All mine.

As if he instinctively understood who the boss was around here, Butch nodded and obediently melted the ice surrounding both Baltasar and Violentia. Balty quickly returned to his usual size, politely cupping his junk until Xander tossed him a pair of sweatpants he'd flown across the ocean just for this purpose.

Baby Hulk goes through a lot of clothes.

During this exchange, my mother had started to inch toward the back room, but Vi blocked her path with a firm shake of her head—clearly choosing a side now that she had all the facts.

Blood is thicker than murder.

Butch had also zeroed in on our opponent in that impressively predatory way of his. "Would you like me to finish Glacial Girl for you, Wolfy? It would be one less thing on your plate."

When I simply stared at the hero in confusion, he shrugged. "We've all heard how Simon schooled Balty and the twins because none of us have ever acknowledged how much you do to protect this family."

It was my turn to blush, but when I turned to Simon again, the unfiltered *love* in his eyes made the embarrassment worthwhile.

"I simply think everyone should appreciate you as much as I do." He smiled encouragingly. "If you truly *want* to kill your mother, go ahead, but remember, you don't *have* to do everything alone."

I don't have to do everything alone…

While I knew Simon would consider it foreplay for me to kill Glacial Girl in front of him, I wasn't relishing the idea. Yes, I deserved my revenge—and my mother deserved to feel the full force of my long overdue rage. But the idea of finishing her as The Hand of Death—the fearsome, emotionless murderer *she'd* molded me into—left a sour taste in my mouth.

It didn't have to be this way.

"Actually…" I cleared my throat, feeling so incredibly out of my element, but appreciating it all the same. "I *would* like to delegate this task... but I think Xanny should do it." My brother looked surprised, so I elaborated, "After all, our parents planned to kill *you* almost since you were born."

"That's right!" he hissed, his eyes narrowing on Glacial Girl as Doctor Antihero came out to play. "Looks like I wasn't a dud after all, hmm? I wonder... whose powers should I pull from to end you, Mother?"

Taking Simon's hand in mine—and giving it a squeeze—I gestured for Balty and Vi to follow us out of the building.

"I'm sorry for what I said back there..." I awkwardly mumbled to my *inventus*, releasing him only long enough to retrieve my suit jacket and gun from where both had been tossed by my mother. "I didn't mean any of it."

He snickered, displaying no regrets—or fucks—as usual. "No harm done, *mon chou*. I'm well aware that I own you for life."

Yes, you certainly do.

As we passed the other bonded pair in the family, I paused to give Xander a hot tip. "Cover her in ice water, trust me. And make sure neither of you are touching the floor when you do."

And with that, I *handed* off my responsibilities, and took the rest of the day off.

After all, I have an inventus *to spoil.*

EPILOGUE
SIMON - ONE MONTH LATER

It's not easy being a mafia queen—but someone's gotta do it.

I sighed heavily as my phone buzzed on the patio table beside me, but dutifully removed my sunnies and squinted down at the screen.

No rest for the wicked, I suppose.

The Mouthy One: *What do y'all think about a pirate-themed cruise ship wedding? Clothing optional.*

The Token Hero: *Why can none of our conversations stay private?*

The Dumb One: *Only if I can be a BUTT pirate!*

Oh, well, there's my opening.

> **My, my, Baby Hulk, you seem quite fixated on butt sex for someone proclaiming how NOT-gay he is at every turn.**

The Dumb One: *Straight people have butt sex.*

> *Not like we do.*

The Mouthy One: *Definitely not. Tell 'em, sweetheart.*

The Token Hero: *I am not getting into this.*

The Mouthy One: *You were more than happy to get INTO it last night. [peach emoji] [villain emoji]*

An amused snort brought my attention to the snack of a man stretched out like a buffet on the lounge chair to my right.

"You named yourself **The Mafia Queen** in the group chat?" Wolfy asked, although we both knew that was a rhetorical question not requiring an answer.

Facts are facts.

I loved how he was following along with **The Rabble** on his phone, but making no move to join in the conversation.

Good.

Because he's retired.

Of course, Wolfy wasn't truly retired. Being clan leader of one of the most powerful supe families wasn't the sort of job that ever stopped, but I'd insisted he back off a bit.

It is a family affair, after all.

Soon after our Icelandic adventure, I urged Wolfy to call for a family meeting to delegate more to his siblings. It was an uncomfortable conversation for him to have—not only because he *enjoyed* taking care of others, but because he'd been taught to never show weakness.

As I'd expected, everyone was more than happy to help.

Butch took over most of the bullshit meetings with other clans, as he could fly anywhere quickly and had experience being diplomatic. In fact, a major reason we decided Captain

Masculine was the man for the job was that he was least likely to murder an important clan leader in a fit of rage.

*Gold stars for our **Token Hero**!*

Having a *hero* represent a notoriously villainous family also demonstrated how the Suarez clan didn't care about outdated labels like *hero* or *villain*… or even *normie.*

Not that anyone knows exactly what I am yet.

After our discovery of the cave paintings, Xander tested my DNA against his, Butch's, and Wolfy's—since we all had *inventus* bonds. Even Smoldering Siren let her future son-in-law *respectfully* cut off some of her hair for testing.

The results revealed we all shared a rare genetic mutation. This was presumably the same gene that allowed us to power-share, or—in my case—simply mimic the power of whatever supe I'd imprinted on.

How lucky Wolfy is to have a parasite like me!

Further testing revealed *all* the Suarez siblings had this gene, which implied it came from both parents. After Xander properly killed off Glacial Girl, he'd taken a few samples for science before Butch torched her body into ash.

Let's see her return from the dead this time

The same was done with Apocalypto Man—since his corpse was at the ready—and the results showed the rare gene was *only* from his side.

Curiouser and curiouser.

Harold Holt's body was exhumed to prove he *didn't* possess the gene—which could explain why he never bonded with Butch's mother.

The legal process to exhume Smoldering Siren's *inventus*—Franco Marisi—was already underway, but it was safe to assume the villain-turned-hero known as Iron Axe had this mutation as well.

What this all meant was still a mystery, and we were keeping the supe heritage bombshell under wraps until we knew more.

In the meantime, that's where Xander was focusing his efforts on behalf of the family. Along with Dr. Lorenzo Torres-Maldonado, our resident scientist was researching our mysterious origins—while preserving evidence of the Argentinian cave paintings in the Suarez family's private archives.

Knowledge is power, after all.

Baltasar still readily served as the family gossip hound—digging up dirt for us to use to our advantage. Apparently, he excelled at this, as there was just something about him that encouraged loose lips to flap when he was around.

It might be his big, dumb face and air of permanent confusion.

Baby Hulk also surprised everyone by offering to be married off so we could align ourselves with another equally powerful household.

The East Coast Salah family is looking like a good match.

Violentia was more than happy to continue on in her previous role as the batshit crazy family enforcer—even if we didn't let her unalive people as often as she was accustomed to.

Ultra Violent's first task—and test—was identifying all the lesser supes who'd sided with her mother, and bringing them in for 'questioning.' Depending on how their interrogations went, they were disposed of or turned into foot soldiers for the rightful leader of the Suarez clan.

As Wolfy would say, you're either with us, or dead.

I was pleased to see the effort Vi was putting into earning back Wolfy's trust while doing my very best to stay out of it—aside from a subtle threat here and there.

Because if she hurts him again, I will kill her myself.

I'd taken over much of the day-to-day business dealings—the scheduling, the mildly threatening emails, the nonstop task of keeping this unruly family in line. I actually found it to be thrilling, since *I* excelled at bossing people around.

It's definitely a superpower!

This all allowed Wolfy to step back—to be the face of the organization you really didn't want to see. From now on, if The Hand of Death paid you a visit, it meant you had fucked up.

Which has truly cut down on the number of fuck-ups we deal with.

The twins were exempt from most family duties until they finished school, but Wolfy said he was working on a post-graduation project for Gabe and Dre. When I asked for more details, he rudely refused, but I edged him half to death until he spilled.

And yes, I meant it like that.

Apparently, Xander had tracked down a local supe with ancient DNA, and Wolfy figured if anyone could get in their head to learn more, it was the combined power of Shock and Awe.

When I hesitantly asked if this supe could be my father, Wolfy simply said he didn't want to get my hopes up.

I suppose we'll leave it at that for now.

Speaking of letting sleeping dogs lie, my murder baby and I were currently in Villefranche, enjoying a mini-vacation by our infinity pool. Wolfy had purchased the cliff house from my mother for a sum so exorbitant, she forgave him for every past, present, and future sin, forever and ever, until the end of time.

Amen.

And because expensive gifts were his love language, Wolfy sold his family's existing Parisian property and purchased an entire apartment building of *my* choosing, complete with a view of the Eiffel Tower.

A simple second home.

In fact, my most recent self-assigned professional task was to sell every one of the family properties, besides the Berlin gallery and the compound outside of Big City. We didn't need the money. I simply wanted to rid Wolfy of all inherited obligations—so he could truly start fresh as the clan leader this family deserved.

And he—more than anyone—deserves it as well.

At another family meeting, we collectively decided to burn down the Suarez family compound and rebuild. This was a new start—for all of us—and an opportunity for the twins to work with a local architect and put their industrial design knowledge to practical use.

I also may or may not have requested a secret lair on the premises.

The infamous archives were below ground and fireproof, so after removing anything else of value from the main house, we had ourselves a barbecue on the Fourth of July.

How very American of us.

I couldn't believe I'd *willingly* returned to Big City—or to the States at all—but true love makes one do all sorts of crazy things.

Like making lifelong commitments that go beyond parasitic bonds.

"Simon..." Wolfy's smooth tone had taken on that growly, angry edge that made me harder than a rock. "Why is Zion Salah texting me GIFs of wolves wearing tuxes?"

That loose-lipped lizard!

I slapped my oversized sunnies back on to hide my face from his searing gaze. "Mmm... I'm not sure. Perhaps Xander blabbed his nudist butt pirate wedding cruise idea to him as well?"

The truth was, I'd decided to marry Wolfy—something that was so out of character for my formerly commitment-phobic self to be almost laughable. And because I was as extra as extra could be, I'd also decided to make it a *surprise* wedding.

Sexy kidnapper vibes!

Lovestruck ally that he was, Butch had helped me appeal to the United Super Nations to expedite my request to marry a supe. Since I was half-supe anyway—and the restrictions on supes and normies marrying would inevitably be lifted once word of our origins got out—my case was unanimously approved.

It helps to have—and embody—friends in high places.

"Tell me what you know," Wolfy growled, suddenly blocking the sunlight as he loomed over me most deliciously.

Tossing my sunnies aside, I boldly met his gaze while tracing a toe up his muscular leg—loving how much gorgeous golden-brown skin was on display with his swim briefs.

The better to mark up, my dear.

"I don't think I will," I brattily replied, shivering in anticipation as he cocked an eyebrow at my disobedience. "Although you're welcome to *spank* the truth out of me."

I'll get that spanking if it's the last thing I do.

With a smirk that almost melted my hot pink bikini bottoms, Wolfy grabbed me around the waist and tossed me over his shoulder like some prize of war.

Here we go!

"I know you're just trying to trick me into getting what you want, Simon," he chuckled, giving my arse a tidy smack that only teased.

He strode through the living room—past Twoey warming herself in the sunlight pouring through the wall of windows—and continued on to the bedroom where we'd first properly touched.

Maybe he'll let me give him another blowie in the onesie someday…

All thoughts of 'Captain Masculine's Favorite Brat' vanished as I was unceremoniously tossed onto the mattress. Wolfy circled the bed before crouching down and retrieving a mysterious metal box I'd never noticed before.

"The problem is…" he continued, rising to stand and setting the box on the bed, "I enjoy giving you what you want too much to ever say no."

Good man.

"What's in the box, Wolfy?" I shimmied out of my bathing suit and gave myself an encouraging stroke—not that I needed the encouragement. "An engagement ring? An engagement *cock* ring, like Xander claims to have given Butch?"

Knowing him, I don't doubt it.

Wolfy narrowed his eyes at me and, for a moment, I wondered if he was onto my secret plan to kidnap and drag him to the altar. But then he used his fingerprint to open the box before pulling out a paddle.

A *leather* paddle.

"Merde..." I whispered, so much feral need shooting down my spine, I was sure he could feel it through the bond. "Is that for me?"

Wolfy graced me with a villainous smile that still held so much love, I almost swooned. "Yes. This box is full of very expensive toys I bought just for you, because if anyone deserves to be paddled with the finest Italian leather, it's my *inventus.*"

He really gets me.

"You truly know the way to a man's heart," I murmured, turning and wiggling my juicy arse in his direction.

He was *mine*—my *inventus*, my precious cream puff, my loyal dog who willingly let me lead. Wolfy gave me everything I'd only dreamed of, including the three little words that only mattered when they came from him.

"Let's play, boss."

With pleasure, murder baby.

Thirsty for more of the super smutty Suarez clan?

Sign up for my newsletter for the BONUS epilogue: **Yes Sir, Sorry Sir**, and preorder Balty's story: **Putting Out for a Hero** (Ignore the Amazon date! I always move them up, promise.)

REVIEWS

If you have enjoyed **Gentlemen Prefer Villains,** please leave reviews! It helps other readers find my work, which helps me as an indie author. *Thank you!*

Amazon
Goodreads
Bookbub

But don't stop there: Tag me in your reviews, stories, edits, videos, and fan art on social. I love to share these posts with my followers!

VILLAINOUS THINGS PLAYLIST

Please enjoy the Spotify playlist that inspired the Villainous Things series (and let me know if you have a song to add):

WOLFY & SIMON PRINTS AVAILABLE

LINK TO ORDER PRINTS ON THE
BOOKS BY C. PAGE

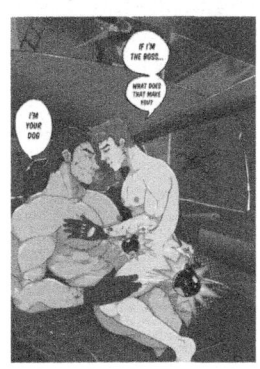

BOOKS BY C. ROCHELLE

Looking for signed paperbacks, N/SFW art prints & bookplates? My NEW store is now live at **C-Rochelle.com/shop** (and **Patreon** members get 20% off art prints plus extra swag and personalized inscriptions in their signed books!)

VILLAINOUS THINGS - SUPERHERO/VILLAIN MM ROMANCE (COMING SOON TO AUDIBLE):

Not All Himbos Wear Capes *(sign up for the newsletter to get the Only Good Boys Get to Top Their Xaddys bonus epilogue)*

Gentlemen Prefer Villains *(sign up for the newsletter to get the Yes Sir, Sorry Sir bonus epilogue)*

Putting Out for a Hero *(sign up for the newsletter to get the Idiots in Love bonus epilogue)*

Enter the Multi-Vers (the twins)

Villainous Book 5 (reunion book)

Want More Villainous Tales? The evil author is already scheming multiple spin-offs!

MONSTROUSLY MYTHIC SERIES (ALSO ON AUDIBLE):

The 12 Hunks of Herculeia (Herculeia Duet, Book 1)

Herculeia the Hero (Herculeia Duet, Book 2) *(sign up for the newsletter for the bonus epilogue: Three Heads Are Better Than One)*

Herculeia: Complete Duet + Bonus Content *(includes Calm Down Monster-Fucker, Three Heads Are Better Than One, & the Thanksgiving Special: Get Stuffed, plus UNcensored art)*

More Monstrously Mythic Tales:

Valhalla is Full of Hunks (Iola's story)

THE YAGA'S RIDERS TRILOGY (ALSO ON AUDIBLE):

Rise of the Witch

A Witch Out of Time

Call of the Ride

The Yaga's Riders: Complete Trilogy + Bonus Content *(The Asa Baby Christmas Special & the Too Peopley Valentine's Day Special)*

More Yaga's Riders Tales:

A Song of Saints and Swans *(Anthia spin-off novella, which includes From the Depths & the Halloween Special: It's Just a Bunch of Va Ju-Ju Voodoo)*

WINGS OF DARKNESS + LIGHT TRILOGY:

Shadows Spark

Shadows Smolder

Shadows Scorch

Wings of Darkness + Light: The Complete Trilogy + Bonus Content *(Oversized Cupids V-Day Special, The Second Coming Easter Special, & the Sexy Little Devil Halloween Specials Pt. 1 & Pt. 2)*

More from the Wings Universe:

Death by Vanilla (Gage origin story novella)

CURRENT/UPCOMING ANTHOLOGIES:

Creepy Court: A Monster Mall anthology (coming Friday, October 13th)

And there will be a bonus Herculeia holiday special in the forthcoming **Snow, Lights, & Monster Nights** charity anthology (coming December 31st - preorder link going live soon!)

ABOUT THE AUTHOR

C. Rochelle here! I'm a naughty but sweet, introverted, Aquarius weirdo who believes a sharp sense of humor is the sexiest trait, loves shaking my booty to Prince, and have never met a cheese I didn't like. Oh, and I write spicy paranormal/monster Why Choose + MM, MFF & MMF romance with dark, naughty humor. #loveislove

Want More?

- **Join my Clubhouse of Smut on Patreon**
- **Subscribe to my newsletter at C-Rochelle.com**
- **Join my Little Sinners Facebook group**
- **Stalk me in all the places on Linktree**

AUTHOR'S NOTE & ACKNOWLEDGMENTS

Okay, so… I did *not* expect Not All Himbos Wear Capes to take off (heh) like it did, or for the *readers* to decide on Wolfgang for the next book (I'd originally planned to just follow the adventures of Xander & Butch), but I am beyond thankful for you maniacs. While I started my author journey in polyamorous Why Choose & monster romance, I truly think I've found my calling with MM, and can't wait to bring you more in this world!

An enormous (as big as the size difference between Wolfy + Simon), thank you to everyone who read Himbos. Not only my existing readers who trusted that I would write an MM romance with the same sweet & spicy care as the MM within my Why Choose books, but to the brand spanking new readers who discovered me through my gay supes. Thank you for taking a chance on this little smut engine that could, and for inspiring me to keep going with this series.

Thank you to my alpha readers—authors Cora Rose, Lily Mayne, Ariel Dawn, and Crea Reitan (can't wait to meet your mom!), and my long-suffering grammar police Lindsay Hamilton and Michaella Dieter. Extra sloppy (spit-kink-style) kisses to Lily for checking my British English, Kitty Siberia for checking my German, and Florence H. for checking Simon's expletive-laden, slutty French.

To my Clubhouse of Smut on Patreon—thank you for continuing to cheer me on through the advanced chapters, NSFW art, cover designs, and all the Wolfy/Simon (and unrelated) snacks and rambles I share. Some might call it excessive, but we have a good time in there.

An extra smutty shout-out to my Va Ju-Ju Voodoo Queens: Adrienne, BobbiJo, Elizabeth R., Elizabeth Z., Emily, Fawn, Kaitlyn, Kayla, Kaylah, Kelly, Kristina, Kyla, Lauren, Melissa, Natasha, Stephanie, Taylor, and Tiffany. Thank you for supporting my author journey in this way!

Some lecherous love to my author friends—whether monsterly horndogs, polyam peddlers, or MM lovers—I can always count on you for inappropriate memes, NSFW art commissions being passed around like candy, legitimate industry know-how, and real-life support. I appreciate you lovelies more than I can say.

And as always, extra butt pats and sloppy kisses to my ARC and Street Team! I appreciate every bit o' hype you loud, proud Weird-Ho's can spare for me and my dirty little books.

Love is freakin' love, y'all!

GLOSSARY

While many people have gone over this book to find typos and other mistakes, we are only human. **If you spot an error, please do NOT report it to Amazon.**

I *want* **to hear from you if there's an issue, so I can fix it.** Send me an email at **crochelle.author@gmail.com** or **use the form** found pinned in my FB group or in my link in bio on TT & IG.

GLOSSARY NOTE: Gentlemen Prefer Villains is an international romp, featuring locations and characters where English is not the first language. Non-English words are written phonetically and italicized. Please use your Kindle translate feature or reference the handy glossary below for definitions.

A NOTE ON SIMON-SPEAK: Simon was born in France - to a Parisian mother who marries well and often - and has lived and traveled throughout Europe. While he's fluent in French (several languages, actually), he chooses to only access it when he's cursing on the streets or getting freaky in the sheets. Otherwise, he's speaking English, with a decidedly British flavor to it.

GLOSSARY

As the author, I did my best to have my characters sound authentic - and brought in British, French, and German authors/readers to check my work - but if something's way off, please contact me directly. Please also keep in mind that this is a work of fiction, people speak uniquely in the real world, and our tiny tyrant especially does whatever the fuck he wants.

SLANG NOTE: There is always a bit of slang peppered into my writing. When in doubt, use Google, or contact me using the methods above if you truly believe it's a typo.

Amuse-bouche *(French):* a small savory item of food served as an appetizer before a meal.
Arschgeige *(German):* Idiot (literally translates to ass fiddle/violin).
Arschloch *(German):* Asshole.
Asado *(Spanish):* The technique (cooking on an open fire/grill) and the social event of having or attending a barbecue in various South American countries.
Arse *(British English):* Ass
Au contraire, mon chéri *(French):* On the contrary, my dear.
Au revoir *(French):* Goodbye (and good wishes - which is ironic with how Simon uses it).
Avale *(French):* Swallow.
Baise-moi à mort *(French):* Fuck me to death (swoon!).
Baise-moi fort *(French):* Fuck me hard.
Blasé *(French):* Bored/disinterested.
Blóm(aggedon) *(Icelandic):* Flower.
Bonjour *(French):* Hello.
Boot *(British English):* The back compartment of a car. What we Americans call the trunk.
Bordel de merde *(French):* For fuck's sake (lit. Shit brothel).
Brut rosé *(French):* A medium-dry, slightly sweet, and fruity sparkling wine. Bunny's favorite.

GLOSSARY

Buenos días *(Spanish):* Hello (lit. Good day / morning, but can be used as a greeting).
C'est bon *(French):* That's good.
C'est des conneries *(French):* This is bullshit.
Capitán *(Spanish):* Captain.
Carte blanche *(French):* Complete freedom to act as one wishes or thinks best.
Casse-toi *(French):* Fuck off.
(Château) Scélérat *(French):* (Large country house of) Villains.
Chorizo *(Spanish):* A cured, or hard, sausage made from coarsely chopped pork.
Choux à la crème *(French):* Classic French pastries made out of choux pastry buns filled with a cream. (See also: **Mon Chou**.)
Chuffed *(British English):* Very pleased.
Ciao *(Italian):* Goodbye (at least to the French. Italians use it for hello, too).
Cueva de las Manos *(Spanish):* The Cave of Hands
Da steppt der Bär *(German):* A place where you're guaranteed to have a great time (lit. 'The bear is dancing here / there')
Du vollidiot hast es ihm verschwiegen. Was hast du dir nur dabei gedacht, du verdammter, wichser! Er könnte verletzt werden! *(German):* "You didn't tell him, you fucking idiot! What were you thinking? He could get hurt!" (You know Erich's mad if he's daring to yell at The Hand of Death)
Eau de *(French):* A perfumed liquid (lit. Water of).
EDM: Electronic dance music.
Enchanté/Enchantée *(French):* Delighted (and, being French, it's either masculine or feminine, depending on who's talking… or who you're talking to… or…)
Entrées *(French):* The main course.
Fils de pute *(French):* Son of a bitch.
Flaugnarde *(French):* A baked French dessert with fruit arranged in a buttered dish and covered with a thick flan-like batter.

GLOSSARY

Gesen *(Japanese):* Arcade (lit. Game center).
Grand-maman/grand-papa *(French):* Grandmother/grandfather.
Hallo *(German):* Hello.
Ikebana *(Japanese):* The Japanese art of flower arrangement. There is SO much more to it than this, but I recommend learning more on your own (and even taking a class)!
Inventus *(Latin):* Find/discover. Perfect passive participle of invenio and the word used to describe supe soulmates.
Jäger/Jägermeister *(German):* Herbal liquor (lit. Hunt Master or master of the hunt).
Je ne sais [COCK] *(French):* **Je ne sais quoi** means a quality that cannot be described or named easily.
Je t'aime à la folie *(French):* I'm madly in love with you/I love you like crazy.
Je te veux *(French):* I want you.
Kamikaze *(Japanese):* Pilot-guided explosive missiles/aircraft flown in suicide attacks during WWII (lit. Divine wind/spirit wind).
Kobun *(Japanese):* The followers in a **Yakuza** clan (lit. Protégés/apprentices; child status)
Konnichiwa *(Japanese):* Hello (lit. Good day/good afternoon).
Krass *(German):* A general exclamation (eg. whoa!).
La petite mort *(French):* The post-orgasm state of being (lit. The little death).
Les petites rues *(French):* The little streets.
Listo o no *(Spanish):* Ready or not.
Loo *(British English):* Toilet/Bathroom.
Magnifique *(French):* Magnificent
Maman *(French):* Mother.
Marunouchi *(Japanese):* A commercial district in Tokyo.
Matcha *(Japanese):* A form of green tea made from a powdered version of the actual tea leaves.
Merci *(French):* Thank you (the only proper response to accepting Wolfy's spit into your mouth).

GLOSSARY

Merde *(French):* Shit (expletive).
Mi lobo *(Spanish):* My wolf.
Minka *(Japanese):* Houses constructed in any one of several traditional Japanese building styles (lit. House of the people).
Modus operandi/M.O. *(Latin):* A particular method of doing something, especially one that is well-established.
Mon chou *(French):* A term of endearment that is used to refer to someone you love (lit. My cabbage, but Simon chooses to interpret it as **choux à la crème** - a sweet little murder baby cream puff)
Mon loup *(French):* My wolf.
Mon vilain *(French):* My naughty one.
Monsieur *(French):* Sir.
No habla español *(Spanish):* I don't speak Spanish.
Noir-Rouge *(French):* Black-Red.
Observatoire Oceanologique *(French):* Oceanographic Observatory.
[Orochi] San *(Japanese):* An honorable suffix to denote respect.
Oui *(French):* Yes.
Oyabun *(Japanese):* The absolute leader of a **Yakuza** clan (lit. Father role).
Palais de la souveraineté *(French):* Sovereignty Palace.
Peckish *(British English):* Hungry.
Plaster *(British English):* Band-Aid. What we Americans call bandages.
Plus fort *(French):* Harder.
Plus vite *(French):* Faster.
Provence *(French):* A region in southeastern France bordering Italy and the Mediterranean Sea, is known for its diverse landscapes, from the Southern Alps to rolling vineyards, olive groves, pine forests and lavender fields.
Putain *(French):* Fuck (expletive).
Putain de bordel de merde *(French):* For fuck's sake to the max (lit. Shit brothel whore).

GLOSSARY

Putains de connards *(French):* Fucking assholes.

S'il te plaît *(French):* Please.

Sake *(Japanese):* A traditional alcoholic beverage made from fermented rice.

Shoji *(Japanese):* In Japanese architecture, sliding outer partition doors and windows made of a latticework wooden frame and covered with a tough, translucent white paper.

Siglufjörður *(Icelandic):* The northernmost town on the Icelandic mainland (lit. Sailing fjord - a long, narrow, deep inlet of the sea between high cliffs).

Signesdottir *(Old Norse):* Traditionally in Iceland, a new-born child takes the first name of their father alongside 'son of' or 'dóttir (daughter) of', depending on the child's gender. In this case, Violentia chose to take her mother's name - Signe - as her civilian name.

Skip bin *(British English):* Large trash dumpster.

Sod *(British English):* An offensive word for a person, especially a man, that you are annoyed with or think is unpleasant. Perfect for all of Bunny's ex-husbands.

Soirée *(French):* An evening party or gathering.

Stinkstiefel *(German):* Surly bastard.

Suce-moi la bite *(French):* Suck my dick.

Sunnies *(British English):* Sunglasses.

Supay *(Incan, etc. mythology):* In the Quechua, Aymara, and Inca mythologies, Supay was both the god of death and ruler of the Ukhu Pacha, the Incan underworld, as well as a race of demons.

Tais-toi *(French):* Shut up.

Tatami *(Japanese):* A rush-covered straw mat forming a traditional Japanese floor covering. (So, yes, it was redundant of me to say "tatami mats" in the book, but I did it for clarity's sake.)

Temae *(Japanese):* The Japanese tea ceremony. Again, there is much, much more to this - have fun researching!

Tempura *(Japanese):* A dish of fish, shellfish, or vegetables, fried in batter.

The Riviera: a Mediterranean coastal region from Marseilles in France to La Spezia in Italy, noted for its beauty and climate, site of many resorts.

Torch *(British English):* Flashlight.

Trackies *(British English):* The bottom half of a tracksuit (can be velour with Juicy printed across the arse).

Trainers *(British English):* Sneakers.

Tratschtante *(German):* Gossip.

Très merveilleux *(French):* Wonderful.

Tu es vraiment emmerdant *(French):* You are so annoying/pissing me off.

Tu me rends fou *(French):* You drive me crazy.

Valensole *(French):* A pretty Provencal town that sits on a hill overlooking a lavender valley (aka. Heaven on earth).

Villefranche-sur-Mer *(French):* (The resort town of Villefranche) on the sea.

Yakuza *(Japanese):* A Japanese organized crime syndicate similar to the Mafia. Can also be used to refer a single member (like a gangster).

Book Club with Wolfy:

> 'Teaism is a cult founded upon the adoration of the beautiful among the sordid facts of everyday existence."
>
> - THE BOOK OF TEA, OKAKURA KAKUZO

Made in the USA
Middletown, DE
09 September 2023